Moths

A trio of dark novellas

Also by Sam Kates

Pond Life and Other Stories
*The Village of Lost Souls**
*That Elusive Something**
*The Cleansing (Earth Haven: Book 1)***
*The Beacon (Earth Haven: Book 2)**
*The Reckoning (Earth Haven: Book 3)**
Strange Shores and Other Stories
Ghosts of Christmas Past & Other Dark Festive Tales
Dying By Numbers: A short story
The Elevator: Book 1
Jack's Tale (The Elevator: Book 2)
The Lord of the Dance (The Elevator: Book 3)
*The Elevator Omnibus: The Complete Trilogy**

* available in paperback as well as ebook

** available in paperback and unabridged audio
as well as ebook

Moths

A Trio of Dark Novellas

Sam Kates

This is a work of fiction.
All characters appearing in this work
are products of the author's imagination.
Any resemblance to real persons,
living or dead, is purely coincidental.

Copyright © Sam Kates 2019
All rights reserved

This paperback edition, August 2019

ISBN 978-1-912718-20-7

www.samkates.co.uk

Contents

The Goldfish Syndrome

*The advantage of a bad memory is that one enjoys
several times the same good things for the first time.*

—Friedrich Nietzsche

Part One: The Mystery of
the Bedraggled Girl

One: A Stranger in the Night

Rain swept in from the moor, driven by swirling gusts. Many of the dour limestone cottages in the village of Ashmoor had stood for three centuries and seen worse. They had rarely, though, witnessed as pitiful a sight that emerged from the darkness as if borne on the wind.

Barefooted, clad only in a full-length nightgown of a woollen material hanging heavy to her feet, she looked at first glimpse to be adolescent. Hair fair and plastered tightly to her skull, clumps dangling either side of her face like strands of a mop. Slight of frame, the weight of her sodden gown appeared to want to drag her to the ground, until a closer look confirmed she was almost out on her feet through fatigue.

That scrutiny would also reveal the error in assuming this was an adolescent. None of the puppy-fat softness of pre-teens remained; the slightness of frame merely disguised, not obscured, the fullness of maturity; the face structure had settled into the angularity of adulthood. Her ponderous, awkward gait, suggestive of somebody not yet fully accustomed to lengthening bones, was more likely a result of her leaden clothing and exhaustion.

The woman, for surely she was in her early twenties, came stumbling through the darkness, wind and rain, from the direction of the moor.

The couple had lived in the stone cottage at the edge of Ashmoor for all of their married lives, a marriage forged in one world war, interrupted by another. Brought together through the exigencies of bloody conflict while she nursed him back to the closest thing he would henceforth know as health, their mutual bond of a shared home county had slowly bloomed into something more. If his inability to sire children as a result of his injuries ever bothered her, she never showed it.

Excused call-up when the world once more went mad, he nevertheless made his contribution, helping to keep the local newspaper in business while the majority of its reporting, editing and printing staff was otherwise engaged in mainland Europe or the deserts of Africa. She, too, played her part, volunteering at a convalescence home where she could resurrect her long-neglected nursing skills.

While the world tried to settle back to an even keel—many wondered if it would ever sail a plain course again after the atomic age had dawned with a bang or, rather, two—they returned to normal married life; or as normal as life could be in post-war Britain.

The cottage creaked and groaned in the gusting wind. Having trained himself to sleep in the foot-rotting mud and thunder and stench of Belgian trenches, a November storm wasn't about to keep him awake. She, on the other hand, was customarily a light sleeper and rarely enjoyed an uninterrupted night when the ancient beams popped and moaned and knocked around her.

Knocked? Her eyes opened. She strained to hear the sound above the howling wind. There it was again, and it wasn't coming from the rafters.

She turned towards him and shook his shoulder.

"Arthur. *Arthur.*"

He was instantly awake, another trick from the Great War once learned, never forgotten.

"Maud? What's the matter?"

"There's someone knocking at the door."

"On a night like this? What time is it?"

"I don't know. Early. Maybe four o'clock."

"Are you sure it was knocking?"

They both lay still, listening. It came again; not a hammering, but unmistakably a rapping on the door.

The bed shifted when Arthur turned over and swung his legs to the floor. She heard grunts and rustling and creaking floorboards as he retrieved his dressing gown from its hook on the back of the bedroom door.

She leaned the other way and fumbled for the switch on the bed-side lamp. It flickered into pale yellow light in time for her to see her husband limp from the room.

She sat upright, arms wrapped around bent legs. A shiver made her clutch her knees tighter.

Arthur hobbled down the short flight of stairs, accustomed to the pattern of creaking wood made by the tread of his feet, paying it no heed. The stairs descended into the main living area of the cottage, which Maud called the parlour, her one vanity and nod towards a desire to attain a class to which he had never aspired.

The room was dark and chilled, the fire long dead in the grate. He tugged the cord on the brass standard lamp. Shadows retreated, but the light wasn't bright enough to banish them completely; sufficient for him to find his way to the fireplace without bashing his shins on the heavy furniture.

The sound of knocking on the front door had stopped. Arthur hesitated by the stone hearth, hand resting on the handle of the iron poker standing upright in the companion set. After a moment's consideration, he grabbed the handle and limped to the door, the poker held upright before him like a ceremonial sword.

He slid back the bolts securing the door. Without pause, he unlatched it—it opened directly onto the pavement—and swung it inwards.

The woman toppled, following the door in, accompanied by a gust of cold air and smattering of rain. She fell headlong to the rug covering the flagstone floor.

Maud clutched her dressing gown to her chin and shivered.

"I've made tea."

Her husband grunted and straightened from the grate; she could hear the click his back made above the storm and spit of the freshly lit fire.

"It'll soon warm up," he said.

She glanced at the sofa. It had taken them minutes of back-breaking labour to manoeuvre the unconscious figure onto it. Although they had closed and locked the door as soon as they had dragged the woman far enough inside, the wind had removed any residual heat remaining in the parlour from the previous evening's fire.

Arthur had disappeared into the kitchenette to put the kettle on, while Maud removed the woman's sodden nightgown and dressed her in a spare one of her own, before swaddling her tightly under layers of blanket. All that remained visible was damp hair and a pinched face. At least her lips were no longer blue.

"Her feet…" Maud turned a troubled expression towards her husband. "They're filthy and torn and cold as blocks of ice. They look like they've carried her for miles. What was she doing out on her own in only her nightclothes on a night like this?"

Arthur shook his head. "It's a mystery, right enough. One I think it's for the constabulary to solve." He took a step towards the telephone table standing beside the front door.

"Wait," said Maud. "She's waking up."

The woman's eyes glittered darkly in the dancing firelight. They glanced about the room and settled on the elderly couple watching her. She watched them back.

Maud took a step closer, and the woman's eyes widened; she began to wriggle, trying to free her arms from their blanket cocoon. Her fingers appeared, clenched into claws. Maud held out a placating hand.

"No, no," she said. "You need to stay warm. I won't come any nearer. Are you hungry?"

The girl stilled, but regarded Maud warily, eyes all pupil like those of a timid cat.

"Can you speak?" asked Maud. "It's all right if you can't or if you don't want to, but can you shake your head or nod?"

The girl's expression didn't flicker. Arthur was beginning to wonder whether she understood English, when her head moved. It was only a small movement, little more than a twitch, but most probably a nod.

"That's good," said his wife. Her tone of sympathy and endless patience reminded him of the pretty nurse who had brought him morphine and changed his dressings while he lay in a hospital bed in Calais within a private hell of agony; during his moments of lucidity, after the drug had deadened the worst of the pain and before it sent him into a fugue, he had been attracted as much by her compassion as her looks. "You must be hungry. There's some mutton stew in the pantry. I could warm a bowl for you. And there's hot tea to drink. Would you like some?"

The woman's tongue darted out and licked her lips. She nodded, a little more emphatically.

While Maud made for the kitchenette, she spoke in a low voice to her husband, "Try to find out her name."

Arthur indicated the armchair the other side of the fire from the sofa. "I don't want to frighten you, but I really need to sit down. I manage around the place without a walking stick, but I can't stand for long unaided. Still carrying a few fragments of German mortar shell in my hip."

He began moving slowly towards the armchair. The woman watched him closely, but made no move to unswaddle herself. He reached the chair and sank into it with a sigh.

"That's better." Warmer, too, now he was closer to the fire. He looked at the woman; her dark eyes stared back, only darting away when a creak came from the ancient beams. "Have you warmed up?"

She nodded.

"That's good. We were afraid you'd suffer hypothermia, you were so cold." He remained silent for a moment, wondering how he could broach personal questions. Arthur had always been a man of few words. The reduced mobility inflicted on him by the Great War had, if anything, increased his reticence. "I suppose I ought to introduce myself. My name is Arthur. My wife's name is Maud. There are only the two of us living in this cottage. The creaks you hear are old timbers settling and groaning in the wind."

The woman seemed to consider this for a moment. Maybe it was

Arthur's imagination, but he fancied some of the anxiety left her. Certainly, her gaze stopped flitting about at every new pop of beam or spit of log in the fireplace.

"It's a foul night. I'm not sure whether you know, but you're in the village of Ashmoor. On the northern edge of Dartmoor." He watched her carefully, but she gave no sign of recognition of the names.

He had pretty much exhausted his repertoire of small talk. Might as well come right out and ask it. "You know our names. Will you tell me yours?"

He didn't expect her to reply so when her lips moved, he was a little taken aback. "I'm sorry," he said, "I didn't catch that." He pointed to his ears. "You'll have to try to speak a little louder. My hearing was also damaged in the war."

The woman's lips moved again. "Jenny. My name's Jenny. Jenny Lewis."

Arthur smiled. "Pleased to meet you, Jenny. So tell me, where have you come from? And where are you heading?"

Jenny stared at him, her lips working soundlessly. Her brow creased into a frown. She shook her head.

"What about the date?" asked Arthur gently. "Or the year? Do you know what year it is?"

She shook her head again. Then, much to Arthur's consternation, her face crumpled and big tears began rolling down her cheeks. A look appeared in her eyes, one with which Arthur was all too familiar: incomprehensible terror.

"I don't remember," she said. "I don't remember…" Her voice disintegrated into a series of hitching sobs.

"It's 1950," said Arthur, before lapsing into silence.

Two: An Inspector Calls

Jenny allowed Maud to sit by her, perched on the edge of the sofa. In that soothing way Arthur so admired, Maud calmed the woman by stroking her hair and murmuring words he could not hear. What a wonderful mother she would have made, he thought, as he so often did, with a stab of guilt. Jenny sat up, keeping the blankets tucked up to her chin, and ate the stew from the spoon held by Maud. She brought her arms free to hold the cup of tea herself.

A little later, without saying another word, she lay down and fell into a deep sleep.

Arthur roused himself; he had been in danger of dropping off himself in the warmth of the fire. He eased forward in the armchair and rose unsteadily. He was so accustomed to the grinding pains in his hip and the aches in other parts of his body that he didn't grimace.

"What shall we do?" Maud stood as though uncertain what to do with herself, her arms folded because she would otherwise be wringing her hands in anxiety.

"We telephone the constabulary," he replied.

"Do you think she's on the run?" Her hand flew to her mouth. "The prison?" She shook her head and lowered her hand. "No, of course not. That's for men only, silly me. From the police, then?"

Arthur shrugged. "Either way, we must involve them."

Maud watched her husband use the telephone. He kept his voice low and the sleeping woman didn't stir. Maud raised her eyebrows when he hobbled back to the armchair, a faint look of puzzlement on his weathered features.

"I spoke to the desk sergeant," he said. "Think I might have woken him up. He didn't sound in the least bit interested until I told him the woman appears to have amnesia. Then he said he'd send someone out right away. He said we must keep her here until they arrive." He grunted. "As if she's in any condition to go anywhere."

~~~

Arthur awoke to a hand lightly shaking his shoulder and looked up into his wife's face.

"The police are here," she said.

He glanced at the sofa. Jenny hadn't moved. Soft snores came from her lips.

Maud crossed to the door and unbolted it. She opened it to two men, one in plain clothes, the other a uniformed Bobby. The rain had relented, but a gust of cold air followed the men into the cottage. Maud hurriedly closed the door behind them.

The detective stepped into the centre of the room, glancing down at the sleeping woman as he passed. The uniformed constable stationed himself behind the sofa, between it and the front door.

"Evening, sir," said the detective, speaking in a low voice. "Please, no need to get up. I'm Detective Inspector Rowe."

Arthur tried to keep surprise out of his voice. An inspector, for a seemingly low-level case of a woman with amnesia? "Arthur Wickens. And this is my wife, Maud."

DI Rowe tipped his trilby to Maud. "Please, Mr Wickens, tell me what's happened."

"There's not a great deal to tell. Around an hour ago, perhaps a little longer, my wife and I were awakened by a knocking at the door. When I opened it, the young woman collapsed onto the rug. She was dressed only in that nightgown." Arthur indicated the fireplace where the woman's nightgown and undergarments had been placed by Maud to dry. "All she had with her were the clothes she was wearing. No bags, no papers, no jewellery."

"Her feet are bare," added Maud. "They were filthy and cut as if she had walked a long way. On a night like this, too."

"We warmed her up," continued Arthur, "and gave her some food. She told me her name. It's Jenny Lewis. But when I asked where she came from and where she's going, she said she couldn't remember and became distressed. Furthermore, she doesn't seem to know what year it is. We've lived in Ashmoor for thirty years and
~~~

we've never seen her before, so I doubt she's local. When she fell asleep, we telephoned the station." Arthur glanced at the constable. He stood gazing stoically into the distance like one of the King's guards outside Buckingham Palace. "Er, shouldn't one of you be taking notes?"

"Don't you worry about that, sir," said DI Rowe. "Is there anything else you can tell us?"

"I don't think so." He looked at his wife. "Maud?"

"There is one thing," said his wife. "When I was smoothing her hair, trying to calm her down, I felt something. Indentations to the sides of her temple. And the residue of something sticky."

The inspector's expression remained deadpan. "Indentations? Perhaps old marks from a forceps delivery at birth."

"Hmm, perhaps." Maud didn't sound convinced. "It doesn't explain the residue."

"I think you can let us worry about that, Mrs Wickens. After all, you didn't call us in—which, by the way, was the correct course of action for which I commend you both—for you to have to continue to concern yourself about this young lady."

"No, I suppose not…" Maud still didn't sound sure, and Arthur felt the same way.

"Nevertheless," he said, "we'd like to know what will happen to her now?"

"We shall of course take her to the station, where every effort will be made to discover her antecedents and return her home."

Before Arthur could ask anything else, the low grumble of a throat being cleared came from the direction of the constable. He was looking pointedly down at the sofa. Jenny Lewis was stirring.

The woman opened her eyes and blinked. Instantly, she came to full alertness, her gaze darting from person to person, as though unsure on whom to settle.

Maud started forward. "It's all right, Jenny. There's no need to be startled."

"Who… who are you?"

Arthur thought the question must be directed at DI Rowe, but then he realised the woman's gaze had settled on his wife.

"You know who I am," said Maud, a note of uncertainty in her voice. "I fed you mutton stew before you went to sleep."

She took another step towards the sofa. Jenny's eyes grew wide with fright and she clutched the blankets tighter to her chin like a shield. Maud stopped in confusion.

DI Rowe, at once all brusque and businesslike, took control.

"Hello, Jenny," he said. "I am Detective Inspector Rowe. My colleague and I have come to take you to the station so we can try to help you. Do you know where you are?"

"I explained…" Arthur began, but broke off when the woman shook her head. Emphatically.

"Who are these people?" Her gaze shifted from Arthur to Maud with no sign of recognition, and back to the inspector.

"Oh, love, we told you our names." Maud sounded as bewildered as Arthur was beginning to feel.

"It's all right, Mrs Wickens," said DI Rowe. "We'll take it from here." He nodded to the constable, who stepped around the sofa into Jenny's line of sight.

She uttered a small shriek and began to shake.

"She's terrified," said Maud.

"As is often the case with people suffering from amnesia," said DI Rowe. He addressed the trembling woman, speaking slowly but in a deliberate tone that brooked no argument. "Jenny, there is no need for you to be afraid. Constable Jones and I are here to help you. We will take you to the station in Totleigh and try to find out who you are and what has happened to bring you to Ashmoor."

"She'll see a doctor?" Maud asked.

"Of course," said the inspector. "Really, Mrs Wickens, she'll be in safe hands. You mustn't concern yourself any further."

They stood on the doorstep and watched the uniformed constable lead Jenny Lewis, still wrapped in blankets, to the black Wolseley parked at the kerbside. Despite his inscrutable manner, the constable handled her gently enough. Once he had settled her into the back seat and closed the door, he walked around the vehicle and stepped into the driver's side.

A pale face glanced at them once from the car's rear window, before looking away.

DI Rowe held up Maud's shopping bag, into which she'd placed Jenny's damp clothes. "I'll have your bag and blankets and night-gown returned," he said. "Thank you for all you've done, but please don't worry about the young lady. She'll be well cared for."

"Can my husband telephone the station later to enquire how she is?" asked Maud. Arthur could detect the same note of concern in her voice that he was experiencing.

DI Rowe's neutral expression didn't alter, but he shook his head curtly. "Best not." He glanced up. The first grey brushstrokes of dawn had appeared behind the low clouds still darkening the sky. "Now we must be on our way." He tipped the brim of his hat.

Arthur and Maud waited until the car had rumbled away, before retreating to the warmth of the parlour and locking the door behind them.

"Well," said Maud. "I don't know quite what to make of that."

Her husband frowned. "They took no notes. We haven't been asked to give statements. It was all most irregular."

"Do you think she'll be all right?"

Arthur shook his head. "I don't know."

Maud glanced at the clock on the mantelpiece. "It's almost seven o'clock. We should go back to bed. Things always look better after a good sleep."

"Hmm." His frown deepened in thought. "First, I think I'll make another telephone call."

Three: Discretion Required

Jonathan Fry hurried through the streets of Totleigh, his overcoat buttoned against the biting wind. At least the rain which had lashed his window through the night had eased. His coat, made of heavy wool, tended to absorb rainwater and make him feel he was wearing a suit of armour.

The offices and press rooms of the *Totleigh Times* occupied a brick building in the tiny business district of the market town. Totleigh, of neither military nor historical significance, had escaped the attention of the Luftwaffe, which concentrated its bombing raids on the nearest city of Exeter, and the cities and towns further south, like Plymouth and Newton Abbot.

The premises, on rather the large side for a regional newspaper with a dwindling readership, hinted at a more affluent past, while its stained and crumbling façade, slate roof patched with inferior tiles, and drab foyer suggested an establishment fighting a losing battle against the big boys from Fleet Street and the new kid on the block, the television.

Fry was under no illusions. You didn't need to be experienced in business affairs to recognise the newspaper was failing and would need to drastically downscale, and soon, if it was to survive the next decade. He also knew he had only been able to obtain the position of indentured journalist due to the number of staff members who had either returned from the war in no condition to resume their former civilian occupations, or hadn't returned at all. He suspected there had been an element of sympathy in the newspaper taking him on as a fresh-faced eighteen-year-old—he had been older by two years than most apprentices, but being a displaced war orphan had probably turned the decision in his favour. Fry was the last member of the journalistic staff to be taken on, another indication all was not well in the world of the regional press.

It was a relief to enter the building and escape the teeth of the wind. For once, he didn't mind the climb up six flights of stairs, past the floors holding the clanking printing press, the stores of syrupy ink and rolls of paper, and the archives, to reach the News Room. This was rather a grand name for a drab space filled with clicking typewriters and tobacco smoke.

He weaved through the maze of desks to his own, pausing along the way to deposit his coat on a stand and retrieve his paper-wrapped sandwiches from the pocket. These he deposited on one of the few spaces on the desktop, the desk drawers already over-flowing with the detritus of almost three years of indentured journalism.

"Morning, Fry."

He glanced at the occupant of the larger desk next to his and nodded. He didn't quite know how to take the Head of Classifieds. The Head was in his fifties, with an almost permanent grin on his face. Fry often felt like a mouse in the presence of a cat who has just eaten but is in playful mood. The Head had escaped active service due to flat feet, he was fond of telling anyone who cared to listen. Not long after Fry began his apprenticeship, the man sent him down to the stores to request a spool of red tape and a length of Fallopian tubing, and Fry hadn't trusted him since.

"The Chief wants to see you."

The Head's grin made it impossible to tell if he was being serious.

"The Chief?" said Fry. "Do you mean the Sub?"

The grin widened. "I thought you'd worked here long enough to know we call the sub-editor the Sub, and the editor the Chief."

"Yes." Fry cleared his throat. "Why does he want to see me?"

"Well, old bean, you'll probably have to ask him that yourself, don't you think?"

The editor of the *Totleigh Times* was a dour man nearing retirement age, with bushy eyebrows that seemed to move independently of the pale, heavy-featured face above which they perched. He had served in the war, but in a hush-hush role in the countryside of Buckinghamshire. Of course, he had a name, but everyone called him the Chief. Fry hadn't spoken to the man since the day he'd been offered the apprenticeship; all his tasks had been assigned to him by the Sub.

Fry stood at the door of the Chief's office, set into the partition which formed the back wall of the News Room. The day shift had all arrived and the room behind him bustled with activity and ringing telephones. Most of the calls would be from businesses looking to place advertisements—the telephones rarely rang with tips of breaking news stories in provincial Devon. Besides, advertising revenue was how the newspaper managed to keep its head above water and why the Head's position was more secure than anyone's.

He took a deep breath before knocking.

"Come!"

The Chief glowered behind the piles of paper covering his desk. Pungent smoke filled the air from the cigar clamped between his teeth. Fry sometimes wondered if the man thought of himself as the Winston Churchill of the newspaper world. Thankfully, he hadn't yet taken to wearing a Homburg.

"Fry," said the Chief. "Shut the door behind you, lad."

If he'd hoped being summoned before the Chief might be for some minor matter, being asked to close the door did nothing to convince Fry this meeting was for anything trivial. Perhaps money had gone missing from the tea kitty again and he, as the most junior member of staff, was under suspicion. He took another deep breath.

"Don't just stand there, lad." The Chief took the cigar from between his teeth and used it to gesture to a leather-bound chair that had seen better days. "Sit."

The chair's padding had compressed through use and Fry sank to the wooden frame. He peered between piles of papers and through drifts of blue smoke at the Chief.

"You turned twenty-one a few weeks ago, correct?" The Chief wasn't one to stand on ceremony.

"Yes, sir."

"Your apprenticeship will be ending in the spring?"

Fry nodded. This didn't appear to be about missing tea money. Perhaps he was about to be told his services were no longer required. If only they would wait until he'd qualified.

"There's no need to look so worried, lad. I don't bite."

"No, sir. No. Um…"

"So what's the Sub been feeding you?" The Chief didn't seem to expect a reply. "Sat in on a few of those shiny new planning committee meetings, I suppose. Some human interest stories about housewives making their rations stretch and the struggles of ex-service personnel to make their way on civvy street. That sort of thing, correct?"

"Yes, sir." The story he was currently working on involved the supposedly imaginative uses some local residents were making of their redundant Anderson shelters. If he was finding it boring to write, he could hardly expect readers to find it interesting.

"Not exactly scintillating, correct?"

"Er, it's not so bad. It's teaching me to write better copy."

"Well said. You strike me as a loyal sort of chap, Fry."

"Do I, sir?"

"That's precisely the quality I'm looking for in my staff journalists. That and discretion."

"Oh." *Staff journalists.* Was the Chief offering him a permanent position after he'd qualified? Fry wasn't sure what to say.

"Yes, discretion. I have something in mind that requires discretion in abundance." He fixed Fry with a steely gaze. "Can I rely upon you, lad?"

"Um, yes, sir. Of course."

The Chief stuck the stub of cigar into the corner of his mouth and spoke around it. "Good. Then I have a task for you."

Fry returned to his desk to collect a notebook and pencil. He had promised to buy himself one of those new-fangled ballpoint pens from his first month's salary as a qualified journalist—they were a little pricey for an apprentice's wage packet—and felt more positive the aspiration might become reality.

He was aware of the Head watching him, but didn't glance his way; the man didn't need much of an opening to be nosy and Fry didn't want to give him any opportunity. He grabbed his coat and made his way back through the building.

Dark clouds scudded and wind continued to gust, casting flurries of stinging raindrops into his face. The police station was on the other side of Totleigh, and Fry had to battle the wind and avoid slipping on drifts of fallen leaves, sodden and treacherous from the overnight storm, while he made his way through the centre of town.

The Chief required discretion. That was no problem; Fry could be discreet. He only wished he had a little more to go on. A young woman appearing in a nearby village in the middle of the night, dressed only in a nightgown and apparently suffering from amnesia, may have a number of mundane explanations unworthy of more than a small paragraph tucked away near the legal notices and obituaries, though none immediately occurred to Fry. The Chief had not said why discretion was so important or why he was handing out this assignment himself instead of delegating it to the Sub.

"Arthur Wickens helped keep this newspaper afloat." The Chief had become wreathed in smoke from his cigar. "If he telephones and says there's something not quite right about this case, then there's something not quite right about it. And I want you, Fry, to find out what that is. Go to the station. Ask questions. Listen to the answers. Unless Arthur Wickens's instincts, and mine, have at last become dulled through age, I suspect what the police *don't* tell you will be more revealing than what they do."

Fry wasn't quite sure what that meant, but didn't have time to ponder; he had arrived at the police station.

The desk sergeant was burly, with a jowly face bearing a neatly trimmed moustache which looked incongruous on such a meaty expanse. *Like a caterpillar on a cabbage*, Fry thought, and had to stifle a smile.

The sergeant looked up from the blotter on which he was writing and his eyes narrowed marginally.

"Can I help you, sir?" His tone suggested he'd rather do anything but.

"Er, yes, please. I'm with the *Times*." Fry fumbled for his wallet containing his staff card.

The sergeant's expression remained deadpan. "Is that so, sir? And what brings a reporter all the way from London to provincial Devon?"

"Um, not that *Times*," mumbled Fry. Any confidence he'd had on entering the station was draining away like water down a plug hole. He held out his card. "The *Totleigh Times*."

"Ah." The inflection the sergeant managed to insert into such a small word was enough for Fry to feel himself colour as though the man had laughed in his face.

Mercifully, there was no one else in the small waiting area to witness what was beginning to feel like his humiliation. He mentally shook himself.

Pull yourself together, man. What chance do you have of becoming a real journalist if you're going to allow yourself to be intimidated by a small-town Bobby?

Fry pushed back his shoulders. "That's right. I'm with the *Totleigh Times* and I'm here to enquire after a young woman whom I understand was brought to this station earlier this morning suffering from amnesia."

"Oh, yes?" The sergeant's expression remained neutral—carefully neutral, Fry fancied—but his eyes narrowed a fraction more. "Mr… Fry, was it?"

Fry nodded.

"And what makes you think anyone answering such a description is here?"

"We received…" Fry had been about to blurt out the telephone call the Chief had taken from a former employee, but remembered himself in time. He took a deep breath and looked the sergeant in the eye. "Come now, sergeant, you can't expect us to reveal our sources."

"Ah. Sources." He nodded sagely as if that explained everything.

Fry waited, but there didn't appear to be anything more. The sergeant gazed impassively at him, rocking gently on his heels.

Take control Fry admonished himself. He extracted his notebook and pencil from his coat pocket, turned to a fresh page and licked the end of the pencil. He jotted down the date and glanced up at the sergeant. The man had resumed writing as though Fry no longer existed.

The sergeant's uniform contained a three-digit number stitched into the shoulder of his tunic. Fry noted the number and cleared his throat.

The sergeant continued writing for a few more moments, before looking up.

"Hello, sir, you're still here?"

"Yes, sergeant. I'm still waiting for you to deal with my enquiry." The sergeant's eyebrows rose as if he didn't know to what Fry was alluding. "About the young woman brought here this morning suffering with amnesia. We understand her name is Jenny Lewis."

The sergeant pointedly placed his fountain pen into the holder on the desk, before allowing his full attention to turn to Fry.

"Let me get this straight," he said, speaking slowly as though to a child. "You say a young woman suffering from amnesia is here in Totleigh Station. Amnesia, of course, being loss of memory. And yet you say she has a name. Sir, in my experience of amnesia, victims don't know their names."

"Partial amnesia, then, obviously." Fry sighed. "Look, sergeant, are you going to answer my enquiry or not?"

"Of course, sir. We're always glad to assist the gentlemen of the press."

Fry nodded and relaxed a little. He held the pencil poised over the notebook. But the sergeant continued to merely stand there, regarding Fry as he would a vaguely interesting insect which had alighted on his desk.

"Um," said Fry. "Well, then?"

"How can I help you, sir?"

"The woman who was brought in this morning? Jenny Lewis?"

"And what time was this, sir?"

"According to our information, it would have been around seven o'clock. Perhaps a little after."

"Ah. I came on duty at eight o'clock. Let's see if the night sergeant recorded anyone coming in before then."

The sergeant shuffled to his right to where a thick ledger stood on the desk. He turned back the heavy cover and began slowly turning pages, pausing frequently to lick his thumb.

Fry stood and watched, resisting the urge to shift from foot to foot.

At last, the sergeant looked back up.

"No, sir, there's no record of anyone by that name or description coming to the station this morning."

"Are you sure?"

"Oh, yes, sir. Quite sure." Without looking down, he closed the ledger with a firmness that said this was his final word.

Fry stared at the man, pencil still poised over notebook. Feeling suddenly foolish, he lowered his hand and slid book and pencil back into his overcoat pocket.

"Ashmoor," he said. "That's where the girl was found. Might she have been taken to a different station?"

"I'm sure I couldn't say, sir, though I suppose you could enquire at Exeter."

"Detective Inspector Rowe," said Fry. "He was the officer who brought the girl in. Could I have a word with him, please?"

"Detective Inspector Rowe?" The sergeant beetled his brows as though in deep thought. "I do believe he's on nights, sir. He's probably at home tucked up in bed."

"Well, could I leave a message asking DI Rowe to contact me?"

"Certainly, sir. I'll see to it the message is passed on." He made no move to jot anything down and didn't ask Fry for the telephone number of the newspaper.

"What about missing person reports? Has there been one filed for a Jenny Lewis?"

"No, sir."

"You seem very sure?"

"Oh, yes, sir." His tone suggested there was no point in pursuing this line of enquiry.

"Um. Right, then. Um. I'd better make my back to the office."

"Very good, sir."

The sergeant picked up his fountain pen and bent his head to the blotter.

Fry paused at the door and glanced back. The sergeant did not look up.

Four: Mere Speculation

The Chief listened attentively, nodding occasionally, while Fry made his report. It didn't take long. When Fry had finished talking, the Chief cocked one eyebrow and fixed him with a piercing stare.

"What do you make of it, Fry?"

"Um, there's nothing to make. They didn't tell me anything."

The eyebrow rose higher. "Sure about that, are you, laddie? Ever hear the expression 'reading between the lines'?"

"Er, yes. It means… ah, I see."

The Chief nodded. "Go on, then. What does your gut tell you?"

"The desk sergeant knew more than he was letting on."

"Good. Go on."

Fry thought for a moment, replaying the conversation in the station. "The sergeant was evasive. Without being openly obstructive, he made it as difficult as possible for me to elicit any information. Although I have no evidence to support this conclusion, I believe he knew the incident to which I was referring. I believe the young woman was indeed brought to Totleigh. Taking her to Exeter from Ashmoor makes no sense, though I suppose she could have been subsequently transferred. The only thing the sergeant said which I believed was that there was no entry made in the night ledger recording the girl arriving at the station."

The Chief nodded. "I suspect you're right."

Fry frowned. "But why, sir? Why would the police want to conceal this?"

"That, my lad, is what you're going to find out."

A telephone call to Exeter Police Station confirmed no young woman by the name of Jenny Lewis, nor anyone suffering from amnesia, had been taken there that day. The constable to whom Fry had been transferred was brusque, but he'd gained no sense the officer was being anything other than completely open in answering

Fry's few questions.

While he talked on the telephone, Fry was aware of the Head watching him, and he'd been glad to shrug back into his overcoat and head for the bus station. A number 16 took him to Ashmoor.

The door to the cottage was answered by a lady of advancing years, wearing a flour-dusted apron. She reminded him a little of the kindly woman who, with her husband, had taken him in as a ten-year-old evacuee from bomb-torn London. Both had since died, he not long after the war had ended, she early last year.

"Mrs Wickens? My name's Jonathan Fry. I'm from the *Totleigh Times*." He showed her his card. "My editor spoke to your husband and he said it would be all right if I called."

"Yes, Arthur did mention it. Please, come in."

Fry stepped through the doorway directly into what appeared to be the couple's living room. A log fire sputtered and spat in a stone hearth, giving the space a welcoming warmth.

"Please, take a seat. Would you like a cup of tea?"

"No, I'm fine, thank you." Fry glanced at her apron. "I can see you're busy. Baking?"

"Yes, I started baking my own bread during the rationing and wheat shortage after the dreadful summer of '46." She pulled a face. "It wasn't what you'd call delicious, mind, bread made with ground semolina."

Fry gave a mock shudder and smiled. "I remember it well."

The woman returned his smile. "Let me get this batch into the oven and I'll join you. My husband shouldn't keep you more than a moment."

Fry slipped off his overcoat so he would feel its benefit when he donned it again to return outdoors. That was something his mother used to say to him and he suspected he'd never forget it. He took a seat near the fire and stared into the flames, his eyes misting with childhood memories. He didn't hear the old man enter until the creaking of the nearby armchair pulled him from his recollections.

"Oh, hello, sir. Mr Wickens?" Fry rose, holding his coat folded over one arm, and stepped to his host so he could shake his hand.

"I'm Jonathan Fry."

"Arthur Wickens. Please, resume your seat. You looked lost in thought."

Fry sat back down and nodded. "The flames in the fire are mesmerising. So, Mr Wickens, you spoke to my editor?"

"Yes. I worked at the paper during the war, you know. He kept me on afterwards, for as long as I wanted, even though enough staff returned to make my employment no longer necessary." Wickens regarded him with an appraising look. "He speaks quite highly of you, Mr Fry. Says you show a lot of potential."

"He does? I do? Oh…" For a moment, Fry was flummoxed; he hadn't been aware the Chief thought of him at all, let alone highly.

"You've come to ask about our early-morning visitor, I understand."

"That's correct."

"It's a bit of a rum do, make no mistake, Mr Fry."

"A rum do? How do you mean, sir? Um, do you mind if I take some notes while we talk?"

Wickens shrugged. "As you like. This is what happened."

The creaking frame of Arthur Wickens contained a sharp intellect. A journalist's intellect. In spare sentences, without flourish or hyperbole, he related what had taken place that morning. Embellishment was provided by his wife, who joined them a few minutes into his discourse, adding a touch of colour, a little flavour, to an otherwise dry tale.

"The girl," said Fry, "Jenny Lewis, gave no hint as to where she'd come from?"

Arthur Wickens shook his head.

"The poor thing was terrified," said Maud Wickens.

"Do you think it was because she didn't know where she was from, or was afraid to tell you?"

"The girl knew her name," said Mr Wickens, "but didn't seem to know anything else. If it was an act, it was a convincing one."

"That was no act," added his wife. "She was trembling with bewilderment and fear." She paused, before adding, "Mostly."

Both men looked at her.

"There was a moment," she continued, "after she'd regained consciousness, when I saw something else in her eyes. Something primitive. Bestial, almost. Her hands clenched into claws. I thought she was going to spring at me like a wild cat."

If Arthur Wickens thought his wife was imagining things, he didn't say so. In fact, Fry thought, he did not, as many husbands might have, regard his wife with a look of scepticism, but thoughtfully, as though not for one moment doubting her word. It confirmed Fry's own impression of Maud Wickens: a level-headed woman not given to flights of fancy.

He cleared his throat. "And the police told you they would take her to the station in Totleigh?"

"Yes," said Mr Wickens. "Detective Inspector Rowe stated as much."

Mrs Wickens nodded confirmation. "The constable returned at about half past nine with the clothes and blankets we'd wrapped the girl in. They'd dried them, too."

Fry opened his mouth to ask a question, but Arthur Wickens anticipated it.

"The constable said the girl was being well looked after and they expected to have returned her home before the morning was old. 'In time for elevenses,' was how he put it. He refused to be drawn any further, although we both tried to elicit more information."

Maud Wickens tutted. "He wouldn't even tell us whether she'd been able to say from where she'd come or why she'd been out in that dreadful storm wearing naught but a nightdress."

"Neither of the police officers opened their notebooks when they came to fetch the girl," added Arthur Wickens. "They didn't take statements from us or ask us to attend the station to give statements at a later time." He harrumphed. "Most irregular."

"Do you have any ideas as to why that should be?" asked Fry.

Mrs Wickens shook her head. Arthur answered for them both. "We've discussed this and drawn a blank. Other than we suspect the constabulary know more about the girl or her origins than they are willing to let on, we have no hypotheses to advance as to what their motives could be."

Fry made a note and looked at the couple, tapping his teeth with his pencil. "We're on the northern edge of the moor here, correct? Where do *you* think the girl came from?"

Maud Wickens didn't hesitate. "Her feet were cut, only superficially, but enough to suggest she'd walked quite some distance, and they were covered in muck to the ankles. The cuts weren't severe enough to suppose she'd been walking far on surfaced roads. The amount of dirt suggested she'd mainly kept to heath. There were also minor scratches to her lower legs which might have been caused by gorse or bracken." She nodded. "I have no doubt she came from Dartmoor."

Her husband was more circumspect. "It's possible she came across farmland. Or maybe from one of the villages on the edge of the moor. South Tawton, perhaps, or Sticklepath. But judging from her state of exhaustion, I'd hazard she came from farther afield. If I had to guess, and I must stress this is mere speculation, I'd say it's most likely she came from the moor. From somewhere deeper in than the villages I mentioned."

Ten minutes later, after Fry had taken his leave of Mr and Mrs Wickens and stood at the bus stop trying in vain to shelter from a sharp breeze, he looked into the teeth of the wind, south, towards the moor.

The elderly couple were too level-headed to suggest there was anything nefarious about the unexplained appearance of the girl and the disquieting way the local constabulary had dealt with the situation, or the likelihood she had come from somewhere in Dartmoor added a dark element to the tale, but Fry possessed an imagination that didn't always sit well with the matter-of-fact attitude required of his chosen profession.

Moreover, he had been raised in a concrete and brick suburb of West London, and there was something about the wild desolation of the moor which raised the hairs on the back of his city-boy neck.

When adding to the mix the Sherlock Holmes tale *The Hound of the Baskervilles*, which had caused Fry nightmares while reading it, it was little surprise he regarded Dartmoor with a touch of superstitious trepidation. Not that he would ever admit it to anyone.

He gazed in the direction of the moor and it wasn't merely the chill of the wind which made him shiver.

Five: Dead Ends

Before reporting back to his editor, Fry spent a few hours ensconced in the gloom of the floor beneath the News Room, which housed the archives. Nowhere in the building, not even in the room containing the clanking, creaking press, was the lack of modernisation more evident. Ancient wooden shelving lined the walls from floor to ceiling and formed poorly lit aisles. The bowed shelves held box upon mouldy box, containing fading editions of the *Totleigh Times* dating back to its founding in the late nineteenth century. No modern microfilm storage here.

The Archivist, a middle-aged man with a habitually morose expression, looked up from his work and peered at Fry through round spectacles as thick as the base of a bottle. He blinked owlishly.

"Hello," said Fry, unable to recall the man's name. "I need to conduct a little research."

The Archivist grunted. "Please be sure to return any cards you remove to precisely the place in which you found them."

"Of course."

The Archivist grunted again and bent back to his work.

The indexing system consisted of cards stored within an array of mismatched filing cabinets which had been expanded piecemeal as the existing drawers were filled. Fry located the drawers marked 'L'—they took up more than half a cabinet—and pulled open the first. Each drawer was long and narrow; each card was sub-indexed with letters of the alphabet. The cards within this one ended at 'B'. He pulled open the fifth; the cards ended at 'I'. With a sigh, he opened the next drawer and began riffling through the cards sub-indexed with a 'J'.

Keeping the system up to date had been interrupted by the war; before that, Fry had been informed, the system had usually been at least six months behind due to its painstaking nature and the refusal of the newspaper's owners to employ additional staff to assist the Archivist. Currently, he had around three years' worth of editions of the *Totleigh Times* to go through and cross-reference. Little wonder he looked morose.

Fry found several references to 'J. Lewis', but only three for 'Jennifer Lewis' and none for 'Jenny Lewis'. He copied the strings of letters and numbers—referring to editions, page numbers, aisles, shelves and boxes—into his notebook, ensuring to slot each index card back into the exact place he'd found it. He felt the occasional regard of the Archivist fall upon him, but gathered from the absence of further admonishments he was doing what the man wanted.

He retired to one of the tables standing at the head of the rows of shelving, sat on a chair which creaked alarmingly under his weight and studied his notebook entries. Both Arthur and Maud Wickens had estimated the girl's age at twenty or twenty-one. If Fry allowed a margin of four years, giving the mysterious girl a maximum age of twenty-five, he could safely disregard any reference to an edition pre-1925. He drew a pencil line through more than half of the entries.

That still left five entries: four for 'J. Lewis', with dates ranging from 1928 to 1941, and one for 'Jennifer Lewis' from 1944.

Fry glanced at the dim aisles and the rickety wooden step-ladder used to reach boxes from the higher rows of shelves. With a sigh, he stood, clutching his notebook, and headed into the dusty shadows.

The Chief peered at Fry through cigar smoke.

"Where does that leave us, Fry? What do we know?"

"Not a lot." Fry, if not completely at ease in his Editor-in-Chief's company, felt a little more sure of himself.

"Summarise what we do know. Only the facts, please."

Fry took a deep breath. "A young woman collapses into an elderly couple's cottage in Ashmoor in the early hours of the morning. She is wearing nightclothes, is bare-footed and appears to have come some distance, judging from the condition of her feet and legs. The female occupier, Mrs Wickens, whilst tending to the girl, notices some indentations to her temples and a sticky residue, which the attending police inspector attributes to a forceps delivery at birth. Mrs Wickens is not convinced by this explanation and points out it does not, in any case, explain the sticky substance. The young woman claims to be unable to remember anything about her recent past, where she is or what year it is, but states her name is Jenny Lewis. Mr and Mrs Wickens summon the constabulary, who take the girl away." He paused.

The Chief nodded for him to continue.

"The desk sergeant in Totleigh Police Station, upon my enquiry, denies any knowledge of the young woman, although he was not on duty at the time she would have been brought to the station. He tells me there is no entry in the desk log recording anybody coming to the station that morning fitting the girl's description. The police tell Maud Wickens, when they return the blankets the girl had been wrapped in, they expect to have her returned home later that morning. They won't reveal anything more to the Wickenses." He paused again to gather his thoughts.

"Arthur Wickens is correct," said the Chief. "The police procedure in this case is most irregular, and that's understating it." He took a drag on his cigar. "Go on."

"A search in the archives reveals nothing except a short paragraph in an edition from March 1944. It's a report of a sixteen-year-old girl running away from a children's home near Okehampton. The girl's name was Jennifer Lewis. It states she had been left an orphan when her mother was killed in a bombing raid on Torquay in 1942. The mother wasn't named in the report and there was no mention at all of her father. I wasn't able to unearth any later mentions of the girl named Jennifer Lewis. Though, of course," Fry added, "there might be something from 1947 onwards, but the editions from those years haven't yet been archived."

The Chief grunted.

"The final piece of information," continued Fry, "is from the children's home, which still exists. It was able to confirm in response to my telephone enquiry that a young girl by the name of Jennifer

Fiona Lewis is recorded as having run away in late February 1944. Her date of birth was given as January 29th, 1928. This was the third time she'd run away. Their records show that on each occasion she was returned by the police after coming to the attention of the authorities for petty theft and drinking alcohol. They said there are no later records relating to the girl and were unable to tell me anything about the girl's character because there are no members of staff remaining from that time, the home being manned during the war by volunteers and retirees, while most of the regular staff were engaged in active service." He shrugged. "And that's more or less it.

"The only thing I can add is that if the Jennifer Lewis who ran away from the children's home in 1944 is the same Jenny Lewis who turned up on the doorstep of Arthur and Maud Wickens, then she is currently aged twenty-two. But what has become of her since running away, where she had come from to appear in Ashmoor, what has happened to her to cause partial amnesia, is a mystery."

Fry stopped talking and sat back. His boss nodded.

"Succinct and accurate. Good job."

"Not enough to run a report in the *Times*."

The Chief shook his head. He looked intently at Fry, who gained the impression his boss was debating whether to tell him something. But all he said was, "Nevertheless, I want you to write up everything we know to date. I'd like it on my desk by close of business tomorrow. Then, you may return to your usual tasks. But keep an eye and an ear open. I have a feeling there will be more to unearth about Mr and Mrs Wickens's mysterious visitor."

Fry nodded and rose to leave.

"Oh, and one last thing," said the Chief. "This remains between us for now."

Fry had the report on the Chief's desk by the middle of the following afternoon. The Chief took it from him, glanced at it, grunted and bent back to the jumble of papers on his desk.

So that's that thought Fry as he closed the Chief's door behind him. *I'll never know Jenny Lewis's story.*

He sank back into his chair with a sigh. The News Room was alive with shrilling telephones and clicking typewriters, the air thick with cigarette and pipe smoke. Through the murky atmosphere, the Head of Classifieds was watching him. Fry had been aware of the Head's sneaking regard while typing up his dead-end report on Jenny Lewis, but had ignored it. Now he glanced up.

"Anything I can help you with?"

The man smirked. Fry considered himself an easy-going chap, able to get along with almost anyone, but there was something about the Head's demeanour, his constant sly, knowing looks, which rubbed him up the wrong way.

The Head nodded towards the closed door of their Editor-in-Chief. "You two have been thick as thieves of late, old boy."

Fry shrugged, but said nothing.

"Ah," said the Head, as if Fry's silence told him everything he needed to know. He laid one finger alongside his nose. "All very hush hush. I understand." He winked.

Fry repressed the impulse to shudder.

Without another glance at the Head, he turned to his neglected regular work.

Six: An Unexpected Lead

The mystery of Jenny Lewis began to fade to the back of Fry's mind during the ensuing weeks while he concentrated on stories that would make it into the newspaper, though he privately wondered whether readers would find the subject-matter particularly interesting. *I mean, who really cares about Mrs Smith turning her Anderson shelter into a miniature tearoom, or Mr Wilson converting his Morrison shelter into a gigantic rabbit hutch?*

Fry didn't, that much was certain, though he was at pains to ensure his true feelings remained concealed when visiting the Mrs Smiths and Mr Wilsons, and translating their earnestly recounted tales into printable copy.

It was during the stormy, dark depths of mid-December that something happened to bring the unexplained tale of the girl with amnesia back to the fore.

One Friday evening, with the weekend off, Fry fancied a couple of pints of bitter. His lodgings paid and what remained of his week's wages burning a hole in his wallet, he decided to indulge his fancy, not something he succumbed to often, particularly on evenings like this when rain swept from the growling sky in torrents.

The interior of The Coach Inn was crowded, smelling of tobacco smoke and damp wool. While waiting for his pint to be poured, he ran a hand through his hair to squeeze out the worst of the rainwater and peered around the bar. The only available space seemed to be at a tiny round table with two empty stools around it in a dimly lit corner of the room. Fry took his glass and shouldered his way to the table.

The stool was rickety, but Fry found that by manoeuvring himself around he could lean back against the wall and feel, if not in the lap of comfort, that he wasn't about to pitch to the floor when the legs of the stool gave up the ghost. He took a sip of bitter and placed the glass on the table. Shrugging off his damp overcoat, he hung it from a wooden peg protruding from the wall. He unfolded the newspaper he'd tucked under his coat for protection and held it up, readjusting it and his position until sufficient light fell upon the print to render it legible.

Fry made sure to read at least one edition of *The Times* each week—not the *Totleigh Times*, but the national broadsheet printed in London. He liked to be informed about world news and the current fortunes, or misfortunes, of Fulham Football Club. He sometimes fantasised about seeing his name on the by-line of a momentous report; during more whimsical moments, he imagined it reading 'by Jonathan Fry, Chief Foreign Correspondent', or '… Senior Football Reporter', or whatever title held most attraction that week.

This edition led with the latest news about the conflict in Korea and President Truman's decision to declare a national state of emergency after the most recent UN setbacks in the Peninsular. Fry tried to keep abreast of global politics, but he didn't pretend to fully understand all the machinations while the main powers jostled and vied for supremacy as the world order continued to be modified following the toppling of Hitler.

He glanced up at the sound of a throat being cleared. A man clutching a full pint glass stood there; he was middle-aged with the rugged countenance of someone who is used to working out of doors. There was something familiar about him.

"Do you mind if I sit here? Only it's a little full tonight…"

"Not at all. Help yourself."

The newcomer sat on the other stool and sipped at his pint.

"I say," Fry ventured, "sorry to ask, but have we met before?"

The man barely looked at him. "Don't think so."

"Oh. Right. I must be mistaken."

Fry returned to the newspaper, but found himself stealing surreptitious glances at the man, who seemed downcast. His expression reminded Fry of the Archivist's. He was certain he had seen the man before, and not long ago, in the past week or so, but could not place where.

The next time he glanced away from the paper, the man was regarding him forlornly and gave a deep sigh. Taking it as an invitation to enquire, Fry asked, "Not having a good day?"

The man nodded. "You could say that. Lost my job today."

"Oh. Bad luck."

"Yes. I was a groundsman out at Cartwell Manor. Of course, it's winter, but there's still gravel and leaves need raking, dead branches to lop, that sort of thing."

"Not heard of Cartwell Manor."

"It's out on the moor, a few miles south of Sticklepath. Used to be a lunatic asylum."

Fry sat straighter. He'd heard the village of Sticklepath mentioned recently. It was where Arthur Wickens speculated the girl with amnesia might have come from.

"Used to be?" he prompted.

"Not sure what it is now, to be honest. I was never allowed into the main building. Very secretive. There's people being treated there for something. Met one of the poor buggers once when he wandered outside. He could barely remember his name. The way a couple of orderlies came after him, I got the impression that…" He cast his gaze about as though afraid of being overheard, and lowered his voice so Fry could barely hear him over the hum of conversation and laughter filling the room. "I think they keep them locked up." The man supped from his glass; it was almost empty.

Fry sat forward so he, too, could speak in a lower tone. "Why do you think he couldn't remember his name?"

The man shrugged. "Memory loss, I suppose." He drained his pint.

"Can I get you another?"

"No, but thanks for asking. I must be on my way." He shot Fry a sideways glance. "Whatever's going on at Cartwell Manor, they want to keep it on the quiet. I suspect that's why they let me go. I can be too curious for my own good."

"Why? What did you do?"

The man shook his head. "Think I've already said too much. Good evening to you." He stood and, without a further glance at Fry, began to push his way past the knots of drinkers.

Fry watched him go, his expression thoughtful.

Arthur Wickens allowed himself the luxury of a private grumble as he made his way downstairs to answer the insistent knocking on the front door.

"I'm coming as fast as I can," he muttered, although he knew the caller wouldn't be able to hear him.

He had been about to begin undressing for bed when the knocking came. At least he was still clothed and didn't have to hobble downstairs in his dressing gown.

Pausing to turn on the standard lamp, he made his way to the door and slid back the bolts. It opened to a gust of rain-dampened wind and two people.

One was a man, but Arthur's eyes were drawn to his companion, a young woman. They widened in recognition.

"Jenny!"

The woman gazed at him, but this was not the frightened girl who had turned up on their doorstep in her sodden nightclothes. She was fully dressed, protected from the elements by a raincoat, but it was her expression that was unrecognisable from the look of bewildered incomprehension which had characterised her first visit. She regarded him thoughtfully, as though sizing him up. Calculating. And there was something else lurking behind the expression. Contempt, maybe. Or malice.

He was so taken aback by her reappearance and, more so, by the change in her demeanour, Arthur instinctively shuffled back half a step, his hip complaining at the unaccustomed movement. The man accompanying Jenny seemed to take this as an invitation to enter and stepped inside, brushing past Arthur, who took another pace backwards, his senses taking temporary leave of absence. The girl followed her companion inside, favouring Arthur with a measured glance as she passed him.

A fresh gust of wind swept drops of cold rain into his face. He blinked, pushed the door closed and turned towards the visitors.

Gathering his wits, Arthur took in the man for the first time.

Tall, angular, with thinning fair hair combed across his head. Drops of rain stood proud, suggesting the strands of hair had been plastered to his skull with oil. The man had stopped in the middle of the parlour and turned back to look at Arthur.

Sharply featured, muddy-eyed, the man had the look of a ferret. A scar, pale even against the wan skin, ran from one corner of his mouth, disappearing beneath the jawline. In contrast to the way the woman had studied Arthur, his expression was dismissive. Disinterested.

Jenny was standing by the sofa, gazing down at it with a frown as though it triggered a memory of the last time she had been in the cottage.

Arthur cleared his throat. "How can I help you at such a late hour?"

"Mr Wickens, I believe? I would apologise for this intrusion, but it hardly seems worth the effort. May I enquire if Mrs Wickens is at home?" His voice was firm, but devoid of character. Banal, almost. The accent was impeccably the King's English; he sounded like an announcer on the BBC's World Service.

Arthur hesitated. He didn't normally take an instant dislike to a person, allowing time to grow to know them a little before making a judgement on their character, but rather felt he might make an exception in this man's case.

There was something else that made him reluctant to admit his wife was upstairs changing for bed; some undefined yet palpable threat.

He shook his head. "She's gone to stay with her sister in Barnstaple for a few days, mister...?"

"Jakes. Timothy Jakes." The man tutted impatiently as though his name was an irrelevance.

"Am I to assume you are the young lady's guardian? Did the police trace you and return her? Is her memory recovered?"

"So many questions and a waste of breath answering them. Either way, you will soon be unable to recall the answers." His mouth, a little crooked due to the scar, drew into a tight smile at the sound of the voice calling from upstairs.

"Arthur? *Arthur?* Who is it?"

"It sounds as though Mrs Wickens has made an unexpected return. Don't you think she would like to come down so young Jenny can thank you both for your kind hospitality?"

Arthur glanced at the girl. She had moved to the fireplace and stood with her back to him, gazing down at the hearth.

"My wife is getting ready for bed." His mouth felt unaccountably dry, making his voice sound hoarse. He cleared his throat. "She's been a little under the weather of late so I'd prefer it if she went to bed. Actually, I was preparing for bed myself so perhaps this can wait until another time."

He stepped to the front door, intending to open it and usher the visitors out. But a sound—a metallic ting—made him look back.

Jenny had turned away from the hearth and taken a step towards him, her expression difficult to read. She was clutching the iron poker.

"Private Lewis," said Timothy Jakes softly, "this is the man who tried to have you imprisoned."

"Private…? What?" Arthur felt his cheeks grow warm with indignation. "That's ridiculous. The girl was clearly suffering with some form of amnesia and I telephoned the police so they could find out where she had come from. They're better equipped…" He tailed away when Jenny took a firmer grip on the poker and another step in his direction.

Jakes was shaking his head and uttering a low sound which Arthur realised was a chuckle. The man reached out and took hold of the girl's forearm, lightly restraining her from moving any closer to Arthur.

"Mr Wickens, allow me to speak plainly. Young Jenny here has completed her treatment. This is her final test before she is promoted. That makes her… hmm, I suppose one could say that makes her someone you'd rather not be on the wrong side of. And, I'm afraid to say, you very much are on her wrong side as things stand."

"How so? We only tried to help her."

He thought about hurling open the door and yelling for help—trying to outrun the girl in his physical condition would be a brief exercise in futility—but instead looked towards the stairs. They creaked as Maud made her way down them, clutching her dressing gown tightly.

"Arthur? I heard voices… oh!"

Maud had caught sight of Jenny. She stopped near the foot of the stairs, wearing a look of confusion.

"Ah, Mrs Wickens," said Jakes. "Returned from your sister's, I see."

Maud's look of confusion deepened. She glanced at her husband. "Arthur, what's going on?"

Being reminded of his lie didn't cause Arthur to blush. He was more concerned about trying to protect his wife, all thoughts of yelling for help gone. The fact he had no idea why they were in danger didn't concern him. He had fought in the Great War, the ultimate exercise in incomprehensibility.

"I don't know," he said simply. He hobbled across the room. Maud came down the last of the stairs and stood by his side.

"I can see you're perplexed," said Jakes, his tone changing to that of a kindly uncle. It didn't suit him. "Maybe I can tell you enough to help you make your decision." He let go of the girl's forearm. She remained standing still, regarding both Arthur and Maud through narrowed eyes, the poker held stiffly before her like a sword.

"It was unfortunate Private Lewis's impromptu night trek ended here. Even then, we might have been able to let things lie if you hadn't decided to notify the local newspaper."

Arthur frowned. "How did you—"

Jakes raised his hand in a terse shushing gesture. "That was foolish of you, Mr Wickens. Foolish in the extreme. You see, Private Lewis is part of an experimental programme. One that is top secret. One that we cannot allow the press to become aware of. You might therefore say my errand tonight is to tie up loose ends of a thread which has become temporarily unravelled. But I'm nothing if not a fair man and thus I give you a choice. You can both accompany us now—I have a van parked outside—and you will later be returned in precisely the same state of physical health you are in presently." He exhaled sharply through his nose. "As for your mental health, well, that's a different matter, but you may prefer it to the alternative."

"That being?" asked Arthur.

Jakes's kindly affectation disappeared and his eyes glinted darkly in the lamplight. "Being bludgeoned by an iron poker is such an ignominious end, don't you think? So messy."

Arthur felt Maud's hand scrabble for his own. He clutched it tightly.

Part Two: The Perils of Practical Journalism

Seven: Dartmoor

Fry endured a restless night, listening to the wind's banshee howl. Rain spattered the window with such force it might have been dried peas striking the glass. While he tossed and turned, his body weary but his mind alert, an idea formed.

The storm had blown itself out by dawn and Fry awoke from a fitful doze to a relatively calm morning. The occasional cluster of bruised clouds drifted across a deep-blue sky, holding the promise of more rain, but of the showery type rather than the deluge which had fallen overnight.

At breakfast, while his landlady stood over a frying pan and the aroma of crisping bacon wafted his way, Fry cleared his throat.

"Mrs Truscott, I won't be here for lunch. Thought I might take advantage of a free weekend and the clement weather to put in a spot of hiking."

Mrs Truscott glanced out of the window. "See what you mean about the weather. The howling wind has dropped away, right enough. Would you like me to prepare you a packed lunch?"

"That would be smashing, if it's no trouble."

"No trouble at all."

Fry smiled. He was growing rather fond of his landlady, a stout widow in her early sixties. When he had first moved in following the deaths of the couple who had taken him in as an evacuee, he had found her rather stern. But she soon seemed to warm to him, especially when she learned he had lost not only his natural parents, but his adoptive ones, too. Fry suspected she felt a little sorry for him and secretly enjoyed mothering him, especially now he was the only lodger in residence.

While he tucked into a plate of bacon, Mrs Truscott joined him at the table. She seemed to take pleasure from watching him eat. Saturday breakfasts were a treat for Fry—it was when he consumed his weekly bacon ration. He sometimes suspected part of his land-lady's ration made it onto his plate, though the one time he had dared to ask her, she had shaken her head with a finality that said this wasn't a topic he should broach again.

"Where are you thinking of hiking, Mr Fry?"

That was another topic out of bounds for discussion: her insistence on addressing him as 'Mr Fry'.

"Oh. Thought I'd head out onto the moor. Get a bus into Sticklepath and strike out from there."

"Sticklepath? That's on the Exeter road. Plenty of buses will pass that way."

Fry nodded, chewed and swallowed his last bite of bacon, and pushed his plate away with a contented sigh.

When he glanced at Mrs Truscott, she was regarding him with a look of mild concern.

"Is anything wrong?" he asked.

"You will be careful, won't you? I've lived on the edge of the moor daughter, wife and widow and seen many lives lost by those going recklessly into its wilds. Especially at this time of year. With all the rain that's fallen, there will be swollen brooks, marshes and bogs where none existed before, mists that rise without warning from the ground and lead the unwary traveller astray."

Fry smiled. "I was ten when I was evacuated from London to Devon." His smile faltered. "Not long afterwards, I was orphaned when my father was killed in France and my mother didn't make it to the air raid shelter in time. Without any other family to return to in London, I stayed here." He shrugged and forced the smile back onto his face. "I've lived away from London longer than I lived in it so consider myself to be more a country boy than a city one now. I don't intend venturing more than a few miles into the moor, I *am* aware of the dangers and I'll be careful." He tapped his stomach. "Besides, I have to take some exercise to counteract the effects of your wonderful cooking."

As he'd anticipated, the compliment made his landlady blush and removed her serious expression. She flapped a hand at him.

"Oh, get away with you." Her tone was stern, but Fry recognised the pleased look in her eyes.

He pushed away from the table. "I shall get ready and make a prompt start."

"I'll have your lunch ready in two shakes of a lamb's tail."

Fry decided not to wear his overcoat since it would make him too warm and, if he was caught in a shower, would become too heavy for hiking. Instead, he put on the old tweed jacket he'd worn—almost worn out—when he became an apprentice journalist. Threadbare at the elbows, frayed at the collar and cuffs, it nevertheless made suitable attire for a brisk stroll across moorland on a calm December day. With sturdy boots, thick woollen socks, notebook and pencil tucked into an inside pocket of his jacket, and a compass in his trousers pocket, he was ready.

Mrs Truscott was waiting for him by the front door. She handed him some paper-wrapped packages and a small tin flask of water.

"Made you a few sandwiches. It's only what was left of last week's cheese ration, but it should keep your belly from rumbling. I've wrapped them separately so they'll fit into your pockets."

"Thank you, Mrs Truscott." The packages and flask slipped comfortably into the pockets of his jacket. "They'll keep me going nicely."

In truth, Fry wasn't overly keen on the cheese produced under rationing. 'Government Cheddar' most people called it. 'Government Shudder' was how the Head of Classifieds at the *Totleigh Times* referred to it. It made Fry feel more kindly disposed towards the cheese.

"There's also this." She held out a stick: midriff-high, gnarled and knobbly. "It belonged to Mr Truscott. It should aid your stride and you can use it to test any ground which looks uncertain. Should help you avoid blundering into any bogs."

Fry took the stick from her. It felt sturdy, the top section smooth from use and the perfect girth to grip comfortably.

"That's splendid. It will be a great help." He smiled down at her. "Well, I'll be on my way."

"Dinner will be at eight o'clock sharp."

"I'll see you then."

Fry glanced back once. His landlady was watching him from the doorstep. The concerned expression had reappeared on her face.

His stroll to the bus station took him past Totleigh Public Library. Fry went inside and made for the reference section. They had the most recent Ordnance Survey map for northern Dartmoor, the 1946 edition.

Fry opened it at one of the reading tables and located Sticklepath. It didn't look very big; more a hamlet than village. He moved his gaze down the map, onto the moor, finding what he was looking for almost immediately. A small rectangle and a one-word legend: asylum. A quick scan confirmed there was nothing else marked within miles that could be what he sought.

If this was Cartwell Manor, the chap in the tavern had spoken truly. It looked to be no more than a few miles south of Sticklepath.

He took out his notebook and made a quick sketch. If he crossed the River Taw at the road bridge in the village before entering the moor, he wouldn't have to worry about having to ford it later. Then a steady south-south-west bearing should bring him to the manor.

The building appeared to be in the middle of nowhere. Two miles or so to the east lay a couple of farms; a few miles to the west, the River Taw. No other buildings were marked on the map in the vicinity; no roads were shown, only a meandering dotted line denoting a footpath or, at best, cart track leading past the manor.

"Hmm, splendid isolation," he murmured to himself.

Hardly surprising, he thought upon reflection. Lunatic asylums tended to be located on the fringes of society, as though the madness of the inmates might otherwise infect the general populace.

Fry folded the map and returned it. Exiting the library, he made for the bus station.

~~~
~~~

Mrs Truscott had been correct: the tiny village of Sticklepath lay along the main road to Exeter. Buses ran through the village regularly—there had been a marked increase in bus services since the end of petrol rationing in May that year. Private motor car ownership remained a luxury for most people in the austerity of the postwar years and the roads were, as usual for December, quiet. So it was Fry found himself in Sticklepath before the hour had long passed ten.

As planned, he followed the main road out of the village in the direction of Exeter until he had crossed the Taw. He could have continued to follow the road for a few more miles until he reached the farms and then struck out westwards across the moor, but he preferred to feel the springiness of grass and heath beneath his feet instead of unyielding road, and yearned to hear nothing but wind and cries of birds in place of the growl of the combustion engine.

The swashing sounds of the river, swollen by rains, behind him, Fry turned from the road and stepped onto Dartmoor.

Eight: Cartwell Manor

The moor did indeed prove to be boggy after the overnight rain, and all that had fallen during the dreary autumn, but Fry found that by exercising caution and using the late Mr Truscott's cane as a testing rod on any patches which looked dodgy, he was able to pick his way safely through the soggiest parts.

Any underlying unease caused by his reading of the Conan Doyle novel did not surface. On such a splendid winter day, there was nothing about the wild beauty surrounding him to cause disquiet. And while perhaps he had overstated his position to his landlady over breakfast, the reality was that he felt at least *as much* of a country boy as a city one.

While the winter sun rode higher and he found his way becoming firmer as bedrock rose to the surface, he settled into a comfortable stride and began to enjoy the exercise. Soon he had jumped over the last of the swollen streams lying across his path and the going became almost exclusively across areas of exposed, lichen-covered granite, broken only by patches of coarse grass and heathland where soil managed to cling to the underlying rock despite its exposure to rain and winds.

He relaxed into the hike, enjoying the breeze in his face—chilly, but not as biting as it would be by January—and the occasional calls of passing birds. Since deciding to settle in Devon, he had put his natural curiosity to use by researching local bird species and, though by no means an expert, fancied he recognised the calls and winter plumage of starlings, golden plover and lapwings.

By checking his compass regularly, he maintained a steady south-south-west bearing, which naturally avoided the forested areas of Dartmoor. He passed through the occasional stand of oaks and stopped for a bite to eat in a copse, sitting on the trunk of a tree which hadn't survived the autumn storms. The remaining trees blocked out much of the breeze and, if not balmy, the atmosphere was unseasonably pleasant. Even the Government Cheddar tasted better than usual.

He struck a rutted track heading in his direction and decided to follow it. Fry did not own a pocket- or wristwatch—it was on his list of things to acquire when he enjoyed the salary of a journalist—but he estimated it wasn't long after midday when he caught his first glimpse of Cartwell Manor.

A high stone wall, constructed from locally quarried granite by the looks of it, enclosed extensive grounds dotted liberally with mature trees, mostly of the deciduous variety, bare and skeletal, but with the occasional green conifer thrown into the mix. Through the trees, at the end of a winding driveway, the manor was visible due to its slight elevation above the surrounding moor. Built of the same material used to make the boundary wall, it presented an imposing sight.

The main building rose to three storeys, with a clock tower—the clock face showed the time as twenty past twelve—rising the height of another two storeys. The walls of the tower were crenelated, like the walls of a castle. Long two-storey wings stretched away to either side of the main construction. The roofs of both manor and wings contained leaded windows, suggesting the attic spaces were used for more than merely storage.

It had been a few years since Fry read *The Hound of the Basker-villes*, but he imagined Conan Doyle might have had Cartwell Manor in mind for Baskerville Hall when he penned the tale. Even on such a pleasant day as this, the manor held a hint of menace, with its blank windows like blind eyes and its wings stretching out like arms ready to grasp the unwitting visitor in its clutches. Add darkness and ground fog and you'd have, he thought, the archetypal haunted house.

The first clammy fingers of unease slipped under his collar. He shivered and forced his mind away from the fanciful. It was then he realised he had no real idea what to do next.

His plan, such as it was, had been to hike across the moor until he located the manor; it had not extended any further. Making sure he avoided marshy areas and kept his bearings had fully occupied his thoughts during his trek. The fine weather and wild beauty of the moor had ensured he remained preoccupied with his immediate surroundings, rather than plan what he would do when he reached his goal.

The entrance to the estate was through a pair of wrought iron gates attached to two tall stone pillars. Carved ornately into the face of one pillar was the word 'Cartwell'; on the other, 'Manor'. The gates stood wide open.

While he pondered, Fry extracted the small flask from his pocket and took a sip of water. It was almost empty. Glancing about to make sure he wasn't being observed—he had seen nobody since leaving the road at Sticklepath—he tipped up the flask and emptied it. He now had an excuse to approach the manor.

The driveway consisted of fine gravel over compressed earth, providing a firm footing. Fry strolled along it, trying to convey the attitude of a casual rambler. He glanced about as though admiring the grounds, while looking for clues as to what went on here.

Between trees and patches of shrubs and flower beds, now winter bare, the grounds were mainly laid to lawn. These weren't the manicured lawns of stately homes, but unkempt areas of rough grass, scuffed and threadbare in places as though trodden on frequently, not merely for the occasional garden party or game of croquet. There was little to indicate the gardens were normally tended by a groundskeeper; perhaps the man he'd met in the public house had lost his job through incompetence.

Away to one side, Fry glimpsed a series of wooden structures and ropes, partly obscured by trees, which reminded him of the sort of assault course associated with military training.

The sun hung low, currently unobstructed by clouds. Weak as it was, it did enough to turn the windows of the manor reflective, making it impossible for Fry to tell if his amble up the drive was being observed.

As he approached the double front doors, one of them opened, giving Fry his answer. An unsmiling woman stood there. Fry forced a smile to his face and strode forward.

"Hello, there," he said, assuming a tone he imagined would sound like that of a stray hiker. "I'm making the most of this fine day to take a stroll across the moor and seem to have run out of water. I've not passed a stream since a mile or two back and so I wondered…"

He fumbled in his pocket and held up the tin flask with an open, hopeful smile.

The woman glanced at the flask. She was probably in her late forties, dressed in a sober brown woollen jacket and skirt. Efficient-looking.

"These premises are not open to the public," she said.

"I'm only asking for some water. I don't need to come in." Fry very much wanted to go in, but could think of no good excuse. Unless… "Having said that, I am in dire need of using the lavatory, if it wouldn't be imposing too much." He began to shift from foot to foot as though desperate to relieve himself. In fact, he had gone behind a rocky outcrop half a mile back, being careful not to point into the breeze.

The woman sighed. "Your name, sir?"

The question took him by surprise—why did she want to know his name merely for him to use the lav?—and the thought of giving a false name didn't cross his mind. "Fry. Jonathan Fry."

"One moment, please, Mr Fry." She disappeared, pulling the door closed behind her.

In case he was still being observed, Fry continued to shift from foot to foot, while it occurred to him he could have used a false name. But, then, why should he? He might be a journalist—at least, an apprentice—but it was his weekend off and he was merely en-joying a ramble across the moor. If he happened to discover something about Cartwell Manor while he was at it, that needn't, and perhaps oughtn't, be under a fake name. Using a made-up name would somehow, he felt, pollute any discovery with the taint of deviousness.

The door opened to reveal the same unsmiling woman. She

nodded at him.

"Please, Mr Fry, come in."

The entrance vestibule opened onto a tiled hallway, unadorned by furnishings except for a plain wooden bench standing against a side wall. A staircase and various plain doors led from the hallway. There was no evidence of a reception area or anything to suggest this was a place accustomed to welcoming visitors.

The woman made no move to introduce herself. She indicated a door next to the staircase.

"The water closet is there. You will find a tap from which you may fill your container."

Fry did not need to use the lavatory, but yanked the chain attached to the cistern above it for form's sake. He held his flask under a tap which shuddered and clanked when he turned it on, but the water it spat out looked clean enough.

While he waited for the flask to fill, he contemplated his next move.

He had found, and gained entrance to, Cartwell Manor, but whether this place had anything to do with the mystery of Jenny Lewis he was no nearer to finding out. There was no evidence to suggest there was any connection, other than the man in The Coach Inn had mentioned meeting someone here suffering from memory loss, and Mr and Mrs Wickens believed it likely the young girl with amnesia had come across the moor from roughly this direction. No real evidence at all; circumstantial, at best, it would be referred to in a court room.

Beginning to feel he was on a wild goose chase, he wondered what he could do to rule out Cartwell Manor from his enquiries. Ascertaining what went on here might be a good place to start.

Besides, he thought, *what's the worst that could happen? This turns out to be a retirement home for the elderly and I've enjoyed a decent hike across Dartmoor.* That wouldn't explain the assault course he'd glimpsed through the trees. *A military training college, then.*

He shrugged and let himself out of the W.C.

~~~

The hallway was empty, with no sign of the woman who had let him in. Fry glanced around, wondering how he could take advantage of his apparent good fortune in being left alone. Before he could decide which of the many doors to try, perhaps with the ready excuse he was merely trying to find his way out—flimsy, he knew, seeing as the entrance vestibule was obvious—one of the doors opened and a man entered the hallway. He was tall and pale, with thinning fair hair and a scar leading from the corner of his mouth.

"Mr Fry, I assume?" He stopped a few yards before Fry, making no move to hold out his hand to shake.

"Er, yes. That's me." There was something about the man's expression, something *knowing*, which made Fry blunder on. "I was taking a hike across the moor when I ran out of water and came across this manor and a lady was kind enough to allow me to use the water closet..." The man's thin lips formed into a smirk and Fry tailed off.

"Indeed."

The man looked away from Fry, as though dismissing him, and to the open doorway through which he'd entered. A couple emerged and Fry gave a gasp of recognition.

"Mr and Mrs Wickens!"
~~~

Nine: Living in the Past

The elderly couple stepped into the hallway. They both wore heavy outdoor coats and their arms were linked, leaning into each other as if for mutual support. Arthur Wickens moved a little awkwardly and with an occasional wince; perspiration glistened on his brow.

Paying no attention to Fry, they shuffled forward until they stood in front of the fair-haired man. They glanced at him uncertainly, before dropping their gazes to the tiled floor. Neither of them made a sound.

Fry took a couple of paces nearer to the couple.

"Mr and Mrs Wickens? Arthur? Maud?"

They didn't look up. Arthur Wickens unlinked his arm from his wife's and passed it around her, pulling her tightly to him. She leaned in to her husband, as though needing his comfort.

The fair-haired man clapped his hands. "I see you are acquainted. How delightful."

Fry moved closer until he was standing a step away from the elderly couple.

"Arthur? Don't you remember me? I came to visit you and Maud a few weeks back."

The old man raised his head and looked at Fry. No spark of recognition ignited his eyes. He stared at Fry without expression.

"You must remember," insisted Fry, feeling a mixture of frustration and disquiet. "I work for someone you know. Um…" So accustomed was he to referring to his senior editor as the Chief, for a moment Fry couldn't recall his name. Yet, for a reason he couldn't articulate which had to do with the fair-haired man, Fry did not want to mention the newspaper. Then it came to him. "George Samuels. You remember George, surely?"

"George…" murmured Arthur in barely a whisper.

Fry nodded encouragingly. He spared a glance at the other man. He was watching the scene, a sneer distorting his mouth, making the scar stand out whiter against his pale skin. Something about the man unnerved Fry, but he turned his attention back to the Wickenses.

Arthur's lips moved and his brow furrowed. "George," he repeated. "The war. I fought with him in the war."

Fry shook his head. "George didn't fight in the war, Mr Wickens. He didn't leave England. He worked for the government in the countryside. Something top secret…" Fry broke off as realisation hit home. "You're not talking about the Second World War, are you? You fought with George in the Great War. That's how you came to know each other."

"Passchendaele." It was still little more than a whisper. "We fought together in the mud. The stink of shit and blood and death. Men and horses screaming. Drowning. Shells exploding…" He grimaced, clutching with his free hand at his hip as though in pain.

His wife turned within his grasp and looked up at him. Her arm came across his chest and hugged him. "There, Arthur, it's all right. It's over. You won't have to go back to the front. Soon you'll be well enough to travel home…" A look of confusion passed across her face.

"Maud?" said Fry gently. "Where do you think you are?"

Her gaze fluttered towards him, then away. It looked haunted.

"I…" she murmured. "I don't know…"

"Do you know who I am? Do you remember me coming to your cottage?"

"Cottage?" She looked at Fry again, the skin around her eyes crinkling with the effort of trying to recall. "I've never seen you before." Her features broke into an expression of utter bewilderment and she turned her face away, hiding it against her husband's chest.

Fry's sense of unease deepened. He turned to the man with the scar. "What's happened to them?"

The man shrugged, the sneer not leaving his face. "They're old. Old people often live in the past."

Fry shook his head. "I went to their home not more than three weeks ago. We sat and chatted over a cup of tea. They might be old but there's nothing wrong with their minds. Something's happened to them to make them like this."

The man acted as though Fry hadn't spoken. He turned to the couple.

"Mr and Mrs Wickens, are you ready to go home?"

"Home?" Maud turned her head to look at the man. "We can go home?"

"Of course. I had intended taking you myself, but Mr Fry's unexpected visit means Miss Danes will be your chauffeur."

The woman who had let Fry in appeared in the doorway. She had donned an outer coat and was tugging on leather gloves.

Maud looked up at her husband. His expression remained faraway and stricken as though he still saw the battlefields of Belgium of more than thirty years in the past.

"Arthur, my love? We're going home."

"Do you know where home is?" asked Fry gently.

"Of course," said Maud. "We are both from Devon. And that's where we'll return."

"To Ashmoor? To your cottage?"

Once more, Maud's expression wrinkled in bewilderment.

"Ashmoor…?"

"All right," said Fry, turning to the man with the scar, anger giving his voice resonance. "I want to know what's going on here. They clearly don't even remember their own home. Who are you? What is this place?"

"My name is Jakes. Timothy Jakes. I work for Dr Emery. And you work for the *Totleigh Times*." He smirked.

"How do you know that?" Fry's anger was seeping away, replaced by a deeper sense of wrongness.

"Oh, we have our sources, too, Mr Fry." He tittered as if pleased by his own wit. "Well, these good people can't linger to chat any longer. They must get home."

"No. Wait." Fry took half a pace towards him and the man's smirk grew wider until it seemed his face must split open. It didn't quite reach his muddy eyes, though. Something in them, some sense of menace, of barely restrained violence and danger, dissipated the last of Fry's anger and made him reluctant to draw any closer to Jakes. "Tell me what you've done to them."

"Dr Emery will answer your questions, I'm sure. I shall take you to him shortly." He gestured to the elderly couple. "Mr and Mrs Wickens, if you'd like to follow Miss Danes."

Fry watched the couple shuffle after the woman. Neither of them spared him a glance.

"Come."

Jakes had already begun to ascend the staircase. He glanced back at Fry. The scar running from his mouth looked paler at this increased distance, like a fault line in a tor.

Fry started towards the staircase and Jakes gave a smirk before continuing to ascend. Trying to tamp down the sense of unease threatening to overwhelm him, Fry followed.

Jakes paused at the landing and stood for a moment, looking out of the window. Fry, too, paused, reluctant to catch the man up.

The encounter with the Wickenses had unsettled him badly, to the extent it almost overshadowed the other discordant note recently sounded. How did this man know where he worked?

He waited until Jakes had started up the next flight of stairs before resuming his ascent. As Jakes had done, Fry paused at the landing. The window began at chest height, allowing a view down into the rear grounds of the manor. Fry had to stifle a gasp.

What must once have been the back gardens were shielded from the moor by rows of trees, sharp granite outcrops and thick stands of gorse. The area—perhaps the size of three football fields—was given over to row upon row of low buildings, occupying half the space. The remainder had been paved. It resembled a military base with barracks and parade ground. It wasn't this which made Fry gasp.

The paved area was occupied by people, many people. Ranks and files of men and women, all dressed in dark clothing, stood with legs apart, hands behind backs, facing a woman who seemed to be addressing them, though Fry could not hear what she said. Not only men and women; some members of the assembly looked to have barely attained puberty.

Fry turned away, troubled. He glanced downstairs at the entrance lobby, at the empty expanse of tiled flooring leading to the entrance vestibule. There was nothing to prevent him from striding back down the stairs, out of the doors and onto the moor.

Nothing except professional curiosity and pride. He had come here to follow up a possible lead on a story entrusted to him by his chief editor. What sort of journalist turned tail and fled at the first sign of discomfort?

Fry rounded the corner and started up the next flight of stairs.

Later, during a rare chance for reflection, he would come to regret his decision.

Ten: Dr Emery

The corridor on the first floor was long and empty. It echoed to their footsteps on the wooden floorboards. And to other, more distant noises. Snarls, as from wild animals, and more piercing sounds.

"Are they... screams?" Fry asked.

Jakes, ten paces ahead of Fry, didn't pause and didn't answer, though Fry imagined his shoulders shook slightly as if in amusement.

Closed doors lined the corridor to either side. Most of them bore sturdy drawn bolts. As Fry passed, one door shook and there came a thud of something heavy hitting the other side of it, making him jump.

Jakes gave no sign he'd even heard the noise.

Fry's unease cranked up another notch.

The corridor was lit by electric lights spaced along the walls. They gave out a weak light which tinged the walls—painted grey, like the inside of a prison—a sickly pallor.

Jakes reached the end of the corridor and paused outside a set of double doors.

When Fry reached him, he opened them and stepped inside. The doors led into an ante-room, set out like a receptionist's office. A desk sat alongside another set of double doors. A typewriter and telephone occupied the surface of the desk, but the chair stood empty.

Without waiting to see if Fry was following, Jakes strode over to the inner set of doors and opened them without knocking. Only then did he glance back.

"In here."

He stood aside and motioned Fry into the room beyond.

The inner office was spacious, a row of windows giving the room a light, airy feel. In front of the largest window, which looked north over the grounds and to the moor beyond, stood a large desk, around which a man was stepping. But Fry's attention was momentarily distracted by the array of jars and strange-looking Bakelite boxes with dials sitting on shelves and cabinets which filled the gaps between windows. Some of the jars contained murky liquid and the suggestion of objects—organic objects—suspended within. Fry had watched reruns of the Boris Karloff *Frankenstein* films at Totleigh's grandly named Palace Cinema; the rows of specimen jars and boxes reminded him a little of Dr Frankenstein's laboratory as imagined in those films.

He dragged his attention away at the sound of a throat being cleared. The man whose office this must belong to had stopped in front of him, holding out a hand.

"Mr Fry? I am Malcolm Emery, the proprietor of Cartwell Manor. Welcome."

Fry shook the man's hand. It was small, matching his stature, his grip weak but dry.

"*Dr* Emery, I understand?"

The man nodded. He was around a foot shorter than Fry, with a bald head and pointed nose. Fry suspected that beneath the neatly trimmed, greying beard the man's chin was also pointed. His three-piece suit and highly polished shoes suggested elegance, despite being brown. If Fry had to hazard a guess, he would place the doctor's age at early fifties.

Fry looked around at a sound behind him. Jakes had closed the doors and positioned himself inside the office to one side of them, like a sentry.

"Please, Mr Fry," said Dr Emery. "Won't you sit down?"

The man strode back behind his desk, motioning to one of the chairs in front of it as he went. After a moment's hesitation, Fry sat, leaning his cane against the back of the desk.

His gaze was drawn to the object occupying a corner of the desk: a circular glass bowl, containing water and an orange fish about the size of Fry's thumb. He had seen a fish like this before while visiting a family to talk about their Anderson shelter.

"I see you've noticed my new pet," said Dr Emery. "Meet Lethe the goldfish."

"Leafy? Strange name for a fish."

"Ah. Not a student of classical mythology, Mr Fry?"

Fry shook his head. "Not really, no."

"His name is *Lethe*, after the Greek god of forgetfulness. Goldfish are becoming popular as pets, you know."

"So I understand. I don't see the attraction myself. Can't take them for a walk; they can't sit on your lap and let you rub their belly; can't throw a stick for them to fetch. Must be a dull sort of existence, too, swimming round and round in an oversized drinking glass all day."

A smile crossed the doctor's face and a sound came from behind Fry, where Jakes stood: the soft snort of a chuckle being repressed.

"Hold that thought, Mr Fry," said Dr Emery, holding up one finger. "You've hit on the crux of the matter. Yes, indeed, the very crux."

Squashed into the bench seat of the Bedford van, the elderly couple continued to clutch hands tightly, as though each providing the other's only grip upon reality. Their driver didn't say a word during the journey from the moor. She dropped them outside a stone cottage and motioned for them to go in, watching them carefully as they hesitantly opened the door. When they glanced back uncertainly, she nodded and waved a hand, shooing them inside like a school mistress directing recalcitrant children.

They closed the door behind them and listened to the van pull away, before turning to take in their surroundings.

They didn't release hands until, with a gasp, the woman pulled away and made for the sideboard occupying one wall. She picked up a framed photograph and stared at it. When she turned to the man, her eyes glistened with wonder.

"Look, Arthur," she said, "it's us. On our wedding day. We're married."

Arthur glanced at her with a puzzled frown, before turning back to the wall mirror in front of which he'd come to a halt.

Maud replaced the photograph on the sideboard and joined her husband in front of the mirror. They gazed at their reflections in silence.

A long moment later, Maud turned to Arthur and held one hand to his cheek. Her voice was little more than a bewildered murmur.

"When did we grow so old?"

Eleven: The Goldfish Syndrome

Fry straightened in his chair. Since encountering Mr and Mrs Wickens in the entrance hallway, and Jakes revealing he knew he was a journalist, Fry had been operating in somewhat of a daze. High time to assert himself.

"Look, Dr Emery," he began, "I don't know why you think I'm here, but I was out hiking across the moor when I ran out of…"

He broke off at the sound of low laughter coming from behind him. Dr Emery regarded him impassively, saying nothing.

Fry sighed. Pointless, he supposed, maintaining the charade of being a casual hiker in need of liquid refreshment. "All right," he continued, "I work for the *Totleigh Times*, as your colleague behind me already knows. I've been working on a story about a young woman who appeared on the doorstep of an elderly couple in Ashmoor. Mr and Mrs Wickens. But this, also, you already seem to know."

Fry watched the doctor closely. His expression didn't change, but he nodded.

"A delightful couple."

Fry waited, but it seemed Dr Emery wasn't about to elaborate.

"Yes," Fry said, "they are lovely, but not usually in such a state of confusion. They didn't know what year this is. What happened to them?"

A flicker of something passed across the doctor's face, but not an expression betraying, as Fry might have supposed, discomfort. It was more a flash of excitement, but gone almost as soon as it had appeared.

"They have forgotten some things." The doctor shrugged. "It can happen with people of advanced age. And some things are better not to be remembered."

Fry hesitated before taking a stab. "Like Jenny Lewis?"

A hint of a smile appeared on Dr Emery's lips. "Ah, indeed. Young Jennifer."

"So she *did* come from here." Fry exhaled loudly. "My hunch was right." Despite the sense of unease continuing to nag at him, Fry couldn't help but also feel a swell of pride. Maybe he did possess the instincts of a real journalist.

Dr Emery's smile grew wider. He looked beyond Fry to where Jakes stood beside the doors.

"Hunch?" said Jakes. "We almost had to draw you a map."

Fry frowned, his sense of pride sinking beneath renewed disquiet. He half-turned so he could look at Jakes. "What do you mean?"

The man gazed back at Fry, his mouth twisting into a smirk—apparently his favourite expression—which tightened and whitened his scar, accentuating it, giving him the appearance of a deformed, satanic clown. But he said nothing.

Fry turned to Dr Emery. "What do you do here? Who are all those people lined up outside like soldiers? What does that young woman have to do with this place?"

"Hmm," said Dr Emery. "I can see you'll have no peace of mind until you know more about Miss Lewis." He looked beyond Fry once more. "Mr Jakes, would you be so good as to fetch young Jennifer?"

When Jakes left the office, some of Fry's apprehension went with him. There was something about the man and his scar which made Fry feel on edge, especially when Jakes was behind him. *Come on*, he told himself. *You're a journalist—start acting like one.*

He reached into his jacket pocket and took out his pencil and notebook. Dr Emery continued to watch him, expressionless once more.

"I'm going to take some notes," Fry said, stopping himself from adding 'if that's all right with you'. "What can you tell me about what you do here?"

Dr Emery did not reply immediately, but gazed at Fry with that peculiar lack of expression. Fry cleared his throat to repeat his question, when the doctor spoke.

"Turpitude."

Fry blinked. "I beg your pardon?"

"Immorality. Degeneracy. Iniquity." Dr Emery leaned forward. Gone was the impassivity; his face was now alive with enthusiasm, eyes glittering with zeal. "They are stains on our society, Mr Fry. That is how my work began. Researching methods to eradicate the causes of depravity. Of course"—he spread his hands—"it has moved far beyond, but more of that soon. For now, let's talk about Jennifer Lewis."

"All right. She's the same young woman who disappeared from an orphanage near Okehampton when she was sixteen, I assume?"

Dr Emery raised his eyebrows. "I see you are truly a journalist. Yes, this is the same Jennifer Lewis. A sad tale is hers, of deprivation of a father figure in her life, of loss and grief at an impressionable age. Of stumbling from the path of decency." His gaze grew more intent. "Alcohol abuse, thieving, sexual proclivity. When she came to our attention, she was living on the streets of London, scratching a living by selling sexual favours. Two unwanted pregnancies by the age of nineteen, with one child given up for adoption, the other stillborn. At risk of a range of sexually transmitted diseases, not to mention a host of other life-threatening conditions to which her malnourished frame would have fallen prey if we hadn't saved her from herself."

"London? How would she come to your attention if she was in London?"

"Our work is well-known among certain higher echelons of society. Well-known and lauded, though not openly, for reasons that will become apparent soon enough."

"Higher echelons? Do you mean the government?"

"Let's say that some members of both the Home and Foreign Offices are sympathetic to our work and ensure we are able to go about it unobstructed by meddling officialdom."

Fry thought back to Arthur Wickens's tale of irregular police investigation into the girl's appearance, and his own encounter with the unforthcoming desk sergeant at Totleigh police station. "In other words, the police have been instructed to turn a blind eye.

Which begs the question: why talk openly to a journalist? You must know I'll be writing a report based on what I learn today."

Dr Emery gave a tight smile which didn't reach his eyes. Instead of responding to Fry's question, he nodded at the goldfish bowl.

"Behold Lethe. Swimming in circles inside a bowl which starves him of oxygen, stunts his growth and is only otherwise remarkable for its singular absence of stimulation. Keeping a living creature so confined might be regarded as rather cruel, don't you think?"

"Um… Can't say I've ever given it any thought."

"Most people don't. If they consider the question at all, they convince themselves the fish suffers no harm. They put it down to the Goldfish Syndrome."

"What's that? I've not heard of it."

"Not surprising. It's the name I give to the excuse people make to absolve themselves of cruelty."

"But if you think keeping a goldfish is cruel, why do you have one sitting here on your desk?"

"To remind myself of the Goldfish Syndrome and how I started down the enlightened path I now tread."

Fry narrowed his eyes. He was beginning to think Dr Emery was as mad as the scientists portrayed in the *Frankenstein* films. "Um, so what, exactly, is this Goldfish Syndrome?"

The doctor motioned towards the fish. "Look at him, swimming round and round and round. The only visual stimulation is the scene outside the bowl and that only changes when there are people in the room. How, then, does Lethe not go out of his mind with the tedium of his existence?"

Fry cleared his throat while he thought of how he could respond, until he realised Dr Emery was no longer paying him any attention and his question had been rhetorical.

"The answer," continued the doctor, "so some scientists believe, is that goldfish are possessed of only the most rudimentary form of memory. They lack the ability to retain anything beyond the past few seconds. They cannot make memories and have no previous remembered experiences to call upon. Thus, they say, when the fish during its constant circling of the bowl passes the same filing cabinet or plant pot or shelf of scientific instruments, each time is as the first time. There can be no boredom, no tedium, because such feelings depend upon repetition of experience or negative comparisons with past experiences. He may have passed that same plant pot a thousand times already today, but he has forgotten each occasion so each new revolution of the bowl brings him only sights which are fresh."

Fry's brow furrowed in thought. "You say 'some' scientists believe this theory. I take it you're not one of them?"

The doctor gave a curt shake of his head. "No, indeed, not as it applies to the humble goldfish. But that's neither here nor there. I *know* the theory is of practical application. One which is of immeasurable benefit to humankind."

Again, the light of zealotry appeared in the doctor's glittering eyes. Fry shifted uncomfortably in his seat, then half-turned at the sound of the office doors opening behind him.

"Ah, good," said Doctor Emery. "Here is Jakes, returned with young Jennifer. It is time for a demonstration of the Goldfish Syndrome in practice."

Twelve: A Practical Demonstration

Jakes entered the office, followed by a young woman. She was dressed in dark trousers and jumper—army surplus, by the looks of them—ill-fitting, baggy, yet she wore them with an easy grace, as though relishing the unrestricted freedom of movement the clothes allowed. Her feet were clad in rubber-soled, canvas shoes, the sort yachtsmen wear.

The woman's fair hair was tied back, giving her cheekbones prominence and lending her expressionless face a degree of severity. She strode to the end of the desk and stood facing it in the classic 'at ease' stance, feet apart, hands clasped loosely behind back.

Jakes remained in the open doorway.

Fry felt doubly uncomfortable with Jakes behind him once more and the young woman in the pose of a sentry, unwavering gaze cast straight ahead, no more than a couple of yards away. Unease cranked towards alarm. He turned his chair so he was sitting side-on to both the doctor and Jakes, and facing the woman. The motion made the cane slide to the floorboards with a clatter. Fry leaned to the side and picked it up, laying it across his lap.

The woman's gaze flickered, darting down to the cane, eyes narrowing, but she didn't otherwise move.

"This," said Dr Emery, "is Jenny Lewis."

Jakes gave a light cough.

"Ah, of course," said the doctor. "Now she has completed her treatment, I should more accurately address her as Corporal Lewis."

"Corporal?" said Fry, unable to keep the incredulity from his tone. "She's in the army?"

The doctor smiled, but again it was a smile born of zeal rather than warmth. "She's in *an* army."

"Those people I saw through the landing window. They belong to an army?"

"Oh, yes. You could call it a secret army, since our work here is a closely guarded secret, as things of such moment must be."

"But… I saw children."

Dr Emery nodded gravely. "Sadly, delinquency knows no minimum age. But we do not accept anyone for our programme until they have attained the age of thirteen. We have many ten-, eleven- and twelve-year-olds keenly awaiting their thirteenth birthdays." He gave a small, humourless chuckle. "Perhaps I should more accurately say their parents or guardians are keenly awaiting their thirteenth birthdays."

"But, children…" Fry's words tailed away; he didn't know quite what to say.

He glanced down at his notebook; the blank page he'd turned to remained blank. He slipped it and the pencil back into his jacket pocket.

Dr Emery indicated the fish swimming around the glass bowl on his desk. "The Goldfish Syndrome, Mr Fry. It's ironic that although I don't believe there is such a thing, I use it as the basis of my work. And at an early stage of the treatment, subjects do indeed display the hallmarks of the syndrome—they are unable to retain beyond an hour or so memories of events that have just occurred."

Fry glanced at the young woman. "Like Jenny forgetting who Mr and Mrs Wickens were an hour after being introduced to them."

"Precisely, although that particular effect is fleeting and passes as the treatment progresses. It is more beneficial to remove the longer term memories. You see, many of our behaviours arise from events which occurred in our past. Sometimes, long in our past. They can influence the way we view the world, the way we react to certain stimuli, the way we interact with those around us, for many years later. Even, perhaps, for the remainder of our lives."

"I suppose," said Fry, finding the journalistic side of him interested despite his misgivings.

"By removing memories of the event, the effect is also removed."

"Removed?"

"Erased, Mr Fry, as easily and as permanently as you can erase a pencil mark in that notebook you carry around. Only, instead of rubber, we erase by the judicious use of electricity. A finely aimed and controlled application of electrical current to the appropriate area of the brain modifies the memory of the subject. After many years of research and experiment with invasive procedures, along came electroshock therapy, the answer to our prayers." He held up a finger as though emphasising a point to a lecture group. "Note we don't use it in the same way our colleagues in the medical professions do, to induce convulsions in their subjects. Instead, it has allowed us to fine-tune our methods to be able to erase memories of traumatic incidents going back to the subject's childhood. At a stroke—ahem, or perhaps I should say, at a bolt—we can remove the causes of delinquency."

He gazed at Fry as though expecting him to applaud.

"Um," said Fry, unable to shake the image of the *Frankenstein* films, "that's all very well, but how does it apply to Mr and Mrs Wickens? They are hardly delinquents."

The doctor chuckled. "Of course they aren't. They are merely bystanders who became involved in something they would be better off forgetting. And so we merely adjusted their memories so they would not remember their encounter with Corporal Lewis."

"I spoke to them. They couldn't remember the last thirty years."

"Their older memories will gradually return. For a short while, they will feel they are younger, which can't be a bad thing for people of their age." Dr Emery flapped a hand as though they were of no consequence. "This isn't about them."

Below his unease, Fry felt a flush of anger at the casual manner in which the doctor had dismissed the elderly couple. He opened his mouth to say as much, then caught sight of the woman. Jenny Lewis had turned her gaze towards him. It was regarding, calculating and cold, devoid of compassion. The words caught in his throat.

"Let me tell you," continued Dr Emery, "what this is about. We are building an army to defend these lands against the sort of aggression we have witnessed in the recent past. To face cruelty and blind hatred with brutality to match and exceed, and ultimately crush it as our oppressors would do to us."

Again he looked at Fry as though expecting him to give a rousing cheer.

"How does erasing a person's memories result in the type of army you're talking about?"

"Ah. We discovered there are certain, erm, other side-effects to our treatments. One in particular, the application of which will revolutionise the way we fight future wars."

"You think there will be more wars after what we've just lived through?"

"Oh, indubitably. And anyone who believes otherwise is incredibly naïve or inestimably stupid."

"Hmm." Fry guessed he fell into one of those categories; he found it difficult to think mankind could be so idiotic as to allow itself to become so fractured again. "All right, suppose you're correct, that there will be more wars. How will we fight them?"

"With soldiers who are incapable of showing mercy. You see, we discovered that as we strip away a person's memories, if we go far enough into their past we also begin to break down their moral compunctions." He uttered a short, humourless laugh. "In people like young Jenny here, morality was not a strong part of their character to begin with. Go far enough back—not so far the subjects forget who they are, but enough to tear away the last vestiges of learned virtue—and the subjects' sense of self-preservation is magnified to the point they will do anything to protect themselves and those who instruct them. For they also become malleable, responsive to orders from those in command, like any good soldier should be."

From his position in front of the open doors, Jakes gave another cough, a little louder.

"Yes, yes," said Dr Emery. "It's time to show you what I'm talking about, to demonstrate what young Jen— ahem, what Corporal Lewis is capable of."

He turned towards her. "Corporal Lewis?"

The woman inclined her head a little towards the doctor.

"This man"—he pointed at Fry—"has come here to cause mischief for you and your comrades. To cause you harm—"

"Hold on one moment," interjected Fry. "I've not come to do anything of the sort."

Dr Emery glanced at him. "Oh no?"

"No! I just came to… I mean, I'm here to…" He struggled to find the words. "I merely came to follow up a story," he finished lamely.

"Indeed," said Dr Emery, looking once more at the woman. "Corporal Lewis, how do we treat those who mean us harm?"

She spoke for the first time, her tone level, uninflected. "We meet menace with aggression. Hostility with ferocity. Inhumanity with destruction."

Dr Emery nodded. He pointed once more at Fry. "This man would expose to the world the great work we do here. He is a menace."

"We meet menace with aggression," repeated the woman.

"He would have us shut down. He is hostile to our work."

"We meet hostility with ferocity."

"He would have you and your comrades cast from your home. He is inhumane."

"We meet inhumanity with destruction."

Her gaze turned once more to Fry.

Jonathan Fry had been in his fair share of scrapes in the school yard. As a refugee, and later an orphan, with a 'funny' accent, he had been the target of local bullies. He stood up to them as best he could, took the bumps and bruises, inflicted one or two of his own. Bullies tend to prefer their victims to be compliant and he had been left alone soon enough. Since those days of short trousers and scraped knees, he had avoided confrontation. Until now.

Jenny Lewis took a step around the end of the desk, bringing her closer to Fry. He pushed against his chair, making it slide backwards with a scraping noise, and rose unsteadily to his feet, almost spilling the cane to the floor. He grabbed it—it felt reassuringly heavy in his hand, though he had no thought to use it as a weapon.

No coherent thoughts at all came to mind; it was overwhelmed by a pressing sense of bewilderment and fear.

Fry had been raised by his parents, and later by the kindly Devonshire couple who had taken him in, to be respectful to all, male and female alike. The idea of physically attacking a woman was abhorrent. Yet, it seemed, he might have to do exactly that.

The young woman did not carry a weapon, but clutched her hands into fists and took a step closer. She stared into his face, her expression neutral but her eyes hard, without mercy.

Fry swallowed, with difficulty; his mouth seemed to have run dry.

"Jenny," he croaked. "What Dr Emery said isn't true. I mean you no harm."

No change of expression showed in her face. She took another step closer; she was now one pace away.

Fry raised the cane and gripped it with both hands horizontally, prepared to use it to try to block the imminent attack.

The woman raised her hands. One remained curled into a fist; the other unfurled and she bent the fingers, drawing the hand into a claw.

Fry tensed.

"Enough!" barked Dr Emery, making Fry jump and involuntarily raise the cane towards Jenny.

She didn't flinch.

"Stand down, Corporal Lewis," said Jakes, crossing from the door to stand by her side. "That is an order."

For a moment, the woman continued to regard Fry, her hands poised for attack. Then abruptly she lowered them and took a few smart paces back to the end of the desk. She moved her hands behind her back and stood once more at ease. Still her expression hadn't altered.

Fry let out his breath heavily and lowered his arms. He continued to keep tight hold of the cane in hands which had started to tremble.

Dr Emery considered him. "I hope this has shown you, Mr Fry, our work here is not something to be taken lightly. Imagine, if you will, an army of Corporal Lewises. Armed and ready to fight on one word of command. Fearless, ruthless, uncompromising. Had we wanted her to, she would have torn you apart with her bare hands."

Fry could think of only one thing to say. "You'd better hope she never turns on you."

The doctor shook his head. "That is simply not possible. After completing the course of treatment, each subject is entirely under my control"—he nodded towards Jakes—"and that of my colleagues."

"Perhaps it would only take one to retain some memory of what you've inflicted upon them. Only one to make the others believe they are victims of a new barbarity."

A flash of doubt crossed the doctor's features, but he quickly recovered his poise. "I'm afraid you couldn't be more wrong, Mr Fry. It is impossible to resist the treatment, as you will soon discover for yourself. Later, when you and Corporal Lewis are comrades in arms, I shall not bother reminding you about this conversation since you shall not, due to the Goldfish Syndrome, be able to remember it." He smiled. It made him look smug.

"Only one," Fry repeated and felt a stab of satisfaction when he saw the same shadow of doubt surface momentarily on the doctor's face, before his features hardened.

"Please do not say that again or I will perhaps, after all, order Corporal Lewis to part your head from your body."

Fry believed the doctor—he had seen for himself in Jenny Lewis's eyes she had only one aim in mind, and that was to hurt him and keep hurting him until ordered to stop. There was only one thing to do in the face of such implacable hostility.

He turned towards his chair as though to move it back into its former position, but continued to turn until he was facing the open doorway.

Fry ran.

Part Three: The Secret Army

Thirteen: Man Hunt

Fry's precipitous flight from Dr Emery's office seemed to catch the other occupants unawares, for he was out of the door, through the ante-room and haring down the corridor without interference. He had almost reached the end of the corridor and the staircase leading back down to the lobby when he became aware, above the thudding of his heart, of the rapid, rhythmic slapping of rubber-shod feet racing after him.

He arrived at the staircase and risked a glance back. Jenny Lewis had almost caught up with him. Light on her feet, unencumbered by heavy outdoor clothing, she moved quickly. It only took a glance for Fry to realise she would overtake him by the time he reached the ground floor.

In desperation, more as a reflex than a conscious decision to act, Fry raised the cane and flung it into the woman's path. It bounced once on the tiled floor, flipped onto its end and tangled in her legs. With a grunt and a clatter, she fell headlong.

"I'm sorry," Fry called out, but he didn't wait to see if she was hurt.

Behind the spread-eagled woman, Fry caught glimpse of Jakes. The man had stopped at one of the doors lining the corridor and was drawing back the bolts.

Fry bounded down the stairs, taking two or three at a time. A glance out of the landing window as he passed told him the massed ranks had dispersed; the parade ground was deserted. He reached the landing and flung himself around the bend. He descended the second flight of stairs in the same devil-may-care manner.

The entrance hallway, too, was deserted. Fry ran across the tiled floor to the entrance vestibule. When he gripped the front door handle, a noise from behind made him freeze. A snarling, baying sound was coming from the stairwell, as though a pack of wild dogs had been set loose. A high-pitched scream arose, which seemed to be the signal for the snarling to grow louder and more feral.

Fry's hand tightened around the doorknob. For a moment which made his stomach lurch, he feared it would refuse to turn. He gripped tighter and twisted. The knob turned easily, allowing the doors to open to a rush of cold air.

The December breeze had freshened. Apart from the occasional bruised cloud, the sky remained clear and wintry pale. The low sun had moved past its zenith and swung beyond the west wing of Cartwell Manor. Praying the mass of people—he struggled to think of them as soldiers—he'd seen at the rear hadn't decamped to the front of the manor, Fry sprinted down the drive. When he risked another glance back, the sun no longer reflected from the manor's windows. From his office window, Dr Emery gazed down at him. It was difficult to be certain at that distance, but it looked as though the doctor was shaking his head as if to express disappointment. Fry didn't hang about to make sure.

He reached the open gates at the end of the driveway and hesitated. Above the rasping of his laboured breathing, he could hear an approaching engine. Bouncing along the rutted track came a dark green Bedford van.

From the direction of the manor, another sound intruded: a howl, rising in pitch like a wolf baying at the moon. Despite the heat generated by his headlong rush from the manor, Fry felt suddenly cold. He darted across the trail in front of the van. The startled face of Miss Danes peered at him above the steering wheel.

The moor stretched northwards away from Fry. Retracing his steps would provide little by way of cover. He didn't know what was coming in pursuit, but he doubted anything that could make such an ungodly noise would be put off the trail by the occasional copse of trees he had passed through on the way here.

Without breaking stride, he glanced wildly in both directions. Away to his left, to the west, he could make out a dark line of trees, something larger than a copse. Perhaps not big enough to qualify as a forest, but it looked substantial enough to be called 'woods'. He veered towards the dark line.

Another howl sounded, carried to him despite the stiffening breeze in his face. Fear lending his legs extra energy, he increased his stride.

Due to its slightly elevated position, Cartwell Manor remained visible as Fry hurried across the moor, casting anxious glances back. The undulations of the heath would soon hide him from view. Before that happened, Fry forced himself to stop and take a proper look from where he had come.

Another howl reached him against the breeze. He fully expected to see one, if not more, hounds being set on his trail, but there were no animals to be seen. There was, though, movement in front of the building. Lots of movement.

A stream of people had emerged from the manor, maybe around twenty, all dressed as far as Fry could tell at this distance in the same manner as Jenny Lewis. Army surplus clothes, dark greys and blacks and khakis, baggy and allowing unrestricted freedom of movement. The figure in front—a man, judging from his build and the way he ran—had already reached the gates. He pointed at Fry, lifted his face to the sky and opened his mouth. Another undulating howl reached Fry, despite the breeze at his back.

The other people caught up with the howler. Without pause, they all took off across the moor, leaping the rutted track like deer, and made directly for Fry.

Fry took to his heels.

The tin flask, sloshing with water, bumped against his hip. His boots, built for hiking not sprinting, felt like concrete blocks encasing his feet. Sweat covered his brow and ran down his back.

Fry shot occasional glances to his right, northwards, while he ran, hoping to see hikers or bird watchers out on the moor taking advantage of the unseasonably pleasant weather. Maybe if there were witnesses about, the pursuit would be called off—Dr Emery had made clear what went on at Cartwell Manor was not for public consumption. He'd talked about a secret army which would no longer be so secret if members of the public were present when a section of this army ran him down in full daylight.

Ran him down, as surely they would, and then what? Fry swallowed and tried to increase his stride, but his energy levels were depleting rapidly and his legs barely responded.

In every direction he could see, the moor was empty of people. Except, of course, behind him. When he risked a backwards glance, the nearest pursuer was only a couple of hundred yards away, and closing.

Fry skidded on a stretch of exposed granite, his feet shooting in different directions, his heart racing like a drum roll. He could not afford to take a tumble—they would be on him before he could reach the woods. He listed to one side, desperately cartwheeled his arms and managed to remain upright. His boots gained traction on thin soil and at last his weary legs responded to the frantic messages from his brain.

The line of trees loomed closer. Seconds later, Fry plunged between them.

Fourteen: Darkness Descends on Dartmoor

In contrast to the sparse stands of trees he'd passed through that morning, the woods were dense and Fry had to slow his pace to pick his way between thrusting boughs. A thick carpet of fallen leaves muffled his thudding footsteps and would make the sounds of pur-suit difficult to detect above his panting breaths. Although the trees were winter-skeletal, their branches often touched and intertwined, providing barriers which impeded rapid progress. The occasional deadfall made matters worse, forcing Fry to deviate right or left. He blundered on, weaving a random path. Before long, he had lost all sense of direction. And he was almost spent.

Rounding a thicket of impassable undergrowth, he came to a halt and listened. If there were any birds in the vicinity, they didn't call. The only sound he could hear above his ragged breathing was the faint whisper of the breeze, that too muted by the tightly growing trees.

Then he sensed it. Not exactly a vibration in the ground, not precisely a thudding, but a sensation nevertheless through the soles of his boots of heavy things approaching.

He could not make out anything through the branches, but his pursuers were dressed in colours which would not readily show up in this environment. Thankfully, so was he.

Then, something. A flash of movement, perhaps twenty yards away. Heading towards him.

Fry edged around the thicket, trying to put it between him and the pursuit. A howl erupted from what sounded closer than ten yards away, it was so loud, and his bladder almost gave way in fright.

Looking fearfully over his shoulder, he stumbled forwards, not paying attention to his footing or the lie of the land.

When the ground gave way beneath him and he pitched forward, he managed to stifle the cry which instinctively rose up his throat.

Fry tumbled headlong in silence, his world a jumbled mass of wet leaves and snatches of pale sky in the gaps between soaring branches.

Until his fall was brought to an abrupt halt by a hard obstacle. And the world went dark.

Fry lay still, trying not to gasp for breath. He'd fetched up against what felt like a fallen tree; leaves had collected against it to form a deep drift, partly covering it. His fall had buried him—leaves surrounded his face, as fragrant as a damp cellar, although he was still able to breathe around them. The collision with the trunk had driven most of the air from him, but he was lucky not to have been knocked unconscious. As it was, the first twinges of pain were making themselves felt in his brow, shoulder and knee, which had borne the brunt of the impact.

A groan wanted to escape his throat; he stifled it. Leaf mould invaded his mouth when he opened it wider to try to replenish his breath quicker. He dared not move, so used his tongue to force the mulch out.

Slowly, gradually, his breathing calmed. Muffled sounds intruded. He tried to ignore the increasing complaints from his bruised body and listened.

Rustling and swishing. Grunts of exertion. Snaps of breaking twigs. Thuds of heavy footsteps.

Fry felt a crazy urge to surge to his feet and run, despite his aches and weariness. He might surprise his pursuers and gain a head start, be away through the woods before they had time to collect themselves. Then a voice spoke and all thoughts of flight were driven from his mind. Though muted by the barrier of leaves covering Fry's head, the voice sounded close; its owner could not have been standing more than six feet away.

"He came this way." The voice was male and strangely without inflection. Robotic almost.

"So where is he?" The second voice was female and passionless. It might have been enquiring the way to the post office.

A grunt. "Must have clambered over this fallen tree."

Fry stifled another gasp as a tremor ran through the tree he was lying against when the speaker thumped or kicked it.

"I'll go this way," said the female voice. "You go that."

Another grunt from the male. Then, in a louder voice, as though addressing someone more distant: "Down here. Somewhere beyond this tree."

The trunk shook as someone heavily built clambered over it. More noises came, louder and closer. Vibrations ran through the ground as others descended the slope. The fallen tree shook to the impact of people hauling themselves over it. Fry brought up a hand and thrust it against his mouth to stop a startled cry escaping when a foot kicked him in the small of his back.

The noises grew fainter as their makers moved away, farther into the woods from where Fry lay.

I'll wait until they're well out of earshot. Then I can go back the way I came until I'm out onto the open moor and head north from there.

He remained still in case there were any stragglers. Although it was dank beneath the leaves, they acted as insulation, trapping his body heat. The increasing warmth combined with his disturbed sleep of the previous night, his physical exertions and expenditure of nervous energy.

His mind reeled with fear and bewilderment. Despite, or perhaps because of, them, Jonathan Fry fell asleep.

He awoke to darkness, a full bladder and a thought running through his mind: *only one.* An image, too, of a steel safe, embedded on its back in a solid concrete floor.

Despite the trapped body heat, he felt damp and chilled. He forced himself to remain still while he strained to hear signs of anyone in the vicinity. The night was calm and silent.

Only one. Although his subconscious mind was clearly trying to hint at the significance of the phrase, it took Fry a moment to recall what it meant. He tried to block out his current predicament while he concentrated, and it came to him—if only one person who underwent Dr Emery's 'treatment' retained sufficient memory of it, maybe he could convince the other victims of what had happened and maybe, just maybe, persuade them to turn on their abusers.

For Fry was under no illusion the people under the doctor's care, people like Jenny Lewis, were being abused. Perhaps they might listen to someone who had undergone the same abuse; they would, after all, be part of the same so-called army. They would, as the doctor had described it, be comrades in arms. That should at least ensure their attention, if not guarantee their belief. If only there was a way for a person undergoing the treatment to be able to remember it later.

The image again: a steel safe surrounded by concrete, a lever-type handle to open and close it, a dial to lock it. That image led to another: a prisoner of war, standing in front of an audience, relating how he'd survived.

Maybe there was a way…

That was a lot of 'maybes' but now wasn't the time to pursue the line of thought. Fry placed it on his mental back-burner; he had more immediate concerns on which to concentrate.

He straightened his legs, grimacing at the sharp flare of pain in his right knee, and turned from his side onto his back. His left shoulder ached and the left side of his forehead throbbed. Gingerly, he raised his hand to his face, forcing aside leaves. He touched his forehead, feeling a lump the size and smoothness of a small pebble. It was sore, but did not appear to be cut.

Fighting against stiffness making it feel he was made of wood, Fry clambered to his feet, shedding a shower of dried leaves and clumps of sodden ones. His knee griped but held his weight. Swaying a little from side to side, he relieved himself where he stood.

His stomach grumbled and his throat felt dry. He felt in his jacket pockets, turfing out more stray leaves. The tin flask was still there; he took a quick swig. The last cheese sandwich was in his other pocket, flat from where he had lain on it, but no doubt still edible— it would take more than a squashing to ruin Government Cheddar. Finding out would have to wait; he wanted to put some distance between himself and these woods before stopping to eat. He also wanted to warm up.

Fry took a futile glance about. The darkness beneath the trees was almost absolute; any star- or moonlight shining onto the moor did not make it to where he stood. He forced himself to stillness and listened once more. Faintly, he heard the distant hooting of an owl on the hunt, but no other sounds came. No voices or rustlings of people moving about.

He turned and began to clamber back up the slope down which he'd tumbled, digging his fingers into the loose surface of leaves and into the moist loam which lay beneath, wincing each time his sore knee came down.

In this way, he reached the top of the slope. Treading cautiously so as not to blunder blindly into thickets or jutting branches, he moved as directly in the opposite direction as the trees and undergrowth allowed.

By the time he emerged from the trees, blinking in starlit moorland, he had warmed up.

Fifteen: Flight Across the Moor

Fry stood at the edge of the woods, allowing his eyes to adjust to the increased visibility afforded by the stars, straining to catch sight of movement or anything suggesting the presence of people. As satisfied as he could be he was alone, he fumbled in his pocket for his compass. By tilting the face of the instrument to best catch available illumination, he was able to establish a bearing of north-east. He set off.

In the brief moments he had stood in the cold, his knee had stiffened, causing him to limp heavily. His shoulder throbbed, forcing him to curtail the natural swinging motion of his left arm. He must, he imagined, have presented a peculiar sight, but thankfully there was no one present to see him. Or so he hoped. At least his forehead had stopped aching.

Gradually, the stiffness in his knee wore off, though it remained sore and he dared not put full weight on his right leg. In this lopsided manner, he made his way across the moor.

Since stepping out of the W.C. in Cartwell Manor and encountering Mr and Mrs Wickens, Fry had not had opportunity to think through events. Now traipsing across open moorland, needing to be alert only to the presence of other people and to avoid blundering into bogs, he could allow his mind to focus on all that had happened since he'd entered Cartwell Manor.

Two things, in particular, bothered him. How did Jakes know he worked for the *Totleigh Times*? And what had he meant when he said they'd almost had to draw him a map?

It was possible the answer to the first question was that the police had informed Jakes about Fry turning up at the station and enquiring after Jenny Lewis. Dr Emery had said the work carried on at Cartwell Manor was of interest to the Home and Foreign Offices—the implication which Fry had voiced and the doctor hadn't denied was that the police had been instructed to turn a blind eye to any peculiar goings-on related to the manor. But Fry wasn't convinced. The desk sergeant had shown a singular lack of interest in Fry and hadn't even made a note of his name. Turning a blind eye was one thing; reporting a name was taking complicity a lot further, and Fry did not want to believe the British police would be involved to such a level in anything untoward.

If not the police... The alternative was obvious and no less palatable: someone from the newspaper had informed Jakes that Fry was taking an interest in the mystery of Jenny Lewis which could lead him to Cartwell Manor. To Fry's mind, there was only one candidate: the Head of Classifieds. While typing up his report for the Chief, Fry had been aware of the Head's surreptitious glances in his direction. And Fry must have left the partly typed report unattended while he'd taken a toilet or lunch break. It would have been a simple matter for the Head to sidle across to his desk, perhaps on the pretext of borrowing a pencil, and take a quick peek at the report without anyone else noticing. Fry had never liked the man—it was easy to think of him as a mole.

Yet Fry's investigations had gone nowhere; they certainly hadn't led him to Cartwell Manor. If the bloke in The Coach Inn hadn't let slip about losing his job at the manor, Fry would never have heard of the place.

He came to an abrupt stop. Of course. That's what Jakes had meant about drawing him a map. Talking to the stranger in the pub hadn't been a random encounter, but a staged one. This also explained why the man had seemed familiar: he had probably been following Fry for days, waiting for the opportunity to engage him in conversation. Fry's visit to the pub Friday evening had presented the perfect chance.

This didn't explain why they'd wanted Fry to learn about Cartwell Manor and link it to Jenny Lewis. Even less so if, as appeared to be the case, they were intent on doing the same to him as they'd done to the young woman and, to perhaps a lesser degree, Arthur and Maud Wickens: the application of electricity and enforced forgetfulness.

The Goldfish Syndrome.

After that, like it or not, he'd join their army. He thought about the ranks of people—men, women and children—lined up as though on parade, their faces expressionless. He thought about the bolted doors and the screams he'd heard inside the manor. Most of all, he thought about the way one of his pursuers had lifted his face to the sky and howled like a beast of the night.

He shivered, his inactivity allowing the cold to creep back into his bones.

A fox loped by, the starlight sufficient to allow Fry a glimpse of glittering black eyes.

He shivered again and set off once more.

The breeze picked up, strengthening to a wind. Clouds began to scud across the night sky, blocking out the stars. Fry had no idea for how long he'd slept under the blanket of leaves; he didn't know whether it was late Saturday evening or early Sunday morning.

He sat on a rocky outcrop to eat the squashed cheese sandwich. True enough, the physical battering hadn't done the cheese any harm. If anything, it had sweated a little in his pocket, improving the flavour.

While he sat munching, trying to work out what he would do when he made it off Dartmoor, a gust of wind cast a flurry of stinging raindrops into his face. He glanced unhappily at the sky. It had turned black. The moor had become a place of deep shadow.

Fry estimated he was around half a mile from the point where he had joined the moor from Sticklepath. He would soon be amongst soggy ground, criss-crossed by swollen streams. It had grown too dark to go blundering about in such terrain and he no longer had the late Mr Truscott's stick to test patches of ground for firmness.

Yet it was too chilly to simply wait for daylight—dawn could be hours away—and the longer he remained inactive the more his injured joints would stiffen, perhaps to the point his knee would cause immobility. No, he needed to stay warm and supple, and that meant staying on the move.

After some moments' deliberation, Fry realised the quickest and safest way for him to return was to strike due east until he hit the road from Sticklepath. That should mean, he hoped, avoiding the streams and boggy ground. It would also ensure he didn't miss the point where he'd entered the moor and end up blundering into the River Taw.

Once on the road, it would be a short walk to Sticklepath. There he could find somewhere sheltered and out of sight to wait for dawn. The first bus service of the day would start around nine o'clock—it being a Sunday—and he could be back in Totleigh for a late breakfast.

He checked his compass. Pulling up his jacket collar against the wind and spattering rain, he struck out due east.

Sixteen: Seeking Sanctuary

He was wrong about avoiding boggy ground. By the time he emerged from the moor onto the road, his trousers were sodden to the knees, his boots squelched and the seat of his trousers was soaked through from when he had been forced to sit down to yank his foot free of a patch of particularly cloying mud.

Rain fell in frequent, squally showers. Water dripped from his hair into his eyes. His knee and shoulder ached. Fry longed for a soak in a steaming bath.

Still, it felt good to stand on solid ground once more. Better yet, the first grey streaks of dawn had appeared on the horizon.

He turned to his left, to the north, and set off once more, a new spring to his step despite his aches and pains. The same thought kept recurring, playing over and over like a mantra: *only one… only one…*

At the sound of an approaching engine, Fry didn't hesitate. He hurried to the side of the road and, leading with his bad leg, stepped over the low drystone wall which formed a notional barrier between road and moor. He crouched low behind the wall and waited.

The vehicle went past from the direction of Sticklepath. When the noise of the engine began to fade, Fry risked a look. A white Austin A40 was disappearing southwards. Fry straightened, wincing at the ache in his knee, and stepped back onto the road, feeling a little foolish.

When he next heard the sound of an engine, he almost decided to ignore it. It was coming from behind him, heading in the direction he wanted to go; perhaps he could thumb a lift.

By the time he thought better of it, it was almost too late. The engine noise had grown louder—the vehicle must be nearly in sight.

At a stumbling run, he made it to the side of the road and flung himself over the wall, prompting a strangled cry of pain when his injured shoulder bore the brunt of his impact with the soft ground.

He lay on his back and stared at the grey sky.

The approaching vehicle was moving more slowly than the Austin had been. Unnaturally slowly. Although not even the most belaboured breathing would be heard above the noise of the grumbling engine, Fry held his breath.

The vehicle seemed to take an age to go past. When he judged it had cleared his position, Fry let his breath out in a relieved sigh and risked a peek above the wall. He immediately ducked back down and pulled himself tighter to the wall.

A dark green Bedford van was being driven slowly in the direction of Sticklepath. The side window in the passenger door was fully lowered. Hands clutching the sill to steady himself, a young man in dark army fatigues was standing in the passenger footwell, his torso protruding from the window. His head, at the level of the van roof, turned from side to side while he scanned the moor.

Once more, Fry found himself holding his breath. But the van's engine tone didn't change to indicate it was slowing down. The rumbling grew steadily more distant until Fry felt it safe to breathe normally again and risk another look.

The van had pulled out of sight around a bend that, fortunately, curved to the right; had it been a left-hand bend, it would only have taken the watcher to turn his head in this direction and Fry's position would have been revealed.

And he would not be able to run away this time. A rapid hobble, maybe, but he would be overtaken within a hundred yards. His only hope of avoiding capture was to avoid detection.

After deliberation, Fry decided to stick to the road. The firm surface made for faster progress and he was keen to reach civilisation again; he felt too exposed and vulnerable out on the moor. He approached bends and crested rises with great caution, edging himself into a position where he would spot a waiting vehicle or person before they spotted him.

In this way, he reached Sticklepath without further incident.

The village was strung along the main road and he approached warily. There was no sign of a green van. In fact, it being early on a damp Sunday morning in December, the place was deserted. That didn't mean there wasn't someone keeping watch from a position of concealment, but it was a chance Fry would have to take. Besides, now he was back in a place inhabited by ordinary people, he felt less vulnerable. If he was attacked here, he could yell for all he was worth and surely someone would come to his aid.

He limped into the village and continued along the main road until he came to the bus stop. Rain was falling again and there was no shelter to wait for the bus. A lane ran from the main road at a right angle. Fry entered the lane and found a recessed doorway to some sort of storage shed in which he could huddle out of the worst of the elements and still see the main road.

He settled down to wait. And allowed his thoughts to return to the prisoner of war...

It had been a low-key affair. Totleigh Town Hall could hold up to three hundred seated guests; it was less than half-full. Fry hadn't been particularly interested in going. He was only there to keep company the kindly lady who had taken him in as an evacuee. She had lost her husband a few months before and was herself in failing health. An evening out at the town hall would do her good, she said. Would help to take her mind off things. Fry smiled and told her that of course he would accompany her.

This had been four years ago, almost a year after the war had finished. Fry hadn't long turned seventeen and worked as a labourer on a local farm. Back-breaking work which would come to an end after the harvest had been gathered. Although he was happy to be able to contribute to his keep, he wouldn't miss the job. He would prefer something office-based, something in which he could exercise his intellect rather than his muscles.

When the soldier stepped out onto the tiny stage to muted applause, Fry barely paid attention. But when the man began to describe his life as a prisoner in a Japanese internment camp in Burma, sometimes in excruciating detail, he found himself listening in horrified fascination.

"Much has been made, and will be made, of the horrific treatment of the Jews and others at the hands of the Nazis," the soldier concluded, "and rightly so. But the atrocities perpetrated by Japan must also never be forgotten. The Japanese nation has been made to pay, and how, by the obliteration of two of its cities by atomic bombs and maybe it is deserving of our merciful forgiveness. But we mustn't forget.

"And now, before I leave the stage, I'll throw the floor open to a couple of questions."

Fry had been impressed by the man's calm demeanour and the dispassionate way he described the torture and deprivations forced upon him. And Fry wasn't the only one, judging by the first question, asked by a man sitting near the front.

"I have seen soldiers like yourself," said the audience member, "who have returned from Japanese prisoner-of-war camps. They tell a similar tale to yours, of appalling treatment and of seeing their comrades die through malnourishment or physical abuse or outright murder. Yet they can only speak of these things haltingly, if at all, for they have returned broken men, their spirits crushed by what they endured and witnessed. You, sir, on the other hand, speak of these horrors with eloquence and fortitude. I know I can't be alone in being hugely impressed by your strength of character—"

"Hear, hear!" piped up someone else in the audience and there was a pause while a round of applause broke out.

When it had died away, the first man resumed. "My question is, how did you manage to endure things that would break most men and come out the other side willing and able to relate what happened in such measured fashion?"

"Ah." The soldier gave a wry smile. "You may not find my answer to your question quite as measured. You see, before the war I was a student of eastern mysticism."

A low groan came from some sections of the audience.

The soldier's smile grew wider. "Yes. That tends to be the sort of reaction those words provoke. But bear with me. I'm not about to regale you with a lecture on Indian transcendentalism, so there's no need to look so worried. Suffice it to say that one of the masters I studied taught a technique for separating certain aspects of the mind from the body. For our purposes, I only need summarise what I did and its effects. The terms the master used I have adapted for western sensibilities. In effect, he talked about compartmentalising the parts of your mind most important to you. If you like, your true essence. In my case, that largely consisted of my memories of my wife and baby daughter." He smiled down at a woman and young girl sitting in the front row. "No matter what they were going to do to me, I wasn't going to let them destroy those memories."

He gazed around at the audience, which had grown rapt once more. "I pictured in my mind a box constructed of solid English oak. The lid of the box was firmly secured by a ruddy great padlock to which I possessed the only key. When I lay on my stinking mat in that seething camp on the first night, I knew what was coming—we'd all heard the whispers of what would greet us if we were misfortunate enough to be taken prisoner by the Japanese. No humane treatment in accordance with the Hague or Geneva Conventions awaited us there. So I took those precious memories—I imagined them as typed on parchment paper and stored neatly in buff manila envelopes—and placed them into the box. Then I firmly secured the lid with the padlock and swallowed the key."

A few members of the audience gasped and he smiled. "Don't forget, this was all taking place in my mind. I didn't actually swallow a physical key. That would have been daft; I knew I would be in the camp longer than it would have taken for a real key to reappear."

The audience tittered.

"When the war at last ended," he continued, "I wasn't in any better shape mentally than my fellow inmates." His expression grew sober. "Those who had survived, in any case. But, unlike most of my fellow survivors, I had the means to make myself better. It was merely a case of instructing my mental self to, ahem, allow nature to take its course, retrieve the key and unlock the box. There were my memories, as intact and unspoiled as when I'd locked them away.

Knowing that my captors had been unable to sully those parts of me that were most precious helped the rest of my mind to heal."

Fry had been entranced. He no longer remembered the other questions that were asked, or the soldier's replies, but he could recall the answer to the first question verbatim.

And something told him the memory might soon come in handy. Along with the steel safe.

When he heard the chug-chug-chug of the approaching bus, he peered out of the lane. The village remained deserted. Rain continued to fall steadily.

Inactivity had caused his knee to stiffen once more. He hobbled painfully to the edge of the road and held out an arm to request the bus to stop.

There were four other passengers on the bus: a mother and her infant, and an elderly couple. Fry studiously avoided looking at them; if they glanced with disapproval at his muddy attire, he didn't notice. He chose a seat away from them, next to the aisle, and sank thankfully into it. The windows were misted with condensation and it would be virtually impossible for an outside observer to see him. For the first time since fleeing Cartwell Manor, Fry dared to relax.

That is, he allowed his body to relax, enjoying the relative luxury of a thinly padded seat, while his mind continued to work overtime. He needed to decide where to go when he reached Totleigh. He needed a place where he could feel safe and plan his next move. He needed sanctuary.

After his experience with the desk sergeant, allied with his suspicion the police were turning a blind eye to whatever was happening at the manor, he dismissed going to the police station out of hand. Returning to his lodgings would also be a bad idea: if these people knew where he worked and somebody in their employ had been following him around seeking an opportunity to engage him in conversation, it would not be a stretch to imagine they knew where he lived.

Hard on the heels of that thought came another: how had Mrs

Truscott reacted when Fry hadn't shown up in time for dinner the previous evening? If not then, when she found his bed unslept in that morning? She was likely to report him as missing to the police since she knew he had been going hiking on the moor, she was fond of him and she was a sensible lady. But there was nothing the police could do, even if they wanted to—they didn't tend to take missing adults seriously until they had been gone for a least twenty-four hours.

Maybe he was making a mistake returning to Totleigh. Perhaps he should have caught a bus to Exeter; from there, left Devon and headed north to Bristol, or east towards London. But he had embarked on his hiking expedition only expecting to need enough money for bus fares for short journeys. What loose change remained in his pocket would barely get him to Exeter, never mind beyond.

No, if he was going to seek sanctuary, it would have to be in Totleigh. And there was only one place he could think of where he might be safe.

Seventeen: The Chief Takes Charge

The bus made three stops before Totleigh. Not many people boarded—nothing much opened on a Sunday and people tended to stay home, particularly when the weather wasn't good—and one or two got off. Each time, Fry huddled into his seat, trying to make himself look inconspicuous, but he needn't have worried; no one spared him a second glance.

The clock at Totleigh station told Fry it was approaching half past ten. After alighting from the bus, he stood to one side to allow the other passengers to go past, while glancing furtively around. He could see nobody dressed in army fatigues, no fair men with scarred faces and no dark green vans.

Rain continued to fall in brief squalls. Fry took a circuitous route to the office, sticking to narrow side streets and alleys, which protected him from the worst of the rain and enabled him to avoid the main thoroughfares. They were largely deserted and he would be in clear view of anyone watching. He did not glimpse anybody acting suspiciously, but his sense of vulnerability had returned as soon as he'd stepped down from the bus and he proceeded cautiously, tensed to flee like an alert hare.

Not that he'd be capable of darting anywhere like a hare; a lame tortoise, maybe. Now he was on the move again, the stiffness was easing in his knee, but it would prevent him from moving faster than at a lopsided trot.

He stopped at the mouth of an alleyway, looking out onto the entrance to the *Totleigh Times* building. A couple of pedestrians moved quickly past, heads bowed against the wind, intent only on reaching their destinations. Otherwise, the street was empty.

Fry waited until there was nobody in sight, before limping hurriedly from the alleyway.

He had been in to the office a few times on a Sunday and so wasn't surprised to see the reception desk manned by a bored-looking chap who helped keep the clanking press working and filled in as a sort of security guard-cum-receptionist on weekends. The press was old and needed regular maintenance and repairs, but it was hardly a full-time job. No one seemed to know what he did for the rest of the week.

"Mornin', Mr Fry."

"Good morning, Clive." Fry nodded towards the stairs. "Is the Chief up there?"

"Aye. You know the Chief. He'll never trust the Monday edition to anyone else."

"The Head's not around, I suppose?"

"The Head? You won't catch him working on a Sunday."

Fry breathed a quiet sigh of relief. He knew the Head of Classifieds worked most Saturdays, and rarely on Sundays, but he felt better for hearing confirmation of his absence. During the bus journey from Sticklepath, Fry had convinced himself the Head was responsible for informing Jakes about him and, most probably, for setting up the encounter with the supposed former groundskeeper in The Coach Inn.

"Er, tell me, Clive, has anyone been in asking about me?"

The man took a moment to consider, as though it was a question to which there could be many answers. Fry had to conceal his impatience. At last, Clive shook his head. "Nope, can't say there has." He glanced down at Fry's muddy trousers and raised an eyebrow. "Been tramping through bogs?"

Fry forced a smile to his face. "Something like that. Right, I can't stand around chatting. There's work to be done."

Clive nodded sagely. "Right you are, Mr Fry. Right you are."

The six flights of stairs presented more difficulty to Fry than normal. By the time he reached the News Room, he was panting from exertion and beads of sweat had broken out on his brow, despite his damp and chilled condition. When he raised a hand to wipe away the perspiration, he winced as his fingers brushed against the lump caused by his collision with the fallen tree.

The News Room was much quieter than during a weekday. Apart from the clackety-clack of one or two journalists tapping away at their typewriters in the shadowy margins of the room, there was little sound. The air was blessedly free of the shrilling of telephones and the smog of tobacco smoke.

The other journalists were too engrossed in their work to do more than glance up at Fry, before turning their attentions back to their machines.

He hobbled across the room to the door of the Chief's office and knocked.

"Come!"

The Chief peered at Fry over the ever-present piles of papers and through a wreath of blue smoke. He removed the cigar clamped between his teeth and used it to gesture at the leather chair in front of his desk. Fry sank into it. For the first time in many hours, he felt safe.

Eyes narrowed against the smoke, the Chief studied him for a long, silent moment.

"Well, Fry, judging by your limp, the state of your clothes, the lump on your forehead and the expression on your face, you have a story to tell."

Fry nodded. "Sir, I'm sorry to barge in on a Sunday like this. I know you're busy with tomorrow's edition..."

The Chief waved the cigar dismissively, before inserting it in the corner of his mouth and talking around it. "Speak, man. Tell me what's happened."

When it came to relating stories, Fry's journalistic training stood him in good stead. The only time he strayed from the unembellished facts was when relating his suspicions—nay, certainty—that the Head of Classifieds must have informed Dr Emery and his henchman Jakes of his interest in Cartwell Manor, although he confessed to not understanding why the Head had given Fry a firm shove in the right direction by putting up someone to pose as a dismissed groundsman.

The Chief didn't interrupt, not even when Fry pointed his finger at the Head. He nodded once or twice, lit a fresh cigar, grunted a few times, but otherwise let Fry's tale run its course.

By the time Fry had finished talking, exhaustion had set in. He wanted nothing more than to return to his lodgings, take a hot bath to soothe his pains and then climb into bed.

He peered through the smoke at the Chief. "We have to do something, but I'm not sure what. It's no use going to the police—according to Dr Emery, they're somehow involved. Their unconventional methods of investigation into the Jenny Lewis case, and the reaction to my enquiries, seem to corroborate his claim."

The Chief nodded, removed the cigar stub from the corner of his mouth and ground it into the overflowing ashtray mostly hidden from Fry by the piles of papers.

"First thing, Fry my lad, is to get you on the outside of something hot and fortifying. Go and make yourself a mug of sweet tea. Never mind the rationing—you have my permission to add an extra teaspoon of sugar." He opened a drawer in his desk and extracted a bottle containing an amber liquid. "Return here with the tea and I'll add a tot of this." He winked.

"Right, sir. Er, would you like a cuppa?"

"I think I'll join you in a small tot, but not the tea. Now, run along. I have a telephone call to make."

The tea urn occupied a gloomy corner of the News Room, well away from where the remaining journalist continued to tap away at his typewriter. There wasn't a great deal of water left and it was barely hot. Fry couldn't be bothered to traipse downstairs to the tiny kitchen on the ground floor to boil fresh water—he would make do. Extra sugar would help the taste deficiency resulting from attempting to brew with water long come off the boil. Any remaining grimace-factor would no doubt be masked by whatever was in the Chief's bottle.

While Fry waited for the tea leaves to steep, he wondered who the Chief could be calling on the telephone. Maybe fellow journalists in one of the main papers in Fleet Street; he was bound to have contacts in the Big Smoke. The police might be unavailable to call for assistance in this particular case, but Fry believed in the power of the press. Involve one of the big boys like *The Times* and have them run a story exposing Cartwell Manor and its peculiar goings-on. Then watch the Establishment (always, when talking about shadowy bureaucracy and cover-ups, with a capital E) squirm. Fry remained unsure quite what was going on behind the Victorian façade of Cartwell Manor, but felt certain it was not something the authorities wanted to be known by the general public. Heck, this could be the sort of exposé to topple the government.

A smile—the first genuine one that day—stole over Fry's features while he daydreamed about the by-line *From our Chief News Correspondent Jonathan Fry* appearing on the day's main news item in one of the London broadsheets.

Happy thoughts making him forget his aches and pains, Fry made a mug of muddy liquid, added two teaspoons of sugar and made his way back to the Chief's office. Even the *only one* mantra had stopped resounding through his head like a stuck gramophone record.

"Ah, there you are, Fry." The Chief waved him to a seat. "Here, lad, let me add a drop to that brew which will grow hairs on your chest."

Fry placed his mug on the desk in front of the Chief and resumed his seat. He watched his boss add a generous glug of amber liquid to his mug. His first sip confirmed his suspicions: the sugar and spirit combined to mask the inadequacy of the tea. He sat back and luxuriated in the warm sensation spreading through his body as the alcohol did its work.

"Did you make your telephone call, sir?"

"Yes, yes. After what you said about Arthur Wickens, I had to call him to make sure he's all right."

"And is he?"

The Chief shrugged. "Seemed a little vague, but knew who I was. He didn't recall you, though."

"No, he wouldn't. Didn't I tell you, sir? His recent memory's been erased. What are we going to do?"

"I made another call." The Chief tapped the side of his nose with his finger. "You don't become Editor-in-Chief, not even of a small regional like this one, without making some useful contacts." He nodded at Fry's mug. "As soon as you've finished your tea, we're going to take a little trip."

They went in the Chief's Hillman Minx Mark III Saloon. Although not the most salubrious of vehicles, it had modern styling and was way beyond Fry's reach on his apprentice wage.

The Chief refused to be drawn on their destination and Fry didn't try to force it. He was happy for someone else to assume control, while he sat back and allowed the motion of the vehicle to lull him into a doze.

So it was he barely stirred when the Chief brought the car to a halt. It was only when both rear passenger doors were opened, letting in a rush of cold air, and the chassis rocked as two people climbed into the back seat that Fry's eyes fluttered open.

He had time to glance behind him, at the army surplus attire of the woman and the white-scarred mouth of the man, then to the Chief, who stared straight ahead through the windscreen, before a powerful hand clasped around his forehead, dragging his head backwards, and a cloth was thrust over his mouth and nose. A cloth with a sweet, chemical odour.

Fry grabbed at the hands holding the cloth, but his arms were batted away. He kicked against the passenger footwell, making his knee sing in pain. He barely noticed. Seconds later, he was incapable of noticing anything.

Eighteen: Ignorance is Bliss

Faint sounds. A muttering of hushed conversation. Then, louder: "He's coming round. Get ready with the bucket."

A bitter taste filled Fry's mouth. He opened his eyes to shifting shadows and his head spun.

He turned his face to the side and stared groggily into the mouth of a metal pail. He was only vaguely aware of hands holding it towards him and noticed nothing about to whomever the hands were presumably attached.

With a convulsive gulp, Fry ejected a thin stream of watery vomit into the pail's echoing depths. His stomach contracted and he retched again. And again, until his stomach was empty.

Turning his head away, he issued a soft groan. He tried to bring up a hand to wipe his mouth, but his arms didn't seem to be working.

Fry lay still, waiting for the world to stop spinning and to make sense again.

It took a while: fifteen minutes, maybe. His grasp of time seemed to have deserted him. At least he was able to gain a better sense of his situation.

He was lying on a padded trolley, in a half-sitting position. His wrists and ankles were secured by straps made, by the feel of them, of leather. The trolley occupied a shadowy space, the size of which was difficult to estimate. The echoey feel could have been due to the concrete walls he glimpsed to one side and beyond the foot of the trolley. What little he could see of the floor was also concrete. He couldn't see a wall to the other side, but whether this was because it was too distant or the light was insufficient he had no way of telling.

The source of light came from somewhere behind him. It was weak and flickered. People—he could not tell how many—crossed to and fro in front of it, causing shadows and making it more difficult to judge the size of the room.

They spoke in muted tones, too quietly for Fry to make any sense of the words.

Then it grew quiet. The light, though still weak, became steadier as though everyone had either left or stopped moving about.

Fry strained to hear any sound, but none came. He cleared his throat and grimaced; it felt as though it had been vigorously scrubbed with a wire brush.

"Hel…" he started, but it came out in little more than a croak. He tried to swallow, but his mouth was dry. Dry and foul-tasting.

"He-hello?" Better. Still croaky, but a recognisable word. "Is someone there? May I have a glass of water. Please?"

A moment's silence. Followed by faint, retreating footsteps. A clanking noise of ancient plumbing shuddering into action and the whoosh of water. Footsteps again, echoing, growing louder.

A hand appeared from behind his head, holding a mug. Fry inclined his head towards it and the mug was raised to his lips. The water was cold and he sipped it gratefully; it tasted heavenly.

Fry's nostrils twitched as a familiar smell hit them. Faint but distinctive. It was coming from the hand holding the mug.

When he'd sipped his way through half of the mug's contents, the hand withdrew.

"Thank you," said Fry, "Chief."

There was a pause, before a man moved into view, chuckling softly. George Samuels, Editor-in-Chief of the *Totleigh Times*, stopped by the side of Fry and looked down at him.

"How did you know it was me, laddie? Lucky guess?"

"Your cigars. I could smell them on your fingers."

The Chief gave a rueful smile.

Fry stared up at him. Now he had quenched his thirst, at the same time removing the foul tastes of chemicals and vomit, his brain processes were returning to normal.

"All along I thought it was the Head of Classifieds. I never even suspected you. But why, sir? Why have me investigate the Wickenses' visitor? Why send that chap to pretend to be the former groundskeeper of Cartwell Manor?" Fry shrugged. "Why any of this?"

The Chief continued to stare down at him, his expression sober. It took a few long moments before he spoke and then it began with a sigh.

"I suppose it was a rather elaborate charade we went through to get you to investigate Cartwell Manor. You would have made a competent journalist, Fry, but lack the dogged tenacity and suspicious mind to become a good one."

"Oh, you'd be surprised," said Fry. "I can be single-minded when I want to be. Becoming an orphan can do that to you, you know."

"Well, laddie, you keep it well hidden. It was a simple matter to have my cousin follow you around for a few days and spin you a yarn about being the groundskeeper here at Cartwell Manor. He's always ready to make an easy bob, is that one. What did surprise me is the initiative you demonstrated by coming out here at the first opportunity. A little rash, maybe, not to have informed anyone where precisely you were going, but the sort of derring-do I like to see in my staff." He sighed again. "Pity."

"You still haven't told me why."

The Chief looked away from Fry and his eyes misted. "Why?" His voice grew fainter as though no longer addressing Fry but musing to himself. "Aye, there's the rub." He gazed off into an unseen distance.

Fry strained against the bindings, but they were securely fastened with no give in them.

A shudder ran through the Chief and his gaze cleared. He looked back down at Fry.

"I've seen the film footage the Americans captured when they liberated the camps. The footage which was shown at the first Nuremberg Trial. Buchenwald, Dachau, Leipzig, Belsen… And the Red Army footage taken at Auschwitz."

Fry narrowed his eyes. "I've heard of the atrocities, of course, but I didn't think the footage was publicly available."

"It's not, but I have contacts."

"Sir, you're Jewish?" Fry could have bitten his tongue off—here he was bound and helpless, and still he addressed this man as 'sir'.

The Chief nodded. "But it's more than that, lad. These were *people*. Weak, helpless. Children, too. Some no more than babes in arms. How do we counter such blind hatred? Such unspeakable inhumanity?"

"That's what this is about? That mad doctor is forming some sort of secret army to fight the Nazis?"

"If they should rise again, then certainly. Or any other regime that would seek to exterminate entire races."

"And," said another voice to the accompaniment of footsteps, "removing delinquency from our towns and cities at the same time." Dr Emery came into view. He gazed down at Fry with narrowed eyes. "I don't appreciate being referred to as 'mad', Mr Fry."

"And I'm no delinquent," muttered Fry.

"True," said the Chief. "But you fit the bill in every other way. Young, fit, healthy and, above all, as you've already mentioned, an orphan. You see, laddie, no one will report you as missing."

"Mrs Truscott will." Fry almost bit his tongue again. Maybe they didn't know about his landlady. Even as he thought it, he knew it was a forlorn hope.

A low chuckle came from behind Fry and a third man stepped into his line of sight. A fair-haired man with a scarred mouth. "Oh, we have plans for her," said Jakes.

Dr Emery looked pointedly at the Chief and cleared his throat.

"Yes, yes," said the Chief. "I'll be on my way." He glanced at Fry. "Good luck, laddie. Thank you for what you're doing for our country. Thank you for what you're doing for humanity."

"What?" Fry stared at his boss in horror. "You can't go and leave me here with these people. Sir?"

The Chief opened his mouth and then closed it as though thinking better of saying any more. He shook his head, before walking away.

"Sir? What are you doing? Please don't leave me. *Please…*"

Tears sprang from the corners of Fry's eyes. He blinked them away as he listened to the Chief's receding footsteps.

A hand came around from behind him, passing a leather strap around his forehead. Before Fry could react, the strap had been pulled tight, forcing his head into the padded surface of the trolley. He tried to pull away, or turn his head, but it was held fast.

He stopped struggling and closed his eyes. It was time.

The soldier who had survived the Japanese prisoner-of-war camp had kept his memories secure in an oak box. Fry had imagined something stronger. He pictured himself standing in an empty room before a safe constructed of steel three inches thick. The safe was set on its back into a solid concrete floor, much like the floor in the room where his physical self currently lay. The door to the safe was closed, but unlocked. Above the combination dial and handle, a series of numbers was engraved into the surface of the door. The numbers were not obvious—there was little light in this imaginary room—but Fry knew they were there; he had engraved them himself. He knelt, held out a hand and traced the numbers with his fingers.

He moved his hand down to the handle and pulled. The door opened easily on well-oiled hinges. He swung it wide; though the door was heavy, comfortingly heavy, he managed it easily and lowered it to the floor. The safe gaped open. He reached inside.

The memories were already there, handwritten neatly on pages cut from a journalist's notebook. Each filled page had been neatly inserted into a brown cardboard folder which fastened with a string tie. Ever since attending the talk by the soldier in 1946, Fry had used the hours of restless wakefulness during sleepless nights, which he frequently endured, to choose the memories he would want to preserve in the event he ever needed to utilise the safe. The safe, too, had existed in his imagination for the past few years. It was he who had kept the hinges oiled.

The cardboard folders almost completely filled the space inside the safe. Handwritten recollections of bouncing on his mother's lap, her scents of lavender and baking making him dizzy with adoration; kicking a battered old football about with his father in their tiny garden; summer trips to Southend and splashing them both in the sea, while across the channel war clouds gathered. These and many like them filled the safe.

There was room for one more. On top of the pile of folders lay an empty one. Inside it, a sheet of blank notepaper and a pencil.

Fry extracted the paper and pencil and began to scribble. There was no time to be elaborate.

Emery. Jakes. The Chief. They destroy memories. It only takes one. Tell your comrades. Make them understand. Remember the Goldfish Syndrome.

He underlined the words 'Goldfish Syndrome' twice, placed the sheet of paper inside the spare folder, fastened the folder with the string tie and placed it onto the pile. The safe was now full. And time was up.

Fry opened his eyes.

Two more people, who Fry hadn't seen before, came into view. Both dressed in white laboratory coats, they held wires which ended in sticky pads.

"No!" said Fry. "I don't consent to this. You can't do this to me."

The only reply was a low chuckle from Jakes. He gazed down at Fry with a smirk that made his scar stand out in the gloom.

Fry's eyes swivelled towards Dr Emery, but there was no compassion to be found there. The doctor regarded Fry with an expression of excitement; more than that, a look approaching ecstasy.

"Your first treatment will now commence, Mr Fry. The first of many. Each one will strip away a layer of your memories until we reach the point where—both for your safety and that of others—you will need to spend some time on the first floor. Behind one of the locked doors about which you expressed some curiosity when you first came to Cartwell Manor."

Jakes snorted.

Dr Emery glanced at him with something akin to distaste, before turning to the two white-coated people and nodding.

Fry reached across and gripped the edge of the safe door. With a grunt, he swung it up and over. It clanged shut with a resounding echo.

The people in lab coats came closer and attached the pads to Fry's temples with a cold, sticky substance, not once catching his frantic gaze.

As a whirring noise began behind him, the light, already dim, flickered and dimmed further. The sharp smell of ozone filled the air.

"Thank you for your sacrifice, Mr Fry," said Dr Emery. "Or should I now call you Private Fry?"

Fry gripped the safe handle and yanked it into the closed position. He grasped the dial and spun it. It whirled around with a series of clacks and clicks, sounding like the spinning wheels of a bicycle when playing cards have been inserted between the spokes.

"Only one," Fry murmured.

"What was that?" The look of uncertainty reappeared on the doctor's face.

Before Fry could respond, a bolt of pain exploded in his head and all he could do was scream.

Jonathan Fry opened his eyes and peered blearily around the room. He lay slumped on a thin mattress. The floor was covered, like the inside of the door and walls, in a thick, padded material. Except in one corner, where a hole in the floor the diameter of a drainpipe emitted an ammonic stench. The room was otherwise bare.

He sat straighter, leaning against the cushioned wall. Noises from adjoining cells reached him: wails, screeches, howls. A line of spittle drooled from Fry's lower lip, but he made no move to wipe it away.

The adjoining cells' occupants wore expressions combining frenzied rage, deep dread and blind incomprehension. These expressions, too, showed on Fry's face from time to time, though he did not, like his neighbours, fling himself wildly at the door or beat himself against the walls and floor.

At other times, though never when anyone else was in his presence, Fry's eyes focused into a steely look of resolve and his hands came up to touch the sticky patches of residue on his temples.

On such occasions, he murmured softly to himself.

"Only one… only one…"

He couldn't remember why he spoke those words over and over as though they had once held great significance. At such times, he felt an unaccustomed sense of wellbeing.

Perhaps ignorance is bliss.

Private Fry lay on his back on a steel cot. The mattress covering was thin and he could feel the canvas straps which supported it through both the mattress and his dark woollen sweater. Around him came the rustlings of his comrades preparing for parade ground manoeuvres. He would not be joining them this morning.

An image came into his mind and he tried to blink it away. It was a recurring image, one that disturbed him in a way he didn't understand. And such a simple thing: an orange fish circling the inside of a water-filled bowl.

His treatment was complete and this morning he would undergo his final test. If he passed, he would rise to the same rank as his comrades. At present, he was the only private in the entire platoon. In the entire army. The only one.

Only one…

The fish circled. It was persistent this morning.

Fry closed his eyes. He needed to concentrate on banishing the image; he did not want to be distracted from completing the final test.

The fish was small and startlingly orange. It continued to swim round and round and round the bowl. If it possessed a mind, it must be bored out of it. Fry stepped forward, intending to pick up the bowl and smash it to the concrete floor. Let the golden fish flap and gasp and expire. Put it out of its misery and be shot of it for good.

Wait a moment. Concrete floor… He could not remember the bowl standing on a floor before. Every other time he'd seen it with his mind's eye, it had been merely a bowl without surroundings, without context. He looked around.

He was standing in a room. A shadowy room of concrete. Bare

except for the fishbowl and a steel door lying flush with the surface of the grey floor. He stepped over the bowl, took a few paces forward and knelt before the door.

A row of numbers was engraved on the door above the handle and combination dial. They weren't visible in the dim light, but Fry knew they were there. He leaned forward and ran his fingers over them, slowing his movements to trace the first number carefully. With his other hand, he turned the dial to match the number. The light wasn't bright enough to show the numbers on the dial clearly, but his fingers moved surely.

He continued to trace the numbers with the fingers of one hand and use the other to spin the dial. The last number moved into place with an audible click.

The fish forgotten, Fry grasped the handle and yanked it up. The door swung open easily and clanged to the floor. He stared at the brown cardboard folders inside the safe. Then reached for the top one.

By the time Private Fry opened his eyes, the barracks had cleared. From a distance, he could hear the barks of the sergeant and the stomping of boots on the parade ground.

"It only takes one," he murmured. "Make them understand. Remember the Goldfish Syndrome."

He swung his legs off the edge of the cot and sat up. It was time to face his final test.

Timothy Jakes knocked smartly on the door and stepped back.

"Yes, yes, I'm coming," came a female voice from inside. A moment later, the door was opened. The face of the woman lit up when she saw her visitors. Her hands came up and clasped together in front of her housecoat. "Why, Mr Fry! I've been worried sick about you. It's been weeks. You must come and sit down and tell me all that's happened over a cup of tea. I reported you missing to the police, you know, but they didn't seem interested." Her gaze lowered to the object Fry clutched loosely in his hands. "And you've brought back Mr Truscott's walking stick." She looked up, her smile of delight beginning to fade when her glance took in Jakes. "And who might your companion be?" Her tone had grown uncertain.

"Hello, Mrs Truscott," said Jakes. "I'm here to ask you to accompany me and Private Fry on a short journey. Although, after today's little test, he will become Corporal Fry."

"Corporal Fry?" The first signs of alarm showed in her expression. "Journey? To where, might I ask?"

Jakes gave a low chuckle. "You might indeed ask. But I fear you'd be wasting your breath. Alas, it seems you might need some persuasion." His tone suggested he was far from regretful. He barged forwards, forcing Mrs Truscott aside.

"How dare you…" she began to protest.

Jakes ignored her. He looked past her to Fry standing in the doorway. "Private Fry. This is the woman who would have you arrested and incarcerated by the civilian police. You heard her say as much moments ago."

Mrs Truscott gasped. "I said no such—"

Jakes glanced contemptuously at her, holding up his hand in a gesture of silence which worked as well as if he'd clamped it around her mouth.

"Private Fry? If you would be so good? And henceforth you shall be addressed as Corporal Fry." His lips parted in an oily smile, the sort of smile a snake might give a mouse before striking.

Jonathan Fry's knuckles whitened where they gripped the gnarled stave. He hefted it as though testing its balance, nodded and stepped forward, forcing Mrs Truscott back into her hallway. When he raised the stick, she began to whimper.

Fry stepped past her and Jakes's eyes widened. "What are you—" He got no further for Fry brought the stick down with a meaty thud onto his head.

Fry stood over the groaning form of Timothy Jakes and raised the stick.

"It only takes one," he said. "Remember the Goldfish Syndrome."

The stick came down again.

Moths

Part One: Larva

One: Single Parenting

There was a boy by the name of Billy. Billy Jenkins. Lived in the flat above ours. He was the first to have roller skates round our way. Steel-framed contraptions with red plastic wheels, held on by red vinyl straps which stretched after a couple of uses. Loved those skates, did Billy. Wore them around the linoleum-floored flat, driving his mother to distraction. Us, too. It was like living beneath a railway bridge.

"Those bloody skates!" Mam would exclaim, raising her eyes to the ceiling from where came the sound of a thousand ball bearings rolling down a tin chute. "They'll be the death of that boy, if he's not careful. If Mrs Jenkins doesn't swing for him, I bloody will!"

She'd attack the loaf of bread with renewed vigour, hacking at it like a miner at the face, while me and Leon grinned at each other. We thought Billy's skates were cool.

Mam was right. Those skates were the death of Billy, though neither she nor Billy's mother played any part in it.

Our block of flats was built at the top of a steep hill. The street leading up to it from the main road below was called Queen Street. How I yearned to take my tricycle and push off from the top of the hill, take it sailing down Queen Street, but that was strictly out of bounds.

After what happened to Billy Jenkins.

Very protective of his skates, was Billy.

"Gissa go," my brother Leon pleaded.

"Nuh."

"Go on. I'll let you have a go of my Frisbee."

"Frisbees are rubbish."

"Gissa go and I won't duff you up." Leon was a boy tall of stature, short on patience.

"Have to catch me first."

Leon was no slouch, but Billy had already kicked off and was picking up speed before throwing out the last taunt. After a few paces, Leon gave up and we watched Billy roll noisily down Queen Street, gathering speed as he went.

Too much speed.

One of my earliest memories is of crouching between Leon's knees as we rocketed down the almost sheer drop of Queen Street on a home-made gambo—what we called a go-kart—Leon's joyous yells drowning out the whoosh of rushing air. This was before Mam put a stop to such goings-on. As we neared the bottom, Leon thrust out his legs and used his feet to slow us down enough to allow the gambo to bank sharply to the left up Jubilee Terrace and avoid shooting out into the traffic on the main thoroughfare of Corporation Road. Corporation Road was not busy by modern standards, but there was a steady flow of fast-moving traffic even back then which loomed ever larger in our wind-blurred vision, adding to the thrill.

Billy Jenkins had neither brakes on his skates nor anything approaching a reasonable substitute. He tried to turn left without slowing, but only succeeded in swinging perilously close to the kerb. Arms flailing, tee shirt and hair rippling, he shot past Jubilee Terrace towards the broken white line indicating that anything approaching the junction must give way to the traffic on Corporation Road. As if anyone with eyes needed to be warned.

Even at the last, as the first scream came tumbling from his throat, Billy was too afraid to deliberately steer into the kerb or simply sit down, the only things which might have saved him.

It was a Jaguar that hit him, slate grey, the same ashen shade as the face of the driver when he saw what his car had done to Billy. I don't know whether the driver ever retrieved the Jaguar emblem which had proudly adorned the bonnet of his car but had become embedded three inches inside Billy's chest. I've often wondered. It bothers me not to know.

I waited until after the funeral before going to ask Mrs Jenkins if I could have Billy's roller skates.

~~~

Frankie Evans was my first friend. He lived down in Jubilee Terrace, though spent most of his time playing with me behind our block of flats. Mam said his mother didn't care where Frankie was so long as he wasn't under her feet.

"Too busy entertaining, is that one," said Mam with a knowing nod to Dad.

Yeah, *he* was still around then.

"Aye," grinned Dad. "She's got right yo-yo knickers, her."

"Hywel, mun, not in front of Karl."

When Frankie came calling, I went out to play in a state of some confusion, images of bouncing panties playing across my mind. As Frankie and I bent over a dusty ring, trying to knock each other's marbles out of the circle, I had to ask him.

"What are yo-yo knickers?"

Frankie looked at me sharply. I was too young to read the warning signs.

"Why d'you ask?"

"My dad says your mam's got 'em."

He punched me hard in the mouth. I suffered a gashed lip. And lost my marbles.

Hit me a lot, did Frankie. Until I started school and learned, of necessity, how to defend myself. The next time he hit me, I hit him back.

Then he wasn't my friend any more.

My sixth birthday party wasn't a great success. Nothing wrong with the jelly, bright red in the shape of an upturned boat, and blanc-mange, a pink quivering rabbit with beady raisin eyes, but Mam was silent and withdrawn while she served them, looking off into the distance, seemingly uncaring if we ate like pigs. So we did. She disappeared soon afterwards, leaving us to it.

Three boys from my class came. They had names, but they might have been Tom, Dick and Harry for all I can now recall. Leon was
~~~

there, too, of course. Despite professing to have outgrown birthday parties—"I'm nine, mun. That stuff's for kids."—he put away two wobbly helpings of jelly and blancmange, and enthusiastically led the games of pass the parcel and blind man's buff.

Mam would normally have taken charge of the games while Dad sat and watched, shouting encouragement around a bottle of Mackeson's. But Mam was in the kitchen, vague-eyed and stony-jawed, doing her best to get on the outside of a bottle of cooking sherry.

And Dad wasn't there at all. He had chosen that day to leave Mam for the wiles of a twenty-something dancer going by the name of Rosie Squire, or something. It wasn't the first time he'd left Mam. It would be the last.

I was the blind man, the thick woollen scarf covering my nose as well as my eyes, but still the smell penetrated. The scuffling and cat calls of the other boys died away; the woody aroma of sherry made my nostrils wrinkle. I dropped my arms to my side and stood still.

The scarf was lifted away and I blinked up into Mam's face. Her eyes were red, her bottom lip aquiver, and I knew she was about to cry. I'd never seen Mam cry before.

Slowly, her face crumpled like plastic in flames the moment before it melts. She dropped to her knees, threw her arms about my neck and buried her face in my shoulder. I held her awkwardly while she shook, hot, against me. Distantly I was aware, beneath the sound of her sobs, of shuffling feet behind me as Leon ushered my classmates out.

A moth flitted past and I watched its erratic flight, momentarily mesmerised.

Leon came up behind Mam. He reached over and placed his arms over hers, resting his head on her neck. I lost sight of the moth.

My father used to believe he was a communist. During the McCarthy witch hunts of the fifties, he would, so I am told, sit by the wireless during reports from the States of the Grand Jury hearings, hurling insults at the 'capitalist pig-dog establishment'. He apparently rooted for Castro during the Cuban Missile Crisis and cheered when Kennedy was assassinated.

Dad was all for the redistribution of wealth. But, then, he could only gain from such an arrangement.

It was not until late into the sixties, around the time of Woodstock, Dad realised that, after all, he wasn't a communist. He was, in fact, a hippy. If Flower Power had arrived a decade sooner, I sometimes wonder whether Leon and I would have been saddled with names like River and Stardust. Would River Jordan have made more of his life than Karl Jordan? At the very least, I'd have had a good opening line at parties.

Jesus was baptised in me.

I was home when Dad tried to come back. He called during a weekday, presumably anticipating Leon and I would be in school. He hadn't banked upon me being home with chicken pox.

I was lying on the settee in the living room, watching television—probably Open University; anything to take my mind off the incessant itching—when the knock came at the front door. Actually, it was the only door. Goodness knows how we'd have escaped from a fire that blocked it. We were three floors up.

Mam put down the iron and went to answer the door. She left the living room door open and I heard every word.

"What do *you* want?" Mam sounded surprised and wary.

"How are you, Meg?" Dad's voice contained a wheedling note, the same which could be heard in mine or Leon's when we had done something wrong and we knew that Mam knew.

"What do you want?"

"I've left her, Meg."

"*You* left *her*? Sure about that, are you, Hywel? Or has she found a younger model?"

"Meg, it's you I love. Always has been."

"Oh, yeah?"

"What do you say, girl? Shall we make a go of it?"

Dad sounded confident. I imagined him wearing that smile, the one he believed melted women's hearts. But it would have taken an industrial blowtorch to melt Mam's heart—she'd had to fix it so many times it was stiff and unyielding.

"Go away, Hywel."

"What?"

"You heard. Go away."

"But, Megan, you can't mean it. Our marriage… The boys…"

"The boys have coped for the last six months without you. They can cope for the next six. For the rest of their lives, come to that. So can I."

"*Meg.* Come on, love. You're upset. You don't know what you're saying."

"Oi! Take one more step and I'll scream blue murder. Mrs Hoskins next door will have the police here in no time. You know what a busybody she is."

"Meg, *please*—"

"Enough! I'm in the middle of ironing. I've got Karl lying sick on the settee—"

"Karl's here? Can I see him?"

I huddled deeper into the settee, not wanting him to come in. Something landed on the corner of the television screen and rested for a moment, before fluttering away. A yellow moth.

"Karl has been here for the last six months, Hywel. Leon, too. You could have called to see them. Or written to them. Or done anything. But you're too bloody selfish. Always have been, always will be."

"I meant to call. I didn't get chance. Let me explain to Karl—"

"You left on his birthday, you bastard. Now *go away.*"

"Meg, you're making a mistake."

Mam sighed wearily.

"Bugger off, Hywel."

I heard the door snick softly closed and Mam came back into the living room. She looked strained, older than her years.

"Mam?"

"Yes, love?"
"Is Dad coming back to live with us?"
"No."
"Mam?"
"What?"
"Can I have his Beatles records?"

Mam found it a struggle. She already had a cleaning job in a nearby office block, rising before dawn and returning, footsore and chap-handed, in time to get us up and ready for school. She found a second job, a few hours a day serving behind the counter of the local newsagents. But there still wasn't enough money. She fell behind with the rent on the flat and had to throw herself on the mercy of the Local Authority.

We were relocated to a council house on the other side of town. The rough side. I didn't mind. To me, the change in our circumstances was for the better. For a start, the house, a solidly-constructed, three-bedroom semi, came with its own garden.

"Leon! Come see. A garden!"

I grabbed him by the hand and yanked him through the kitchen towards the back door. Mam looked on, a rare smile on her face.

The garden went back a long way, a jumble of overgrown lawn, concrete paving, tangled brambles and weeds. To an adult, the garden probably looked like hard work. To a seven-year-old, it was a place of exploration and adventure.

Leon and I were poking about, his excitement not perhaps as great as mine, when the ground began to shake. I glanced up, startled. Leon was looking down the garden and I followed his gaze.

With a hiss and a roar, a diesel locomotive shot into view, no more than a few yards beyond the cross-wired fence which marked the rear boundary of the garden. Behind it came a line of rattling carriages that were gone in a blur of grimy windows and white faces.

"That train goes all the way to London," said Leon.

"Wow!" I exclaimed. "London… where Dick Whittington went."

"Aye. But the streets aren't really paved with gold, you know."

"I *know*. I'm not a kid any more."

Leon went inside to help Mam unpack. I stayed in the garden, my gaze turning to the east, in the direction the train had gone.

Leon had been less than enthusiastic about moving across town to the council house since it meant us having to change schools. Leon had been attending our old school three years longer than me and did not want to leave his friends. Since I had no friends in school, I couldn't have cared less about leaving.

It was with a sullen Leon I walked to our new school on our first day. When we walked home again that afternoon, Leon was sporting a black eye and had torn the knee out of his new trousers. Mam was furious.

"*Leon Jordan*! First day in a new school and you come home in this state. What's the matter with you, boy? Look at those trousers! Money doesn't grow on trees, you know." Mam threw up her arms in exasperation. "Who were you fighting with?"

Leon stood straight, bottom lip quivering.

"Dunno," he muttered.

"What do you mean you don't know? How can you not know who you were fighting with?"

"Dunno his name. He's in standard four." Standard four was what the top year in junior school was called then. Leon was in standard three.

Mam sighed, some of the heat gone from her.

"Why were you fighting?"

"Dunno."

"Don't give me that. *Why* were you fighting?"

"He…"

"Yes?"

"He said his dad knows my dad and his dad said my dad's a waster not interested in anything if it can't be drunk or screwed." The quiver in Leon's bottom lip quickened. "He said me and Karl are bastards 'cause Dad don't live with us." The first sob escaped Leon's clenched lips. He tried to hold it back and snorted a glob of snot onto his top lip. He raised a hand to wipe it roughly away. "The other kids were laughing..." His last defences crumbled and he bowed his head, shoulders shaking.

Mam crouched and clutched him to her.

"He was wrong, love," she said softly. "Your father not living with us any more doesn't make you and Karl bastards. You do know that, don't you?"

Leon pulled away, his face flushed and damp, and looked into Mam's eyes.

"Yes," he said. "But the rest of it was true, wasn't it?"

Mam didn't answer.

Two: Art

Brian Lewis lived in our street. My age, he walked to school with me and Leon, and later, when Leon had graduated to comp, just me. Brian was big and ponderous, in adults' shoe sizes in junior school, and the most flatulent person I have ever met. Leon and I would wait for him at his garden gate. He'd lumber down the path, trumpeting a greeting which he'd repeat two or three times on the way in case we'd missed the first one.

It was always a mad dash to get seated in class before Brian. The last place anyone wanted to sit was in the desk behind him. Our teachers were willing accomplices. They were happier with Brian sitting at the back of the room where he could explode to his bowels' content without causing too much disruption.

I lost touch with Brian when we went to comp. He was streamed in the C band, while I was in the B. The A band was for the bright kids; B for the thickies who cared and the more intelligent who didn't; and C was for the real no-hopers.

Only now do I wonder what became of him. I'd like to think he settled down and raised a family because, dim-witted as he was, he wasn't a bad kid, though presumably he'd have first needed his ailment treated.

I only mention Brian Lewis because it was through him I met Art Llewellyn. He also lived in our street, so he said, a few doors down from Brian. It's funny, mind, looking back, that not once did I see him come out of or go into any house, on our street or anywhere. And there's another thing which seems odd now: not once did he come to my house for tea or to call for me, nor I to his. We always met up at one of our usual haunts, though we had rarely arranged to beforehand. It was almost as though we shared some sort of psychic link, like in an episode of *The Twilight* Zone or something, that told us when it was time to meet up and where.

Although he was the same age as us, he did not go to our school. A bus collected him each morning, he told me, from the far end of the street and delivered him to the Welsh-medium school at the top of town.

The Saturday we met must have been an extraordinarily dull day since I only played with Brian outside school if I had exhausted every other possible avenue of entertainment. Brian and I were mucking about in his front garden when I became aware of someone slouching over the gate, watching us.

I had been about to go home anyway. Playing with Brian was like playing that card game patience: it was all right for a while, but grew tedious pretty quickly.

The boy stood aside when I opened the gate.

"See you Monday, Bri," I called. He raised a hand in farewell but didn't look up from whatever boring activity had him engrossed.

I looked at the stranger.

He was of above-average height, with signs in his narrow legs and gangly arms that he would later sprout to more than six foot. His hair was brown and grew below the collar of his faded tee shirt. In his teenage years, that hair would cascade lower than his shoulder blades in a tangled mass of curls. Nobody ever found out how his mane would cope with advancing age and changing fashions because Art never made it into his twenties.

He returned my regard, a cool gaze from narrow eyes.

"Who are you?" he said.

Something about his manner annoyed me.

"What's it to you?"

He shrugged. "Just being polite. I couldn't give a toss who you are. Another idiot, I suspect. This street's full of them."

"Hey, who are you calling an idiot?"

"I can only see one idiot right now and, strangely, I'm not referring to Brian."

That was it. I sprang forward, my arms stretching to encircle him in a bearhug. He was expecting me and stepped back, using my momentum to bring me on. I ended up face down on the pavement. He watched me, the grin on his face making me madder.

It didn't last very long. He was quick and agile, dancing lithely out of my reach. Although he didn't lay a finger on me, I couldn't get close enough to wipe the ever-widening grin off his face.

By the time I came to a standstill, my fringe was dangling over my eyes, sweat dripping from it.

"What's your name?" I said, panting hard.

"Art."

"Art? What sort of name's that?"

"Short for Arthur. I prefer it. Like Art Garfunkel. What sort of name's Karl?"

I grimaced. "As in Karl Marx."

"Harpo Marx, more like." His grin grew even wider until it seemed his face must split apart like an overripe plum.

I couldn't help myself. I grinned back.

Later, when I thought back over our meeting, I could not recall telling him my name.

The pupils at our junior school were in the main a dysfunctional collection of thugs, hoodlums and bullies.

Most children, including me, came from broken backgrounds of some sort. The Education Authority encouraged families of such children in the town and surrounding villages to send them to our school by providing free transport for those living too far away to walk, and resettled any such families who required rehousing in the estates which had grown up around the school, so bringing them within its catchment area. Other schools in the area, including my old one, defined their catchment areas to exclude the council estates, thereby ensuring the undesirables were all herded together into one seething melting pot.

Circumstances varied from kid to kid, but there were common themes: poverty, broken marriages, domestic violence, alcohol abuse and below-average levels of intelligence. But those in themselves could not account for the singular lack of academic achievement or the sheer scale of thuggery that went on in the playground. I believe it was the system itself that engendered it.

They say cream will always rise to the top. Not when it's constantly stirred, it won't.

Of course, I can only see these things clearly with the wisdom that age and hindsight allow. At the time, all I knew was that I went to an uncommonly rough school where survival depended upon anticipatory cunning, fleetness of foot and, when all else failed, strength of fist. There was no rising above the common herd by dint of sporting or academic prowess, nor indeed any expectation placed on us to do so.

I felt no urge to try to exceed anybody's expectations.

Mam's money worries eased, ironically through incurring a debt. It was the divorce. Dad seemed to have disappeared off the face of the earth. Mam's solicitor had to advertise the divorce in various newspapers before the court would allow it to go through, thus delaying the process by many months and increasing her legal bill to hefty proportions.

It was a tense period in our house. By then, Mam worked on the industrial estate on the edge of town in a small, smelly factory which made steel ball bearings. She'd rouse me and Leon each morning before she left to catch the first of two buses that would take her to work. She'd return at four in the afternoon, hollow-eyed and heavy with the stink of oil. Her job was to pack the finished bearings in large wooden crates and smother them in grease to protect them in transit. No matter how long she soaked in the bath, the oily smell would never quite leave her and she could never remove all traces of ingrained grease from beneath her chipped fingernails.

And she was only paid a pittance.

"What am I going to do?" She sat at the rickety kitchen table, wringing her hands on the scruffy Formica surface. Black they were, too. She'd been to see her solicitor straight from work, grease-streaked face and all. "I'll have to work at that bloody factory for the rest of my life to stand any chance of paying Mr Dennis's bill."

Leon and I glanced at each other, unsure what to say.

Mam sighed, long and hard. It held the sound of defeat.

"Have you told him you can't afford to pay him?" said Leon.

"Yes. Mr Dennis knew from the start I'd be struggling, even if everything had gone through smoothly." She sighed again. "Trust your father, boys, to make things difficult. If he'd at least kept in touch with you two, we'd know where he is and could have avoided most of the expense." Her face broke into a bitter smile. "Only one thing for it, I'll have to go on the game."

"Mam!" said Leon, shocked.

"What's on the game, Mam?" I asked. "Like football?"

"Never mind." Her smile grew warmer. She glanced at Leon. "Only kidding, love. Besides, I wouldn't be much good at it, would I, smelling like an old rag."

"Mam, what will you do?" said Leon. "Really."

"I don't know, love. Mr Dennis doesn't seem bothered. He just pats my hand and tells me not to worry. He said today we could come to some arrangement."

"What does he mean by *that*?" Leon's voice dripped with suspicion.

Mam snorted. "He's old enough to be my father, mun. No, he's a gentleman is Mr Dennis. I've no fears on that score."

"What do you mean, Mam?" I asked, trying hopelessly to follow the latest thread.

"Nothing, love. Look, boys, there's no need for you to worry, right? We'll get out of this mess somehow. Now, I'm going to run a bath. Then I'll make tea."

She was right. We did get out of the mess and Mam stopped having to work in the factory. All thanks to Mr Dennis and his arrangement.

Art Llewellyn was my first true friend. My only true friend.

At first, it was the three of us: me, Art and Brian. On the weekends, or during school holidays, we'd leave town, Art and I singing the latest T-Rex hit, Brian accompanying us on his peculiar inbuilt trumpet. We'd go tramping over the fields which lay beyond (and that are probably now covered in the squashed-together boxes of a modern housing estate) until we reached Deadman's Woods.

It wasn't its real name—that was something quaint like Foxglove Wood—but it's what we kids called it. Local legend had it that in olden times, the road from town to Cardiff was terrorised by a dark rider who went by the name of Dic Du; that's Black Dick in English. He targeted the English industrialists who had poured into South Wales to grow rich on its treasures of coal and iron, relieving them of the gold in their pockets and, sometimes, their lives. His reign of terror lasted a year until soldiers in the employ of a local ironmaster shot him in the shoulder. He was dragged bleeding but proud, refusing to plead for mercy, to the woods and hanged from the great oak which stood like a sentinel at the centre of the first line of trees marking the start of the wood.

The legend did not bear close examination. For starters, the centre of the iron industry was in Merthyr, fifty miles or so away up the valleys. But we didn't know and wouldn't have cared if we had. When we stood at the foot of the great oak, peering up at the thickest branch, we could make out the narrow groove in the bark caused by the swinging rope and the dead man's weight. We stretched up and ran our fingers over the knotted hole in the gnarled trunk where a soldier contemptuously thrust Dic's dripping sword after he had used it to make sure all life had fled the dangling body. We *knew* the spirit of Dic Du roamed the woods after dark, calling to his horse Romany, hunting for his sword and cursing the English in wailing tones of eternal anguish.

The three of us spent hours in those woods, climbing trees, making dens in tangled undergrowth, using ferns to re-enact the Battle of Rourke's Drift and playing hide 'n' seek, at least until Brian grew bored with not being able to find me or Art. And, of course, it took no effort to find Brian. All we had to do was stand still and listen. It sometimes took minutes, but he'd always give away his position sooner or later.

"Mob, mob, Brian," I'd call.

"But you didn't see me," came his plaintive response.

"No, but I heard you, Bri. You need to bring a cork with you next time."

There weren't many next times as far as Brian was concerned. Art made sure of that.

It was a humid afternoon towards the end of summer. Deadman's Woods was thick with midges that made our heads itch. Moths, too. They particularly bothered Brian, who moaned constantly as we roamed through the trees. Art and I were able to escape the flying menace by shinnying up trees and standing on branches that swayed in a light breeze which was non-existent at ground level. Brian wasn't so lucky. Big and cumbersome, he struggled to haul himself up into the most climber-friendly beech and stood casting increasingly sullen glances up at us, scratching his head.

"Hey, Brian!" called Art. "Come and stand over here, will you? I need your help to get down."

Brian glanced up at Art, shrugged and slouched over to the foot of the tree in which Art perched. Art climbed down to the lowest branch, about a foot above Brian's head. He stood, his left arm curled around the trunk, his right hanging by his side. I was carving my initials with a penknife high on the trunk of a nearby tree. I stopped what I was doing and turned to watch, assuming Art was simply trying to take Brian's mind off the midges and moths. He certainly didn't require any assistance from Brian to climb down. I had seen Art descend from much taller trees without any help, swinging from the lowest branch like a monkey before dropping lightly to the ground.

"A bit closer, Bri," said Art. "Come right underneath me so I can lower myself onto your shoulders."

Brian did as he was bid without question, hunching forward to take Art's weight. Brian rarely questioned. Perhaps he deserved what he had coming.

Art made no attempt to lower himself from the tree. Instead, he stood straighter, his free hand fiddling with the front of his trousers. I realised what he was about to do in time to warn Brian, but I said nothing.

Art's aim was true. A stream of urine hit the crown of Brian's head, splattering onto the back of his shoulders, staining his sky blue tee shirt navy.

"Huh?" Brian straightened, putting one hand to his head. The steady stream splashed on his hand and down his arm.

I might have mentioned that Brian's mental circuits weren't the quickest at making the necessary connections. Instead of stepping away from the tree and *then* looking up, he only looked up. To make matters worse, he opened his mouth to say or shout something.

Only then did he stumble out of the flow, spluttering and swearing.

Art shook himself and did up his flies. He glanced at me. He didn't smile with his mouth, but his eyes were in hysterics. That's when I realised my mouth was gaping and I shut it hurriedly. I looked back at Brian.

He was standing a few yards away, bent forward, spitting and shaking his head. Drops flew as though from a wet dog. When he looked up, there was murder in his eyes.

Brian shouted, darkly but incoherently. The only word I could make out clearly was, strangely, my name. He ran to Art's tree and jumped at the lowest branch. Art had already scuttled up out of reach. Brian's hands wrapped around the branch and he stopped shouting while he strained to pull himself up. For a moment, it looked as though he might succeed. Art must have thought so, too, for he clambered higher up the tree to where the branches were becoming dangerously thin, the hysterical light in his eyes extinguished. In fact, he looked positively scared and I could see why. Brian was in a rage the likes of which I have rarely seen. If he managed to reach Art, I have no doubt he would have caused him serious harm.

Aware that the situation was out of hand, I started to climb to the ground. I had some vague notion of trying to calm Brian down, although there was nothing I could have said which would have pacified him right then.

It was therefore fortunate indeed for Art that, just when it seemed as though Brian must be in position to swing his legs onto the bough, he lost his grip and fell back. He landed on his feet, but stumbled, dropping to one knee. He stayed in that position for a moment, sopping head bowed, then slowly straightened. The rage had disappeared from his face. It had been replaced by something worse: abject misery.

Without looking at either Art or me, he turned and lumbered away, the first sob escaping before he was out of earshot.

I finished my descent and took a few steps in the direction Brian had gone.

"Let him go," said Art. He dropped lightly to the ground.

"That wasn't a very nice thing to do," I said.

"Oh, fuck him. He's a boring bastard."

"Yeah, maybe he is. But it still wasn't nice."

Art shrugged. "Maybe I'm not a nice person. Who cares?"

I looked at him. Moths fluttered about his head in a small cloud.

"I wouldn't want to be in your shoes when he catches up with you."

Art shrugged again. "He's all brawn, no brains. Forget about him. He's no loss. We can have far more fun without him."

He was right about that. We did have more fun without Brian tagging along. But I felt guilty about what had happened, knowing I could have prevented it by calling out a warning to Brian as he hunkered at the foot of the tree.

By the time we made our way home towards town across the meadows, my sense of guilt had faded. Disappeared entirely, actually. That's being a kid for you. It's as easy to shed guilt as it is to climb a tree.

We were nearly home when it occurred to me.

"Hey, Art, did you notice something about Brian earlier? Something unusual as he was trying to climb your tree?"

"What, other than being covered in piss?"

"Yeah."

"Um… I give up."

"He went nuts, didn't he? Straining to climb that tree. Busting a gut almost. But not once—*not once*, mind you—did he fart."

~~~

"Come and sit down, boys."

Mam had just come in from work. She was later than normal because she had detoured to see Mr Dennis, her solicitor, on the way. Leon and I joined her at the kitchen table.

"Leon, Karl, your old Mam's worked her last in that stinking hole of a factory." She dug a black hand into the pocket of her stained and torn dungarees and extracted a pitiful handful of notes and change. "There! My last wages."

"Mam… how will we manage?"

Leon's face looked pale and drawn, a smaller version of Mam's usual countenance. Not today, though. She was tired and dirty, yes, but did not seem as drained as normal. In fact, she was positively chirpy.

Mam looked from one to the other of us, smiling.

"I'm going to work in an office, boys. A clean, warm, safe office. A solicitors' office."

This was Mr Dennis's arrangement. Mam would join the firm of Clancy, Strick and Dennis as office junior. It was one of the oldest law firms in town. Mam would be the oldest junior in town, probably in the country. Her initial duties would involve making tea, filing, learning how to operate the switchboard and putting up the mail, whatever that meant. But she wouldn't be a junior for long.

The firm were to pay for Mam to attend evening classes in the college where she would learn to type and do shorthand. If that went well, she would be promoted to a secretary. And it did go well. Mam took to typing as though she was born to it.

"Strangely enough, boys," she told us with a grin, when she came home from college proudly clutching her typing certificate, "I owe a lot to that factory. Packing those damned ball bearings one by one made my fingers so dextrous typing was a doddle once I'd learned which key was where."

So Mam became a legal secretary. She left the house at the same time as us each morning and turned towards the town centre, looking
~~~

smart as a new pin in her black business suit she'd bought from a charity shop. It would be a while yet before she could afford to buy new clothes. And as she worked, she paid off her debt to her employers. A small amount was deducted each month from her wages until the bill for her divorce was settled in full.

The brown envelope arrived one month into her new job. She opened it at the kitchen table where Leon and I were eating breakfast. She extracted a sheet of paper and stared at it, before turning to us. Her eyes were doleful, but her jaw was set firmly.

"That's it then," she said quietly. "Your dad and me are no longer married."

I glanced at Leon. He glanced at me. Bending our heads, we continued with our breakfast in silence.

Three: First Love

I didn't pay much attention to girls until I started attending comprehensive school. There had always been too many distractions in junior school, like self-protection, and I guess I was a slow starter when it came to affairs of the heart.

Crompton Price Comprehensive was a rambling, red brick affair, named after the nineteenth century philanthropist who had it constructed as a grammar school and donated it to the, then, Parish Council. It was the nearest comp to my house, not much farther a walk than to the junior school, and it was the one where the kids from my junior school went.

God forbid we should be allowed anywhere near the town's other English-speaking comprehensive, Brynhill, a purpose-built edifice erected six years or so previously at the end of the Decade of Love. Brynhill, we were told in tones of hushed awe by older kids, had modern facilities like language labs and dark rooms for photography and projection rooms for screening pupil-shot ciné films; it had weight-training equipment and woodwork rooms with electric lathes and circular saws.

Not so Crompton Price, or Crumbly Place as most of us called it. That was a warren of echoing block-floored and porcelain-tiled corridors smelling of polish and disinfectant. We sat in draughty classrooms at all-in-one wooden desks and chairs, scarred with generations of stains and carvings. The desks still had inkwells, in some of which could be seen the encrusted remains of long-dried ink.

No projection rooms or language labs for us. We had a gymnasium, of sorts: a small, windowless room with a creaky floor, which exuded the constant odour of sweaty feet, and ceiling lights dimmed by the cages enclosing them to protect them from misdirected basketballs. We had three science laboratories with dodgy gas taps and chipped, drip-stained sinks. There was also a cookery room for the girls and a woodwork room for us, though the only things which ran on electricity in there were the overhead lights and the teacher's hearing aid.

Outside we fared better: three rugby pitches, a football pitch with virtually vandal-proof metal posts and two tennis courts that doubled as a five-a-side pitch in the winter. Still not a patch on Bryn-hill's hockey pitches, cricket squares, indoor tennis courts and swimming pool, but then they didn't have The Arches.

Kay Williams. My first love. Crush, anyway. She was in Form A5, I was in B1 and the two classes had PE and games together. The girls would go off and play hockey or netball or whatever girls did, but we'd all crowd together in the corridor outside the changing rooms before the lessons, waiting for the teachers to come along and unlock the doors.

I was slouching against the corridor wall, observing a game of Top Trumps without much interest, when I noticed her. She had her back to the wall opposite me, chattering girls in front of her. She seemed bored, only half-listening to the talk. Through the bobbing heads of her companions and occasional melee of boys which pressed up and down the corridor, I watched her.

Her hair was long and straight, so blonde it was almost white. Two slides, one at each side, kept hair from her face. Some strands had come loose and tumbled down her clear brow like the finest icicles. Her eyes were wide and blue, their impression of innocence tempered by dark, curling lashes that spoke to some deeper instinct in me. So did her lips. Full and naturally blushing, I wanted to press my own against them.

Momentarily oblivious to the noise and crush around me, I was only aware of her and the quickening of my pulse. It started to flutter and race, like the wings of an agitated moth, when that azure gaze turned and settled upon me. I looked away quickly, heat flaring in my cheeks. When, after a few moments, I dared to look back, she was still watching me. Her eyes had narrowed slightly, but otherwise there was no change to her expression, except maybe for a hint of upturn at the corner of her mouth. Or perhaps I imagined it.

Either way, I was smitten.

~~~

Mam arrived home from work late one evening. She came in singing, shopping bag in hand, newspaper-wrapped fish and chips under an arm. It being a dank November evening, both Leon and I were in. We sat at the kitchen table, Leon poring over maths homework or, more often, staring into space, while I flicked through a Beano.

"Hello, my loves," trilled Mam, flinging our dinner onto the worktop.

"What you got, Mam?" I asked, eyeing the carrier bag.

She grinned and withdrew a navy dress that she held up against her. It was made of a thin material which gave it an insubstantial, willowy look, the sort of dress someone in her early twenties might wear to a disco when her hot pants or jumpsuit were in the wash.

"Well," she said, holding out an arm and sticking out a leg so she could see the dress better. "What do you think?"

"Very nice, Mam," said Leon.

"You'll be able to see your knees," I added. "And your shoulders."

"I know, love," said Mam. "That's the point."

She giggled, a throaty sound which seemed alien coming from her.

I made faces at Leon as Mam clattered about with plates and cutlery. He shrugged and shook his head.

While we ate, I couldn't help thinking about that dress. It looked quite expensive, although that wasn't what worried me. Mam was now earning a legal secretary's salary which, though hardly a king's ransom, had eased her financial worries considerably. We'd even had a telephone installed.

"Ma—am," I started.

Leon cleared his throat and shot me a warning glance.

"What's the, er, special occasion?" he said.

Mam put down her knife and fork. She looked at us, carefully, as though weighing us up.

"I've been asked out," she said.
~~~

"What, like a date?"

"Yes."

Mam didn't lower her gaze, but pressed her lips tightly together and waited.

I opened my mouth, then closed it when Leon's stockinged toe met my shin.

"Good," said Leon.

Mam raised her eyebrows.

"Really?" She gazed intently at Leon.

"Yes," he said. "Really."

Mam turned to look at me.

"What about you, Karl? Do you mind if I go out on a date?"

Again I felt Leon kick me. I looked at Mam and shook my head. She let out her breath in a deep sigh. Her eyes glistened.

"Thank you, boys," she said.

Crompton Price Comprehensive School was built in an age when cost was not always the determining factor. The school site sloped but, instead of simply levelling the area as would happen today to make the project more cost-effective, the architect had incorporated the slope into the design. The building was erected backing onto the slope, allowing a basement to be constructed into the side of the small hill. The boiler house and caretaker's storage rooms and workshop were housed in the basement, the heavy doors reinforced with steel cladding and secured with sturdy bolts and padlocks, not only to discourage potential thieves but, more importantly, to resist the most tenacious pupil. The doors faced out onto a small paved area above which jutted the back of the school. Two smooth brick pillars supplemented the support provided by the side walls of the basement, forming three perfect curves which gave the area its name.

Teachers rarely ventured down to The Arches. Neither did the caretaker during school hours, unless something went wrong with the boiler. Thus the area became a popular haven for smokers and lovers.

I was only occasionally one of the former. My attempts at joining the ranks of the latter were disastrous.

Has ever a more overtly asexual method of covering the female form been invented than gym knickers? The girls in Crumbly Place wore brown undergarments for PE that clung where they didn't need to and sagged where they needed to cling. Not that it stopped us boys from looking. Our gazes would start at the feet, clad in the ubiquitous black daps we all bought from Woolworth's, and work their way slowly up to the knee, the normal limit of our view when the girls were wearing their uniforms. From there, our gazes would travel slowly upwards to the forbidden levels, ever upwards, seeking answers to what to twelve-year-olds was one of life's great mysteries. But the promise offered by long, bare limbs would be cruelly dashed against the unrelenting barrier of the gym knicker.

Kay Williams could even make gym knickers look mysterious and alluring, which probably says more about the pubescent me and my state of perpetual sexual anxiety than it does about her. To my testosterone-addled mind, Kay would probably have looked fetching in a cardboard box.

I didn't even know her name at first. I'd hurry to every PE and games lesson to gain a good vantage point in the corridor from where I could watch her. After games, I'd always be the first off the rugby field to rush back to the changing rooms in case I happened to see the girls returning from the hockey field. They always finished before us—I suppose because it took them longer to shower and dress, another female mystery.

It took me weeks to get to know any of the boys from Form 1A5 well enough to enquire, as off-handedly as I could, as to her name. It took me months to talk to her, although, as it happened, I didn't have time to think about it. Just as well—there was no time for my courage, such as it was, to desert me.

"Leon," I said, keeping my voice low, "she's only going on a date, right? It doesn't mean we're going to have a new dad, does it?"

My brother looked at me, half-smiling. We were in the living room while Mam was upstairs getting ready.

"Don't be soft," he said. His expression became grave. "And don't let Mam hear you saying stuff like that. It's been six years since Dad went. She's worked her fingers to the bone to keep us clothed and fed. It's about time she did something for herself."

"But supposing she gets married again. Will he be our new dad?"

"No. Well, he'd be our stepfather, I suppose. But, for chrissake, mun, it's only a date."

"Who is he, anyway?"

"Dunno his name. He's some divorce client of Mam's boss. He asked Mam out a while ago, but she couldn't say yes until his divorce was over. Something about ethics."

"What are ethics?"

Leon rolled his eyes.

"You'll understand when you're older," he said smugly.

"So you don't know, either."

"Yes, I do. But I ain't telling you. You're only a kid."

"Oh, yeah? And you've got stray pubes on your lip."

Leon coloured, his hand coming up to his mouth where a sandy moustache was trying its best to lend him an appearance of maturity beyond his fifteen years. I knew he was sensitive about the moustache—it annoyed him that it wasn't thick and dark like some of his friends' efforts at cultivating facial hair—and so it made an easy target when I wanted to get at him.

He was quick. In one movement, he dropped his hand and lunged forward out of his chair, bringing his right fist down onto the top of my thigh. The pain was bright and deep, but faded quickly as my leg went numb.

I gritted my teeth and blinked back the tears which sprang hotly to my eyes. Leon sat back in his chair, but he was tense, ready for me if I reacted. I didn't. I knew there could be only one winner in a fight between me and my brother. Leon was serious about his rugby and had filled out, while shooting upwards to touch six foot.

"That'll teach you not to cheek your elders," he said. "And just remember, there's plenty more where that came from."

I ignored him, trying to concentrate upon not crying while sensation, hot and thumping, returned to my thigh.

Despite the occasional incident like this, Leon wasn't bad as big brothers go. Since Dad walked out of our lives, we had become closer. Leon must have often felt tempted to play the role of father figure but, to his credit, resisted most of the time, though he asserted his seniority like all older siblings do. My resentment at such displays of power never lasted long.

At the sound of a car horn tooting outside the front window, Leon and I glanced at each other, the fight already forgotten. I also forgot about the fading pain in my leg as we both rushed to the window.

We lifted the net curtain over our heads and peered into the darkness, our breath fogging the glass.

"Wow," I exclaimed quietly as I took in the sleek contours of the Ford Capri that sat idling by the kerb.

"Flash bastard," muttered Leon.

There was a clatter behind us as Mam rushed downstairs. I glanced back to see her pulling a coat over shoulders which were bare in her new dress. A whiff of perfume wafted over to us. And there was something not quite right with her face. It took me a moment to realise it bore more, far more, than her usual touch of make-up.

"I'm off then, boys. Karl, there's school tomorrow so I want you in bed by ten. Leon, make sure he is."

"Yes, Mam," we chorused.

"Tarra, then."

"Bye, Mam," I muttered.

"Good luck," said Leon. "Enjoy yourself."

His fingers dug into my ribs.

"Yeah," I mumbled. "Enjoy yourself."

Try as I might, I can't recall the name of the maths teacher I had in Form One. I *can* remember his thick sideburns and foul breath, and the way small sprays of spittle were ejected from his mouth when he leaned close to me.

Once he'd finished his lecture about paying more attention in class and trying harder to hand my homework in on time, he let me go. I didn't bother rushing, although it was lunchtime. We first years had to scamper across to the block containing the dining hall as soon as the lunchtime bell went if we were to stand any chance of getting towards the front of the queue, although 'queue' doesn't accurately describe the heaving mass of shoving, squawking boys. And the girls' line was no more orderly.

Resigned to standing at the very rear of the boys' line, which meant a thirty-minute wait and little choice of food when I eventually made it into the dining hall, I stopped off at the toilets to wash my face free of maths teacher's spit. Making my way across to the other block, gaze turned to the floor, I didn't notice her approach until she was almost on top of me.

I stopped dead in my tracks. She was a few paces away, hands thrust in the pockets of her jacket, bag slung around her shoulder.

"Aye, aye," I said, mouth outstripping brain comfortably. "Mitching, is it?" Instantly I blushed, realising how foolish I must have sounded.

"Dentist, actually," she said. "Though it's no business of yours."

She had barely broken stride and had almost gone past me. I put out my hand and laid it on her arm. She stopped, but glanced down at my hand, eyes narrowing.

"It's Kay, isn't it? You're in A5."

She looked at me, eyes still narrow. I removed my hand from her arm.

"What's it to you?"

Her tone was cool, but not icy. Encouraged, or at least uncowed due to not having rehearsed any of this, I blurted on.

"My name's Karl. I've seen you in games. I'd, er, I'd love to see you some other time."

I stared at her, horrified, thrilled, scared and hopeful all at the same time.

Kay returned my gaze, no sign of what she was thinking showing on that wonderful face.

"One o'clock. Tomorrow. The Arches."

Before the response had sunk into my brain, she had walked on. I turned and stared after her, replaying her words, satisfying my cynical mind I had heard correctly.

When eventually I made my way to the dining hall, it was with a sick, yet strangely elated, feeling in my stomach. By the time I made it into the hall, I could have eaten a horse. Sadly, there were none left.

Four: Custard

It wasn't so much trains that fascinated me as their destination. True, the hissing of the rails when a train approached always gave me a little shiver of excitement. The impact of air rapidly departing the space briefly occupied by an engine, and the clatter of speeding coaches or trucks transmitting itself into my feet by a rumbling shake, never failed to give me a rush. The fleeting aroma of burning diesel and axle grease made my stomach flip, but with thrill not nausea.

I was never so stimulated by the sight, sound and smell of a train to want to go to the station in town and obtain a timetable, or to note the name and type of each engine, or even to purchase an anorak.

No, it was where the trains ended up which tweaked my imagination. Leon had told me the railway line beyond the wire fence at the end of our garden, a fence that now sagged in the middle from the hours I had spent leaning on it, was the main Swansea to London Paddington line. And I wanted to go to London.

I had mentioned it to Mam more than once.

"Aw, love, I can't afford to take you to London yet. Perhaps next year."

She'd ruffle my hair or hug me, while I bit back my disappointment.

I'm not sure quite what it was that attracted me to the big city. I'd visited Cardiff and Swansea which, although a lot smaller then, hadn't left too deep an impression on me. We had touched upon London in geography—one of the few lessons in which I'd paid close attention—and images of the city were now commonplace with the increased popularity of television, but my fascination had its roots much further back. It was down to the fairy tale qualities conjured up by a school trip to see the pantomime *Dick Whittington*, and the Ladybird book about London, one of the few books I read and re-read from cover to cover.

Ladybird books were a common birthday and Christmas present for kids in the early seventies. Fairly inexpensive, they covered a range of wholesome educational topics like *Flags of the World* and *What to Discover Along the Seashore*, and were suitable for children of all reading abilities due to their simple language and prominent, colourful pictures. They were in durable hardback format and slim, twenty of them taking up little space on a shelf. I know because that's how many I had, though the titles of most of them have long flown my mind.

I must have spent hours with that Ladybird book about London, thumbing past the vivid drawings of the Houses of Parliament and Big Ben, reading about St Paul's Cathedral and Speakers' Corner.

London called to me with its history and its vastness and its opportunities. In so much as I dreamed of fame and fortune, it was always in London the dreams were set.

And that's where the trains went.

I did my best to like Derek. I really did.

Mam had been seeing him for months before deciding the time was right to introduce him to me and Leon. She laid the groundwork carefully, mentioning the possibility of inviting him to tea off-handedly, before slipping it into conversation as something that would be happening, and finally graduating to setting a date.

"You'll like Derek, boys," she said with conviction, though I wonder who she was trying to convince. "He's lots of fun. He makes me laugh."

"Basil Brush makes me laugh," I muttered, ignoring Leon's glare and moving my shins out of reach of his toes.

Mam placed a hand, the skin on which had become much softer since escaping the factory, on the back of one of mine.

"Give him a chance, love," she said quietly. "That's all I ask."

The appointed night arrived. Mam called in the supermarket on her way home from work.

"Steak tonight, boys," she said, smiling at us nervously.

I was glad she didn't wear the frock which revealed her knees and shoulders. She dressed conservatively in a high-necked blouse and slacks. Leon and I were dressed as we always were after school: torn jeans and tee shirts. Mam looked at us and opened her mouth as though to say something. Then she shook her head.

"He'll have to take us as he finds us. If he— oh, is that a car I hear? Karl…"

But I was already in the living room, rushing to the window. I peered through the net curtain at the now familiar contours of his Capri.

"Yeah," I called. "It's him."

I slouched back into the kitchen as Mam went to open the front door. Leon was sitting at the table. He winked at me, but didn't smile. He looked as nervous as Mam.

There was a murmur of conversation from the hallway, a brief silence, then Mam entered the kitchen, followed by Derek.

He was tall and smelled of aftershave that must have been splashed on liberally since it overpowered the aroma of cooking vegetables from the stove. He had narrow shoulders, the collar of his shirt nearly stretching past them. The top three buttons of the shirt were undone, despite it being cold outside, revealing a thick tangle of greying hair and a twinkling gold medallion.

Mam nodded at us.

"Derek, these are my sons. Leon and Karl."

Derek raised his right hand in a salute-like wave.

"All right, dudes," he said.

"Yeah, er, cool," said Leon.

"Huh?" I said.

Mam smiled uncertainly at us.

"Let me get these steaks under the grill," she said. "Make your-self at home."

Derek stepped to one side and leaned nonchalantly back against a work surface. It must have been disconcerting to stand there with Leon and I staring at him, but he seemed completely unfazed. He grinned at us, showing two rows of even white teeth, except for one gold incisor.

"So, Leo," he began.

"Leo*n*," said Leon.

"Yeah, right. So your mother tells me you play rugby."

"Yeah, I do." Leon sat straighter. "I play blindside flanker for the school firsts. We're doing well. Only lost three games so far."

"Really? I'm more of a football man myself. Less likely to mess up your face that way. Got to keep your looks for the ladies, know what I mean."

He winked at Leon, grinned and stretched out a hand to smack Mam lightly on the rump. She giggled like a girl. I noticed he allowed his hand to remain in place for a second or two longer than necessary. Mam made no attempt to move it.

Leon also noticed. He cleared his throat.

"Football's for— ow!"

Leon glared at me. I smiled sweetly back.

Derek had apparently exhausted his repertoire of conversation with a teenager who played rugby. He turned his attention to me.

"So, er…?"

"Kevin," I said.

"Of course. Kevin. What do you do?"

"Oh, I collect radishes and play the accordion."

Leon snorted. I dared not look at him for fear of collapsing in a fit of giggles. It was Mam's turn to glare at me.

"Don't listen to *Karl*," she said. "He's only having a bit of fun."

"I see," said Derek. "He's a joker, is he?"

He smiled at me, or at least his lips curled up at the edges. His eyes, however, did not twinkle. They had gone a dull grey, like slate. My urge to laugh dissipated.

Derek turned to Mam.

"He's not the only one who likes a bit of fun," he said in a husky tone.

He grabbed Mam about the waist, yanked her away from the grill and swung her round as though performing a tango. Mam blushed and dropped her gaze from mine and Leon's. She caught Derek's hands and pulled them away.

"No. I, er, the steaks will spoil." She lowered her voice, but I caught her words. "Wait until next week."

Leon had half-risen to his feet, a dark look on his face. I cleared my throat and he took the hint, sinking slowly back into his seat.

After that, Derek ignored us. He chatted away to Mam while we ate, not so much as sparing us a glance. Whenever Mam tried to include us in the conversation, he fell silent but gazed doe-eyed at Mam while me or Leon muttered some reply. When Mam caught his expression, her breath would catch in her throat and her nostrils would flare. Then he'd be off on some new tack and Mam would join in like an eager pupil, her sons forgotten.

It quite put me off my food, I can tell you, though not to the extent it prevented me from clearing my plate. It wasn't every day we had steak.

Derek called goodbye to us as he was leaving. Leon barely grunted and I raised a hand in farewell, but he and Mam were already at the front door. Low murmurs and rustling noises drifted in to us in the living room.

When Mam returned, she looked as though she'd been standing too close to a furnace and her hair was sticking up at the back.

"Well," she said cheerfully. "That went okay, didn't it?"

"Yes, Mam," I said dutifully.

Leon glanced up from the settee.

"Mam, tuck your blouse back in," was his only comment.

Not all the trains which passed behind our house on their way to London sped by as though desperate to get there. Occasionally, a freight or coal train would trundle past at little more than walking pace, and still slowing. I asked Leon why.

"There's a siding 'bout three hundred yards further on," he explained. "Sometimes a goods train will pull in there to make way for the express."

"Why?"

"'Cause a goods train is slower than an express, shit-for-brains.

That's why it's called an express. It means fast. It wouldn't be much of an express if it had to crawl along behind twenty trucks of coal or something, would it?"

Sure enough, whenever I noticed a goods train passing at less-than-urgent pace, I'd watch until, three or four minutes later, a passenger train would tear past like a demented serpent. If I stayed and listened, moments after the hiss and rumble of the express had faded I'd faintly hear the chug and groan of the goods train picking up speed.

Not that I did this very often. After four years of having a main track railway line at the foot of the garden, trains had lost their novelty, although my fascination with their destination burned as bright as ever.

I didn't dwell long upon Mam's new love interest and my dislike for him. I had more important things on my mind. Like meeting Kay Williams down at The Arches.

That lunchtime, I fought to maintain my place towards the front of the queue. I dithered over what food to choose which would not make my breath stink—kids at Crumbly Place went to The Arches during lunch break for only two reasons, and I didn't think Kay Williams was a smoker. By the time I had made my choice and carried the tray to a vacant table, I could not face eating.

My Timex read ten to one when I arrived at The Arches. That didn't necessarily mean it was ten to one. The watch was old and I often forgot to wind it up.

Half a dozen kids of varying ages stood around the pillars which supported the arches, puffing on cigarettes. The breeze whipped away their smoke, but still the dim space behind was thick with its acrid smell.

I stopped in the middle of the smooth floor, hands in pockets, wondering what to do. Four couples were clinched at regular intervals around the inner wall, mouths suction-padded together, arms encircling and exploring, tentacle-like. One female head broke off long enough to glance at me, and I heard a snigger. I waited a moment longer, then turned and strolled back out into the open air.

The smokers barely spared me a look while I walked to the foot of the steps leading up to the yard. I slouched against the wall, hands firmly tucked in pockets, hoping that nonchalance would disguise my turmoil.

My watch said ten past one and I was wondering how much longer to wait, when she appeared. I watched her bounce lightly down the steps, noticing from my low vantage point how the hem of her skirt billowed out as her legs moved, offering glimpses of creamy white thighs. I swallowed.

"Hi," I said, trying to appear casual.

She mimicked my stance, leaning back against the wall beside me, hands tucked into the pockets of her skirt.

We stood like that for a minute or two, me desperately trying to think of something to say which would not reveal my acute state of anxiety. I turned my head towards her.

Her head was turned in my direction, but inclined to look back up the stairs. Her mouth was moving, though she made no sound. Her eyes swivelled down to look into my face as I started to turn away to follow the direction of her gaze.

She grabbed me by the hand.

"Come on," she said.

I forgot all about trying to see what she had been looking at. When her fingers clutched mine, all the spit in my mouth evaporated and my heart started pounding simultaneously in my head and my groin, but not in my chest.

She yanked me towards The Arches. I went willingly, almost trotting to keep up with her. This time the smokers did look at me. I thought I caught more than one expression of admiration. Envy even.

Then we passed through one of the arches and into the gloom beyond. She led me to a gap in the wall between two couples and stopped. She released my hand, turned and looked at me, her back to the wall. I stared back, my breath coming in short gasps. Her lips were slightly parted and I could feel the warm sweetness of her breath when I moved my face closer. I pressed my lips to hers and the rushing sound of a honeyed waterfall filled my ears. My eyes closed. I had never kissed a girl before; I never wanted to stop kissing this one.

My eyes snapped open when I felt her hand flutter at my belt. I brought my own hands down and grasped her wrist.

"What are you doing?" I pulled my face away from hers.

"Shh," she said.

She reached out and pulled me firmly forward until out lips met once more. This time, I did not resist when I felt her hand on the buckle of my belt.

I was too caught up with my own racing passion to realise there was somebody standing behind me. Kay slid to one side and I was left pursing my lips at the blank wall. My trousers were yanked down from behind. Although the metal clasp and flies were fastened, she had undone my belt and this was enough to allow my trousers to slide down to my knees under the force of the tug.

I yelped, my hands shooting down to my waistband to yank the trousers back up. I turned as I did so, straightening and fumbling at my belt to fasten the buckle. That's when the first damp coldness seeped into my buttocks.

My right hand crept around to the seat of my trousers. It was sagging like a sodden nappy and something gooey was flowing down my thighs. My hand came away wet. I raised my fingers to my nose.

"Custard?"

The laughter made me look up. Kay Williams stood before me, a smirk spoiling her perfect features. A brown moth fluttered around her head, though it wasn't the season for moths. Next to her stood two of her friends. They were giggling. One of them held a plastic carton, its rim coated in yellow gunk. The other couples had broken off their clinches to stare and laugh. Even the smokers had come in to see what the fuss was about. They pointed and sniggered, smoke coming off them like steam.

"Why?" I said, looking at her through the first tears of shame.

Her voice was as cold as the custard running down my legs and filled with contempt.

"D'you really think I'd go out with a thickie from the Bs?"

"Yeah," said one of her friends. "She's far too good for you, Custard Pants."

Tears traced a burning path down my cheeks. I stumbled forward, head bowed. Congealing custard clung to my legs and collected at my ankles.

Their laughter followed me as I squelched up the steps. When I reached the top, I broke into a shambling run that didn't end until I'd reached home. It was the first time I'd played truant from school. It wouldn't be the last.

Five: Mitching

Most of my leisure time during my early teens was spent with Art Llewellyn. He attended the Welsh-language comprehensive, a twenty-minute bus ride away. Reckoned he'd end up working for the BBC. He said he liked the school, though I didn't believe him when he said the girls were all stunning and mad for him. I didn't believe a lot of things Art said, but I liked him because we had much in common. For a start, he didn't appear to have any other friends either. At least, none who lived locally. We came to depend upon each other, like tired old lovers too accustomed to each other's ways and too afraid to break apart.

He was the brains of the outfit, or thought he was. I was always the Sundance Kid to his Butch Cassidy, the Robin to his Batman. It was always Art who came up with ideas for new things to do. I didn't usually object. Sometimes I too grew bored with wandering through Deadman's Woods or traipsing across fields in search of horse chestnut trees.

It was Art who had the idea to catch the bus to Cardiff. We were a week into the summer holidays and Mam was quite happy for me to spend the days as I wanted, so long as I kept out of mischief. She even gave me the bus fare.

"Here's a little extra," she said with a wink, pressing a pound note into my hand. "Don't spend it all at once."

Art and I caught the nine-twenty from the town centre bus station. We sat at the back, poking out our tongues at people as the bus wound its tortuous way through the narrow streets of town. When it gained the relative freedom of the A48, we settled back in our seats and chatted about girls and sport and television and the latest phenomenon due to hit Britain, a film whose very title caused us to discuss it in hushed tones of reverence. Art reckoned he knew everything there was to know about it.

"It'll be really good, see?" he said, speaking to me in that way he had sometimes as though I was his younger brother. "Apparently you can't even see the strings."

"Strings?"

"Yeah, you know, like in *Thunderbirds* and *Captain Scarlett* and all those old kids' programmes. You can see the strings, right?"

"Yeah, but they're puppets. *Star Wars* isn't puppets. It's sort of… *real.* Like *Star Trek.*"

"Course it's real. The people are, anyway. But the spaceships or the aliens can't be real, can they? Stands to reason."

He smiled sadly at me and looked away, shaking his head.

Leon took me to see *Star Wars* when it arrived on these shores the following year. I sat in the packed cinema peering up at the screen with my mouth wide open. I had never seen, or imagined, anything like it before. When we got home that evening, I went straight to my room and lay on my bed, hands behind head, reliving the experience and determining to become a film director or a science fiction writer. But I did not possess the drive or talent to do either.

I tried to write a story about spaceships and bug-eyed aliens and purple planets. It starred a space ranger named Jake Duet who had to fight his way through hordes of evil galactic troops led by the dastardly Arthur Death in order to save Princess Nia, and it was complete crap. No matter how hard I sucked the end of my pencil, trying to come up with something original, my plot could not break away from the film's. I showed my effort to Mam. She read it carefully, ignoring the atrocious spelling and lack of grammar, and pronounced it a worthy first attempt. But I knew she thought it rubbish and she knew that I knew.

"Come here, love," she said, drawing me close with her hand about my waist. "Everyone has a special talent. Perhaps writing's not yours."

"But what is my talent then, Mam? I'm useless at everything."

She laughed and hugged me tighter.

"Love, you're only twelve. You might not discover your talent until you're much older. You have to keep trying different things until you find something you enjoy and you're good at."

"But I want to be good at something now."

"You are good at something now."

"I am? What?"

"You're good at being a son."

"Aw, Mam."

She was wrong about that. I turned out to be not such a good son. And that started through my discovery that I did in fact already possess a special talent, one which needed the right set of circumstances to enable it to reveal itself and flourish. Art was the catalyst who brought those about.

Mitching, or bunking off or playing truant, was easy at Crumbly Place. Like the day I was christened Custard Pants, I simply walked out of there. A steep flight of concrete steps led up to the school's main entrance. Anyone descending those steps would quickly drop from sight of any watching eyes. Unless a teacher happened to be in the vicinity—and it was easy to check without being seen— skipping school for the day was a doddle.

You only had to ensure you were present for registration. This was taken once each day immediately after assembly. Each class had a form room where a teacher would mark in red pen the attendance register, before dismissing us to the first lesson. Then, or at any of the lesson changeovers during the day, it was the easiest thing in the world to slip away unnoticed amongst a milling throng of a thousand or so pupils.

Most of the teachers didn't give two hoots. They were, as a rule, either uncompromising control freaks or apathetic paper shufflers. As Crumbly Place was populated by the lower dregs of society's children, so the teaching staff was made up of the incompetent and the psychopathic. The only thing truly comprehensive about Crumbly Place was its level of dysfunctional people, children and adults alike. In that sense, I was ideally suited to it, and it to me.

I began mitching on a regular basis after the incident with Kay Williams at The Arches. Word quickly got around and for days I was met with sniggers and smirks wherever I went. Shouts of 'There goes Custard Pants' would follow me down the corridor and hilarity greeted the lunchtime menu whenever it contained custard. Even some of the teachers joined in.

Our biology teacher was grey-haired and short, with a habit of sniffing loudly at the end of each sentence. Mr Cornish was his name. Of course, we all called him Pasty, though not to his face.

"Today, 1B1," he announced in a loud voice, "we are going to look at infections, their causes and effects." *Sniff.*

One or two members of the class mimicked his nasal affectation. If he noticed, he didn't say anything. Pasty was one of the indifferent ones.

"Now then," he said. "Who can tell me what we call one of the classic signs of infection in humans or animals? It's a substance with an offensive smell. It's usually quite thick in consistency and is green or yellow in colour." *Sniff.*

At this point, he fixed his gaze upon me and a smug grin appeared on his face.

"And, no, Jordan," he said triumphantly, "I'm not talking about custard."

While the class fell about laughing, I hunched my shoulders and slid down in my seat, trying to disappear into the floor.

I ignored the comments and jibes, hoping they would eventually die away and, of course, they did, though the nickname would stick in some peoples' minds for the rest of my school days. But the first PE lesson following The Arches incident, to have to stand in the corridor with Kay Williams and her cronies, was more than I could face. So I mitched. That and every other PE lesson for the rest of the school year.

Cardiff was noisy and smelly. We climbed down from the bus at Wood Street Station and headed for the city centre through a scrum of shoppers, office workers and vagabonds. Our nostrils were assailed by exhaust fumes from crawling cars and lorries, sour yeast and hops wafting from the Brains' Brewery, and musky odours exuded by rushing people. Art and I were invisible to them. They only saw things at eye level and then only if those things affected them. If a passer-by's gaze did happen to inadvertently alight on us, it would slide off again as easily as a warm dab of butter.

Art nudged me in the ribs and pointed up at the grubby side of the tall building we stood by while we waited for a break in the traffic to cross St Mary Street. I looked up to see a sign reading 'Prince of Wales Theatre', before my gaze moved down to the glass-fronted cabinet Art was giggling at. Behind the glass was a collage of grainy pictures which seemed to be poor quality stills taken from films. They showed a variety of men and women in a variety of poses, most involving few, if any, clothes. Crude black stars had been added in strategic places to prevent the pictures offending obscenity laws, but failing to prevent stirrings in my pubescent instincts.

"This place shows dirty flicks." Art sniggered. "I know somebody who's been in there. He says the seats are sticky."

An inexplicable warmth was spreading from the pit of my stomach. Dark images of damp skin and taut features and grunting rhythms flashed through my head. As part of me tried to impose a sense of grubbiness and distaste upon my mind, so a more primordial reflex flooded my body with a deep longing and promise of unbounded pleasure. It wasn't a fair fight.

"Let's go in," I breathed.

"Yeah, sure," I heard Art say as though he was not standing by my side but ten yards away. "The boy I know is sixteen, but he's got a tash and stuff. We'll never pass for eighteen. Besides, it's only ten o'clock. It probably doesn't open till the afternoon."

It took quite an effort to tear my gaze away from those pictures of cheap lust. Something inside me that had only turned over and grunted during my close encounter with Kay Williams had now awoken fully.

When recounting events that took place forty or more years ago, it is difficult to be confident about their chronology. Some incidents can be fixed by extraneous events, like that first trip Art and I took to Cardiff. I know it was the summer holidays and we discussed *Star*

Wars on the bus. Since the film didn't come to Britain until early 1978, our trip must have taken place the previous summer when I had just completed my first year at comp.

But I can't recall precisely when the incident involving Mam and Derek happened. If it was before the Cardiff trip, it would be easy to blame them for what followed. If, however, it occurred later, then I had already strayed from the straight and narrow without their help.

Everyone looks for somebody to blame. It makes life easier to bear if it's someone else's fault.

Some days I didn't leave the school premises when mitching PE or games, though I never hid out at The Arches. Who willingly returns to the scene of their humiliation? There were other places to be out of sight or, at least, out of mind, which pretty much amounted to the same thing. Take the school library, for instance. I'd march in as though I had every right to be there, grab a book and a chair, and while away the lesson in peaceful solitude, attention wandering far and wide, though rarely settling on the book. If the school librarian ever wondered whether I ought to be there, she never challenged me.

Another good place was the toilet block next to the staff room. Troublemakers tended to avoid it, preferring blocks further away from the teachers, and so the teachers didn't bother checking them often. It was possible to spend a double games lesson locked away in the end cubicle, trousers around ankles for the sake of appearance, reading a comic while my feet grew tingly and numb.

I'd reappear amidst my damp-haired classmates as they jostled outside the classroom door for the next lesson. Nobody ever remarked upon my earlier absence. I doubt they even noticed. There was nobody in form 1B1 from my old junior school and, following The Arches incident, I had become withdrawn and solitary, any first shoots of friendship withered by my indifference.

On other days, when the sun was shining or conkers were ripening, or I hadn't done homework, I'd shoot off immediately after registration, keeping to back streets and alleys where I was less likely to be spotted by a policeman or questioned by an over-inquisitive adult. For I stood out like a suntanned vampire. Not that the school uniform was overly loud—grey trousers and shirt, navy jumper, grey tie with thin green stripes—but it was still a uniform. It marked me as belonging elsewhere, no matter how strongly I'd protest I didn't belong.

The day that ended with me trying to run away to London began clear and fresh. Even before I reached the school gates, I had decided it was far too nice to spend shut away amongst the smell of floor polish and disinfectant. The rustling colours of autumnal Deadman's Woods called to me.

After registration, while the rest of my class headed off to double maths, I made for the main door and joined the stream of children pouring around the front of the main building towards the science block. Nobody noted my presence, even less my absence when I ducked away and trotted down the stone steps and out of the front gate. I crossed the road and headed down the side street opposite.

Two hundred yards down that road stood a shop selling home-made sausage rolls, which were both delicious and well within my dinner budget. I often went to Deadman's Woods armed with provisions of sausage rolls, crisps or chocolate bars. Maybe a can of pop, too, if my dinner money would stretch that far.

But that day I was fated to travel empty-handed. As I approached the shop, somebody I recognised went in and I muttered an annoyed curse. Next door to us lived an old lady. Miss Smith or Jones or something unmemorable. None of us liked her, though Mam tolerated her for the sake of pleasant relations.

"She might be an old busybody," Mam would say, fixing me and Leon with a stern eye, "but she's lonely and hasn't much else to do except gossip. So try to be nice to her."

Something must have shown in our expressions because she sighed. "Well, keep out of her way then. Don't give her any reason to include you in her topics of gossip."

That's what we did. Leon and I kept out of the old lady's way, giving her no cause to notice us. But, just my luck, there she was in her furry ankle boots, checked overcoat and headscarf, disappearing into the shop. She would notice me immediately if I followed her in—those knowing grey eyes noticed everything—and word would reach Mam I wasn't in school when I should have been. I could probably have thought up some excuse to satisfy Mam this time, but I didn't want to use up good excuses unnecessarily. The alternative was to wait for the old dear to leave the shop and the vicinity, but she was likely to be a while. She wasn't the sort to simply collect her purchases, pay for them and leave. She'd probably engage the shop-keeper in chit-chat for twenty minutes and I didn't want to hang around the streets that long. Someone was bound to notice me.

With a shrug and a sigh, I headed away from the shop towards Deadman's Woods, missing the comforting weight of a sausage roll in my pocket, trying not to wonder what I would do for lunch.

I needn't have worried about food. By the time I reached the wood, the wind had freshened, dragging in low clouds, ominously dark. It wasn't long before drops of rain the size of marbles were spattering the trees. My fold-away anorak wasn't designed to keep out rain of that intensity and soon water was seeping into my clothes, cold was seeping into my bones and the soles of my shoes had doubled in thickness with cloying mud.

Peering up through swaying boughs, I guessed the rain was set for the afternoon. My stomach rumbled. I decided to go home.

Six: Shopping

It was in one of the big department stores—Howell's or David Morgan's or British Home Stores—where Art Llewellyn opened my eyes to a new world. A world in which being twelve and skint didn't necessarily mean having to go without nice things.

We were in the clothing section and I was bored. I had no interest in clothes and the pound note Mam had given me was burning a hole in my pocket.

"Let's go to the toy section," I said. "Or find somewhere they sell sweets."

"Half a mo." Art stopped by a rack of black tee shirts. "I could do with a couple of new tee shirts for the summer." He glanced at me, his eyes taking in my battered plimsoles, torn jeans and faded shirt Leon had outgrown. "So could you."

"Yeah, but I can't buy a tee shirt for a pound. Even if I could, I ain't gonna."

Art turned back to the rack and rummaged through the tee shirts, picking one out, holding it against his torso and nodding. He held one against me. Then he removed the hangers and replaced them on the rack. He folded the tee shirts and handed one to me.

"What are you doing?" I said. "I can't afford that."

"Who said anything about paying for it?"

Art glanced from side to side, then yanked his shirt from the waistband of his jeans and stuffed the tee shirt down the front of them.

"Oh, shit," I hissed. "Put them back."

"Too late."

He was looking over my shoulder. I turned. A large man in a grey suit was striding towards us, a frown on his face.

"Run," said Art.

"What?"

My gaze didn't move from the approaching man, who was now lengthening his stride and would be upon us within moments.

"Run, you idiot!"

I felt a tug at my shirt that made me stumble back a step and broke my paralysis. As the man broke into a shambling run, I whirled around and took to my heels after the rapidly disappearing Art.

"Hey! Stop!"

I ignored the shout.

We ran like ferrets, dodging shoppers and sales assistants who, alerted by the shouts of the pursuing man in the suit, made half-hearted attempts to halt our flight. Art headed for the down escalator.

"No," I shouted. "This way."

I veered towards a set of double doors marked 'Fire Exit' in green paint. I thudded against the metal bar, which yielded easily, and the doors burst open. Glancing back to ensure Art was following, I bounded down the stairs two and three at a time. Another set of doors opened when I crashed into them and I was in the open air.

Art burst out of the building behind me and we paused, panting. The slapping of heavy footsteps descending the steps made us take to our heels again, up the alleyway in which we had emerged and into the stream of people crowding the main street. There we slowed to a swift walk which soon took us away from the department store.

I glanced at Art. His hair was sticking up where it wasn't sweat-slickened and his eyes were bright. He looked at me and started to giggle. I turned my head but could see no signs of pursuit. I grabbed Art by the arm and ducked down a less crowded side street.

"You bloody idiot!" I hissed. "We nearly got caught."

He shook his arm free and doubled over, laughing so hard tears spurted from the corners of his eyes. I watched him, uncertain whether to laugh with him or thump him. As his hilarity died away, he straightened.

"Oh, man," he said. "How cool was that?"

"Cool? I nearly wet my pants."

That almost set him off again. While he struggled to contain his mirth, he nodded at my left hand. I glanced down to see I was still clutching the tee shirt from the store. I held it up, shook it out and gazed at it. It was black, with a printed skull and crossbones motif splashed across the chest. It was far cooler than any other shirt I owned. After yanking off Leon's cast-off, I shrugged it over my head and ran my hands down the front, smoothing it. Then I looked back at Art.

His eyes had grown brighter while he watched me, but his expression had become calm and strange. Although our respiration had returned to normal following our exertions, his breathing had grown short and ragged.

He leaned forward and kissed me.

Although Mam didn't normally return home from work until five-thirty, I didn't usually go home when mitching in case one of the neighbours—most likely the nosy old bat next door—spotted me and reported me. That day I was so cold, wet and hungry, I decided to take the chance.

Head hunched into shoulders, ineffective hood yanked forward to shield downcast eyes, I trudged along our street and up the path to the front door, failing to notice Derek's Capri standing by the kerb.

As I closed the front door quietly behind me, I heard noises. They were coming from upstairs. Leaving my bag at the foot of the stairs, I began to creep up.

Of course, I knew about sex. I was going on thirteen and we'd giggled about it in the yard in junior school. I'd even attended one or two sex lessons—'health education' lessons were their official title—in comp. But I swear, as I made my way stealthily upstairs that lunchtime, the notion the sounds I could hear might be connected to the sexual act did not once enter my head.

I paused twice, holding my breath, when the tread creaked beneath my feet. The sounds from above continued unabated: panting exhalations, low moaning and rhythmic grunting of bedsprings. They emanated from Mam's bedroom, the door to which stood ajar.

Gaining the landing, I paused once more. The certainty growing in my mind that Mam was being attacked was confirmed when I clearly heard her moan, "No… no…"

Yes, I should have realised what was going on. It would have been obvious to anyone with an ounce of common sense, even to me on any other day. But not that day. Besides, it was my mam. How could I possibly conceive of her having sex?

I sprang forward into her bedroom.

Art's eyes grew wider, impossibly wide, as he pulled away. He looked as shocked as I felt.

"Karl, er…" he mumbled, face reddening.

I brought my hand up to my lips and fingered them gingerly as though he had smacked me with his fist.

"I'm sorry," he said, dropping his gaze to the floor. "It was the heat of the moment, or something…"

As he tailed off, his eyes flickered up, looking at me with a mixture of anguish and self-loathing, and something else. Longing? His expression made me want to thump him more than the kiss had. He must have read my thoughts because his colour deepened and he glanced hurriedly away, taking a step back.

My flare of anger subsided.

"Forget it," I said brusquely.

"Yeah. 'kay." He did not look up.

"Really," I said. "Let's forget about it."

"Yeah."

We both knew a small but significant barrier had been erected between us.

Mam lay on her back, arms bent over her head, hands gripping the headboard so tightly her knuckles had whitened. Her head was thrown back over the pillows, revealing her smooth pale throat, and her eyes were screwed tightly shut as though she endured excruciating pain, an impression strengthened by the low whimpers escaping between her clenched teeth.

A man moved on top of her, his arms clamped over hers, his bare body forcing her legs apart. Lank hair flopped between the man's shoulder blades and he grunted in time to his movements. The man was wearing socks of a washed-out shade of grey. One of them had worn so much, the pink ball of one foot poked through.

I took three or four running steps to the edge of the bed and leapt, tucking my knees beneath me. My landing was firm and centred upon his calves, driving his legs into the mattress and bringing his rump into the air. Before he had time to react, I brought my teeth together in the fleshiest part of his anatomy that presented itself.

The man shrieked. He jerked backwards, arms flailing. One of them caught me across the side of the head and sent me spinning from the bed. I landed heavily amidst a jumble of discarded clothing. Only when I glanced back did I realise the man was Derek. He knelt on the bed, twisting his torso and straining his neck in an effort to see where my teeth had connected.

Mam squirmed up the bed into a sitting position. She tugged at the bedspread, desperately trying to free it from beneath Derek to cover her nakedness. She only partially succeeded. The bedspread came up to her waist, but no higher. She stopped struggling to free it when she realised my horrified gaze was upon her chest.

"Oh, love, what—" she began, only to be drowned out by Derek's shout.

"The bastard bit me on the arse!" His voice was high, cracking with incredulity.

He swung around to face me, bringing his still engorged member to bear upon me like an accusing finger.

"You little shit." The outrage had gone from his voice. It had turned low and menacing. "It's about time someone taught you a lesson."

I shoved trousers and blouse aside as I began to scrabble backwards.

"No, Derek." Mam put a hand on Derek's bare shoulder. "He didn't know what was happening. He probably thought—"

"I know exactly what he thought." Derek glanced back at Mam. "'Here's my chance to have a go at Mam's boyfriend while his attention's elsewhere.' The little bastard's never liked me. And the feeling's mutual. Now it's time he had a bloody good hiding. He's got it coming."

"No, Derek! He's only a kid. He's—"

Mam screamed and her hand slid off Derek's shoulder as he came for me. But he'd missed his chance. When he'd turned his head to speak to Mam, I had wriggled towards the door and now stood by it, hand on doorknob. I nodded at his deflating member and yelled at him.

"What you gonna do with that, you great ponce? Gonna pick a lock?"

His face contorted and, with a bellow, he charged. I was through the door, slamming it shut behind me. I heard a heavy thud and the door rattled in its frame, followed by a muffled oath. Then, fainter, since I was already at the foot of the stairs, the sound of the door being yanked open and the pound of angry footsteps and what might have been another cry from Mam.

I paused, debating which way to run. I was about to head through the front door when I felt the familiar vibration through the soles of my shoes which heralded the approach of a train. I wheeled and made for the back door.

Mam accepted without question my explanation that we had found a backstreet shop in Cardiff selling tee shirts on the cheap, but I could tell by Leon's expression he wasn't so easily fooled. He waited until Mam was out of earshot.

"Wanna tell me how you really got that tee shirt?"

I looked away from him and shrugged.

"Okay," he said. "Have it your way. But stay out of trouble, you hear me? If I find you've been thieving…"

He left the threat unspoken, but it had some effect.

After that, I was very careful not to let him or Mam see the fruits of my new hobby.

The train passed the fence at the bottom of the garden as I ran towards it. It was a goods train and it was slowing.

I reached the fence and stopped, glancing back over my shoulder. Derek emerged from the house and lumbered perhaps half a dozen yards down the path towards me. It must have been the steady drizzle on his bare shoulders which made him remember he was only wearing socks. He came to a halt and glanced from side to side at the neighbouring houses. With a final glare at me, he dropped his hands to hide his modesty, turned and scuttled back indoors. My gaze moved to the upstairs window. Mam was there, her face pale, hair awry, mouthing something at me.

That's when the reaction set in. I began to shake and the first scalding tears blurred my vision. I turned and vaulted unsteadily over the fence. The sound of the goods train idling in the siding reached me clearly. Soon it would be drowned by the roar of the approaching express. I didn't have much time.

For now I had a plan. I was going to run away. To London.

I couldn't even do that properly.

Part Two: Pupa

Seven: On the Run

"Let's go shopping," I said, arching my eyebrows suggestively. Art's eyes narrowed. He didn't like it when I proposed ways to spend our time.

"Where d'you wanna go?"

"Town will do. They've got *Star Wars* action figures in Woolies."

"Town? Haven't you ever heard of not shitting on your own doorstep?"

"What do you mean?"

Art sighed and reverted to his school ma'am voice.

"Town is small, right? Compared to somewhere like Cardiff. The shopkeepers may recognise us. And someone we know might see us. It's far too risky."

I shrugged. "Cardiff then."

"Got any money?"

I rattled my pocket. "Aye. Still got the pound Mam gave me on Saturday, plus the change from the bus fare. Enough for another return ticket. Besides, it's not as if we'll be spending anything when we get there, is it?" I giggled.

We were walking through our council estate towards town. Art stopped and his eyes narrowed further as he peered at me.

"Got it bad, haven't you?" he said. "Look, if we get caught…"

"Yeah?" I stopped, too, and we stood facing each other on the pavement.

"You know when I leave school I'm gonna work for the BBC or the Welsh Office or something, right?"

"So?"

"What are *you* gonna do, Karl?"

"I dunno. What's that go to do with anything?"

"Don't you see, mun? If we get caught nicking stuff, I'll never get to work for the BBC. But it probably wouldn't make any difference to you. They won't stop you from working down the mines or in the steel works just 'cause you've got a record."

"I suppose…"

"And my dad'll kill me. Yours won't, will he?"

"Mam would go spare. And Leon." I shuddered.

Art raised one arm and placed his hand on my shoulder.

"It wouldn't be so bad for you as it would be for me. You've never met my father."

"No, but—"

"Believe me, Karl, if I was lucky enough to survive what my dad would do to me, I'd still be finished. I'll end up in the foundry with you."

"That wouldn't be so bad."

"Yes, it would. It would be worse than hell." He removed his hand. "I've got prospects. I'm going places. I can't be caught nicking stuff."

"So…?"

"So, if we're caught, let's say it was all your idea and you made me do it, even though I was dead against it."

I looked at him long and hard. The memory of him leaning forward to kiss me popped into my mind and something must have shown in my face because a shadow of doubt flitted across his. Then I shrugged.

"Makes no difference to me," I said. "Okay. If we're caught, I'll say it was all down to me."

"And you made me go along with you against my will."

"Yeah, yeah."

Art's face broke into a grin.

"All right," he said. "Let's go shopping!"

The train was carrying sheets of steel from the works at Port Talbot. They were loaded onto flat-bed trucks, each sheet protected by a swathe of hessian, secured to each other and the truck by nylon straps, the whole covered in a tarpaulin blanket.

I approached the idling train at a crouch, though due to the curvature of the tracks there was little risk of being seen by the driver. The tarpaulin on the second truck from the end had come loose at one corner and it was simple to slacken it sufficiently to enable me to wriggle under. As I did so, two moths, which must have been hiding in the gloom, took to the air. At the same moment, the express shot past with a rattling, whooshing hum.

The goods train lurched into motion while I settled myself onto the sacking that, despite its prickly texture, was surprisingly comfortable and insulated me from the iciness of the steel sheeting. While the train picked up speed, I lay down and listened to the increasing tempo of the sleepers passing beneath me, shielded from the wind and drizzle by billowing canvas.

The image of Mam and Derek writhing in her bed pushed into my mind. With an effort, I forced it out and thought instead of London. Closing my eyes made it easier to see streets paved with gold, where happiness could be found around the next corner. Course, I knew it wasn't like that really. I knew it was a city a fraction the size of Wales with two or three times Wales's population crammed into its grubby streets.

All the better for losing myself in.

The wrapped sheets of metal cushioned my body from excessive bouncing, the tarpaulin muffled my ears to the worst of the rattling, my mind walled off my sensibilities against bad memories.

I lay thinking of London, lulled by the rhythm of the tracks.

And slept.

Shoplifting was my thing, my talent. I was better at it than Art. With him it was stuff goods up your jumper and scarper. I adopted a more subtle approach. Casual was the keyword. None of this suspicious loitering for me. No shifty glances that could attract a shop worker's attention. No sudden outbreaks into stiff-legged trots which screamed, 'Look at me! I'm nicking your stuff!'

I'd act naturally, confidently, behave as though I were an ordinary shopper going about his business. Small items—sets of Top Trumps cards, sweets, tapes, action figures—were easy. First I'd buy something in another shop, something small and cheap, and ask for a carrier bag. Handles looped over my left wrist, I'd browse in the target shop, casually dropping items into the bag as I went. If I caught anyone staring at me, I'd smile disarmingly and they'd smile uncertainly back before looking away in confusion, as though wondering how they could possibly have suspected such a friendly young man of being up to no good. Sometimes, I'd approach the store manager or checkout operator, my bag heavy with stolen goods, and ask for directions to a different department or enquire as to the availability of a particular item. Not that I really wanted to know. Purely for the hell of it.

Larger items presented only an insignificantly higher degree of difficulty. Mind you, I am referring to items which could be concealed on the person. Even back then it would have been tricky to walk out of a shop carrying, say, a box of Meccano the size of a tabletop or wheeling a bicycle without raising suspicions. But clothes were a doddle. Usually, I'd pop into the changing room to try something on under the watchful eyes of a shop assistant. I'd emerge and hand the item back to her with a rueful smile. "Too tight," I'd say, or, "It looks better on the hanger than on me." I'd politely decline her offer to find something else and stroll away, wearing the tee shirt or jumper or jeans, which I had concealed beneath the item I was supposedly trying on, underneath my jacket or baggy cast-off jeans that had once belonged to Leon.

In those days it was easy. There were no electronic tags on goods. No CCTV cameras. Few shops employed security guards, though most of the department stores had a plain-clothes detective or two roaming the floors. They were easy to spot. Nearly always dressed in suits, they'd try to appear nonchalant, but were nowhere near as good at it as me. And there were certain dead giveaways: their eyes following shoppers rather than being focused on the goods for sale, their familiarity with the other staff and their complete lack of shopping paraphernalia. They never wore raincoats or carried umbrellas, even if it was tipping down outside. They never carried shopping bags. They never bore the harassed air of someone attempting to find that elusive present for a relative's birthday. Evading them was simple. A child could do it and I was better than any child.

I was masterful.

Until the day I was caught.

The train juddered and clanked as it slowed, waking me from my unplanned slumber. I shivered; the coldness of the steel had worked its way through the sacking and into my bones. Raising the loose corner of tarpaulin, I peeped cautiously out.

The train was pulling into a yard containing rusting, corrugated iron sheds and small cranes. I knew that a goods train wouldn't pull into Paddington, but this place looked nothing like I imagined London to look. Perhaps I was in the docklands. I sniffed at the air, trying to detect salt, but could smell only diesel. No cries of gulls came to my ears, only the clanking of the slowing train.

I raised my torso, so my shoulders emerged from beneath the canopy, and craned my neck, straining for a glimpse of domes or spires, anything that would confirm I had reached my destination. All I could see beyond the hulking sheds was the top floor of a grim building which could have been anywhere.

Cursing my foolishness in falling asleep and missing the names of the stations through which I must have passed, I decided to stay put and see if the train was going to continue its journey or whether I had already reached the end of the line. But as I started to withdraw under the canvas, I saw the man and realised that staying put was no longer an option.

Flushed by my own success, I became cocky. Too cocky by half.

I must have stolen stuff from every high street shop in Cardiff. Toys, books, costume jewellery—not the real stuff; *that* was kept under lock and key—clothes, trinkets, gadgets… whatever took my fancy that would fit into my bag or pocket or beneath my clothes. Had I chosen to sell my plunder to the kids at school, I might have had a profitable little business on my hands. But that would have meant lowering my guard sufficiently to interact with my peers. So it wasn't entrepreneurship for me.

Instead, I squirreled away my ill-gotten gains beneath the removable bottom drawer in my old oak chest of drawers, or behind the jumble of comics and board games and jigsaw puzzles with pieces missing at the back of my wardrobe, or in plain sight to anyone who cared to poke about amongst the tangle of old laces, foreign coins, broken cigarette lighters and other juvenile odds and ends occupying the drawer and cupboard of my bedside cabinet.

Whenever both Mam and Leon were out, I'd take out the stuff, spread it over my bed and finger it, play the tapes, flick through the books, salivate over the dirty magazines, put on the clothes and parade around my bedroom to no audience other than my delight at my own cleverness.

And that was enough for me. I had discovered something at which I could excel. It didn't matter that only Art knew of my talent. It was irrelevant that I couldn't tell Mam or Leon. Especially Leon. It was enough that I knew.

Art had been displaying less and less enthusiasm for shopping. He wanted to go traipsing around Deadman's Woods or play Top Trumps—"After all," he said, "it's not as if you don't have plenty of packs to choose from."—but I would have none of it.

"What could be more fun than shopping?" I said. "The thrill of the hunt, homing in on the prey and then in for the kill, never knowing who could be waiting to pounce on you. Who wants to play Top flamin' Trumps when we could be doing that?"

Art sighed, cowed by my uncharacteristic vigour.

"Yeah, but—" he started in half-hearted complaint.

"But nothing. Don't forget, butty boy, this was your idea in the first place."

He glanced about guiltily and I knew I had him.

"We agreed, remember? If we're caught…"

"Yeah, yeah. I put you up to it. Trouble is, shopping keeps me sharp. On my toes, like. If we don't do it so often, I could get sloppy. Forget who put who up to what."

He'd always cave in and we'd head for the station to catch the next bus to Cardiff or, if the mood took us, west to Swansea, though the pickings there didn't seem quite as good and security was even more lax than in the capital, making it easier to shop and thereby removing most of the fun.

To pay for the frequent bus journeys, I did chores for Mam. Mowing the lawns, cleaning the windows, polishing the few brass ornaments on the mantelpiece, that sort of thing, for which Mam was now well-equipped to reward me in more than motherly gratitude. She had finished paying off Mr Dennis's bill and had moved out of the typing pool to become secretary to one of the junior solicitors. We were still not exactly what you'd call comfortable, but we got by with fewer financial difficulties.

It pleased Mam to see me so keen to earn a few bob of my own; it showed I was developing a sense of responsibility, I overheard her say to a sceptical Leon. It pleased her even more that I was apparently happy, content to go off with Art each weekend to the pictures or to a football match or to hang out in a park or to perform any other activity I could think of that she wouldn't enquire too closely into and which she would consider unlikely to involve getting into fights or trouble with the police or getting drunk or becoming caught up in the increasingly accessible, shadowy world of drugs.

To Mam, I was a model son.

The man was short and old, wearing a grease-stained boilersuit, his face wrinkled in astonishment at the sight of me peering from one of the trucks pulling slowly past him. I heard a shout as I ducked back under the tarpaulin and, when the train juddered to a halt, the scrunch of heavy, booted feet on gravel.

The corner of the tarpaulin was yanked free and daylight flooded onto my face.

"What the bleeding 'ell are you doing in there?"

Close up, his face was as brown and lined as a shrivelled conker, streaks of black grease accentuating the deep creases. It was a gruff face, though not an unkindly one. Something else about him struck me as wonderful. I beamed up at him.

"You're a cockney?"

His wrinkles deepened as his thick eyebrows met.

"Not a cockney, no. Londoner, yes. But what in 'eck's—"

"I made it!"

He took a pace back and disappeared—he must have been standing on the side of the truck to have been able to peer into it—while I struggled to my knees and thrust my torso once more into open air. I glanced from side to side proudly, like some ruler surveying his kingdom, and sighed happily.

"Ah, London."

"No, son."

I looked down. The man's face was still crinkled in suspicion, but there was another expression lurking beneath. Pity.

"What?"

"This ain't London, son."

"It's not?"

"Nope."

"Then where is it?"

"Swindon."

"What?"

"Swindon." He held up one grimy hand. "Come on, you'd better come with me."

His rough hand caught mine as I jumped down from the truck in a daze. He moved it up to my elbow and gently steered me away from the idling train towards one of the decrepit-looking sheds. The crunching of our feet on the gravel brought me round.

"Where's Swindon?" I asked.

He shook his head gravely.

"The back of beyond, son. The back of beyond."

Eight: Caught

By the next summer holiday, Art had grown tired of me calling the shots. It was the first Monday of the six-week break and, as usual, I was all for going to Cardiff shopping. He shook his head and stopped walking towards town.

"I've had enough of shopping."

"Don't be daft, mun."

"And so have you."

"I have not."

"You don't even nick stuff you want any more. And you chuck most of it away."

I shrugged. "I haven't got any more room to stash it."

"Then why carry on? It's pointless."

"No, Art." Rage had appeared from nowhere and I heard my next words as though they were uttered by somebody else. "It's *you* who's pointless."

I saw his fists clench and I tensed. But he simply turned and walked away.

"Where you going?" I shouted after him.

He tucked his hands into his pockets and continued walking.

"Coward!" I yelled.

There might have been the slightest break in his stride, but he reached the street corner and turned out of sight.

"Right," I muttered. "I'll bloody go shopping without you."

I headed towards town.

The man—Arry he introduced himself as—picked up the telephone standing on the desk inside the draughty Portacabin, which apparently served as the railway yard office. He bounced the handset reflectively in one grubby hand while looking at me.

"Come on, son," he said softly. "I don't want to call the Old Bill. But you leave me with little choice. It's a criminal offence, you know, hitching a ride on a train, aside from being fool'ardy. You could get a record."

I stared at him, biting my lip, finding it difficult to think clearly through the buzzing inside my head. A moth took off from somewhere behind Arry and circled the space above his head, before flying off towards the ceiling.

"Last chance," said Arry.

With a heavy sigh, he looked down at the dial and rotated the first number. The dial clicked rapidly while it returned to its starting position. He placed his finger in the hole for the second number.

"Wait," I said.

He replaced the telephone and turned to me, settling his bulk against the edge of the desk.

"My name's Karl Jordan," I said in a flat tone. "I was trying to reach London."

Arry's eyebrows arched.

"I'm running away from home," I said.

"How old are you, Karl?"

"Thirteen."

"London's no place for a thirteen-year-old on 'is own, believe me. Wanna tell me why you're running away?"

"No."

"Fair nuff. But there's nothing that can't be sorted out by talking to your parents. It's something to do with your parents, yeah?"

I shrugged. "I haven't got a dad. Well, not one to speak of."

"Okay. Talk to your old woman, then. I bet she's worrying herself sick over you."

I shrugged again.

"What's your phone number? Let's put her mind at rest."

After only a short pause, I told him. As he dialled, I burst into tears.

The centre of town consisted mainly of shoe shops, banks and pubs. The few shops selling clothes catered only for the very young or the very old. The stock in the only specialist toyshop was hopelessly outdated, the proprietor presumably refusing to become caught up in the hype surrounding *Star Wars*, or believing it would be a here-today-gone-tomorrow fad, since he did not stock one item to do with the film and was therefore shunned by most kids my age. There were a couple of bookshops, but they held little interest for me as I had already acquired a large enough stock of comics to see me through to my twenties, and I could not conceive of reading a book for pleasure.

Only two shops in town held any attraction for me, though I would have shopped in any, even a shoe shop, at a pinch; it was all in the act, not the acquisition. Flipside was a record shop that stocked a wide selection of singles and cassettes, both current and oldies, and was my first port of call.

Second, rather. My first was a newsagent where I purchased a pop magazine, not because I was particularly interested in reading about pop music—what's the point of *reading* about it?—but because it was big enough to come with a carrier bag.

Then I went into Flipside. Immediately, the biggest difference between shopping in town and shopping in Cardiff became apparent. The shops in town were much quieter than their city counterparts, and so the shop workers were able to keep a closer eye upon their customers and their stock. Not that I was going to let such details stand in my way. I considered myself a master shopper and the match of any small-town sales assistant.

The record shop was manned by two men in their mid-twenties with unkempt shoulder-length hair, black tee shirts proudly displaying their preferred bands—one Pink Floyd, one some group I had never heard of, The Jam—and scruffy jeans. Pink Floyd stood behind the counter, nodding his head to the track blaring from the overhead speakers and watching the few customers through thick-lensed black spectacles. When a woman came to the desk with an album, he served her without speaking. Meanwhile, The Jam wandered the shop floor, straightening records in display cases, exuding a sour odour like turning milk and watching customers as they browsed. Whenever I turned from one rack of singles to another, or looked up from flipping through a bundle of old albums, one of them was studying me, expressionlessly but unwaveringly.

I was unfazed. Casual was my accomplice, confidence its partner.

Next time I caught The Jam watching me, I smiled and walked towards him.

"Hi," I said. "When's the next Sex Pistols single due out?"

He didn't blink.

"July," he said in a tone that was the antithesis of my jolly greeting. "'My Way'."

"Sorry?"

"It's called 'My Way'."

"Oh. Right. Thanks."

I turned towards the rows of cassettes and began to flip through them. When I next glanced up, The Jam's attention had been diverted by a youth who had requested a particularly rare record judging by the concentrated expression of determination upon The Jam's face as he riffled through a stack of coloured-vinyl singles. I brought my gaze round in a casual sweep, as though wondering in which place to look next—enough to reveal Pink Floyd was also momentarily engaged with a customer at the counter.

Without pausing or twitching or blushing, acting smoothly and naturally—fluidly—I dropped the tape I was holding into the carrier bag. I can't remember what tape it was. That didn't matter. All that counted was the thrill of getting away with something I knew to be wrong. The thrill which made the blood pound fiercely in my veins, making me feel more alive, more *real*, than at any other time in my life.

Ironic, really. There I was congratulating myself on how real my life had become, when the truth lay a considerable distance in the opposite direction. Even then I didn't always find it easy to distinguish reality from fantasy.

Before leaving, I approached Pink Floyd and asked him some inane question, like when the *Grease* soundtrack would be released, as if I cared a monkey's arse. He answered me in blank monotone and with blanker expression.

With light heart, I stepped onto the pavement and headed for town's other interesting shop, Woolies.

I had to wait in that Portacabin for over three hours. Arry insisted upon waiting with me.

"Me shift's finished, anyhow," he said, pouring two mugs of tea from a chipped and stained teapot.

I sipped at mine. It was strong and hot and sweet, and drove away the last of my tears. When he'd finished speaking to Mam, Arry did not look at me until my sobbing had quietened. He made no mention of it, for which I was grateful.

But I wasn't so glad he wouldn't let me step outside to stretch my legs.

"My boss might see you," he said. "If that 'appens, he'll insist on making it official like. Right stickler for form the boss is. Right pillock, if you ask me."

He gave me an exaggerated wink. Hesitantly at first, I smiled back.

By the time Leon arrived, me and Arry were as thick as the custard Kay Williams's friend poured down my trousers. We were laughing uproariously about a TV programme we both loved—*Fawlty Towers*, maybe—when there was a rap on the door and it opened to reveal my brother. His expression killed my chuckles dead in my throat.

Arry looked from me to Leon.

"You must be Karl's brother." He made it sound like 'bruvver'. "Found us okay, then?"

"Yeah. It's like you told my Mam, turn left a hundred yards out of the passenger station." His stony glance fell on me. "You ready?"

I nodded and rose to my feet.

Arry held out his hand and I shook it. "Don't forget what I said. Talk to her." He turned to Leon. "You can find your way back to the station?"

Leon nodded curtly.

Arry smiled. "Good luck, boys."

"Thanks, Arry," I said.

"Er, yeah," said Leon. "Thanks."

Then we were outside in the dark and wind and drizzle. Leon strode briskly away, following a muddy path which led between sheds and dilapidated stock. I trailed in his wake, awaiting the explosion.

No sooner had we left the yard and emerged onto a deserted pavement than Leon turned on me. He grabbed my shoulders, digging his fingers under my collarbone, and hissed into my face.

"What the hell d'you think you're playing at? Mam's going fucking spare wondering what's happened to you. She rang school and I had to go home. I had a match this afternoon. And do you have any idea how much it's cost to get up here, and get us back again?"

While he ranted, his fingers dug deeper into my flesh, and I squirmed. But I was determined not to shame myself with tears twice in one day.

When I failed to reply, Leon shook me, snapping my head back and forth like a boxer's overhead punch ball.

"Answer me, you little shit!" He brought his face right up to mine. I could feel the heat in his breath. "Why did you do it?"

If his hands hadn't been gripping my shoulders so tightly, I would have shrugged, probably pushing his wrath to its outer limits. Instead, I spoke.

"I… I went home lunchtime."

"Yeah? So?" Leon's spittle wet my face.

"Mam was there. In bed. With Derek."

Leon's face withdrew an inch and the vicelike grip of his fingers slackened marginally.

"I thought…" My voice hitched and I had to swallow deeply to continue. "I thought he was hurting Mam. I… I went for him."

Leon stared intently at me, saying nothing, but his features softened.

"Derek was angry," I said. "He came after me. I thought… I thought he was going to kill me."

A low whistle escaped Leon's lips.

"That bastard. No wonder Mam was so subdued. I should have realised, but I was too caught up in having to miss the rugby."

"I'm sorry you missed your match."

Leon looked hard at me, his face contorting into something between a smile and a grimace. His fingers tightened once more on my shoulders as he tugged me to him.

"Sod the rugby," he whispered over my shoulder. "You're my brother."

My resolve crumbled and I sobbed into Leon's shoulder. But I didn't care. After a minute or two, I pulled away, swiping my sleeve across my cheeks.

"I was going to London," I said.

Leon smiled. "Didn't get very far, did you?" He ruffled my hair in a way I normally hated, but at that moment I found comforting. "Come on, little bruv. Let's go home."

Side by side, we walked through the rain to the railway station.

Woolworth's occupied a prominent position in town's high street, one of the few magnets for young and old alike. A veritable grotto of toys, sweets, electrical hardware, records and tapes, kitchenware, games and novelty gifts, and much more, all at affordable prices. Not that cost worried me.

This was the first time I had been shopping, in the sense I now used the word, in Woolies, and so the first time that my senses were attuned for store detectives. I spotted him straight away. Very different to the city detectives, he was good, very good. He was dressed casually, scruffily almost, in jeans and sweatshirt, and carried a bag from another shop under one arm. He did not stare at other shoppers, did not stop to chat to any of the checkout girls. But he still gave himself away. Twice my gaze swept innocently past him and twice he was stealing sneaky glances at me. He had obviously marked me as a potential miscreant.

I wandered the aisles, browsing goods at random, floating on a tide of purpose. Being the best that I could be at something. Fulfilling my destiny.

The detective wasn't that good, after all. I easily manoeuvred myself into a position where he could not observe me and began to slip things into my bag.

That familiar sensation of superiority was so euphoric, made me so light-headed, I initially thought I was imagining the heavy hand on my shoulder and the gruff voice that boomed in my ear.

"Would you accompany me to the manager's office, please, sir."

I glanced back into the grim face of a man in a dark suit I had not previously noticed in the store. My eyes swivelled to the tills at the front of the shop. The scruffy man in jeans was standing in line, clutching a bag of pick-n-mix.

The manager's office was at the back of the shop. It was hot in there, windowless. A fly buzzed somewhere; a moth fluttered around the harsh overhead light. They made me empty the carrier bag onto the manager's desk. Dark Suit sorted through the items, handing me the pop magazine without a word.

The manager, a grey-haired man in shirtsleeves, watched and sighed.

"This belongs to the record shop, I believe, sir," said Dark Suit, holding up the cassette tape I had acquired in Flipside.

The manager nodded. "They were right, then. I'd better ring them back and thank them for the warning. Perhaps you can pop that tape round to them, Wilson."

"Yes, sir." Dark Suit nodded towards me. "And see if they want to press charges against this one?"

The manager sighed again, heavily. "Yes, I suppose."

I cleared my throat. "I was going to pay for that stuff. I don't know how that tape got there, though."

Two sets of eyes turned to me, one sad, the other harsh.

"It's too late for that, son," said the manager.

"Yeah," added Dark Suit. "Save it for the police."

Nine: Burying Hatchets

School passed me by without my really noticing. If I learned anything during those years in Crumbly Place, it was that academia and I were not well met. When I could be bothered to stay within the establishment's walls, I was sullen and withdrawn, finding favour with neither teachers nor fellow pupils. Apathy ruled me in class. On rare occasions when I knew answers to teachers' questions, I never volunteered them. They had to badger me to hand in homework. It was seldom correct. I spent more time during lunch and break times writing out sheaf after pointless sheaf of lines of spidery writing—'I must complete my homework on time', or 'I must pay attention in class'—under the bored gaze of the chemistry teacher or the baleful glare of the maths teacher than I spent on the homework itself.

Gradually, I slipped down the forms, from B1 to B5 in three years. If Mam ever noticed, she said little. Since the Derek and shoplifting incidents, she treated me with kid gloves, torn between a desire to force me onto the straight and narrow, and her guilt at the part she fancied she might have played in making me stray.

I played on that guilt like a virtuoso violinist. If Mam attempted to cajole me into sitting down to my homework or raised the subject of my atrocious school reports or began to mention my descent towards the oblivion of the C forms, I'd drop my gaze to the floor, allow a trembling to begin in my shoulders and wait for her to subside into stuttering confusion.

That tactic didn't work on Leon.

"What are you playing at?" he'd shout, waving my school report in my face. "Another shite report. D'you want to leave school with nothing?"

"Oh, hark at bloody Mastermind," I'd retort, bringing colour to his face.

"Look here, clever dick, I've passed enough exams to get into the army. I don't need to do any more. What are you going to do?

Become a rent boy?"

"What's it to you? You're not my father."

That was my trump card. Leon would always back off when I said that, glowering and muttering under his breath. Except once, the time when I was caught shoplifting. Even though the police let me off with a caution—since neither Woolworth's nor Flipside had lost any stock, they weren't keen on pressing charges—Leon showed no mercy.

"We may not be… the best looking… or the strongest… or the brightest… in the world… or even this tiny part… of the world… but there is one thing… *one thing*… we… *do*… *not*… *do*… and that's… thieve… Understand… me…?"

He spoke calmly, but each pause was filled by a resounding clout to my head, back, arms, legs, whichever part of me was most exposed. I cowered on the floor of my bedroom, curled up like a foetus.

I heard the door open—I dared not look up—and Mam started to say something.

"Mam! Out! He has to learn and this is the only way he understands."

"Mam!" I cried. "Make him—"

My shout was curtailed by another heavy blow to the back of my hands where they cradled my head. Below the ringing in my ears, I heard the door snick closed.

That was the most angry I ever saw Leon. We had fights on occasions, like all brothers do, though perhaps less often than some, and I had begun to fill out to provide some level of resistance to Leon's powerful bulk. But there was no opposing him that day. Had I tried, I'd have probably ended up in hospital.

It went on until, through runnels of snot and blood, I was able to convince my brother my thieving days were over.

I meant it, too.

Unlike Leon, I had no goal for when I left school. He had wanted to join the army since he was ten, and had gone through school keeping himself in top physical shape by playing rugby and any other sport he could, and studying with a dogged determination subjects that might help his future career: things like maths, English language (*not* literature; "What's the use of reading? Why make believe when there's real life out there to be lived?"), physics and chemistry (to keep the engineering option open and to help understand the mechanics and reactions involved in firing a bullet from a gun or a missile from a silo), and computer science.

At sixteen, Leon departed Crumbly Place, the proud possessor of a clutch of CSE passes in his holy subjects and an acceptance letter from the Ministry of Defence.

I, too, looked forward to leaving at sixteen, but that was my sole aim. Nothing sticks in my memory about my final two or three years in school. I kept myself to myself, remaining quiet and withdrawn at school, when I was there, but things must nevertheless have happened to me. I must have got into a few adolescent scrapes, become embroiled in the occasional pubescent entanglement, indulged in the odd youthful caper but, if I did, they left no lasting impression upon me.

And I left no impression upon Crumbly Place. It sucked me in at the age of eleven as though I were one tiny niblet on a giant's platter of corn, passed me unnoticed through its gullet, before expelling me the other end, larger and untidier but otherwise little changed by my experience.

Trouble is, where does an undigested piece of corn end up?

For a few months after he refused to join me shopping in town, I didn't see much of Art Llewellyn. Part of me had always suspected we would drift apart sooner or later. He, after all, had his life planned out: O levels, sixth form, university, then a career with the BBC or in the civil service. He was a boy with prospects. And I was a boy whose sole aim was to leave school as quickly as possible. Ask me about anything beyond that and I'd most likely shrug and crack a joke or change the subject. Since I was never going to rise towards Art's standards, it was more likely he would be dragged down to my level. He would be better off without me.

After we had known each other for about a year, he told me he was moving house. Dismay must have shown on my face.

"It's all right, mun," he said. "We can still be friends. I'll still knock round with you, if you want."

"You're not going far, then?"

"Nah. My dad's been promoted and we're moving to a nicer part of town. It's not far away. I won't be changing schools or anything like that."

"What's the name of the street?"

"Talbot Close. Number twenty-three."

"Never heard of it. Sounds nice, though."

"It is."

"Perhaps I can come round for tea or something?"

"Dunno. My dad doesn't like me having friends round. Hey! Have you heard the new Queen single? It's bloody amazing!"

True enough, Art moving away didn't really affect our friendship. We still saw each other as much as when we lived in the same street. The row over my shopping expedition caused the first true rift between us, but that didn't last long.

It was a rare dry day during the half-term holiday in October and I was bored, so bored I was even contemplating calling for big Brian Lewis, who still lived down the road from me. I hadn't bothered with Brian since that day in Deadman's Woods when Art emptied his bladder over Brian's head, and he hadn't bothered with me. Although Brian wasn't the sharpest tool in the shed, he knew as well as I did I could have prevented him getting sluiced.

I stood on the pavement outside our house, leaning against the front wall, hands thrust in pockets, wondering how to break the ice with Brian, when I became aware of someone standing next to me. I glanced up.

"All right?" said Art.

I shrugged. "You?"

He shrugged. "Been shopping lately?"

I felt the flush rise above my collar and dropped my gaze to the pavement. "Nah. Given it up. It was, er, kind of forced upon me."

"I heard. Caution, wasn't it?"

"Aye."

"You should have been called Harpo, you know that?"

My fists clenched inside my pockets and I looked up sharply. But instead of the goading smirk I expected to find on his face, I saw only merriment dancing in his eyes and the beginning of a warm smile on his lips.

"Toss pot," I said companionably.

"Fuck wit," he replied in the same tone.

Art shoved his hands in his pockets and leaned against the wall next to me. After a few minutes, he broke the silence.

"What shall we do, then?"

I opened my mouth to make a suggestion, then closed it again. I shook my head.

"You decide," I said.

Of the two of us, Art looked closer to eighteen, though we were both within touching distance of sixteen. With his gangly six-foot frame, flowing curls and dark stubble, he could pass upon cursory examination as an adult. I was, and remain, an inch or two shy of six foot and did not have to shave regularly until my late teens. My only attempt at cultivating facial hair ended with the first jibe from Derek.

The truce between Derek and me was an uneasy one. He had stayed away from our house for months following my attempted bolt to London. Mam had once again to gradually introduce him into the conversation, until she could pluck up the courage to invite him round.

"No, Mam," said Leon. "Don't bring him here. Not after what happened."

Mam looked at me, eyebrows raised.

I shrugged.

Leon also looked hard at me.

"Suit yourself, then," he said to Mam.

When Derek came, Leon greeted him stiffly, before excusing himself upon some pretext of a training session. Derek turned to me, hands in pockets.

"Karl," he said.

"Derek," I replied.

I was aware of Mam watching us as though we were two dogs eyeing each other for the first time.

"Well, then," said Derek.

I said nothing.

Derek shuffled his feet. I remained still, trying to keep my expression neutral.

Derek held out his hand.

"It was a misunderstanding," he said. "By both of us. Let bygones be bygones?"

I looked at his hand, only reaching out to grasp it fleetingly when Mam pointedly cleared her throat.

Derek withdrew his hand and thrust it back into his pocket. He turned to Mam.

"There, Meg," he said in that smarming manner I hated. "All friends again." He removed his hands from his trousers and held them out towards Mam. "Now how's about a cuddle, girl?"

Mam shot an embarrassed glance to me, but I was already turning away, fighting an urge to kick him sharply near the place I'd bitten him when last we'd met.

I was proud of my moustache. It was light, much lighter than my hair, and thicker beneath my nose than it was above the ends of my lips, but it was far more noticeable than the pitiful efforts of some of my peers.

Derek called round for tea, as he was doing with increasing regularity. As usual, Leon disappeared as soon as Derek arrived, leaving me to suffer mealtime with Derek and Mam on my own. I was pretty much ignored while I ate methodically, the sooner to leave the table so they could flirt and talk innuendos without embarrassing me or Mam. I believe there was nothing that would embarrass Derek.

I had only a few chips and half a sausage remaining on my plate when I became aware of his gaze upon me.

"What?" I mumbled, quickly forking another mouthful in and chewing.

Derek grinned playfully. "There's something crawling on your top lip. Dunno what it is. Could be a starving caterpillar or something."

The food stuck in my throat and my cheeks flared with heat.

Derek's grin faded. He leaned towards me as though to share a confidentiality.

"I'd get rid of it if I were you," he hissed in a stage whisper. "The ladies don't like them. Tickles their thighs."

He sat back, grinning wolfishly at Mam. She blushed and dropped her gaze, but could not completely stifle the schoolgirl titter.

It took an effort, but I managed to swallow the last of my meal, mumble my excuses and leave the table. They didn't notice me go.

I gazed at myself in the bathroom mirror. Raised a hand and ran a finger over the hair clinging sparsely to my top lip. Then I reached for the razor.

Without the bumfluff I had fondly imagined constituted a moustache, there was no way I would ever pass for eighteen. So it was Art who went into the shop and purchased our cider.

Mam gave me pocket money each week in return for mowing the lawns and weeding the flower borders and other odd jobs. I would have done them willingly enough without payment, but I wasn't one to look a gift horse in the mouth. Art never seemed short of money. That's what came from having a well-to-do father, I supposed. Between us, we had enough cash to purchase two or three flagons of cider each week.

At first, we'd only buy the one. Art would emerge from the corner shop, a broad grin on his face, clutching the paper bag tightly to his chest. We'd scurry off to Deadman's Woods where we'd find a suitable log upon which to squat. With great ceremony, Art would unwrap the paper and remove the brown bottle of Bulmer's Woodpecker or Olde English or whatever else was available that was cheaper. So long as it was cider. Always cider. As he loosened the cap, I'd mimic the escaping gas by sighing in anticipation.

We'd pass the bottle back and fore, swatting absent-mindedly at the incessantly circling moths, lifting the bottle to our lips and pouring the sweet, cloying liquid down our throats. A warm glow would ignite in the pit of my stomach and spread outwards like a lava flow, down through my legs and up to my head.

Before the flagon was half-empty, we'd be chuckling, the log rocking beneath us. By the time the last drop was tipped between numbing lips, one or both of us had fallen off the log and lay giggling at the leaf-dappled sky.

Until we started to grow accustomed to it. Then we'd graduate to a flagon each. Perhaps accompanied by a packet of ten Woodbines or Player's and a box of Swan Vestas matches.

It wasn't long before making the trudge to Deadman's Woods carrying heavy, sloshing flagons seemed like too much effort. Instead, we'd find a piece of quiet wasteground or, in the evenings, a deserted schoolyard or a little-used bus shelter, and get sloshed.

While the cider flowed, our talk grew louder and more outlandish. We'd fantasise about girls and Art would tell me about his conquests at school. I'd sometimes make stories up about my adventures with the fairer sex, and Art would gasp and coo as I did to his tales, though I doubt he ever believed my claims.

Sometimes we'd talk about what the futures held when we left school. Rather, Art would. Apart from the occasional mumbled contribution, I tended to keep quiet when the subject came round to such obscurities. No matter how much we'd had to drink—and we soon increased our intake to three flagons, sometimes four at a session; Art always seemed to have enough money for the additional purchases—Art would speak about what subjects he would choose for A level, which university he hoped to attend and the range of career options he would have open to him in grave tones with no hint of alcohol-fuelled jollity. When it came to his future, Art could be intense. Desperate even.

How ironic, then, that he had very little future ahead of him.

Ten: School's Out

Derek's Capri became an almost permanent fixture, parked against the pavement outside our house. He came to tea nearly every evening, then sat and watched television with us, snuggling up to Mam on the sofa. He would always leave at around eleven o'clock. Leon and I would raise our eyes to each other as we heard him and Mam rustling away on the doorstep.

She would return to the living room after the Capri had gunned away from the kerb, dishevelled and flushed, and would sigh as she sat down.

"What's up, Mam?" Leon would ask.

"Nothing," she'd reply, but she'd glance at the place next to her where Derek had been sitting. Sometimes, she'd reach out a hand and pat at the spot wistfully.

She waited until Leon had left home for the army before dropping her bombshell.

"Karl," she said, clearing her throat.

I glanced up from the television. She was sitting forward on the edge of an armchair, not looking at me, wrapping a piece of cotton distractedly around her fingers. She always fiddled with a piece of cotton when she had something difficult to do. She must have carried strands of the stuff around with her just in case.

"Yeah?" I enquired casually, though I could tell this was not a casual moment.

"I have something to tell you."

"Go on then."

She paused, breathing deeply. Without looking up from her twiddling fingers, she blurted it out in a rush.

"Derek and I have been talking. It's no good you arguing 'cause it's already decided. What with your excuse for a father and now your brother leaving home I want to have a man around. And Derek's losing his flat 'cause they want to redevelop the building or something. So we've decided. He's moving in with us. Next week."

For the first time, she looked at me. I could read the defiance in her eyes and knew she was right: it would be no good my protesting. Her mind was made up.

I thought furiously, striving to keep my expression neutral, hunting frantically for a loophole. There wasn't one, so I did the only thing I could in the circumstances. I tried to make the best of a dire situation.

"Okay," I said.

Mam's eyes flared with relief as though she had been expecting stiff resistance.

"But," I continued, "there's one condition."

Mam's jawline hardened and her lips tightened.

"Oh, yes?" Her tone was cold, indicating she was more than ready to meet my resistance head-on and there would only be one winner.

"Yes," I said. "Can I have Leon's room?"

There were no fanfares when I walked out of Crumbly Place for the last time as a pupil. Except in my head. I had just turned sixteen. I had no qualifications, no skills, no purpose.

The careers teacher had not been able to bring himself to look me in the eye. Which was fine by me. I could barely bring myself to attend his office, until I learned a meeting with him was compulsory in order to obtain the release from the education system I so craved.

"Er, Jordan, is it? Or do you prefer Karl?"

He glanced up from the papers on his desk long enough to see me shrug.

"Right, right…" He shuffled some papers around, picked up a pen and started to jot notes. "Sixteen three weeks ago. Eligible to leave school at Easter. Er, that's next week. Failed three CSEs. Didn't sit three more. Passed none."

When next he glanced up, I was gazing intently at him and he hurriedly bent his head again. It was his head that was fascinating me. It was round, like a football, and the dome was completely bald in a perfect circle the size of a side plate. Hair grew in grey profusion from the edges of the circle as though the bald patch had always been there. The hair looked stiff and wiry, like the bristles of a scrubbing brush. I felt a strong urge to reach out and rub my fingers over his head to experience the contrast between the baby-smooth pate and the static-inducing scrub. My hand was already on the move, fingers flexing in anticipation, when I realised it might not do my chances of getting out of there as quickly and painlessly as possible any good, so I yanked my hand back hurriedly.

He glanced up again and I caught a hint of consternation in his frown before that perfect circle was turned up to my view once more.

"Hokey-dokey," he said. "Apprenticeships. Interested in learning a trade? Bricklaying? Carpentry? Oh, perhaps not. I see that woodwork was one of the CSE failures. What about plumbing? Or car maintenance?"

He did not look up, but stopped writing as though waiting for an answer. I tore my gaze from the crown of his head and cleared my throat. Then I cleared my throat again.

He looked up and now the impatience in his expression was unmissable.

"Um," I said.

"Yes?"

"Um."

"Come on, boy. Spit it out. Do you want to enter an apprenticeship or not?"

I stared at him, my mind a complete blank. His eyes flickered away from my face, directing themselves somewhere over my shoulder. He sighed deeply in exasperation and bent back to his notes. That circle smiled at me.

"Er, sir?"

He did not look up.

"What?"

"I want to become a monk, sir. Like you."

I found Art in the café where we sometimes hung out. He was in his usual spot, in front of the Space Invaders machine, tongue poking out while he concentrated on blowing the advancing aliens into oblivion.

I stood and watched until the sneaky invaders moved too quickly and he was done for.

"Damn!" he said.

He was reaching into his pocket for another coin when something in my expression stopped him.

"What's up?" he said.

"Nothing," I replied. "Except that dickhead Derek is moving in with us. Mam told me last night."

"Oh." He stood looking at me for a moment, then threw one arm about my neck and swung me towards the door.

"Come on," he said. "I know just the thing to banish the blues."

Art was loaded as usual and emerged from the shop struggling under the weight of a box containing six flagons of the sweet stuff. Taking it in turns to lug the weight, we headed for Crumbly Place. Leaving Art and the cider by the gates, I went ahead to scout out the lie of the land. Sometimes on Saturdays, the janitor was busy in the workshops which opened off The Arches, but that day all was quiet.

I scurried back to the top of the steps leading down to the gates and beckoned to Art.

Moments later, we were sitting in the shadows beneath The Arches, breaking the seal on the first of our flagons.

Art raised his bottle to his lips and paused, eyes glittering blackly in the gloom.

"Down the hatch?" he murmured.

"Down the hatch," I agreed.

We tipped back our heads and drank.

The lecture Mam attempted when she learned I had not turned up for three exams, had abjectly failed the three I'd sat and I was intent upon leaving school at Easter did not run smoothly. It didn't help that she learned these things and acted upon them in the presence of Derek.

"Have I brought you up to be a good-for-nothing dropout?" A red spot burned brightly in the centre of her forehead.

Derek rubbed her forearm in what he no doubt intended as a comforting gesture but that, to me, looked like one of his usual gropes.

"Course you haven't, Meg love," he cooed. "He's done it all on his own."

I bit my tongue. We were sitting in the living room, Mam perched on the edge of the settee, her lapdog slouched next to her and me facing them from an armchair. Thus far I had only grunted and shrugged in the face of Mam's rant, but if Derek continued to stick his oar in, I knew I was going to boil over like an unwatched saucepan.

Mam waved the letter from the headmaster at me. Of course, I had considered chucking it, but that wily old bastard had warned me he would be telephoning Mam before the end of term and if she hadn't received his letter then he would expect me to report for lessons on the first day of summer term.

"Mitching exams?" she said or, rather, shouted or, rather yet, squeaked since her voice had a tendency to rise higher than her vocal cords could comfortably bear when her emotions were running away from her. "How... when? I thought the exams weren't until the summer."

I shrugged again and her eyes flared. I felt it politic to say something at this point.

"We had the chance to sit some at Christmas. Thought I might as well put my name down."

Derek chortled. "Why, if you weren't going to bother to turn up?"

I waited for Mam to snap at Derek, tell him to butt out. When she didn't, but continued to glare at me, my inner pressure gauge cranked up another couple of notches.

"Well?" she demanded.

"Well what?" I said. "So I missed a few exams. Big deal. It saved me failing all of them."

"But you're not stupid, boy. Or at least I thought you weren't."

"You thought wrong then."

"But I didn't even know you had exams. I would have helped you."

"Helped me? You don't even know I'm here half the time. You're too wrapped up in him."

Mam recoiled as though slapped.

"Hey!" said Derek. "Don't talk to your mother like that or you'll have me to answer to."

"Hush, love," said Mam. The anger had gone from her voice. She sounded defeated, but made one last effort. "It says here"—she waved the letter again, but without enthusiasm—"you would benefit from seeing the year out. Try the exams again in the summer. I'll help you."

I shook my head.

"*Please*, Karl."

"Mam. Listen. There's only one thing I want and that's to get away from that dump. And that's what I'm going to do next Thursday when it finishes for Easter. I'm sixteen. You can't stop me."

The skin around Mam's eyes crinkled and I knew it was over. But I reckoned without Derek.

"You little shit!" he hissed. "What sort of son upsets his mother like this, after all she's done for him? What sort of son cares so little for his mother?"

I rose to my feet. The pressure that had been building inside my head had dispersed, leaving me with a sensation of deep tiredness. I glanced at Derek. He was itching to lay one on me, but Mam had tight hold of his wrist. Her head was bowed and damp stains were appearing on the headmaster's letter dangling loosely from her other hand.

Perhaps I should have walked away, but there was still an ember of rage lurking somewhere inside.

"Up yours, dickhead," I said, clenching my right fist, middle finger extended at Derek.

He was on his feet in an instant, letting out a cry of fury, but Mam wasn't about to let go of his wrist. With her other hand, she yanked at his shirt, crumpling the headmaster's letter, and pulled him back onto the settee. The back of the settee faced the living room door and Derek used his momentum to twist and lunge at me.

But I was already through the door and running.

It was a warm spring evening. As the sun set, the security lights attached to the walls above the arched entrances flickered on. It grew dark and the unseasonable balminess brought out the moths. While we drank, we watched them flutter about the lights.

"Silly sods," I remarked. I was at that relaxed state of inebriation where the mundane seems engrossing. I waved my flagon airily towards the moths. "Look at 'em. What's so bloody fascinating about a light?"

"Perhaps it's not the light which draws them." Art's voice was quiet. Contemplative.

"What d'you mean? They always fly around lights."

"Yes, they do. But maybe it's not the light that attracts them. Maybe it's the darkness which lies beyond."

"Huh?"

"Look, the brighter the light, the more moths are attracted, yeah?"

"I s'pose."

"Well, the brighter the light, the deeper the darkness appears the other side of it. I reckon the moths are trying to reach that darkness. They fly round and round and round but the darkness always stays just out of reach."

I took a long swig of cider. "Okay. Then why do they want to reach the darkness?"

Art didn't answer for a moment and I glanced at him. It had grown shadowy beneath The Arches and as far as I could tell in the gloom his expression was serious. Grim.

"Isn't there something about absolute darkness which attracts us all?" he said softly.

It was my turn to fall momentarily quiet. He may have been onto something there.

I grunted. "So the moths are like us."

He shrugged. "Or we're the moths."

It was a momentous year for me, that first year of a new decade. It was the end of punk and the beginning of New Romanticism. Thatcher had not long begun her iron-fisted reign that would last much longer than many would have predicted, far less wanted. It was the year the Americans boycotted the Moscow Olympics, the SAS stormed the Iranian Embassy in London and some nutter ensured there would be no more possibility of a Beatles reunion.

It was the year I grew up, that I stepped into the wide world. I learned more during the second half of that year than I had learned through all the years I had been forced to attend school. It was the year I felt the first cruel barbs of love, or something approximating it. The year I was first stroked by death's cold fingers. I learned about loss and grief and emptiness and shame.

Most of all, I learned about hatred.

I was well past the giggling, tipsy stage. Well beyond the hiccupping, revealing confidences stage. Even the morose, the world-doesn't-like-me phase was behind me. Next stop was catatonia.

As I unsteadily tipped back the last of my three flagons, barely aware of the cool stream running down my chin to splash onto my chest, I peered groggily at Art. He had almost finished his third bottle, though was in a far better state than me.

"Feeling better?" He grinned. His teeth looked radioactive in the gloom and my state of altered awareness.

"Mush berrer." I raised the bottle jerkily, spilling more cider down my tee shirt. "Up Derek."

"Aye," agreed Art. "Up Derek."

We lapsed into silence while I concentrated upon trying to make the world stop wavering. I only partially succeeded, having to settle for it ceasing to resemble the opening title sequence to *Dr Who*.

"So you've left school," said Art.

I nodded and waved my arms about expansively, spilling yet more cider. "Thish dump and me… finished."

"You know, Karl, I envy you. You're free to do what you want. Get a job. Don't get a job. Lie in bed. Get up. Go for a walk. Stay in. You haven't got to write essays and memorise stupid dates and regurgitate pointless formulas. Or should that be formulae? Who gives a shit."

Some quality in his voice, some note of wrongness, pierced the fog fast enveloping my brain. I looked at him, sitting shoulders hunched, near empty flagon clutched between his knees.

"So, leave school," I said.

He looked away from me, out through the arches to the darkness that lay beyond the lights. The deep darkness that always stays just out of reach.

"Father, huh?" I said.

"Yeah," he whispered. "My father. Right."

"Well, bottoms up." They were the last coherent words I spoke that evening. I swigged long and hard and the world wavered beyond recall.

Somehow, I made it home. I awoke in my own bed the next morning, screwing my eyes tight against the glare of daylight, some dim recollection of pausing during the stagger homewards to eject burning streams of used cider from my overworked stomach reinforced by the sickly-sweet smell which cloyed in my nostrils and in the depths of my throat.

Yes, I had been blindingly drunk during those moments with Art beneath The Arches. Nevertheless, I *can* recall them. You see, I've had reason to replay those moments over and over in my head so that, even if alcohol's distortions have been so extensive as to render my memories unreliable, they have become reality to me. They are what actually happened.

They were my last lucid moments with my one and only true friend. That night, Art Llewellyn died.

Part Three: Adult

Eleven: Man About the House

Derek and I reached some sort of impasse. An uneasy one, right enough, but an impasse all the same.

He moved in on a Saturday afternoon in mid-April, not long after I had finished school for good. I would have offered to help, for Mam's sake, but what Derek owned fitted into the tiny boot of his Capri: a small battered suitcase, a bulging leather briefcase and a box of books on car maintenance. Derek was not what could be called a man of property.

I sat in front of the television, not paying much attention to Grandstand, listening to him making the two or three trips upstairs with Mam chattering away in the background like an excited schoolgirl.

There was silence for a while, then a clatter on the stairs and the living room door burst open. Mam's face was flushed and her hair disarranged as though she had just crawled out of bed. Derek clutched a bottle and three glasses, a goofy grin on his face.

"Join us in a little celebration drink?" said Mam.

"Aye, Karl lad, this is the start of a new era in the Jordan household," said Derek. "Or should that be the Burton household?"

I shifted in my seat and opened my mouth, but Mam was too quick. Shooting me a warning glance which only dented her smile marginally, she said smoothly, "As long as this is Karl's home, this will remain the Jordan household. Are you going to open that bottle, love?"

Derek's eyes narrowed but his goofy grin didn't waver. He popped the cork and sloshed the fizzing liquid into three glasses.

"Cheers," he said, raising his glass. "To the good ship Jordan and all who sail in her."

Mam giggled and raised her glass.

I grunted.

"Come on, Karl," said Mam. "Drink."

I lifted the glass and took a sip. Derek watched me over the rim of his glass, the smile never leaving his lips, but long departed from his eyes.

I wasn't entitled to claim any handouts until I was seventeen for reasons I didn't understand. Old enough to leave school but too young to be supported by the state.

But I was old enough to register at the job centre. Not that I wanted a job. Having been forced into spending the last ten or eleven years cooped up in stuffy classrooms trying to block out the droning of teachers' voices, I wanted to enjoy my freedom before even thinking about earning money. But Mam was insistent.

"You're the one who was so adamant about leaving school," she said, the first spots of colour appearing high in her cheeks. "If you think you can laze about all day while I'm out working to support us both, you've got another think coming. You get yourself down the town centre and put your name down with the employment people."

"Perhaps I'll go tomorrow," I mumbled.

The red spots grew deeper. "You'll get yourself down there now. I will not sit back and watch you become a good-for-nothing layabout like your father."

I didn't argue. Why waste energy on debating a point towards which you feel complete indifference? Besides, I couldn't see any harm in simply putting my name down on the job centre's books. Unemployment levels were rising steadily and jobs for which I was suited were hardly going to be falling out of trees. And, if by some twist of misfortune they did manage to find an employer willing to take me on, I could always turn it down.

The woman in the job centre was greying and grim. She had a habit of continually raising a finger to press her spectacles tight against the bridge of her nose, though they didn't appear to be slipping.

"Name?"

"Karl Jordan."

"Address?"

"Seventeen Mayhill Rise."

"Age?"

"Sixteen."

"School?"

"No."

She raised her head from the form and looked at me for the first time.

"What do you mean, no?"

"I've left school."

"I gathered that from the mere fact of your presence here. Which school *did* you attend?"

"Crumb— er, Crompton Price."

She pressed a finger tight against her spectacles, then bent her head towards her desk.

"Qualifications achieved?"

"None."

Up came the head.

"None at all?"

I shook my head.

"Not even a CSE in woodwork?"

"I failed it."

Press spectacles, lower head. Her hair resembled a tangled mass of grey wiring.

"Any special skills?"

I briefly considered telling her about my talents as a shoplifter. "No."

"Work experience?"

"None."

"What about voluntary work experience. Helping out charities or churches?"

I shook my head again when she looked back up.

"How about community work orders?"

"No."

"Do you have any criminal convictions?"

"No."

"Well, that's something." She bent her head and scribbled. She lowered the pen, raised her head, gave the obligatory shove to her spectacles, then folded her hands on the desk. "So. What sort of job are you interested in?"

"Um. I'd quite like to be an astronaut."

Her impassivity didn't waver. She must have heard it all, and worse, many times before.

"Nasa's space programme is rather heavily subscribed at the moment, I'm afraid," she said. "Anything else?"

"A cowboy?"

Again, not a flicker.

"You should consider emigrating to the United States." She raised a finger to her spectacles. It was starting to annoy me. "Until you do, is there any particular job you'd be interested in doing locally?"

"I want a job that pays lots of money for doing very little, that requires no qualifications or talent and allows me to sit on my arse all day being rude to people. I want to work in the job centre."

She didn't so much as blink. "I'm very sorry," she said, "but you have to have developed a high boredom threshold and hold a degree in cynicism to work here. We'll be in touch if anything comes up. Good day, Mr Jordan."

If Art's death was reported in the newspapers, I never saw it. A sense of wrongness had been growing in me since the night Art and I got drunk at The Arches. I didn't see him the following day, despite visiting our usual haunts, like the corner shop where Art bought our cider or the café where we played Space Invaders.

The feeling that something was out of kilter became stronger as the day drew on. An unshakeable heaviness settled into my bones, a sense of overwhelming loss. As if part of me had been torn out. I knew, without being told, Art had gone.

That evening, I waited until dark before leaving the house. Mam, cuddling up to Derek in front of the television, didn't even notice me go.

I walked across the field towards Deadman's Woods. A full moon bathed the scene in a milky light, while making the shadows beneath the trees deeper.

I approached the first line of trees, in the centre of which stood the great spreading oak from whose bough Dic Du was reputed to have been hanged. Something dangled there now; I could hear the creaking of a rope against the bark of the branch as its load swayed in the night breeze.

Dread filled me, but I forced myself on. It wasn't until I was standing almost directly beneath the body—for that, of course, is what it was—I could make out the face. The branch was high; part of me marvelled at the feat of climbing involved to have scaled the tree to such a height while carrying a length of thick rope.

I gazed up into the peaceful features of my best friend.

It took me days to pluck up the courage to pay a visit to the public library. Not that there was anything about the library requiring courage, only to what the visit might lead.

The interior was dim and cool, the only sounds the rustling of papers and muted conversations between staff members and customers. I hadn't been inside the library since I was a young child, but it smelt the same as I remembered: of dust and floor polish.

I headed for the local reference section and took from the shelf a large-scale map of the town centre. Finding a vacant table, I unfolded the map and laid it out in front of me.

"Talbot Close… Talbot Close…" I murmured as I pored over the map, tracing streets with my finger.

"Help you, love?"

I glanced up into the kindly face of a woman who, judging from the bundle of books balanced in her hands, either worked in the library or was a prolific reader.

"Er, just trying to find a street," I muttered.

She glanced down at the map.

"Well, you've got the right plan," she said. "Let me reshelve these and I'll lend you a hand. This is a lending library, after all."

She walked away, chuckling softly, and I returned to my task. But it was hopeless. Town looked much larger than I had realised when all laid out in black squiggly lines, forming roads that led into avenues, that branched into crescents and drives, that in turn became streets and ways and lanes. My eyes were beginning to ache from unaccustomed concentration on small print. What I really needed was—

"Ahem. Have you tried the index?"

The woman had returned, minus her load.

I shook my head, not lifting my eyes from the map.

"Can't see one," I said.

She moved to my side and I caught a whiff of a clean, flowery aroma as she leaned over and lifted the map.

"Here," she said in a low voice. "It's on the reverse."

She placed the map face down on the table, revealing the index laid out in neat columns.

"Now, then," she said. "What are you looking for?"

"Talbot Close."

"Talbot Close… Talbot Close…" she murmured, much as I had been doing minutes earlier. "Here it is."

She turned the map over and located the reference given in the index. She pointed it out to me. "There, see. In one of the oldest parts of town, by the looks of it. Next to the old industrial estate."

I frowned. That didn't sound much like the street Art had described to me. I rose to my feet. "Near the old industrial estate. Thanks."

"That's all right. We're here to help."

I left her to fold the map. Striding down the stone steps to the street with a renewed sense of purpose, I almost ran into a boy my age, but twice as large, coming up the steps.

"Watch it," he said. Then he stopped. "Karl."

It was Brian Lewis, the windy boy who lived down our road and my one-time playmate. Until I'd met Art, after which Brian hadn't stood a chance. I stared at him, taking in the grim eyes and set mouth.

"Have you heard something?" I asked. "Something about Art?"

His brow creased into a frown and he opened his mouth to speak. At once, I was afraid to hear what he might say.

Whatever Brian said, or if he spoke at all, was lost beneath the pounding of my feet and the rushing noise in my ears as I took to my heels to get away from him. I ran until my breath came in short, burning wheezes and my side felt as though someone was holding a hot poker to it.

I ran until I was too exhausted to think.

Twelve: Interviews

Talbot Close turned out to be a dump.

Stuck at the top end of town, before the residential district gave way to the fume-churning chimney stacks of the ageing industrial estate, the street looked like a set from a drama about inner-city decay.

Two lines of brick terraces faced each other across a tired strip of tarmac as pitted as the surface of the moon. The Close ended in a small turning area bounded by grey stone walls that, in case anyone was foolhardy enough to attempt to scale their forbidding ten-foot faces, were topped with coils of rusting barbed wire as though something of more value than a builder's yard lay beyond. Many of the houses were blind, windows bricked in and doors replaced by sheets of corrugated iron.

I stepped off the pavement around a rusting Cortina balanced on four crumbling towers of bricks, and paused to look closely at the doors of the houses.

"There." I crossed the road and walked along the opposite pavement until I stood in front of number twenty-three.

Like its neighbours, the house had seen better days. Where stone cladding remained on its walls, it was obscured by moss and grime; where the cladding had fallen away, water-stained pink bricks showed through like scars. The three window frames I could see—one next to the front door and two on the first storey—were in an advanced state of decay, flecks of once-white paint clinging stubbornly to the rotting wood. It was difficult to tell which was more grubby: the windowpanes or net curtains drooping behind.

I stared at the front door. It had once been green. Damp had made the wood swell into boil-like mounds and, in other places, sag like wet cardboard. The number twenty-three had been painted on crudely in black. I raised my fist to knock, but hesitated, part of me still refusing to believe Art had lived here.

Taking a deep breath, I brought my fist sharply forward, aiming at a spot where the wood looked to be relatively sound, and rapped on the door.

"Gonna find yourself a job then, Karl?"

I kept my eyes fixed on the television screen and grunted.

"Gonna be a layabout for ever, is it?" Derek's tone was almost openly contemptuous. Almost, but not quite: Mam was in the living room with us.

"Yeah," I said. "I want to take after you."

I still didn't look away from the television, but I heard the settee creak as Derek stiffened.

"Now, Karl," said Mam. "You know full well Derek can't work with his back. Otherwise he'd be out there working as hard as the next man, wouldn't you, love?"

"Course I would, Meg," said Derek. "Still, we get by all right on my disability, don't we?"

"On Mam's wages, you mean." Now I did look at him. He was staring at me, lips tight.

Mam looked at me, too, frowning.

"What is it with you, Karl? There's no need to be rude to Derek. Besides, he's right. You can't just sit in front of the telly all day. You need to find a job."

I looked away from them, but not before Derek's lips curled into a triumphant sneer. Gritting my teeth, I rose and strode from the room.

The door to number twenty-three Talbot Close opened jerkily and partially to reveal a tired face perfectly in keeping with the setting. The face was old, the flesh shrunken, skin pooling in creased yellow pouches beneath the eyes, making them appear sunken and vague, and around the lips, giving the mouth a permanent pucker. The face looked at me without much interest.

"Yes?" it said.

"Um, is this where… er, did Art Llewellyn live here?"

The face creased further, like scrunched linen. Before I could mumble something else, another voice came from inside the house.

"Mam! Who is it? Mam!"

The door was opened wider from within, but only so far—it had swollen through water ingress and decay, and stuck fast with barely enough room for a person to squeeze in. A girl pushed herself into the opening alongside the old face. I say girl, but she was a young woman, around eighteen or nineteen. At first glance, with her slightness and pale complexion, and her juxtaposition to the old face, she did appear as no more than a girl.

She looked at me from beneath a brown fringe which, with her dark eyes, increased the impression of paleness to the point she appeared to be frail and ill, an impression that was banished the instant she spoke.

"Who are you?" she said, her voice strong and confident. "What do you want?"

Confusion thickened my tongue, making it feel too big for my mouth. I parted my lips, trying to speak, but I had no idea what to say.

The girl's eyes narrowed to black slits.

"Are you simple? We're not buying anything, if that's what you're trying to do. And we're not interested in Jehovah." Her glance turned from me to the old face. Tears ran down it, following the lines of the grooved wrinkles. "Go on in, Mam," she said, her voice softer. "I'll get rid of him."

The sunken eyes in the old face slid away from me as the head turned, revealing lank strands of grey hair. I watched as it shuffled away into the gloomy interior.

"Can you talk?" The girl's expression had grown hostile, her voice sharp. It matched her features.

I nodded.

"Go on then."

I took a deep breath and willed my tongue to work. "Is this number twenty-three?"

The girl's eyes flickered to the black number on the door beside her head.

"Can hardly deny it, can I? You look too young to be a debt collector." She sighed. "Tell me what you want or go away. This isn't a good time."

"I…"

"Yes?"

"I, er…"

"Come back when you've learned how to string a sentence together." She took a step inside and started to tug at the door.

"Wait. Please!" At last it came out in a rush. "I'm looking for Art Llewellyn's house. He was my best friend."

She paused. Her eyes grew darker, her skin paler, while she considered me. Then she sighed again, but softly.

"You'd better come in," she said.

Against my expectations, the job centre arranged an interview for me. A Japanese company was opening a new factory on the edge of town to manufacture televisions, radios and new-fangled video cassette recorders. They were looking for production operatives to sit at a conveyor belt and solder small bits of metal to bigger pieces of metal while they moved slowly past. It was, according to Derek, the lowest job available in the factory and one 'a trained monkey' could do.

The bloke conducting the interview wasn't, as I had expected, Japanese. He was thickset and greying, a bushy moustache hiding his top lip like a furry pelmet. He wore a sky blue boilersuit and spoke with a Cardiff accent. He used a shiny gold fountain pen to jot notes on the clipboard on the desk in front of him.

The interview took place in a brightly lit Portacabin alongside the factory. Construction work was still ongoing in there, judging by the sounds of drilling and hammering, and the hard-hatted activity in the vicinity.

A makeshift work bench had been set up in the Portacabin and the man in the boilersuit waved me to a stool the opposite side of the bench from where he sat. He glanced up from the clipboard.

"Jordan? Karl Jordan?"

"Yep."

"No qualifications? No work experience?"

"Nope."

"Ever used a soldering iron?"

"Nope."

"Well, here's your chance."

He nodded to the surface of the bench. To one side stood a metal stand, holding a thin implement, slightly longer than his fountain pen. The bottom half of the implement was made of heavy plastic; the top half was of shiny metal, tapering to a bulbous point. Next to the stand was a thick plastic tray. I pulled it towards me. It contained a misshapen lump of plastic clad in a grey wire mesh. Odd lumps protruded from the mesh here and there, and blobs of shiny metal dotted the floor of the tray like spilled mercury. A small container of assorted metal slivers occupied one corner of the tray. A pair of tweezers lay alongside.

I picked up the soldering iron. It was surprisingly light. An electric cable protruded from the plastic base and snaked over the man's side of the bench and out of sight. I glanced at him.

He nodded encouragingly.

"The on switch is on the handle. See?"

I pushed the sliding switch up with my thumb. A tiny orange light was revealed that glowed brightly.

"Now what?" I said.

"Solder."

Clutching the soldering iron in my right hand, I used my left to pick up the tweezers and extract a sliver of metal from the container. I brought my hands slowly towards each other until the piece of metal touched the tip of the soldering iron.

At first, nothing happened. Then, as though made of wax, the sliver began to shimmer and run. A silvery drop fell to the worktop surface and a wisp of smoke curled upwards.

"Oops," I said.

"Don't worry," said Mr Boilersuit. "But try to do it over the tray. The drips won't burn that."

I moved my hands above the tray and brought them closer to the wire-meshed lump of plastic. I touched the molten end of the metal sliver to the mesh and held it in place. It solidified within moments. When I let go, the sliver protruded proudly from the lump like a plasticine bird's beak.

I grinned.

Mr Boilersuit nodded.

"Easy, isn't it? So do you reckon you could do that on the production line? Course, the work will demand more precision, but we'll start you on the components that will be permanently concealed. When you've mastered those, we'll move you to the more visible stuff where the quality of finish will matter."

I shrugged.

He bent his head and began to scribble on the clipboard with his gold pen. When it caught the light from the overhead strip, the pen glinted like a sunbeam.

He stopped writing and half-turned in his chair as though expecting something to be behind him. There was nothing there.

"Damn," he said. "They've moved the document cabinet to the new office already. It's opening tomorrow, see. I've got to nip over and fetch a new employee form for you to complete. Won't be a moment."

When the door closed behind him, I was still staring at the fountain pen lying on the desk. If I moved my head slightly, I could make it sparkle like orange crystal as light shot off its shiny barrel. A shadow flitted across it as a moth circled the ceiling light.

I reached out and picked it up. It was surprisingly heavy and the barrel wasn't as smooth as I'd imagined. It was engraved with an inscription. I held it to the light and read:

To the Best Dad in the World, Love Bethan & Marc

When the light caught the pen again, it glinted with almost the same intensity as the orange light still showing on the soldering iron, which I had returned to its stand without switching off.

Still holding the pen, I reached for it.

~~~

"You got a name?"

I nodded, clenching my hands tightly on my lap and trying not to fidget.

She frowned impatiently. "Are you going to tell me what it is?"

"Karl. Karl Jordan."

"And you were friendly with Arthur?"

I nodded. "I called him Art."

Her lips pursed. "Yeah, that sounds about right for my brother. Full of pretensions."

It was my turn to frown. "He told me he was an only child."

"He probably told you a lot of things which aren't true." She sighed and dropped her gaze. "He was a dreamer. A hopeless dreamer." She looked back up. Her dark eyes glinted. "What else did he tell you?"

The door to the front room where we were sitting swung open to reveal the wrinkled old face I had seen earlier. I could now see the face was attached to a wizened neck perched upon a slight body clad in a grey cardigan of a material so fluffy it resembled fur.

"Cuppa, love?" the old lady enquired of the girl.

"No ta, Mam."

"What about your friend?" The wrinkled head turned toward me and a vague smile revealed small pointed teeth protruding from baby-pink gums.

The girl spoke before I could. "He won't have one either. This is Karl, Mam. He was a friend of Arthur's."

"Oh. That's nice." The old lady produced a crumpled tissue from the sleeve of her cardigan and held it to her nose. More tears welled in her eyes and began to run down her cheeks, turning the crevices to streams.

The girl rose quickly and put an arm around the old lady's shoulders. "There, there, Mam," she cooed. "Come and have that cup of tea."

She led her out to the back of the house. I glanced around the
~~~

front room.

It was clearly not used much. The filthy net curtains cast the room in gloom, but there were no lamps to lighten the space. I perched on the edge of a sagging two-seater settee. The girl had sat on a similarly dilapidated armchair. A mantelpiece of dark wood framed an empty fireplace.

The girl came back into the room.

"What's your name?" I asked.

"Karen."

"Where's your father?"

"I don't have a father."

"Art said—"

"Let me guess. Our father was in some high-up job and wanted him to follow in his footsteps. We've got loads of money and lived in some posh house in the sticks."

I sighed. "Something like that."

"Our father died when Arthur was a baby. He never knew him. I remember him though." Her face twisted into a brief grimace before tightening. "He was an alcoholic. When that alone didn't beat the spirit out of Mam, he finished the job with his fists. Bastard! Arthur was lucky not to know him."

"Did Art… Arthur, go to the Welsh comp?"

"Yes. Until he failed every exam and they kicked him out."

"He said he was going to go to university."

She uttered a high-pitched, squeaky laugh and glanced around the room. "Do you think our mother could afford to send him to uni? She can just about afford to feed herself. If I didn't send money home…" She tailed off, staring into the distance.

"You don't live here?"

Karen shook her head. "I moved away two years ago when I got a job in Cardiff. They've given me a week's compassionate leave. I'm going back after the funeral." She looked at me. "That's the day after tomorrow. We thought it might be delayed because of the inquest, but the coroner has released his body as the cause of death is not in doubt. 'Asphyxiation'. At least he wouldn't have felt any pain. His body was too full of alcohol to have felt anything." She sighed.

"I… I was with him. The night it happened." She glanced at me sharply. "Not when he, um, climbed the tree, but earlier. We were drinking to drown my sorrows."

Karen's lips tightened. "The police have been asking us what Arthur was doing that day. We haven't been able to tell them anything." She stood. "I think you should go."

At the door, I stopped.

"The funeral. *Please*. Where is it?"

She told me, then scraped the door closed behind me.

Thirteen: A Farewell

I was so engrossed in what I was doing, I didn't notice Mr Boilersuit come back into the Portacabin.

Holding his fountain pen lightly in my left hand, my right used the soldering iron to attach metal slivers to the pen's barrel. They protruded at regular intervals, like fins, and gave the pen the appearance of a sleek and deadly missile. It looked like something out of *Thunderbirds*.

The first I became aware of Mr Boilersuit's presence was a strangled spluttering noise.

I glanced up from my work. He was standing inside the doorway, staring at me, his mouth moving, soundless except for that weird spluttering which sounded like a shortwave radio being tuned.

Smiling, I held up the pen.

"Look," I said. "I'm really getting the hang of this soldering lark."

I wasn't offered the job.

The police didn't come knocking, although I expected them. They still hadn't been by the day of the funeral. I don't know why, but I guessed she hadn't told them about me.

It started to rain when I was halfway to the chapel. I was dressed in an old-fashioned woollen suit that had been my father's and fitted me well enough. Mam had insisted on buying me a pair of black shoes to attend interviews, but cheap ones. Her legal secretary's wages were sufficient to cover day-to-day bills, but didn't stretch to expensive shoes for me.

By the time I reached the chapel, the suit jacket hung from my shoulders like a lead apron. My shoes squelched and pinched my toes. A blister was forming on my left heel.

I sat in the back pew of the chapel, brushing dripping hair from my eyes, trying to wiggle feeling back into my toes and ignore the damp odour wafting from my suit.

Most of the pews in front of me were empty. Art's mother sat huddled in the front row, her shoulders shaking gently, head bowed. Karen sat next to her, back straight, staring ahead. An elderly couple sat behind them. At the other end of their pew sat a middle-aged man. A moth fluttered from the vaulted ceiling and settled onto the back of his dark coat.

I was the sixth member of the congregation. Not even Brian Lewis, that windiest of boys, had shown up.

The only others present were the vicar and, of course, the star of the show.

Art was hidden within a plain pine coffin resting on a trolley before the steps leading to the altar. He wasn't doing anything. Just lying there in that box.

As the service started, I ignored the request to stand and join in some hymn; I ignored the mumblings of the vicar and the mumbo-jumbo responses from the other five members of the congregation.

I sat and dripped and stared at the coffin.

The woman at the job centre was not the same one who'd taken my details when I signed on; younger and not unattractive. She regarded me stonily. I returned her gaze.

"Well?" she said.

"Yep," I replied. "You?"

Her lips tightened. "As you know, I meant, well, what have you to say for yourself?"

"About what?"

"About the interview, Mr Jordan. For the factory job."

"I thought it went well."

Her jaw sagged slightly, but she quickly recovered her poise.

"*Went well?* You were lucky they didn't report you to the police for causing criminal damage to that poor man's fountain pen. I would have." She glanced down at the papers on the desk in front of her and ticked a box with a biro. "Your benefits, when you become entitled to them at seventeen, will be suspended for six weeks. If you deliberately sabotage any future interviews, they may be suspended indefinitely."

I stared at her. She was in her low-thirties, with auburn hair and deep brown eyes. She raised her eyebrows and I felt a fluttering in my lower stomach.

"Yes?" she said.

"Er… would you… um, will you go out with me? Like, on a date?"

Her expression didn't flicker.

"Goodbye, Mr Jordan."

The funeral service must have ended because four men in black appeared—the undertakers, I guessed—and began rolling the trolley down the aisle towards the chapel doors.

The other mourners rose to follow the coffin. I kept my gaze fixed upon the back of the pew in front of me.

I didn't look up until the last of the small party was stepping through the chapel doors. Only then did I stand and trail outside after them.

The rain had eased to a light drizzle, but the low, grey sky promised more heavy rain to come. The mourners clutched their coats and huddled their shoulders as they trudged slowly behind the coffin.

The tiny procession wound through the chapel grounds, along a worn concrete path, passing old headstones, leaning and lichen-faced, until coming to a halt near the stone boundary wall. The branches of a huge tree growing beyond the wall extended above us and dripped down our necks drops of water the size of marbles.

My suit sagged as though trying to drag me into the ground to join Art. I shivered.

The undertakers guided the trolley towards a coffin-sized hole.

My feet had grown numb with cold; at least the blister and squashed toes had stopped hurting.

The vicar stood at the head of the grave. Art's mother and sister stood at the far side, while the other three mourners stood opposite. I stopped a little behind them, and stared at the hole.

At this close range, I could see shovel marks in its steep sides. But I was not near enough to be able to see the bottom. I longed to step forward and peer in to see how far down it went. The undertakers were in the way.

They lifted the coffin from the trolley and lowered it until it was somehow suspended above the hole. They retired to stand behind the vicar.

As the vicar started the committal service, I stared again at the coffin. In the chapel, I had been curious as to what Art looked like. Did he still appear as tranquil as when I'd last seen him, dangling from Dic Du's tree, or were his features running, turning green, with furry stuff growing on his cheeks? It seemed important that I know.

And now we were beside the hole that was about to swallow Art, I needed to know how much water was in there. Was the coffin waterproof? Would it float?

Without realising it, I had taken a step towards the coffin. A strong sense of being watched made me glance up.

Karen was regarding me through narrowed eyes. She gave an almost imperceptible shake of her head.

I stepped back and lowered my gaze.

The committal service drew to a close. The rain fell heavier. Drops from the tree bounced on the coffin lid.

The undertakers stepped forward. By means that were a mystery to me, they lowered the coffin hand over hand, before moving off, followed by the vicar.

The elderly couple moved to the edge of the grave. They glanced down, nodded to Art's mother and walked away. The single man was next, stepping briskly to the graveside without looking down, then moving away without any acknowledgement to Art's mother or to Karen. After he'd gone, I realised I'd only ever seen him from the back.

Karen was looking at me again, her mouth set firmly in a straight line. I looked away and didn't move.

When I looked back, Karen was standing at the edge of the hole, clutching her mother's arm. Art's mother was sobbing, holding a handkerchief to her mouth. She held a red rose in her other hand. Before they left, she threw the rose into the grave.

I waited until they had reached the concrete path before stepping forward, the grass oozing beneath my feet.

The coffin fitted snugly into the hole, with barely a flat hand's width at either side. Muddy water filled the space between the coffin and the grave wall; it was almost level with the lid. At least that answered one of my questions: the coffin didn't float.

The red rose lay on the lid, its petals flat and bedraggled in the rain.

I stared, trying to imagine Art lying there, grinning up at me, but all I could see with my mind's eye was a blanched, weeping corpse, clutching a posy in broken fingers.

The incessant drip-dripping of water faded. The rain-spattered lid of the coffin loomed to fill my vision, which wavered. I swayed.

A sensation overcame me of drifting away, of falling, toppling forward to join my friend in his watery pit.

Fingers dug painfully into my arm. Senses came back into focus as my head cleared.

I took a stumbling step backwards and turned to see who had saved me.

Karen was looking at me closely, with something approaching concern.

"You okay?" she said.

I nodded. "Er, thanks."

She glanced to where her mother was standing in the rain, waiting. "I have to go."

Letting go of my arm, she turned, but then hesitated. Without looking at me, she said, "Come back to our house for a while, will you? My mother could do with someone being there. Someone who knew him. Please."

She walked away.

I glanced at the grave, but did not step back to its edge.

"Goodbye, Art," I murmured. "It was fun knowing you."

Then I, too, turned and walked away without a backwards glance.

Fourteen: Death

Leon was killed while manning a checkpoint in southern Armagh. Shot through the chest by a sniper, he survived for two tortuous minutes lying on his back on the rain-slickened road, while a fellow private tried desperately to staunch the flow of blood.

I wanted to know what he had been thinking about while lying there gazing at the sky. I wanted to know if he could glimpse the infinite darkness that lies beyond. I wanted to know what it was like to feel your life bleeding away, one heartbeat at a time.

I wanted to know his emptiness.

I trudged through the rain from the chapel. Water seeped into my underwear.

Art's mother and sister had been driven away in a sleek black limousine. I'd hung back in the chapel grounds until they'd gone in case they offered me a lift. The other three mourners had long disappeared.

It was the middle of the afternoon in August and would be hours before the sun set. Yet the sky was so low and grey and full of rain it seemed twilight must be setting in early.

I headed vaguely back towards home the opposite side of town. Art's house wasn't far from the chapel, but I would need to deviate if that's where I intended going.

My stomach fluttered, then erupted into a grumble. I hadn't eaten since breakfast and then had only picked. I'd left the house without any money, leaving the few pound notes I'd meant to bring on my bedside cabinet. This was the early 1980s, before the pound coin was introduced.

Probably just as well. The notes would have become a soggy lump in my pocket. Besides, they wouldn't have been sufficient to buy a large enough quantity of what I really needed right then: forgetting-juice.

Briefly I toyed with the idea of 'shopping' for alcohol, to see if

I still possessed the old knack of acquisition without cost. Then I remembered I hadn't been very good at that, either, and dismissed the idea.

Maybe there would be booze at Art's house. There often is at wakes.

I changed direction and made for Talbot Close.

The heavy rain had made the door to number twenty-three swell more. Karen had to lean against it to open it sufficiently for me to squeeze through. I wondered how her mother gained entrance but let the question remain unasked: I am possessed of some sensitivity. I guessed there must be a back entrance.

We sat in the front room, me on the sagging settee, Karen on the armchair. There was no sign of her mother.

"Mam's in bed." Karen twitched her nose. "This has been hard on her."

I nodded. A smell surrounded me like an aura, dank and putrid, like rotting vegetables. If she noticed—and she must have, the way her nose continued to twitch—she said nothing.

"Drink?" She nodded to the floor beside me.

I reached down and picked up a bottle of wine. It was a cheap brand I recognised from the shop where Art bought our cider. Ignoring its sour taste, I welcomed the warmth it sent through my limbs.

We sat in silence. I drank and she watched me.

When I'd drained the bottle, I glanced down to see another full bottle awaiting my attention. It didn't come as a surprise. I was halfway through it when I asked the burning question.

"Who were the other mourners?" To this day, I'm not sure why that was important, but I needed to know.

Karen shrugged. "The elderly couple are friends of Mam. The middle-aged bloke…" She broke off, gazing at me with dark eyes.

"Yes?" I sat straighter, raising a fresh waft of damp putrescence.

"You already know."

Her gaze was unflinching and in that instant I knew she was right. I already knew who the other mourner was. He had been dancing around the edges of my thoughts for years, never letting me see him completely, skipping back to the darkness whenever I tried to bring my regard fully to bear. To see him, if only from behind, at the funeral of my best friend was, putting it mildly, unexpected.

I sagged back into the damp depths of the settee, raised the bottle to my lips and took a deep slug. He had come and I had barely spared him a second glance.

"Moths," I murmured. My tongue had grown thick, like a piece of wood, and had trouble forming the word.

Karen's mouth twisted into a curious expression. The wine had done its work, numbing my senses. The sight of her front teeth, grown long and pointed, barely caused me pause.

She nodded. "Reaching for the darkness. The unattainable darkness."

At that instant, I knew love for the first time. The only time.

Her head twitched to one side as though she had heard something. "I must go and see to Mam. Let yourself out."

"I love you, Karen."

She didn't look back as she scurried through the doorway. "Don't be so fucking ridiculous," she said, and was gone.

I never saw her again.

That night, I dreamed vividly of Art. He lay in a lidless, water-filled coffin, his face barely protruding above the surface. Three moths— two brown, one yellow—had settled high on Art's cheeks, just beyond reach of the brimming water. Their eggs clung to his pallid skin in blood-coloured clusters, like clumps of cheap caviar. The middle-aged man from his funeral stood the other side of the coffin, staring at me. I wanted to return his gaze, see him fully at last, but I could not tear my attention away from Art.

Art opened his eyes. No whites remained, no irises. They had become all pupil, two black pits staring up at me.

"Karl…" Art's voice came in a cracked whisper which reached me as though I knelt with my ears pressed to his lips. "I've found it."

I nodded, knowing full well to what he referred.

The moths took off from his cheeks. It was only as they

fluttered towards me that my dream-self felt the first twinge of unease. When they landed on my eyelids and crawled into my unblinking eyes, I awoke in a thrashing sweat.

The news about Leon came while Mam was in work. Derek rang her, the prick, instead of going to fetch her. One of her co-workers brought her home. When she arrived, her eyes puffy and black with run mascara, Derek swept her into his arms.

If she'd wanted to come to me, he hadn't given her chance. Perhaps as well—how could I have offered her comfort when I possessed not a crumb of compassion? I sat, numbed, and watched them.

Derek watched me back, peering down at me over Mam's quivering shoulder. It only appeared for a moment—it could have been a suppressed belch that twisted his face into the smirk, but I doubt it.

He had been wary of Leon during my brother's visits home. The snideness and sniping were kept hidden away, tended until he could bring them to bear upon me once Leon had returned to the army.

Leon had stopped growing upwards, but his frame had taken on a mean sort of leanness. Not that he had ever possessed much of a devil-may-care outlook on life—he had always been too focused on his goal of being accepted into the army—but none now remained. He had grown serious and edgy. Though apparently content to sit in front of mindless television programmes and allow Mam to fuss over him like an over-protective hen, an air of palpable danger hung about him and he exuded an impression of being ready to fly off the handle at the slightest excuse. Not even I dared rile him. Derek, the cowardly twat, kept well out of his way.

I understood what Derek's smirk meant. The main obstacle to his becoming the main man, the ruler of the roost, had been swept away by a paramilitary bullet.

It was then, as the smirk left his mouth but remained in eyes which continued to watch me, I made my decision.

It was then I decided to kill Derek.

Fifteen: Moths

"That's all," I say. "No more."

Dr Bharata reaches out a finger. It is long and brown and tapered, like a fine cigar. It pauses over the 'stop' button on the recording machine, but withdraws as though he's had second thoughts.

He looks at me and I have to blink. His mouth has grown long and thin—it protrudes like a proboscis. Eyes have expanded to the size of dinner plates and become multi-faceted. Neck has thickened and armoured; a thorax. A pair of wings form a brown, gauzy backdrop.

Next moment, he is a slight man in a knitted pullover and open-necked shirt, a small head the shape of a lightly squashed pumpkin perched on thin shoulders, neatly trimmed facial hair compensating for the paucity of hair clinging to the asymmetrical slopes of his upper skull. Behind him is nothing more than the tall back of his chair and the cream-painted wall of his office.

"Karl, don't you want to talk about what you did to Derek?" Dr Bharata's voice is soft, soothing. It is the sort of voice it's pleasing to obey, even when it encourages you to talk about things you'd rather not acknowledge.

I shrug, making the chains of the restraints clink together like the sound of two glasses raised in toast. "Told you all about that last time, didn't I?"

My voice has taken on a sullen tone, but I'm tired. I have talked for hours without pause, except to sip from the plastic beaker of water and once to use the loo. Accompanied, of course. The table on which the beaker of water sits is, naturally, attached to the floor. Not that I could hurl it far in these restraints.

Besides, there isn't that much to tell and it's the least interesting part of my tale. I mean, knife murders are a dime-to-a-dozen these days, or so I understand from the telly.

That's where I long to be now, lying on my cot, gazing up at the screen fixed high on the wall, watching some mindless crap about people with more money than I can imagine, wanting to spend it on a converted barn in the countryside.

Dr Bharata nods. "So you did. In any case, I find certain other aspects of your life more interesting. Potentially more revealing."

He wavers between man and insectoid. Blinking doesn't help, but I continue to do it anyway.

It must be the drugs they force me to take. Far from redressing the chemical imbalance in my brain, they are altering reality, like some crazy hippy trip.

I raise a hand to rub at my eyes. The wrist restraints allow me that much movement, but little more. The ankle restraints are loose enough to let me stretch out my legs and cross them. Not enough to let me leap across Dr Bharata's desk and sink my teeth into his thorax, or throat, as I sometimes fantasise about doing. Should the opportunity ever present itself, I wonder whether I would take it. Dr Bharata's okay. He really is. Except, perhaps, when he's trying to make out I'm a looney.

"I can see you're tired," continues the doctor in that voice as comforting as soft toffee. "Hardly surprising. But we need to continue for a little longer."

I half-stifle a groan.

"It's important, Karl," he says. "What we determine today about the nature of your world might mean the difference between remaining locked in a cell for the remainder of your natural days, or…" He shrugs his slight shoulders. When the vision shifts, he is flapping his wings a little. "Or perhaps being prepped to return to society."

No flicker of excitement stirs within me. I've heard it before, how I might be repatriated into the real world if only I can get a grip on how that real world looks and behaves. It doesn't bother me. Being completely frank, the thought of going out into the wide world scares me. It's not that I have anyone to go out there for. Mam died three years ago, well into her eighties. Slipped away in her sleep, so the old people's home informed the secure unit's staff.

The only thing that used to bother me about being locked up

was the thought of Mam having to spend all those years alone. That, at the end, she was with other people gladdens me.

"Okay," I say. "What do want to hear about, Dr Bharata?"

Maybe I should have waited until after Leon's funeral to sort out Derek. That way I could have stood by Mam's side while they lowered her child's body into the ground. Unless he was cremated. Perhaps it should bother me that I don't know.

Here's the understatement of the century: Leon's funeral couldn't have been much fun for Mam. I mean, having to attend your elder son's funeral must be bad enough, without your other son being banged up in custody charged with the murder of your boyfriend. And as if that wasn't sufficient, the more sensationalist tabloids were gleeful in their lurid descriptions of how I'd left Derek's body. 'Mutilation', they called it. I prefer 'rearrangement'.

They even gave me a nickname.

"You see," I explained to Dr Bharata during our previous session, "I didn't want to disfigure Derek as a means of torture or anything like that. He was already dead when I rearranged him. I did it for the moths."

Dr Bharata raised a thin eyebrow which made the dinner-plate eye below it bulge. He was mostly taking insectile form that day; it made it easier to tell him about Derek.

"That's why you left the windows open all around the house? To allow the moths in?"

I nodded.

"Ah, I see. It certainly drew in the flies according to the police report."

I shrugged. "It was the moths I wanted to come in. I had done it for them."

"Done it? You mean, killing Derek?"

I shook my head. "That was for me and for Mam. I thought she might even thank me for it one day. No, I mean the rearranging. *That* was for the moths."

Dr Bharata leaned closer, bringing his proboscis almost into contact with the surface of his desk. His outstretched wings shivered like muslin in a breeze. "Tell me, Karl. Describe what you did. Explain why you did it."

"Well, when he'd stopped twitching, I removed his shirt and vest." I chuckled. "He wore a string vest like an old man. Then I turned him onto his stomach. You see, I wanted to make wings."

Dr Bharata's thorax bulged briefly as he swallowed. Going into grisly detail about how I'd made Derek's wings didn't bother me, but I didn't know how strong the doctor's stomach was and, feeling reasonably well disposed to him that day, preferred to spare him every in-and-out of my struggle. And it had been a struggle; it's surprising how uncooperative Derek's cooling skin and flesh proved to be. I might not have been completely satisfied with the result—I'm no surgeon and Mam's carving knife could have been sharper— but it wasn't a bad effort, even if I say so myself.

I gave him the potted version. "I sliced Derek open down the length of his spine and across his lower back, peeled back the flesh into two triangles and stapled them to his outstretched arms."

Dr Bharata swallowed again. He touched the buff-coloured file sitting on the desk before him. "I've seen the police photos of the scene. You propped him up against a wall and nailed his hands to it."

I nodded. "It was the only way to get his arms to stretch and stay there. Lucky it was an old house. Solid walls. Will hold a nail and support a lot of weight."

"Hmm. And you removed his ears and eyelids…"

I nodded again. "Insects don't have ears. As for the eyelids, it was the best way I could think of to make his eyes seem bigger." I stared into the doctor's bulbous eyes.

"And the length of tubing you attached to his mouth?"

"Proboscis."

"Why, Karl? Why did you want to make Derek resemble a giant insect?"

I sighed. "I've already told you. For the moths." I thought for a moment. "Look, it isn't easy to explain, but I've told you Art's theory about how moths are attracted to light not because of the light itself, but to the infinite darkness which lies the other side?"

Dr Bharata nodded.

"Well, that seems insufferably unfair to me. I mean, they're harmless enough creatures, right. They have this reputation for destroying clothes, but some of them are beautiful and delicate and they deserve better than to spend their existence trying to reach something that's not even there. So I wanted to give them a god."

The doctor cleared his throat and blinked as though he hadn't heard me correctly. "A god? For moths?"

"Exactly."

He shifted a little in his chair, making his wings quiver. When he next spoke, he wasn't addressing me. "Session terminated at 15:42." He pressed the 'stop' button on the recording machine before glancing at me.

"Well, Karl, I've been doing this job for more than fifteen years, and this is the first time I've heard a post-mortem mutilation justified as a means of providing a deity for a group of flying insects. Quite frankly, I don't know if you believe what you're spouting or whether you're taking the fucking piss."

His language shocked me a little. I opened my mouth to protest, then closed it again. What difference did it make if he believed me or not? If he did, it would merely confirm what he already thought; if he didn't, he would think I was being contemptuous and dismissive of the process to try to heal and rehabilitate me. Either way, the end result would be the same.

Moth-Man would continue to languish in a padded cell in a high-security institution for the criminally insane.

Moth-Man? Yes, that was the nickname the tabloids gave me. Pity, really. It would have been better suited to Derek.

"Let's talk about Art Llewellyn," says Dr Bharata.

I shift uneasily, making the restraints clink again. "I'd rather not."

"Okay. His sister, then. Karen."

I shift some more, but say nothing.

"What about his mother, or his house? Twenty-three Talbot Close. You've been consistent throughout this was your friend's address."

I nod. *Here it comes again* I think. *This is where he makes out I'm a complete nutjob.*

"You claim to have visited your friend's family, with the surname Llewellyn, at number twenty-three in 1981. However…" He pauses, staring at me as though inviting me to recant. I stare back at him mutely.

"However," he continues, "the last residents to move out of Talbot Close were a family by the name of Hughes. That was in 1979. The houses remained locked and shuttered until the whole street was demolished in 1982 to make way for new development." He taps the file in front of him. "It's all in here, Karl. Copies of closure and demolition orders, legal notices, contractor invoices. Most of it is a matter of public record. Do you have anything new to say about this?"

I shrug. I've heard all this before.

"You see," continues Dr Bharata softly, "you *did* visit a house in Talbot Close. A derelict one. The police found a property where the boarded-up front door had been forced open enough to allow a person to squeeze through. Inside they found a couple of empty wine bottles next to a rotting sofa. The bottles were covered in your fingerprints, Karl. The property was infested with rats."

Still I say nothing. I know what's coming next.

"As you are aware, Karl, the police spoke to your friend Brian Lewis. The one you say Art Llewellyn urinated over in what you refer to as Deadman's Woods. Brian denies knowing anyone by the name of Art or Arthur. He says it was only the two of you that day in the woods; that it was only ever the two of you. That it was you, Karl, who urinated over him and is the reason why you stopped being friends."

He stares intently at me, before tapping the file again. "Don't you find it odd that you say he was your best friend, that you spent a lot of time with him, and yet your mother never set eyes on him?

She told the police she found herself wondering on occasion whether he even existed." He pauses, but I'm not about to fill the silence. "There is no record of his birth or death. The Welsh-medium school has no record of a pupil by the name Arthur or Art Llewellyn. No inquest was held into the death of a person by that name. The chapel at which you say you attended Art's funeral has no record of the funeral service or burial. No gravestone marked with that name stands in the chapel graveyard."

Dr Bharata is, for the moment, in human form. I stare back, refusing to be cowed. It is at moments like these, when he is trying to fuck with my mind, I can see myself ripping out his throat with my teeth, laughing around his spurting blood while I do so.

"Speaking of Art's funeral," continues the psychiatrist, "what fascinates me most is the unexplained mourner. The middle-aged man. Karen said you knew who it was. I believe it is another person conjured up by your sub-conscious mind."

He gives a long pause as if to allow me time to interject, to come clean. I remain silent.

"Okay," he says, "as you wish. You, Karl Jordan, come from a broken home. By all accounts"—he once more taps the file; it is beginning to grate on my nerves—"your mother did her best by you in trying circumstances and little blame can attach to her for what happened. Your older brother was a focused young man with whom you enjoyed if not a close relationship, then not a bad one as sibling relationships go. It was his untimely death that I believe finally pushed you over the edge."

He pauses, as though to allow me opportunity to nod wide-eyed in epiphany-esque agreement. I maintain a steady, mute gaze.

He sighs before continuing. "But what about the other adult in your life? What about your father?"

I can't help myself; I give a snort of disgust.

Dr Bharata nods. "I tend to agree with you. It sounds like he was a waster. Perhaps in many ways you were better off without him in your life. But you secretly yearned for a father, isn't that true, Karl?"

Still, I say nothing.

"I think it is only natural that you did. And that is who the fifth mourner was at Art's funeral. It was your father, Karl. Or, rather, your father as you wished he'd been."

Dr Bharata's theories are not new to me. He figures he has me all worked out and I'm not about to disabuse him. Like I said, most of the time he's okay.

I can't help, though, but think back to Art's funeral, to the smartly dressed, middle-aged man who'd been there, but whose face I never saw. I'd like to think I might have had a father who would come to my friend's funeral as a mark of respect not only to my friend and his family, but to me.

"However," says Dr Bharata, "that funeral never took place. For how could it? Although I have to say I admire the detail with which you describe the non-existent event. The shovel marks on the side of the grave—that's a nice touch. Neither did the shoplifting sprees to Cardiff take place. Or they did, but you went alone. And the cider. You claim it was Art who bought the alcohol. Let's see, you said that due to his height and long, curly hair, he could pass for eighteen." He clears his throat. "You've never explained the wig and platform-soled shoes the police found in your bedroom, Karl. A wig of long, curly hair. And the stash of cash. Not a fortune, it's true, but enough to keep you in flagons of cider and bottles of cheap wine."

I say nothing. In truth, the wig and shoes and cash worry me. I've never offered an explanation because I don't have one. Unless the wig and shoes were part of my thieving stash I've since forgotten about—possible, given the amount of stuff I nicked—but the cash... Images intrude of Mam's purse lying on the coffee table, Derek's wallet on a bedside cabinet, Leon's loose change flung carelessly on a work surface. No. I refuse to allow myself to consider that I might have stolen from my own. Derek, no problem, he was fair game. But Mam and Leon? Never.

The psychiatrist gives another long pause and I know he's gathering himself for the final denouement, the scene where Poirot has everyone gathered in one place and lays out all the evidence and red herrings before unmasking the killer.

"I believe you invented Art Llewellyn as the sort of person you'd like to have been. The boy with all the advantages. Though even he, in the end, was a fraud, wasn't he?" He sighs and gives a small shudder I think is intended to make me feel sympathy for him but that only makes me think *he*'s the fraud.

"Accept it, Karl," he continues. "Art Llewellyn, his sister and mother, his suicide, the funeral, are all figments of your imagination." His eyes, still human or else they'd take over the office, widen to their fullest extent as he attempts with the force of his will to make me see his version of reality. "Accept it, Karl, and be free."

I almost feel sorry for him. Almost.

"Art Llewellyn…" I begin.

Dr Bharata leans forward. "Yes?" he breathes.

"Art Llewellyn was the best friend I ever had."

The doctor's face collapses in on itself. His shoulders sag. He glances at his expensive wristwatch. "Session terminated at 17:12," he says.

Alone in my cell at last, I find the evening television doesn't interest me. I lie on my back and wait for lights out.

Exhausted though I am from spending most of the day delivering a monologue, I don't crave sleep. To stave it off, I think about Dr Bharata and his theories.

Very keen on his theories, is the good doctor. Anxious to explain my behaviour by blaming it on external sources. It will make his reports neat and efficient if he can box me away under 'Dysfunctional parenting' or 'Traumatic childhood'.

He has attributed the root cause of what I did to Derek to various incidents. There was Billy Jenkins and his roller skates, for a start. Witnessing him being impaled on the bonnet ornament of a Jaguar must have left a lasting scar on my young, impressionable self.

Then there was my ritual humiliation at The Arches at the hands of Kay Williams and her cronies, with the help of liberal dashings of custard. How could I have gone through such an experience without it shaking my faith in human nature?

Or, his favourite, the one he returns to time and again: the disappearance of my father from my life. "How devastating that must have been to a child," he says, gazing upon me with a look of profound sympathy I'm sure is fake. "And on your sixth birthday, too. To lose the only adult male in your life at such a tender age…" He shakes his head in feigned sadness, while watching me closely for signs I was as traumatised as he seems so desperate for me to have been.

While he expounds these theories, he sits forward excitedly, his dark eyes aglitter. When I fail to affirm how badly I slept in the weeks following whichever incident is currently his chief suspect, or how withdrawn I became as a result, or how I wanted to pull the wings off insects, or any of the hundred other signs he is barking up the right tree, but merely give an indifferent shrug, he sits back, the zealous light fading from his eyes, his face slumping into a hang-dog expression of disappointment.

For all his eloquence, his framed certificates hanging on the wall, the strings of letters after his name, he's ducking the obvious.

Maybe some of us are born to be moths.

At last, the lights on my wing flicker off and I am nearly cast into darkness. Only one source of light remains. On the ceiling above my bed is a pale night light. I kicked up a fuss about having one until they installed it. When they realised it keeps me docile throughout the hours of darkness, they readily agreed to it becoming a permanent fixture. If I move cells, the night light comes with me.

Pale though the illumination it delivers, it serves its purpose. I asked them to position it near the wall, where the shadow is deeper.

I gaze at the light. Rather, at the infinite blackness which lies beyond.

The blackness that my best friend Art found. The blackness that I, too, will reach one way or another.

Returned

The dead man answered thus:
'What good gift shall God give us?'

The boards answered him anon:
'Flesh to feed hell's worm upon.'

—Algernon Charles Swinburne *After Death*

Part One: Earth

One: Tequila

It started, as most things end, with a funeral.

This seemed a perfectly ordinary funeral. At first.

The sun could not pierce the glowering clouds, which cast the day in a sullen greyness as befitting a solemn occasion. A greyness to match the stone from which the church, a sombre backdrop, was constructed. The hearse had come to rest in the turning circle at the end of the driveway—opened to vehicles only on such occasions—near the yawning hole waiting to be filled. Rolls of green tarpaulin had been draped over mounds of earth huddling discreetly in the background. The tarpaulin rippled and snapped in the stiff October breeze.

Parked cars lined the roads outside the church grounds. They disgorged people dressed darkly, who huddled themselves against the wind and walked in slowstep along the church drive towards the funeral cars. Two Daimlers, black and stately, stood behind the hearse, far enough away to allow space for the coffin to be extracted when the time came.

Two black-overcoated men stood at the rear of the hearse, faces expressionless, nothing about them worthy of note. Anonymity suits their profession.

From the crowd now assembled behind the Daimlers, six men stepped forward. They, too, wore black overcoats, but their faces were animated with expression: a mix of deeply ingrained sorrow and apprehension. These men approached the rear of the hearse and formed two lines facing each other with grim gazes.

One of the undertakers released the latch on the rear door of the hearse and raised it silently on well-greased hinges. The other removed a black, plastic object from the floor of the hearse and placed it on the roof, behind the erect tailgate. His expression seemed carefully neutral, as though he had stood before a mirror for hours practising how to look impassive. The first removed sprays of flowers from the coffin and placed them aside. They both stood poised at the open door as the action shifted to the Daimlers.

The rear doors to the furthest Daimler opened and four people stepped out. The oldest was stooped, arthritic, her gaze permanently cast down due to over-curvature of her spine. The youngest, also female, around two generations more youthful, stayed by the first woman's side, watchful and ready to offer support. The remaining two, a couple, looked to be in their fifties, greying and lined.

From the nearest Daimler, three people emerged. The older woman, also greying, stood erect, face set as though determined to see this last ordeal through, or expressing stony-faced disapproval. The man—balding, face crumpled like yesterday's newspaper— grasped her arm, though it was unclear whether it was a gesture of support for her or it was he who sought strength in contact. The third person was younger, the grey light unable to dull the chestnut glow of her hair. Her eyes were dry, but red-rimmed and puffy. She stood, hands clenched tightly, a little apart from the older couple. Neither of them made any move to comfort her.

Came the moment for the main player to take centre stage. The undertakers each gripped a gleaming chrome handle and began to slide the coffin off the raised floor of the hearse. The men standing at the end of the two lines turned towards the vehicle and bent at the knees. The undertakers guided the coffin onto their shoulders. The action was repeated down the lines and the men straightened, the coffin perched securely on six shoulders, steadied by six hands bracing the teak sides. The men's free arms linked beneath the casket and, as one, they shuffled around to face the yawning hole. But they did not move towards it. Not yet.

Here the funeral departed from what is considered normal on such occasions.

The undertakers closed the tailgate of the hearse. The one with the practised expression held a hand towards the object on the roof and paused, looking to the three mourners from the nearest Daimler. The older woman grimaced and her lips pursed into a tight nest of wrinkles. The man lowered his gaze. Only the puffy-eyed younger woman responded to the enquiring glance of the undertaker. She took a deep breath and nodded.

The undertaker depressed one of the buttons on top of the object and stood back. If anything, his expression became too guarded and, perversely, expressed volumes.

At first, nothing happened and the tableau was frozen: the bearers, coffin on shoulders, arms entwined, eyes straight ahead; the chief mourners as motionless as freshly hewn statues; the sixty or so people who made up the rest of the mourners also unmoving; and, finally, the undertakers, who had resumed their carefully deferential stances and oh-so-guarded expressions at the head, and to either side, of the bearers. For moments, all was still, all was quiet. Even the persistent breeze faltered and no traffic could be heard passing along the main village road beyond the churchyard walls.

The sound which broke the spell was as unexpected as a peal of raucous laughter. It came from the black object on the roof of the hearse and at such a level the snapping of the tarpaulin covering the mounds of earth as the breeze picked up went unheard.

It was the sound of a guitar playing a snappy riff to the accompaniment of clapping hands. The riff was repeated and a bassline added. Drums and cymbals joined in, complemented a bar or two later by lead guitar.

As the music filled the churchyard, a shiver ran through the assembled mourners, breaking their apparent paralysis. There came a shuffling of feet on the driveway, furtive glances were cast at one another, coughs and the clearing of throats could be heard above the music.

When the distinctive sound of a saxophone broke in with a Tex Mex line, completing the melody, the bearers began to move. Taking small, deliberate steps, they shuffled forward. After the first few hesitant paces, they fell into the music's beat and stepped to its rhythm.

The undertakers marched slowly alongside the coffin, guiding the bearers between grey headstones.

The chief mourners followed, the puffy-eyed younger woman alone in front, one older couple a pace or two behind, their faces mirroring each other's in distaste. Behind them came the other greying couple, followed closely by the women separated by two generations in age. The younger of these, it might be remarked, bore a sibling resemblance to the woman at the head of the procession.

All others fell in behind. Many affected airs of grim neutrality as though there was nothing unusual in what they were doing. Some were unable to hide their feelings of aghast at taking part in a funeral procession to a tune their expressions made clear they felt was so misplaced.

The bearers paused when the music reached its first bridge, causing those following to also halt their forward shuffle. All were once more still as the saxophone crescendoed, all instruments fell momentarily silent and one word—in keeping with the tune but not the occasion—resounded across the graveyard.

The music kicked back in and the saxophone soared. The bearers resumed their rhythmic stride and the mourners shuffled along behind, beginning to fan out as the coffin approached its journey's end.

The undertakers quickened their step to beat the coffin to the graveside. They busied themselves laying wooden slats, like railway sleepers, and nylon straps across the waiting hole. The straps were, of course, grey since this was a sombre occasion in spite of the upbeat accompaniment.

The bearers came to a halt alongside the grave. The chief mourners formed a loose huddle at the foot of the grave. The rest of the mourners continued to fan out, some, perhaps subconsciously, stepping in time to the music still playing from the roof of the hearse. They came to rest, standing three or four deep, spread out along each long side of the grave.

The bearers, assisted by the imperturbable undertakers, lowered their burden carefully until it rested upon the wooden slats.

To the relief of many present, the music was coming to an end. Instruments dropped out in the same order they had come in: first, the saxophone went, followed moments later by the lead guitar, then the drums; next, the bassline faded, leaving only the catchy guitar riff and clapping accompaniment.

Three bearers stepped around the grave and took up position opposite. All six stooped and straightened, clutching the grey nylon straps in their hands. The occasional apprehensive glance passed between them. One of the undertakers muttered something and the bearers pulled tightly until the nylon webbing bore the coffin's weight. The undertakers, one each side of the grave, effortlessly removed the wooden slats and secreted them beneath the tarpaulin. At a nod from one of the undertakers, the bearers began to let out the straps, inch by careful inch, and the coffin started to descend.

The guitar and clapping stopped and there was an instant's silence, before a group of voices shouted the title exultantly:

"Tequila!"

The CD player fell silent and the coffin settled into its dank home. The bearers allowed the straps to fall to the ground, before moving away to blend once more amongst the mourners. The undertakers tugged the straps out of the hole and rolled them into muddy, grey rolls that disappeared into the huge pockets of their overcoats. They stepped into position at the head of the grave, a gap between them, and resumed their carefully neutral poses.

The coffin was interred, the mourners in place; the orchestra awaited its conductor. A tall figure of advancing age detached itself from the crowd and stepped forward to fill the gap between the undertakers. He faced the mourners, dog collar visible beneath the tightly buttoned overcoat. His hands emerged from the coat's pockets, clutching a small black book. He opened it, lifted his head and began.

"Family… friends… we are gathered here together to commit the soul of Paul Duffy to our Lord…"

The priest's voice was low, yet contained such timbre no one had difficulty hearing him above the gusting whoosh of the ever-freshening breeze.

When the priest reached the line 'Ashes to ashes, dust to dust', one of the undertakers tossed a handful of soil onto the lid of the coffin. It scattered with a sound like sand hitting glass. Clearly, the undertaker kept a supply of desiccated soil in the seemingly vast pockets of his overcoat since the ground upon which they stood, in the midst of a Welsh autumn, could never yield such a dry specimen.

It was then the funeral severed all links with conventionality. For it was then, amidst the priest's recitation, the whipping wind, and the muffled sobs and sniffs from the congregation, another sound intruded. It was low, too soft to be heard by anyone other than those standing at the immediate graveside, and so incongruous the few who heard it preferred to ignore it.

The priest was one of those. His face blanched and he stumbled over a word, but he was an old hand at this game and recovered so quickly no one present would later remark upon the stutter.

The undertakers were also standing close enough to the grave to hear the noise clearly. It was a regular, insistent noise, one that is commonplace in so many other situations except here. Never here.

It was the sound of knuckles knocking on wood. Gently, tentatively, but unmistakably bone on wood. And there was only one item made of wood in the vicinity which could be the source of the sound.

The undertakers' expressions didn't flicker and they didn't so much as glance at each other. But, as one, they took a step back from the grave.

Two: A Wake

David Owen flicked the end of his cigarette over the garden fence into the scrubland lying beyond. He gazed down the hill towards the church. Between the swaying branches of the maples and fir trees which ringed the graveyard like ancient sentinels, he caught glimpses of white marble and grey granite, crosses and slabs and angels.

But not the grave of his friend. Not from this angle. It was obscured by trees. They spared him the sight of the grave being filled. He imagined what it felt like to lie inside a coffin, in complete darkness, and hear the thuds and slither of fresh earth being thrown in. Would he be able to sense the weight of soil pressing down like a lead blanket? He shivered and tugged his suit jacket tighter.

"Beer, Dai?"

David turned. Ian Griffiths stood there, looking ill at ease in his charcoal suit. In one hand he clutched a can of bitter. The other held out a bottle of Stella. David took it.

"Ta, Griff."

Griff took a swig from his can. "We promised Paul we'd get pissed. Least we can do."

"Yeah. Suppose."

"You okay?"

"Apart from having just buried my best friend, fine."

Griff sighed. "He was my friend, too. I stood beside you carrying the coffin, remember?"

David took a long pull from the bottle. As he lowered it, he gestured towards the house. "What's happening inside?"

"Paul's parents just left."

"What! Already?"

"Aye. Think Cath's relieved, mind."

"I bet. They're an odd couple. Paul was the white sheep of that family."

"True enough. And he's the one who gets ill." Griff tipped up his can and drained it.

David raised his bottle and drank deeply. "What are the rest of the boys up to?"

"Let's see: Rhys is trying to get into a theological debate with Father Moran; Mikey's chatting up Cath's sister; Steve's chatting up Cath's mother; and Wacko is getting stuck into the whiskey."

David grimaced. "Cath's gran better watch out then." He emptied the bottle. "'nother?"

"Why the hell not?"

David took Griff's empty can and dumped it and his bottle into the recycling bin standing beside the back door. He went into the kitchen.

Two or three people were occupying the cramped space, not saying much. As David squeezed between them to reach the fridge, they nodded and smiled at him in the half-embarrassed way that strangers acknowledge each other at weddings and funerals. The muffled burble of more animated conversation came through the door leading from the kitchen into the rest of the house.

David extracted a can of bitter and a bottle of Stella from the fridge. He reached for the bottle opener on one of the work surfaces, forcing one of the kitchen's occupants to change position, no easy task in a room that small.

"Sorry," muttered David. He prised off the bottle top and quickly raised the bottle to his lips as foam bubbled from the neck. Wearing that same half-embarrassed smile, David eased himself back outside.

"So," said Griff when he'd popped the can and taken a swig, "you gonna tell me what's really up?" He held up a hand. "Don't give me any more of that 'just buried my best friend' crap. Paul was dying for months. We all had time to get used to the concept. Something else is bothering you."

David sighed. "How can you tell?"

"Skulking in the back garden alone in the cold. It's getting dark and it's going to rain soon. Doesn't take a bleeding psychologist to work out there's something up. Besides, we've known each other since we were, what, six? That's over twenty-five years. So tell me. What's up?"

"Hold this." David passed his bottle to Griff while he took out a cigarette. "Want one?"

"Aye."

David took out another and lit them both. He placed one between Griff's lips and took back his bottle. "Okay. But you must keep this to yourself. It's too weird. Way too fucking weird." He blew out a long stream of smoke which was instantly whipped away by the strengthening wind.

"Go on."

"You're gonna think I'm nuts."

"I already think you're nuts."

"You and me both." David took a deep breath. "There's no easy, or sane, way of saying this so I'll simply come straight out with it."

"That'd be good."

"Okay. Well, you know we just buried one of our best mates. Stuck him in a box in a hole in the ground six feet deep and then covered him with earth."

"That's how dead people are traditionally buried."

"That's just it. I don't think Paul's dead."

"Huh?"

"Griff. I think we buried Paul alive."

The village of Taiwyn owed its name and existence to the building that served as the village pub and unofficial community centre. Now called *The Poacher's Rest*, the pub had been built as a farmhouse in the late fifteenth century when industry meant nothing more than diligent work. Liberally washed with lime to preserve the stonework, the house was named *Ty Gwyn*—White House. This name came to be applied collectively to the straggling assortment of stone cottages which gradually appeared over the next twenty years to house the farm labourers and associated trades that fed off a thriving farm—millers, weavers, slaughterers, tanners—and the businesses which fed off them: brewers, butchers, grocers, bakers, blacksmiths, ma-sons and cobblers. As centuries rolled by and the farm became a hamlet that became a village, the name stuck and was bastardised into its current form.

Taiwyn's tiny Baptist Chapel dated back to the early sixteenth century, built to serve a small community, its graveyard long-since filled. The gravestones marking the resting places of its earliest occupants leant at crazy angles, the inscriptions barely legible beneath centuries of moss and lichen. The late nineteenth century builders of Taiwyn's Anglican Church were blessed with better foresight. They located at the edge of the village where there was already a derelict stone chapel and, more importantly, ample room to ensure the church's cemetery was large enough to serve the villagers for centuries to come. Their forward planning, coupled with double, sometimes triple, plot occupation meant that Taiwyn's inhabitants could die safe in the knowledge there was plenty of room for them amongst their forebears. The church from the outset adopted a liberal, open-ground policy of not refusing a Christian burial to anyone, provided only they had lived in the village at some point during their lives.

Paul Duffy had been a non-practising Catholic, but a village boy all his life. The Anglican vicar had readily acquiesced to his widow's request, made some months previously, that Paul spend his eternal rest in the churchyard.

The cemetery was laid out in a grid system. When one square was filled, another some distance away was started. That way, more recent graves lay next to ones a century old. Paul's grave was next to one of a child who had died in 1898 of consumption.

As the light faded and the first drops of rain began to fall, the gravediggers tamped down the mound of earth with the backs of their shovels.

"Just in time," one remarked as the rain began in earnest. He shouldered his shovel and tucked under his arm the green tarpaulin used to mask the grave spoil from mourners. "Stick the cross in and let's get out of here."

His colleague removed a simple wooden cross from a canvas

sack and thrust it into the soil at the head of the grave. The grave-stone wouldn't be installed for another six months or so, when the earth covering the coffin had finished settling.

The men walked away to stash their equipment in the store shed behind the church before heading into the village to the *Poacher's* for their customary after-work pint or two.

Rain spattered the newest grave in the cemetery, runnels carving channels into the earth on each side of the mound. That wouldn't cause a problem; the coffin was interred so far down not even a tropical downpour would be sufficient to wash all the topsoil away.

The cross grew darker as water soaked into the wood. The inscription had been burned on with a soldering iron and would still be quite legible to anyone braving the rain. It read:

Paul Tyrone Duffy

Resting peacefully

Inaccuracies can be found in the strangest places.

"Are you sure it was *knocking* you heard?" Griff had lowered his voice, although they had the back garden to themselves.

David nodded. "Absolutely positive. It wasn't long after the service started. I was standing nearer to the grave than anyone except for the priest and undertakers. It wasn't a loud noise; I could only just hear it. But there's no doubt in my mind it was the sound of someone knocking on wood."

Griff swallowed hard. "And it was coming from…?"

"Yep. From the hole in the ground. And there was only one person in there."

David returned Griff's stare levelly. He couldn't detect any obvious disbelief etched onto his friend's face. Not that it would have mattered; it felt good simply to have unburdened himself.

"Paul Duffy was the most single-minded bugger I've known, but not even he could cheat death." Griff emptied his can down his throat and nodded as if coming to a decision.

"What are we going to do?" Having shared the problem, David was quite happy for the moment to let Griff make the running.

"Inside," said Griff firmly, taking a step towards the house.
"Why?"
"One: it's starting to rain."
David glanced up and felt raindrops hitting his cheeks.
"Two?"
"Two: we're gonna talk to Father Moran."

Three: A Likely Story

Father Moran was standing by the front door in his overcoat, clutching Cath's hands. From somewhere he had produced a battered old trilby which was pulled low over his ears, making him look like a down-at-heel private investigator. As Griff and David approached, Father Moran let go of Cath's hands, turned and let himself out of the front door. Griff darted through after him.

David stopped as Cath turned to him. Her face was pale and drawn, her eyelids swollen. David placed a hand on her arm.

"Holding up?"

She nodded. "It's been easier since *they* went."

David didn't need to be told she was referring to Paul's parents.

"What was the journey to the church like? Being cooped up in close confinement with them couldn't have been much fun."

"Oh, a right bundle of laughs it was. My parents wanted me to travel with them and my sister and gran in the other limo, but I wouldn't give *her* the satisfaction. Do you know, we only spoke once during the journey. She looked at me with her lips all pursed in that way she has, like she's just bitten into a lemon, and said, 'Are you still intent on continuing with this ridiculous charade?' When I nodded, she looked away and hasn't looked at me since." Cath breathed out heavily. "It was what her son wanted, for goodness' sake, yet all she could think about was how it might reflect on her. Well, fuck her."

David reached out and squeezed her forearm. "You need a good rest, my girl."

Cath sighed. "Don't think I've ever felt this tired."

David glanced at the front door, which stood ajar. "Me and Griff are going to have a quick word with Father Moran. Then we'll start rounding everybody up. Who's staying with you tonight?"

"No one." She shook her head quickly to forestall his objections. "Mam's tried to persuade me that she should stay, but I want to be on my own. I'll be fine." She forced a thin smile.

"Well, if your mind's made up, I know it's no good trying to un-make it."

He let go of her arm and watched her make her way slowly back towards the living room from which came louder sounds of chatter and laughter, suggesting a large dent had been hit in the supply of booze Cath had laid on. Then he turned and followed Griff out of the front door, pulling it closed behind him.

"Here he comes," said Griff. He was standing on the pavement with the priest. "Hurry up, Dai. Father Moran wants to get back to his parish for evening mass."

David tugged his jacket tighter against the rain. He stopped in front of the priest and nodded.

"Father Moran. Thanks for waiting."

"What's this about?" asked the priest. "As your friend here, er…"

"Griff," said Griff.

"Ah, yes. As Griff was saying, you have something to ask me?"

"Um…" For a moment, realisation that what he was about to say would sound like crazy talk paralysed his tongue.

"*Dai*," urged Griff. "Come on. Spit it out."

"Um. Okay. Look, Father, this might sound crazy, but I know what I heard. In the cemetery. By the graveside."

The priest sighed. "A knocking sound?"

"You heard it too!" David felt a rush of relief wash over him.

Griff looked from one to the other and muttered something under his breath.

Father Moran held up a hand, palm outwards, to quell David's enthusiasm. "My son, my son. I can guess what you think might have caused the sound, but you must banish such thoughts at once."

"Huh? We both heard the knocking and it was coming from the coffin. If Paul's alive—"

"No!" The priest shook his head so vehemently drops of rain from the trilby spattered David's face. He gazed at David intently. "Listen to me and put this madness to rest. I have conducted many,

many burials and this isn't the first time I've heard such sounds at the graveside. But not once—not *once*, mind you—has it meant we were interring a soul that hasn't departed this life. There are other, mundane explanations for the sound you heard."

David frowned. "Like what?"

Father Moran glanced at Griff, then back to David. "Forgive me—I know he was a dear friend to you both—but I understand his body didn't undergo a post mortem and wasn't embalmed at the express wishes of the widow. A cadaver still containing blood and internal organs will quickly begin the decomposition process once removed from refrigeration. Gases can be expelled, sometimes quite forcibly, with the result that an echoing noise might be heard which could be mistaken for, er, knocking."

David glanced at Griff—who looked as sceptical as he felt. David shook his head. "No. That can't explain it. Paul only died three days ago. We all knew it was coming and Cath made the arrangements months ago. An early burial slot became available when the planned funeral was delayed by a last-minute decision to hold an inquest. And Paul died of cancer. By the end he was barely skin and bone. He would only have been out of cold-storage for a matter of hours. Hardly likely his body would start giving off gases that make the sounds of knuckles on wood so soon."

"Perhaps not likely," said Father Moran. "But possible. I have also known the wood of caskets to expand or contract when hitting cold or wet earth. The sound of the wood creaking or settling can sound exactly like the noises we heard earlier."

"Oh," said Griff. He looked deflated, like a child who's had his sweets taken away.

David once more shook his head, but said nothing. He could tell when he was fighting a lost cause.

Father Moran smiled sadly at him. "I can understand why you'd allow a glimmer of hope to pierce the gloom of grief, but the soul of your friend now dwells with the Lord. Be assured." He nodded sagely. "And now, boys, I must be on my way. My parishioners are expecting me." He touched his trilby, turned and walked towards a car parked a little further up the road.

"Let's get out of this rain," said Griff. "I feel another beer's in order."

David stared after the departing priest. "You believed that bull-shit?"

"You didn't?"

"A likely story." David looked at his friend. "I know what I heard coming from Paul's grave. It wasn't gas or expanding wood. It was knocking."

Griff's eyes narrowed. "Ah, shit. I know that expression. What are you about to do?"

Reverend Will Hopkin sat by the desk in his study and stared out into the darkness. Night had fallen earlier than normal for October, hastened by the storm. Rain spattered against the window, echoing the crackling of burning logs from the open hearth behind him.

The Anglican church vicarage of St Illtyd's was a rambling stone grandfather of a house, grey at the temples, a little stooped and ar-thritic, but with many years left in it before it would require major surgery. It stood within its own modest grounds across the road from the west boundary of the church. Reverend Hopkin could see the dark shapes of the trees which screened the cemetery swaying in the wind.

A funeral had taken place that afternoon conducted by Father Moran, the priest from the Catholic Church of St Roberts in the adjoining parish. A kindly old man, though capable of being a little brusque. Reverend Hopkin sometimes wondered, though would chastise himself for a lack of generosity of spirit, whether the true focus of Father Moran's faith still lay in God and the Catholic Church or had been deflected to something far more earthly, some-thing that could be found in a bottle. Or perhaps it was the vow of chastity which made the elderly priest a touch grouchy on occasion. Such an enforced unnatural state could not be good for a man over so many years, thought the reverend.

He turned his attention back to the manuscript lying on the desk before him. It was bound in leather, once black but faded to a streaky grey by age, its pages yellow and waxy. The language of the handwritten lettering on the pages was a translation into Old Welsh of a series of petrified-wood carvings in Brythonic, the language of the British Isles before the successive invasions of the Romans and Anglo-Saxons.

Reverend Hopkin sighed heavily while his gaze followed the script. He already knew it by heart, as had his predecessors. Studying it more would not cast any further light on what was to come. The question was not if or how, but when.

He raised his head and looked out into the wild night. He could just make out the church as a deep black silhouette outlined against the inky sky and the trees which swayed more violently than before. It was too dark for him to notice the two shapes that detached themselves from the foot of the trees and made their way into the graveyard.

Four: A Grave Situation

"You do realise what night this is?" Griff sounded anxious.

"Friday night." David shrugged. "So what?"

"It's October thirty-first. Halloween. Not the best of nights to be blundering about a bloody graveyard."

"Seriously? You need to grow a pair."

"I have a big enough pair," Griff said stiffly. "But I don't like messing around with the supernatural. So, what's the plan? Stand around the grave and call to him? Draw a pentacle and find a goat to sacrifice? Take off all our clothes and dance naked in the rain?"

"You really are nervous. You always gabble when you're worried about something." David sighed. "This is starting to feel a little ridiculous. Look, we're almost there, as far as I can tell in this dark."

"We could use our phones to light the way."

"We could be seen. How would we explain what we're doing in a cemetery after hours?"

"It's not like we're equipped with shovels, or anything. We can say we've come to bid our last goodbyes to our dearly departed mate."

"I suppose. Still, I'd rather not have to explain anything about this to anyone. Let's just satisfy ourselves—"

"You, you mean. I'm already satisfied."

"Okay. Let's satisfy *me* there are no noises coming from the grave, then we'll piss off to the *Poacher's* and meet the others."

Griff sniffed. "But first let's get out of these sodden suits. Mine's made of wool and I'm starting to smell like an incontinent sheep."

Catherine Duffy saw her parents off, brushing off their attempts to stay and help her to tidy up.

"*Really,*" she told them for the fifth time as she shepherded them outside. "The worst is done and the rest can wait until tomorrow. I want to be alone."

Cath closed the door with a sigh, locked it and turned to survey

her home. *Her* home. What had been hers and Paul's now only belonged to her. Her face began to crumple and she waited for the
surge of sorrow to pass. She had cried so much over the past six
months, there couldn't be many tears left.

A couple of dark overcoats lay over the back of a chair where
their owners had discarded them.

*They belong to Dai and Griff. Strange they never came back after going to
speak to Father Moran.*

Cath shrugged. The boys would no doubt return for their coats
in the coming days.

She found a clean glass and sloshed the remains of a bottle of
red wine into it.

It was ridiculously early to go to bed; barely past six o'clock. But
she wanted to be somewhere that reminded her of Paul. Although
he hadn't slept in their bed for weeks, having spent his last days in
hospitals and hospices, she could still imagine him lying next to her.
Right now, she craved that crutch.

Nursing the glass like a comforting hand, she trudged upstairs.

David came to a halt. In the darkness, with rain gusting into his face,
the cemetery had become a place of shadow and vague shapes.
Gravestones and crosses and marble angels seemed monstrous and
alien and forbidding in the gloom.

"I think we're in the right place."

"Look, mate," said Griff, "I'm bloody drenched, I need a pee
and I'm fed up. We should be in a warm pub toasting Paul's memory,
not arsing about in the dark looking for his grave."

David sighed. "You're right. What was I thinking? But we might
as well be sure now we're here."

"Then let's be sure. I don't care who sees us. We need light."

David didn't object when Griff fumbled in his pocket, drew out
his phone and activated the torch function. Blinking in the bright
light, he glanced around.

"Yep," he said. "We're almost there."

Being careful to avoid other graves, shoes squelching on the sodden turf, they moved across the same ground over which hours earlier they had carried their friend's coffin to the accompaniment of a pop tune.

When the light of Griff's phone illuminated Paul's grave, they drew to a halt at the same time.

"Huh?" Griff squinted against the rain. "They haven't finished filling it?"

Behind the grave, barely picked out by Griff's phone, lay a muddy area where earlier a large pile of waiting soil had been masked beneath green tarpaulin. That pile had been shifted to form a neat, fresh mound of wet earth covering most of the hole into which they'd lowered their friend's remains. But near the head of the grave, in front of a crooked wooden cross, the mound had been disturbed. Clods of mud lay on the surrounding grass. A steep-sided hole, a couple of feet across, spoiled the uniformity of the mound.

Without speaking, David took Griff's phone from him. Griff didn't object; his eyes looked large and frightened. David stepped forward until he could shine the torch into the hole. The hole was deep, its sides glistening with rain, and falling earth had partially filled it, but the contrasting lightness of broken, splintered wood was unmistakable in the harsh gleam of the phone.

"They finished filling it, all right. But someone's come along and dug him up." Even as he spoke, David knew there was something not quite right with his words; something that didn't fit with what he had seen.

Griff's eyes grew wider and his mouth opened and closed like that of a stranded fish. He stepped to David's side and peered into the hole.

"Look at the coffin, Dai." His tone had changed from shock to something approaching awe. "Look at how the wood has been broken. It's splintered *up*wards. Paul hasn't been dug up. The coffin's been broken from the inside."

The wind howled around the old building, finding gaps in the crumbling mortar holding the stack together, whistling through rotting window frames. Reverend Hopkin switched the television off with a sigh. He couldn't settle to anything this evening.

A photograph on the mantel above the cold fireplace showed a dark-haired, fresh-faced, smiling version of himself alongside a young woman holding a pink, chubby baby in her arms.

The woman and child had long gone, at first to her parents in Chester. After that, who knew? He had never made any effort to find out and she had never tried to contact him, other than through solicitors to obtain her divorce. The child could by now be a mother herself. Perhaps he was unknowingly a grandfather. The thought lent him no cheer.

As though it had happened yesterday, he could still see her standing in front of the fireplace, her cheeks flushed, trying to keep her voice low so not to wake the toddler sleeping upstairs. The toddler suffering with tonsillitis who would come sniffling into their bed at three in the morning, forcing him to move to the put-up couch in the spare room. Not that this was a big deal—he and she might have continued to share a bed, but hadn't slept as man and wife in over a year.

"Will," she said. "We can't stay. It's stifling. It would do your sanity good to come with us, but my mind's made up. We're going with or without you."

"You *know* I can't leave. The Burden—"

"Pfft!" She silenced him with the force of her frustration. Worse was the contempt he saw in her eyes. "All that mumbo-jumbo, sacred task, passed down the centuries bull*shit!*" Spittle flew from her lips in a fine spray. She glared at him, her cheeks aflame.

He didn't trust himself to speak for fear of inflaming her further, but gazed back in mute appeal, imploring her to stay with his eyes. Besides, he had tried all the words he knew.

Her shoulders sagged as the fire in her died. "Will, you should hear yourself." The lack of passion in her voice was worse; it made the contempt deeper, more cutting. "You sound like a fucking lunatic."

The next day, she walked out with barely another word spoken.

The child peered back at him over her shoulder, expressionless.

He mentally shook himself, forcing his mind back to the present.

The present. All Hallows' Eve. The night when the ancient Celts, who once inhabited these lands, believed the boundary between this world and the next grew thin enough to allow passage between the two.

He shivered, stood and walked into his study. There he kept the fire banked in inclement weather, making it the cosiest room in the house. The leather-bound manuscript lay on the desk where he'd left it, but he barely glanced at it. A sense of foreboding had been growing all day. A sense that something was approaching with the unstoppable force of a tumbling boulder.

It could, at last, be happening.

Five: Footprints in the Dark

G riff clutched David's forearms, his fingers digging in painfully. "Ouch! Let go, mun."

Griff's eyes were wild in the light from his phone. "Fucking hell, Dai! It's not even possible." He let go and peered into the hole. "Look at that coffin. Remember how heavy it was. It's made from oak or teak or something. Wood, anyway. Solid bloody wood." He turned back to David. "We both went to see him before the end. It was, er…"

"Six days ago," said David quietly. "And I know what you're going to say. There's no way he would have the strength to break out of that coffin."

"Too bloody right. He was barely seven stone soaking wet. He was being fed by drips. Even if it's possible they somehow mistook him for dead when he was alive and he survived three days of being kept in a fridge, he couldn't have punched through solid wood. And never mind the coffin. How in the hell could he have pushed through six feet of wet earth?"

David shrugged. "He couldn't, but it looks like he did."

Griff shook his head slowly, like a bewildered bear.

"So where is he now?"

David handed Griff's phone back to him. He took out his own phone and activated the torch function.

"You look in that direction." David nodded towards the disturbed head of the grave. He shone his light beyond the foot. "I'll look this way."

"What? We can't split up. Don't you ever watch horror films?"

David began to smile until he saw his friend's expression. "You're really terrified, aren't you?"

"How are you *not*?"

"It's our friend. It's Paul."

"Our dead friend."

"Come on, mun. I've seen you down blokes twice your size on a rugby field. And like you said, Paul was seven stone soaking wet."

Griff's eyes narrowed and he exhaled heavily. "Whatever came out of that hole in the ground, whatever burst through that coffin and six feet of mud, it wasn't Paul."

"Well, there was nobody else in there." He thought for a moment while Griff turned away, aiming his light beyond the grave. "You're right. Maybe it would be better if we approached him together."

"There's no need to split up." Griff's tone had turned flat, inflectionless.

"What d'you mean?"

"Look." Griff nodded at where his light illuminated the grass beyond the crooked cross.

The area alongside the grave was a little churned, the grass flattened and patches of mud showing through, presumably from where the gravediggers had been working.

Beyond the dishevelled area, something different showed at the limit of the light cast by the phone. Glistening wetly, a little faint as though partially washed away by the rain, a line of muddy footprints led away from the grave.

"Oh."

Since discovering the disturbed grave, David had felt oddly calm, as though this was an everyday occurrence. Only now, at the sight of the footprints, did the first sensation of something being fundamentally wrong make itself felt.

Griff stared at the footprints. "What are we going to do?" His voice remained oddly devoid of emotion.

"We have to follow them, of course."

"Yeah. That's what I thought you'd say."

Sleep eluded Cath Duffy. Though emotionally drained and despite the glass of red wine, her mind stubbornly remained alert. It didn't help that that bloody song with its catchy sax line kept playing over and over in her head. Hardly a song, she supposed, with its one-word title cried exultantly a few times throughout. Tune, then.

She reached out and switched on her bedside lamp. When she could focus again without blinking, she turned to her side and gazed at the photo standing on the bedside cabinet the other side of the bed. The surface of the cabinet was otherwise empty. Gone was the tottering pile of books about apocalypse and alien invasion and space colonisation—he'd loved his science fiction, had Paul—and the scattering of shrapnel, as he'd called loose change.

Stripped of the minor trappings of a life cut short, the cabinet looked impersonal. Sterile. Apart from the photograph.

It was her favourite one of her late husband, snapped on her iPhone during their honeymoon in Corfu, printed off and framed when he had gone into hospital for the last time three weeks ago. Deep down, where the truth can't be denied, she had known he wasn't going to return home.

Paul grinned out at her, sunglasses pushed onto his head preventing his thatch of normally tawny hair, bleached to straw by the sun, lifting in the balmy breeze. The two weeks of unaccustomed sunlight had turned his eyes from their usual pale ice-green to a deep emerald above a nose adorned with a scattering of freckles. He looked the picture of health and happiness.

"My love," she murmured, "you didn't half cause a stir with your choice of funeral music."

Not so much a choice as a steadfast insistence.

"It's a chirpy tune," he'd said, during one of his lucid moments when the cocktail of painkillers allowed a glimpse of the real Paul to emerge.

"It's inappropriate," said his mother from the foot of the hospice bed, her lips tightening into a white line.

Paul glanced at her. "Mum, I love you dearly, but this isn't your call." He grinned; with his sallow, sunken cheeks and deathly pallor, it might have been construed by those who didn't know him as a grimace, but Cath recognised the cheeky, almost impish character she'd fallen in love with. "You're missing a chance at a great one-liner, you know, Mum. This is where you shrug and say, 'It's your funeral'."

"Really, Paul, this is *not* a joking matter." Even in the extremes of her son's suffering, she couldn't set aside her stone-carved, prudish convictions of what best befitted any occasion. Cath found her dislike for the woman edging towards contempt and worse.

"Mum, you couldn't be more wrong," said Paul. "Death is the ultimate joke."

"Come now, son," said Paul's father. He sat next to his wife on a padded bench drawn up to the foot of Paul's bed. "Don't upset your mother like this."

Cath had to bite down hard to prevent the response flying from her lips. *You wimp. You* fucking *wimp. Always taking her side, letting her take the lead and following along like a lost lamb. Man up and dare to think an original thought.*

Paul turned to her and grasped her hand. With rare strength, he held it tight and gazed into her eyes. "Never mind what they say. Never mind what anyone says. I want to go into the ground to that tune, not to some dirge which will make everyone depressed." For the last time, his gaze grew more intense; over the final days he had left, during rare periods of consciousness, his eyes lost their glint, the lively personality within cowed at last beneath the weight of decay and pain and chemicals. "Promise me, Cath, you'll sort it. *Promise* me."

She whispered loud enough for him alone to hear, "I promise."

And she'd kept her word, despite stern opposition.

She smiled back at Paul's image and closed her eyes, the jaunty tune still in her head now a comfort rather than an irritation.

The muddy footprints led them towards the edge of the cemetery, which was bounded by a high stone wall. A mature alder towered higher than the wall, still retaining most of its leaves. A bench had been placed next to the wall to enjoy peaceful views of the cemetery and to take advantage of the summer shade provided by the tree.

David and Griff approached side by side, their phone lights illuminating the sopping ground ahead. The footprints grew fainter but remained visible, glistening wetly in the rain. They didn't lead in a straight line, but meandered a little from side to side as though whoever had made them was intoxicated. The occasional small clod of mud had fallen to the ground alongside the marks.

By unspoken consent, they slowed as they neared the boundary wall. A narrow concrete path led from the church to the bench; the footprints joined the path and then remained, in a weaving sort of way, on it.

Griff noticed the bench first. He gasped and came to a dead stop. His hand once more gripped David's forearm painfully.

"Ouch! Will you stop…" David's words tailed away as he, too, saw.

The light from their phones reached the small concrete hardstanding upon which the bench had been placed. A pair of mud-caked shoes and the lower portion of dark trousers legs, liberally spattered in mud, were revealed by the light.

"Oh crap shit fuck," muttered Griff.

David grabbed his friend's hand and tugged it loose from his arm. "Come on."

It looked as though it took a tremendous effort for Griff to tear his gaze away from the shoes and legs. He turned wide-eyed to David.

"I don't know if I can go any further."

"That's okay. You stay here. But I'm going." He took a step towards the bench.

"Wait! You're not leaving me here on my own." Griff took a few exaggerated breaths. "Oh dear God. Come on then."

Together they moved slowly forward.

Six: Returned

A slight, hunched figure of a man was revealed by the light of their phones. He sat on the bench, huddled over, arms supported by thighs as though he did not possess the strength to sit upright. A dark suit, daubed liberally with mud, clung loosely to an emaciated frame. The head hung forward, muddy water dripping from lank, tawny hair.

The wind was slackening, no longer spattering rain into their faces. They drew to within a few yards of the bench and came to a stop.

Griff took short, sharp breaths, like a panting dog. David, by contrast, had grown calm once more. The sense of wrongness remained, but he did not feel afraid. Paul Duffy had been his best friend since they had sat next to each other in infants' school in short trousers, scraped knees bumping together when they turned to each other to discuss in excited whispers the latest episode of *The X-Files*. They had got up to mischief and into trouble side by side. They had got each other out of countless scrapes. Once or twice, they had fought each other, but the rare fallings out made their bond stronger.

And best mates didn't freak out and run in the opposite direction, even when the other appeared to have arisen from the grave.

"Paul?" said David hesitantly. "Is-is that you?"

The figure on the bench lifted its head slowly. Griff uttered a low moan.

Paul Duffy looked up at them.

The sense of foreboding growing inside Reverend Will Hopkin changed in nature. What had begun that morning as a general sense of unease cranked up a notch at a time as the afternoon wore on, like a spring being slowly ratcheted taut. The darkness of a stormy autumnal evening turned the vicar's disquiet to apprehension. From there, it was a short step to full-blown trepidation.

The fire crackled in the hearth. Reverend Hopkin gazed into the flames.

Fire. That, according to the ancient manuscript lying on his desk, was the only thing which could end this once and for all.

Purification.

The one who first held this ancient office—who had, in effect, inaugurated it—had employed another of the elements, earth, in the mistaken belief it would be as effective as flame. Not so; earth imprisoned, not destroyed.

So said the record and so Reverend Hopkin believed. He was, if nothing else, a man of faith.

He recognised the dichotomy. A man of the church with a deep belief in writings that predated Christianity. A vicar whose creed was shaped by a mandate laid down when paganism held sway in these lands. A man of God following the testament of what would be described as druidism.

It made no difference—he had no trouble squaring it with himself. Reverend Hopkin's church might be named after a Christian saint, but it occupied a site which had been holy for centuries before the eponymous saint trod these parts. Christianity, Islam, paganism, the Old Testament, ancient Egypt, the Greeks, the Romans, they all had certain things in common. The number of deities might differ, but they all preached the existence of a higher power that shaped the lives of mortal man.

He held an unshakeable belief in the powers of goodness, of mercy, of compassion. Whether you called the embodiment of that belief Yahweh or Allah or The Dagda or Apollo or Zeus was, in Reverend Hopkin's considered and private opinion, irrelevant. It was the belief that was all-important.

And if you held faith in goodness, it followed that you believed in the opposite. For without evil, there could be no balance.

Reverend Hopkin needed no faded manuscripts to convince him of the existence of evil. He merely had to watch the daily news. But what he believed he would soon have to face was not something that would make the evening news. An ancient evil had returned.

This was no longer a matter of faith to Reverend Hopkin—it had grown to become a certainty.

He gazed into the flames and waited.

Rain washed rivulets of mud down sunken cheeks. Strands of hair lay straggly along the brow. Pale eyes, seeming impossibly large in such a diminished face, gazed at them uncomprehendingly.

"Paul?" A flicker of doubt passed through David like a shudder.

"He doesn't look like he knows who the fuck he is," said Griff in a low voice. "Maybe because it's not really him…"

David glanced at Griff and silenced him with a curt shake of his head. He looked back to the figure on the bench and took a step closer.

"You're Paul. Paul Duffy. And you must remember me. It's David. David Owen." He motioned towards Griff. "This is Ian Griffiths. We've called him Griff for as long as I can remember. We…" David's voice tailed away.

The blank face staring up at them didn't change expression. No flicker of recognition showed.

David felt Griff step to his side.

"Look at his hands." Griff's voice remained low.

Paul's hands hung down loosely between parted thighs. Or what remained of his hands. They were misshapen, mangled, skin broken in countless places allowing splintered bone to show through. A thick substance, which looked black in the light from their phones, oozed around the protruding bones. The rain struggled to wash it away. Only in the drops falling sporadically from the tips of what remained recognisably as fingers did the substance appear red.

Griff raised his voice. "Paul? It's us. Your mates. We carried your coffin this afternoon and lowered it into the ground. You died and we buried you. We've just come from your wake."

Still nothing except a blank stare.

Griff breathed out heavily. "Dai, what are we going to do? We need to call someone. But who? The police? An ambulance? Who the hell do you call when your dead friend busts out of his grave—

Ghostbusters?"

David shook his head; he was beginning to think Griff might be right and they needed to call someone. The thought of ringing Cath crossed his mind, but he quickly dismissed it. Until they knew the figure sitting before them was Paul in spirit as well as body, and not some empty shell—a word tried to force its way into his mind and he pushed it away—they ought to keep Cath out of it.

He looked at Griff and shrugged. Griff opened his mouth to say more, when a noise made them both turn back to the bench.

Paul's mouth was trying to form a word. All that came out was an incomprehensible croak, the sound the hinges of an unoiled gate might make.

He tried again, face contorting with effort. And again, and at last something discernible could be made out amidst the guttural noises.

"Few…null…"

"Few-null?" David repeated.

Paul gave an almost imperceptible nod.

"Few-null," he said, his speech growing more recognisable with each attempt.

"Ah," said Griff. "Funeral. Is that what you're saying?"

"Ess. Fewnull."

"This afternoon," said Griff. "Your funeral was this afternoon."

Paul's face bore a look of intense concentration while he struggled to get the words out.

"Did…yew pay… Tuh… kluh…"

"Did we pay…?" repeated Griff.

"No," said David. "He's trying to say 'play'." He nodded vigorously. "Yes, Paul. We played 'Tequila' at your funeral. Cath insisted on it."

The corners of Paul's mouth turned up into a ghost of a smile.

Part Two: Water

Seven: Cats' Eyes

David stepped to the bench and sat next to his best friend. He raised an arm with the intention of hugging Paul, but thought better of it: the man looked frail enough to be crushed like a brittle meringue. He adopted the same pose, sitting forward with his forearms resting on his thighs, and turned his head to regard Paul.

"What happened, mate?" David asked softly. "How have you, er… come back?"

Paul turned his head towards David. Tendons in his neck creaked like old timbers. His mouth worked.

"De-d."

David nodded. "You succumbed to the big C three days ago."

"Sti…"

"Go on, mate. Try again."

"Sti-ll."

David felt his brow crease in puzzlement. "Still?"

Paul's head jerked as he gave another nod; they were becoming more vigorous, perhaps as the tendons in his neck stretched.

David glanced up at Griff, who was watching them warily. "What does he mean? Still what?"

"Isn't it obvious? Still dead."

"No…"

David's denial faded. Paul's head was making the small, jerky motion again. More insistently.

He looked up at Griff once more. "That's bullshit. He's sitting here talking to us. How can he still be dead?"

Griff hadn't moved from his position some yards away. He nodded curtly towards Paul.

"You heard him say it. From the horse's mouth, so to speak. Or should I say from the mouth of the—"

David raised his hand, palm out, so sharply Griff's words cut off as though the hand had clamped around his mouth.

"Don't," said David. "Don't you dare say that word."

"You know me, Dai. I call a spade a spade."

"Not now, Griff." David let out a heavy sigh. "Let's get him away from here."

"Get him away…? What are you talking about? We *have* to call somebody. And now, before our phones run out of juice."

David shook his head so vehemently drops of water sprayed over Paul. He didn't seem to notice.

Griff's expression hardened, turned stony. He opened his mouth to speak, but David beat him to it.

"No, Griff, don't say any more. I know you're right. Of course we have to call somebody."

"Okay. Good. So who?"

"Let's get him away from here first. Somewhere warm and out of this rain. My place is the closest."

Griff's eyes narrowed in suspicion. "Why?"

"Why what?"

"You know very well what I mean. We're in a graveyard with a man who's risen from the grave and, by his own admission, is still dead, and you want to take him home? We're not discussing an abandoned puppy."

"No, he's not an abandoned puppy, Griff, he's our *friend*. And friends look out for each other."

"When they're alive, yes. When they're dead, not so much."

"He's not dead, Griff. I don't care what he says. If he's sitting up and talking, he's alive. If we get him back to my place, get him cleaned up and into dry clothes—and we could do with the same—*then* we can decide who to call. All right?"

Griff breathed out heavily. "I don't know about dry clothes. I could do with a beer or ten."

David slipped his arm under Paul's and helped him to stand. It was like lifting a bushel of dried sticks. Cracks and pops came from Paul's knees, back, hips; if it moved, it made the sound of a spitting fire.

Griff did not offer to help. He seemed reluctant to get within two yards of Paul. It didn't matter. Paul had never been of bulky build. The disease had eaten away at him until he'd resembled a neglected scarecrow. David suspected his weight, such as it was, largely consisted of the soaking suit hanging from his wasted frame like a wet towel draped over a hat stand.

David had deactivated the torch and slipped the phone back into his pocket to free both hands to assist Paul. They proceeded in the light of Griff's phone. He went a couple of paces ahead.

David ran his arm around Paul's back and under his furthest arm. With Paul's nearest arm draped around his neck, kept there by gripping his wrist, being careful not to grip too hard and break something, being even more careful not to touch the ruined hands or the dark gloop dripping from them, David steered him along the path. Paul moved jerkily, accompanied by a series of crackling, popping sounds. But he was compliant and light, and David managed to support him easily.

A couple of things nagged at him; things out of kilter over and above the general sense of wrongness. He tried to push the thoughts away but they were insistent.

First, the smell. On the edge of detection, but present, like something in the fridge starting to spoil. Second, Paul's armpit. If someone were to grip David beneath his arm, it would feel feverishly hot, despite the rain and cold. Yet he sensed no heat emanating from his friend. He might have been supporting a mannequin.

He tried not to think and concentrated on keeping Paul on the path. Until the muddy prints coming towards them deviated away across the grass.

He came to a stop. "Wait!" he called to Griff.

"What's wrong?"

"Come and hold Paul for a moment. I need to do something."

"What do you need to do?" Griff's eyes narrowed to slits.

"Nothing much. I'll be a minute. Two, tops. Come and hold him."

Griff shook his head. "Uh-uh." He looked at Paul. "Sorry, mate, if it really is you. I'm really sorry, but I'm not coming near you." He looked back at David, the expression in his eyes approaching shame, but his jaw set in a determined line.

David sighed. "Okay." He half-turned so he could look at Paul. "Paul, listen to me. I'm going to let you go. Can you stand on your own?"

A slight jerk of the head.

David brought Paul's arm from around his neck and allowed it to dangle, and slipped his arm from around him. Paul swayed, but remained upright. His head drooped forward as though he lacked strength with which to hold it upright.

David glanced at Griff. "I won't be long."

Griff shrugged. "Whatever."

David used the torch on his phone to find his way back to Paul's grave. He surveyed it for a moment, wondering whether he could achieve his task without getting his suit covered in mud; it was the only one he owned. With a shrug, he sank to his knees. He propped his phone against the crooked cross so its light spilled across the disturbed head of the grave.

Using only his hands at first, then his forearms, too, he swept clods of sticky earth into the hole. Apart from the cloying nature of the mud, it was easier than he'd anticipated.

Before long, the grave looked whole once more. He patted down the replaced soil and retrieved his phone. He straightened the wooden cross and reviewed his work. Perhaps the gravediggers would notice the site had been disturbed, but he doubted anyone else would. And maybe the continuing rainfall would help to heal the scar left by the displaced earth. Already, the soil he'd replaced was melding into its surroundings.

The arms of David's suit felt as though they'd been dipped in treacle. He rubbed the excess mud from his sleeves and hands on the wet grass.

With a satisfied nod, he made his way back to the others.

They were standing in darkness. That is, Griff was standing on the path where he'd left him. Alone.

"Where is he?" David hissed. "And why are you in the dark?"

"My phone's out of juice. As for your mate, he's over there."

Your mate, David noticed, but made no comment. He shone his phone towards where Griff had indicated.

Paul was sitting on a raised concrete grave. In his ruined hands he somehow clutched a container. It looked like a vase in which mourners placed flowers. He held the vase to his face and was drinking from it. Greedily. Water ran from his chin and down the front of his shirt.

"He's on his second," said Griff, his voice without inflection.

"I know that tone," David said, tearing his gaze away to look at Griff. "What's wrong?" He held up a hand. "I mean, what's *particularly* wrong? Something's happened since I left you."

Griff gazed back at David, his skin looking washed out in the stark light from David's phone. His mouth worked soundlessly as though rehearsing what he was going to say. No; that wasn't it. Drawing in a sharp breath, David realised his friend was struggling to talk due to paralysing fear.

He glanced about. Apart from Paul sitting on the gravestone glugging dirty water from a vase, there was nothing unusual to see. He turned back to Griff.

"What, Griff? What happened? Tell me."

Griff's mouth worked again and this time words came out.

"His eyes."

"What about them?"

"I don't care what you say, but whatever that is over there, it's not human."

"*What happened?*"

"His eyes," Griff repeated. "Just after you'd left me on my own with him, before my phone died, he suddenly went all stiff. Like a poker. His head turned from side to side, making his neck sound like breakfast cereal when you pour the milk on."

"Huh."

"He was looking for water. I was glad he wasn't looking for me." Griff shivered.

"His eyes? What about his eyes?"

"That was the worst part. Oh, Dai, they were frigging horrible."

"How?"

"You ever looked closely at a seagull? Seen their eyes? All yellow and alien. That's what his eyes were like, only a sickly yellow, like something you'd get out of an infected wound. But…"

"Go on."

"The *absolute* worst part was they were all lit up. Glowing like cats' eyes in headlights."

David frowned. He was seeing a new side to Griff tonight, one he hadn't suspected existed. A fanciful, slightly hysterical side.

"Yellow, glowing eyes?" He couldn't keep the scepticism from his voice.

Griff uttered a short laugh, completely without humour. "Scoff all you want, but I know what I saw." He glanced towards Paul, who looked to have emptied the vase of water; he simply sat on the grave, head bowed once more to his chest. "Whatever that is sitting on that grave, it isn't Paul. I don't know what it is, but it isn't Paul."

Eight: Healing Hands

Griff carried David's phone to light their path until they had exited through the little-used side gate. When they were standing on the pavement in the pale wash of sodium streetlights, Griff turned off the torch and slipped the phone into a pocket of David's jacket. He scooted back a yard or two as soon as he'd let go of the phone.

The breeze dropped and the rain turned to drizzle, shrouding the evening in a fine mist. It remained wet enough, David hoped, to discourage anyone from being outside. At first, he was in luck. The streets were deserted. If they had earlier been busy with children in damp ghost and witch outfits, and fussing parents struggling to hold umbrellas against the wind, the evening was drawing on and the trick or treat activity had subsided. The only social attractions in the village which might draw pedestrians—the pub and rugby club— lay in a different direction. The village shop would have closed more than an hour ago. The only engines they heard sounded distant; no vehicles passed them.

As though the water he'd consumed acted like lubricant, Paul's joints stopped making the noises of a log fire. His walking motion became steadier, more natural, and David no longer needed to support him as if Paul was drunk. Instead, he linked his arm through Paul's and bent his arm to his chest, so Paul's was held lightly but firmly in his own and he could steady him should he stagger. Griff trudged along a few yards behind them, saying nothing.

David lived in a terraced house in a small row of identical properties at the edge of the village, overlooking common land. The road petered out into a dirt track leading onto the common. Except for those belonging to residents or delivery drivers, vehicles rarely went down there—any driver who took a wrong turn would either have to perform a three-point turn and retrace his steps, or enter the narrow lane that ran behind the terrace parallel to the road. David gave a silent sigh of relief when they turned into his street. They had encountered nobody thus far and it was only another fifty yards to his front door.

"Aw, shit." He came to a halt. "It's Mrs Jones. One of my neighbours."

Along the pavement towards them came a woman. In one hand, she clutched her headscarf tight beneath her chin against the rain; in the other, she held a lead. The lead ended in a Jack Russell, which trotted along beside her.

"She's a right nosy one is Mrs Jones," said David in a low voice. "What shall we do?"

"Give her the fright of her life?" said Griff.

"Ha frigging ha."

David blew out his cheeks and cast around for an idea. There was no time—Mrs Jones was almost upon them, slowing down no doubt to pretend to be neighbourly while trying to find out what they were doing out and about on a foul night such as this.

In desperation, David stepped off the pavement and into the road, swinging Paul around to face out towards the common. He let go of Paul's arm and stepped in front of him. Gripping him by his wasted biceps, he lowered him to a seated position on the kerb. A salvo of mini firecrackers went off as Paul's knees bent beyond the right angle.

"Lower your head," David hissed at Paul. "And don't try to speak."

Paul's head bowed forward, arms resting on his raised thighs. This meant his mangled hands were out of sight, hidden by the shadows of his legs.

David glanced at Griff. "Pretend he's pissed, okay?"

Griff didn't reply. He was watching the approaching woman, his face set into an unnatural smile.

"Good evening, boys," said Mrs Jones cheerfully, coming to a stop.

"Evening, Mrs Jones," said David.

"All right, love?" said Griff, his tone matching the woman's for cheeriness.

David took a sideways glance at Griff. He never called anyone 'love'. The smile had grown wider, becoming ghastly, like the grin of a clown with sharpened teeth. His eyes were big and round, glittering darkly in the muted glow of the streetlights.

"It's a wet night for you boys to be out," said Mrs Jones. "And in your best suits, too. But, bless you, it was your friend's funeral today, wasn't it? That poor boy." She clutched her headscarf tighter. "Oh, and that poor, poor girl. So young to be a widow."

"You knew Paul then, love?" said Griff.

"Only by sight and name," Mrs Jones replied. "The same as I know you, Ian. It's a small village, isn't it? The sort of place where everyone knows everyone."

You make it your business to know David thought. Before the onset of his illness, Paul had been a frequent visitor to his house. Griff, too, and, less frequently, Cath and most of his other friends. Many had remarked that the curtains of Mrs Jones's house had twitched as they'd passed.

Her gaze lingered for a moment on David, resting upon the muddy sleeves of his jacket, before sliding to Paul's back, also streaked with mud, where it remained.

David cleared his throat to say something, but a noise intervened. A low, rumbling noise, like an engine distantly idling.

"Hisht, Scamp," muttered Mrs Jones, without moving her gaze from Paul's back. She gave an impatient shake of the lead. The noise died away as quickly as it had started.

David glanced at the dog. At the scruff of its neck, the fur stood up like the bristles of a brush. It stared at Paul, its teeth bared in a silent snarl.

"Your friend," said Mrs Jones, "looks familiar."

"Oh, you'd be surprised," said Griff. "Not necessarily a pleasant one, at that."

David shot his friend a dark look and spoke hurriedly. "He's Paul's cousin. I suppose there is a family resemblance."

Griff snorted. "A striking resemblance, you could say."

Mrs Jones tore her gaze from Paul. It moved between David and Griff, her eyes narrowing.

"Does he speak?" She took half a pace towards the kerb as though to step out into the road so she could look at Paul face-on. But her dog began to growl again and set its claws to the pavement. She would have to physically drag the creature to get it to move any nearer Paul.

"Hisht now, Scamp," she said. "I don't know what's got into you this evening. It must be all the spirits roaming the land on this Eve of Hallows."

Silently thanking the dog, David stepped into the road. "He's had a little too much to drink," he told Mrs Jones. "We're taking him home to sleep it off."

Paul's head came up to look at him. For a moment, David imagined he saw a flush of colour bloom in Paul's eyes. The colour of rancid custard. "Food…" Paul said in a croaky voice. "Water…"

"Yes, yes," said David. He shot Mrs Jones an uncertain smile. "He's got the munchies."

He stooped to place his arms under Paul's and heaved. "Up you come, Pa—ul's cousin."

David glanced at Mrs Jones. If she'd noticed his mistake, she didn't remark upon it. She watched him with a neutral expression. Guarded. She made no move to continue on her way.

Paul stood with his back to her, swaying gently. David stepped around him to stand between him and Mrs Jones, and linked his arm through Paul's. He turned Paul to face forward, being careful to keep her view obstructed.

"Must get him home," he said. "Bye, then, Mrs Jones." He looked beyond her to where Griff stood, and made a pointed expression. "Come on, Griff. Let's get Martin back to my place."

"Martin?" Griff's face became so filled with puzzlement David could cheerfully have slapped it.

"Yes." David was afraid to catch Mrs Jones's eye. "Martin. You know, Paul's cousin Martin."

"Oh." Griff's expression cleared as comprehension dawned. He turned to Mrs Jones. "Yes, we'd better get, um, Martin home. 'Night, love. Watch out for all those roaming spirits."

Without daring to look at Mrs Jones again, David got Paul moving. The road between them and his house was clear.

He waited until the front door was firmly closed behind them, before rounding on Griff.

"What the hell? What the bloody hell did you think you were doing? You might as well have come right out and told that woman Paul's come back from the dead."

Griff shrugged. His glance kept darting to Paul. "This is not something people aren't going to find out about. You know that, right?"

All at once, David felt dog-tired, lacking the energy to remain angry with Griff. He let out a deep sigh. "I suppose."

"Besides, we're going to call someone soon, aren't we?"

David grunted and looked away. "We need to get him out of those wet clothes."

Paul's head turned towards David. "Food…"

"Right, okay," said David. "Food first." He looked at Griff. "What do you give someone who's been dead for three days?"

"Bread? Fish?" Griff's voice rose in pitch and his eyes took on a manic glint. "Give him a glass of water. Perhaps he'll turn it into wine."

David frowned. "You need to stop freaking out, man. He isn't the Second Coming. It's Paul. Our friend."

"Nah, you're right. I went to Sunday School. They never mentioned Jesus's eyes glowing like a freaking alien's."

"Griff, chill, okay?" David thought for a moment. "I guess soup is the safest bet."

After installing Paul in an armchair in the living room, David heated a tin of soup and tore up some bread into small chunks, which he placed in the bowl, before pouring the soup over it. When he returned to the living room carrying the bowl of soup and a glass of water, Griff had removed his soaking suit jacket and sat down in the chair furthest away from Paul.

When Paul saw the glass, he sat forward, reaching for it with his mangled hands. The dark substance seemed to have stopped oozing and had congealed, giving his hands the appearance of those of a severe-burns victim.

Paul clutched the glass awkwardly and raised it to his lips, draining half of the contents in one go. David knelt on the floor in front of the armchair. He began spooning soup and bread into Paul's eager mouth.

A damp odour came from Paul. Beneath it lay the other smell. Faint and unpleasant.

"I thought they gummed their lips and eyes," remarked Griff.

"Huh?"

"Undertakers. I thought they gummed the lips and eyes of corpses to make sure they don't spring open during viewings in the chapel of rest and frighten the shit out of everyone. Or sew them shut, even."

David shook his head, not looking away from Paul. He ate greedily, slurping the contents from the spoon as soon as David raised it to his lips. "He wasn't put on view. Cath didn't want it."

When Griff spoke again, David was relieved to hear the manic note had gone. "We need to call her, Dai. If we don't call anybody else, we need to call Cath."

"Not tonight. You saw her after the funeral. She's exhausted. We can't spring this on her in that state. She needs a good rest."

"Then we tell her tomorrow." It wasn't a question and David knew Griff was right.

"Yes. Tomorrow."

The last of the soup disappeared into Paul's mouth. Paul raised the glass and drained it. Spilled water washed away the soup which had dribbled from the corners of his mouth.

"Well, that didn't touch the sides." David carried the empty bowl and glass into the kitchen. He returned to the living room with two opened bottles of beer. He handed one to Griff.

"Cheers," Griff said, taking a deep slug. He belched. "That hits the spot."

David raised his bottle and took a long sip. Griff was right.

"I suppose I should get him some dry clothes," he began. "And perhaps we ought to…"

He tailed off as he noticed his friend's expression. Griff had frozen with his bottle half-raised, his gaze fixed on Paul. David turned to follow it and let out an involuntary gasp.

Paul sat back in the armchair like a satisfied diner, looking down at his lap. The off-yellow glare coming from his eyes spilled down his chest, giving his white shirt a sickly pallor.

"See?" said Griff. "I told you they fucking glow."

David ignored him. "Paul?" He took a hesitant step closer.

Paul did not look up. He seemed intent on his lap, where his hands lay. And there came new sounds…

Crunching, grinding, followed by an earthier, meatier sound, similar to the one made when tearing a drumstick from a roasted chicken.

"Look at his hands." Griff sounded breathless. "Fuck me, Dai, look at his hands."

Paul's hands were changing. The dried, black gloop had gone, concealed by new skin. The bones were knitting, moving beneath the surface like a tangle of worms. The fingers straightened, crackling and popping as they moved back into place.

Bathed in the tainted glow spilling from Paul's eyes, the skin covering the transforming phalanges and metacarpals appeared stained, like parchment over which yellow ink has spilled. Then the light faded and the skin of his hands took on a pink hue.

Robustly pink. And the hands no longer writhed and made sounds. They lay lightly on Paul's lap, whole and undamaged.

Nine: Not Alone

Bright spots of colour appeared high on Griff's cheeks. He stared at David with a mixture of incredulity and fear etched across his features.

"Dai, you saw what just happened. His hands were like raw mincemeat. Now look at them. We have to call someone. Whatever's happening here, it's too big for us to handle." Griff tipped back the bottle of beer and drained it. He set the empty bottle down on the coffee table in front of him with a bang.

Paul remained sitting back in the armchair, head bowed.

"Look," said David, "I've already agreed we should call Cath tomorrow. But, seriously, who else can we call?"

Griff shrugged. "The police."

"Why? No crime's been committed."

"How do we know that? An ambulance, then."

"I agree he should probably be checked out by a doctor, but it's the weekend. It can wait until Monday."

"His parents. Surely they have a right to know their son has apparently returned from the dead."

"Yeah, I agree. But I think that's Cath's decision, not ours."

Griff threw out an arm in frustration. "A fucking priest, then."

"What, like Father Moran? He wouldn't believe us. And what could he do, anyway?"

"What do *you* suggest, Dai?"

"I suggest sleeping on it. Decide about contacting Cath in the morning."

"Hold on. We've already agreed we *will* call Cath in the morning. If we don't involve anyone else, she *has* to know."

David said nothing.

Griff breathed out heavily and his shoulders sagged in resignation. "Where's he going to stay tonight? Here?"

"Don't see why not. I don't have a spare bedroom but he can sleep on the sofa. It's comfy and he doesn't take up much room."

"Don't you have work in the morning?"

"Nah, got tomorrow off, as well as today. I had time coming."

"Well, rather you than me, mate." Griff stood. "I'm going to leave you to it, then."

"Where you going? To the *Poacher's*?"

Griff shook his head. "Can't face seeing the others right now. And I'd never be able to keep this from them. Think I'll head home." He gave a short laugh. "Just as well we're both between relationships right now."

David pulled a face and nodded. "You're welcome to spend the night here, if you want. Leave Paul in the chair and you can have the sofa."

Griff's face twisted. "You've got to be fucking kidding. Spend the night with a frigging zo—"

"No! *Don't* call him that."

"Okay, man, okay. But, no matter how much you object, it's what he is."

David felt the flush rise above his collar. He could barely manage to keep his tone level. "No, Griff, you couldn't be more wrong. I don't know how you can say such a thing about one of your best friends."

Griff stared at him for a long moment. "My friend didn't have glow-in-the-dark eyes. My friend didn't have bones and flesh which heal themselves in seconds when broken. My friend died." He pointed towards Paul without looking at him. "Call that thing sitting in the chair whatever you want. Call him Paul if you like. But don't call him my friend."

Griff turned to David standing in the doorway. "I'll come back in the morning to make sure he hasn't eaten your brains in the night." He held up a hand. "I'm kidding." His eyes narrowed. "But we'll call Cath, yeah?"

David glanced away into the darkness and sighed. When he looked back, Griff's eyes had become slits. "I agreed we would."

Griff considered him for a long moment, before nodding. "Okay.

See you in the morning." He turned and strode away into the drizzle-misted night.

David shut and locked his front door. He shivered; he needed to get out of his damp clothes.

Paul remained sitting in the armchair, hands dangling loosely between his thighs. Hale, healthy hands. He looked up as David entered the living room.

"Food?"

Again a flash of yellow in his eyes, gone almost as soon as it had appeared. David could almost convince himself he'd imagined it. Almost.

"Yeah," he said. "Soon. But we have to get out of these wet clothes first and get clean. Your hair is covered in mud and I've not been this dirty since I first attempted to change the oil in my car without knowing what I was doing. Oh, man, I learned a few things that day." He gave a half-hearted chuckle, but Paul didn't respond. David shivered. "And I'm cold."

He went into the kitchen and switched on the central heating. The chill seemed to be seeping into his bones. Maybe part of it was his body's reaction to the evening's events. It wasn't every day you buried your best friend, only to later have him sitting in your living room asking for food.

He poked his head through the living room doorway. "Come on, Paul. You need to take a shower while I find some clothes that might fit you."

Paul's gait had improved, though he continued to move stiffly. He managed to climb the stairs with only a minimal amount of popping and creaking. He didn't speak, but once they'd reached the bathroom he began to undress without David having to tell him to or offer assistance.

David stepped around him and turned on the shower. He waited for the water to run hot. "There," he began, turning, "the shower's…"

His words tailed away. Paul stood facing him, naked. It had been a couple of years since they'd last shared a changing room after playing football or squash; participating in sport had been one of the first things to go after the treatments had begun. David had watched his friend waste away as the never-ending radio and chemical bombardments stripped the flesh from his frame. But this was the first time he had seen him naked since the diagnosis.

Painfully thin didn't come close. Sunken chest; concave stomach beneath xylophone ribs; pelvic bones and shoulders, resembling coat hangers, supporting twig-like legs and arms. Paul might have been slight before falling ill, but he'd been wiry, with tight muscles like knots in rope. No muscle definition remained; he appeared to consist entirely of skin, bone and sinew. The only fleshy looking part of Paul was his penis, hanging limply between two thighs denuded of muscle.

Worse was his colour. Or lack of it. The entire front of his body looked as pale as a plucked chicken. His limbs, too, but not his hands. They looked normal, incongruously pink amidst the paleness.

If Paul was discomfited by David's shocked regard, he didn't show it.

"Right then, Paul. In you get. There's shower gel and shampoo. I'll fetch you a clean towel and some clothes."

David waited for Paul to shuffle past him and step into the cubicle. He slid the acrylic door closed behind his friend and gasped. For a long moment, he could only stare.

It wasn't the skinniness of Paul's rear view—he'd fully expected that—but the stark contrast in colour from his front. As though recovering from the effects of a full-body bruise, his back, especially between his jutting shoulder blades, and buttocks bore large, vivid stains of blueberry-coloured purples, fading to violets and pale reds.

The door began to mist up with condensation. David tore his gaze away, stooped to gather Paul's discarded clothes in his arms and left the bathroom.

David took a clothes hanger from the airing cupboard on which to hang Paul's suit. As he folded them, the trousers made a crinkling sound. He peered inside and extracted a rectangle of plastic-backed, padded material about the size of the cover of an encyclopaedia. The material felt heavy, like a soiled disposable nappy, he guessed, though he didn't have children; had never been in a relationship long enough for the issue of issue, so to speak, to arise. He sniffed at it dubiously and immediately regretted it. The pad was clearly, from the smell, soaked through with bodily fluids, including faecal matter.

Holding one corner of the material gingerly between thumb and forefinger, David carried it downstairs, Paul's muddied shirt tucked under his arm. Into the main dustbin outside the back door went the pad. Into the washing machine in the kitchen went Paul's shirt. His own shirt, the sleeves looking as though they'd been dipped into a dirty canal, joined it.

He hung Paul's suit in the airing cupboard, alongside his own. Both suits were liberally streaked with mud and he'd have to get them dry-cleaned before they could be worn again. He could brush the worst of the mud out of them when they were dry.

A couple of minutes later, dressed in a towelling shower robe, a clean bath towel tucked under one arm, a small pile of clothes in the other, he returned to the bathroom.

It resembled a steam room.

"Paul, you done? My turn now. I've brought a towel and some clothes. Paul?"

David dumped the towel and clothes onto the floor, and crossed to the shower. He slid open the door a fraction and peered in.

Paul stood beneath the shower nozzle, head leaning back, water pouring from his hair. His lips were widely parted, allowing the spray to fall into his open mouth. His Adam's apple moved up and down as he swallowed.

"Paul? You shouldn't drink that stuff, mate. It's come from the hot tank. It isn't drinking water."

Paul lowered his head and turned towards the door. The glint of yellow in his eyes was fading.

~~~
~~~

David tried not to stare, but it was difficult to tear his gaze away and, besides, Paul appeared oblivious of his regard. Paul stood with his back to the shower cubicle, patting himself dry with a towel. Minutes earlier, that back had borne the vivid colours of a fading bruise. The occasional darker patch of skin remained, but otherwise Paul's back and buttocks appeared almost normal. Almost healthy looking.

The pinkness of flesh returned to life had spread to his front, too. When Paul had stepped from the shower, David thought maybe the new ruddiness of his chest and stomach had been caused by the hot water, but now he felt certain Paul's body was returning to something approaching normality after... After what?

The answer came to him like a light slap. After lying on his back, dead, for three days, that's what. He hadn't been subjected to a post mortem, hadn't been embalmed. His blood must have pooled and coagulated. Now, after being active, after replacing lost fluids—he had been glugging hot water as he'd once, pre-cancer, glugged beer—his blood had thinned and was being pumped around his body once more.

David was no doctor and suspected that any doctor would say such a thing wasn't possible. Well, he was standing in a bathroom looking at living, moving proof which gave lie to such an assertion.

"Paul, there's a pair of boxer shorts and sweatpants on the floor for you to put on. The pants'll probably be too big on you, but they have a drawstring waist so tie it tight and they should stay up. And there's one of my old tee shirts. It's a Sabbath shirt and I know you don't share my taste in metal, but let's be honest"—he shrugged— "do you really give a shit at this point?"

"Thank you." Paul's speech no longer sounded strained, or croaky.

"No probs. That's what friends are for."

David slid shut the cubicle door and stepped under the shower to take advantage of whatever hot water remained in the tank.

By the time he stepped out, Paul had disappeared. The clothes David had left for him had gone, too. A damp towel lay in a heap on the floor.

David dried himself and dressed in much the same way as Paul, in baggy sweatpants and tee shirt, a Zeppelin one. The house was cosy and the chills had been driven from his bones. His stomach rumbled and, with a start, he realised he hadn't eaten since breakfast. There had been plenty of buffet food on offer at Cath's during the wake, but the knocking sound he'd heard coming from the grave had driven all thoughts of eating from his mind.

He went downstairs to the kitchen. Paul was already there, sitting at the tiny table, the only light coming from the open fridge. No, that wasn't the only source of illumination. Yellow light spilled down the Black Sabbath tee shirt from Paul's inclined head, casting the faded charcoal of the material in a sickly glow.

David switched on the overhead light, banishing the glow. He shut the fridge door and turned to the table.

Paul's hands were raised to his mouth, holding something pink. On the tabletop in front of him was an opened carton of chicken breasts David recognised as having come from his fridge. Raw chicken breasts. Paul was tearing at one of the breasts with his teeth. Two breasts remained in the carton; it had contained four.

"Hey, man," said David.

Paul ignored him and continued tearing, chewing and swallowing.

"Paul? You might want to let me cook those first."

Paul slowly raised his head to look at David. The light faded from his eyes to be replaced by a look of confusion.

"Huh?" he said.

David stepped forward and gently removed the half-eaten meat from his unresisting hands. Hands that felt warm to the touch, if not a little feverish.

"You shouldn't eat raw chicken. You'll get salmonella or some such shit." It occurred to David how ridiculous what he was saying sounded. He was, after all, addressing someone who had died of cancer three days ago. Salmonella was unlikely to feature high on his list of what to avoid. "Look, I'm hungry, too. Let me put what's left of this chicken in the oven. I'll do some chips, as well. They'll have to be oven chips, mind. I'm a mechanic, not a chef."

Paul nodded and the look of bewilderment passed.

"Let me get the food in the oven and then we can have a beer while we're waiting for it to cook."

Paul nodded again.

A few minutes later, David pulled up the chair opposite Paul and passed him an opened bottle of lager. David took a long pull on his own; it helped tamp down the building sense of unease threatening to bubble to the surface. Paul sipped at his bottle without comment.

David let out his breath in a heavy sigh. "So, man," he said, "what the hell's going on?"

Paul's thin shoulders moved; it took David a moment to realise he was shrugging.

"Do you have any idea what's happened?" he asked. "As we told you in the graveyard, you died three days ago. We buried you this afternoon. Griff and I were two of the bearers. We carried your coffin to 'Tequila'. We lowered it into a bloody big hole in the ground. Then everyone headed back to yours where Cath did you proud."

David watched Paul closely when he mentioned his wife's name. Maybe there was a slight widening of the eyes—now, thankfully, returned to pale green—but otherwise he gave no reaction. Except, a hint of a smile, no more than a hint, turned up the corners of his mouth. A strand of raw chicken protruded from one corner and lay down his chin. David tried to ignore it.

"'Tequila'," Paul said. "I knew Cath would do it." The suggestion of a smile had gone. His words should have sounded wistful but, although his voice was now similar to the old Paul's, it remained flat and inflectionless, stripped of emotion.

"She insisted, despite stern opposition. Your mother was quite, er, vocal in her disapproval."

"Yes. She made her feelings known in the hospice, too."

"You remember everything? Your final days and hours?"

Paul nodded without hesitation. "But it's like watching a film. That stuff happened to someone else."

"What happened? How are you here?"

Again the shrugging motion. "I came back."

"What does it feel like?"

"It doesn't feel like anything."

David stared at him for a moment. "How the hell are you sitting here, drinking beer, talking to me? How the fuck did you come back?"

"I was brought back."

"Brought back? What d'you mean? How can you be brought back?"

"Something brought me back."

David felt the hairs on his neck stand to attention. "Something?"

Paul nodded. "I'm not alone."

Ten: Saturday Morning

David slept fitfully. If it wasn't dark dreams which awoke him from brief interludes of snatched slumber, it was imagining the sounds of doors opening and closing, or hunger pangs. While Paul had scoffed everything placed in front of him—the cooked chicken, most of a bag of oven chips, almost an entire loaf of bread—David had only picked at his food and ended up giving most of his to Paul. It was the strand of raw chicken. Every time David glanced at Paul and noticed the pink meat sticking to the side of his chin, his stomach lurched.

Paul might have been dead for three days, but he ate with the appetite of a bodybuilder. And with a singular lack of apparent enjoyment. He forked food into his mouth, chewed and swallowed, all the time wearing an expression of focused concentration. Slice after slice of bread accompanied the meat and chips. He didn't seem to care whether the bread was buttered or not. He interrupted eating only to wash a mouthful of dry food down with water. He had drunk the bottle of lager, but without any outward relish. When David offered him another, he'd shaken his head and asked for water.

David tried to engage Paul in further conversation, but his friend was unresponsive, too distracted by the process of eating. A mechanical process, it seemed, entirely lacking in aesthetic pleasure. If his stomach had shrunk, Paul showed no signs—no evident discomfort, no gagging, no struggling to swallow.

When, at last, his appetite had apparently been sated, Paul said one word. "Sleep." When David asked if he'd like to use the bathroom first, his only response was a shake of the head.

After digging out an old duvet and a couple of pillows, David made some sort of bed on the sofa in the living room. Paul clambered into it—showing no evidence of remaining stiffness—and closed his eyes.

"'Night, then," David said, but there was no reply.

David had gone upstairs to bed, stomach empty, mind filled with misgivings.

Morning came as a relief. When he opened his eyes after the latest bout of napping, infested with images of walking, talking corpses, and found light spilling around the edges of his curtains, he decided to get up.

David Owen wasn't the only one to endure a restless night. The Reverend Will Hopkin tossed and turned, listening to the creaks and groans of the vicarage around him. The old building sounded as unsettled as he felt.

Unlike David, Reverend Hopkin did not greet daylight with any sense of relief. The feeling of dark foreboding had grown stronger throughout the endless night. By morning, it pressed down on him and against him, more oppressive than an imminent electrical storm.

The prospect of a Saturday morning off did not, as it normally did, cheer him. He would have welcomed the distraction of officiating at a wedding.

He had afternoon visits scheduled to elderly and sick parishioners, but nothing planned for the morning. Often, at such times of leisure, he would don thick-soled walking boots and set out into the countryside, following narrow lanes and obscure-looking footpaths, with no particular aim in mind other than to enjoy the never-ending wonder and beauty of God's creations—for any given value of God.

But not this morning. Apart from having no urge to do anything so frivolous as ramble through the countryside, a nagging sense told him not to stray far from the church. Not until whatever was approaching had arrived and whatever was to happen had happened.

After breakfasting unenthusiastically, Reverend Hopkin retired to his study. He looked over Sunday's sermon and made a few desultory amendments, more for the sake of keeping his mind busy than to improve the words.

It wasn't working; his mind was not distracted. His gaze kept lifting from his notes and wandering through the window, to the church. At this angle, he could see the tops of its grey walls where they rose above the trees screening the cemetery. The trees swayed gently on this first day of November beneath a becalmed sky across which clouds, the fluffy kind, moved sedately, allowing the occasional glimpse of the blue infinity which lay beyond.

The church roof was covered in slate of a marginally darker grey than the stone from which the walls had been constructed. Most inhabitants of Taiwyn would be surprised to learn both stone and slate had been quarried locally. The stone quarry had been filled in long ago; the rugby club and pitch now inhabited the site. The tiny slate quarry had been left to nature, which had done its job well. All that remained was a depression in the centre of Bluebell Wood, that children who played in the woods called The Dip, filled with mulch and rotting treefalls. Dig down deep enough and it was still possible to retrieve a fragment of grey slate.

The constructions which had occupied the ground upon which the church stood had always been formed of local materials: stone, slate, wood, wattle, daub. It was a vital part of the Binding.

St Illtyd's Church was cruciform, with an imposing square tower rising from the intersection of transept and nave. The clock on the tower face told Reverend Hopkin the time had long passed nine.

He put the sermon to one side. Sometimes, there was only one place to go; only one place he felt at peace. He needed to be in the church.

David opened the front door and beckoned Griff inside.

"Everything okay?" Griff looked at him with concern.

David nodded. He pointed at the living room door. "He's fast asleep."

"Can I see?"

"Sure."

Griff opened the door and they both peered into the gloom. A huddled shape could be made out on the sofa beneath the duvet. A suggestion of tousled, tawny hair poked out. Griff sniffed.

"What's that smell?"

"I'm not sure." David motioned for him to withdraw and pulled the door closed behind them.

"It's him, isn't it? The smell's coming from him."

"He had a shower. He's clean."

"It's coming from inside him." Griff raised a hand to his mouth as though to cover a wave of nausea. "Bloody hell, Dai, you know what's happening, don't you? He's decomposing."

David opened his mouth to contradict his friend, then closed it. The same thought had been nagging at him all morning. "How can that be?"

"Easy. Because that's what happens to dead bodies."

"But his blood is circulating again. It had pooled—his entire back was one giant bruise—but he stood under the shower guzzling hot water like you guzzle beer, and it must have helped his circulation return to normal. So the smell can't be his flesh."

"His internal organs, then."

They stared at each other for a long moment. David let out a long sigh. "Let's go into the kitchen. I need coffee."

While he busied himself boiling the kettle and spooning ground coffee into the cafetière, Griff sat at the table. David was aware of his intense gaze following his every movement.

Griff waited until he had filled the cafetière with hot water before speaking.

"So tell me, what has he had to say for himself?"

David turned to face Griff, leaning back against the work surface.

"Not a lot. He's eating me out of house and home, mind." An image of half-eaten raw chicken popped into his head. He pushed it away. "He ate like a horse last night. Polished off almost a whole loaf of sliced bread. And when I came down this morning, I found he'd been at the boxes of cereal. You know what I'm like with breakfast cereal. I'll try something new, go off it after a couple of days and leave the box in the cupboard alongside all the other opened boxes. Well, the cupboard door was wide open when I came down this morning and all the boxes had been emptied. He'd scoffed the lot. And dry, no milk."

Griff stared at him, then grunted. "Well, on a scale of weird shit that's been happening since yesterday, I'd say that ranks quite low. Come on, Dai, he *must* have said something."

David turned away to pour the coffee. He didn't speak until he had sat down opposite Griff and they both nursed mugs of fresh coffee.

"He did say something strange. But, first, let me tell you about the shower."

While they sipped at their drinks, David related to Griff the paleness of Paul's front and the vivid contrast of his colourful back. He told him about the soiled pad he'd removed from Paul's trousers, and finding Paul still in the shower, drinking the hot water. He described how Paul's body looked to have returned to something approaching a normal, healthy colour.

Griff shook his head firmly. "There's nothing healthy about the smell in your living room."

"No, there's not." David paused. "He said he could remember before. Being in the hospice."

"Yeah, right."

"Really, Griff. He said something about his mother only he would know. It really is Paul, you know, but changed. Different. It's as though he's lost all emotion."

Griff continued to gaze at him. "There's something else, isn't there?"

David nodded. "He also said something about having been brought back. I gained the impression it was against his will. And he said…" David drew in a long breath. "He said he hadn't come back alone."

Griff sat with his back to the door leading through to the hallway and living room. He glanced behind him as if expecting to see someone—or something—standing in the doorway.

"What in holy shit does that mean?" he said, his voice low.

David shrugged. "I couldn't get any more out of him."

Griff said nothing for a minute or two. David could almost see the cogs of his brain turning. At last, he spoke. "I still think we have to tell Cath."

"What? No, we can't. Think about it, mun. She's spent the past few months having to come to terms with her husband's impending death, watching him waste away before her eyes. She held him while he breathed his last. And yesterday she buried him. How the hell are we going to tell her he's back? 'Hey, Cath, a funny thing happened. We bumped into Paul. Yeah, *that* Paul. The one we stuck in a six-foot hole in the ground yesterday. Except he can now heal miraculously and his eyes glow occasionally. Oh, and he smells a bit funny.'" David grimaced.

Griff sighed. "Yeah, I can see how that would be awkward, but I still think she has a right to know."

David shook his head vehemently. "Not until we know more about what's going on. Cath has gone through hell these past months. But she's pulled through them and was bloody brilliant yesterday. I don't know many who'd have coped with not only losing her husband but having to deal with the constant disapproval of his witch of a mother. And if you're right and Paul's body or organs are rotting, he's hardly going to be back for long, is he? Think what it will do to Cath, seeing him like he is now, and then losing him again in a matter of, what, I don't know, weeks, days? If she has to go through all that once more, this time it could destroy her."

Griff stared at him and his expression softened. "All right, then, but what the hell *are* we going to do? We can't simply keep something this big to ourselves." He gestured behind him. "Whether that thing through there is truly Paul or not, it's a marvel of modern science."

"What about Rhys? He's an intelligent bloke. He might know what to do."

Griff shrugged. "I sometimes wonder about his intelligence, but okay. He might be with Sarah. *She* will definitely want to tell Cath."

"Hmm. If she's with Rhys, then she's going to have to be let in on it, too. That's okay; if anything, she's brighter than Rhys and more grounded. She might have some sensible ideas. But get them to agree not to involve anyone else until they've at least seen Paul."

"I'll try. I'll go fetch them while you stay here with the dearly departed."

Catherine Duffy awoke from a deep sleep, blessedly free of dreams. She yawned and stretched and patted Paul's side of the bed with a sad smile. A glance at the bedside clock told her it was approaching ten and she had slept for almost fourteen hours. She couldn't remember the last time she'd slept for so long. Probably not since a babe in arms.

She lay for a while, enjoying the cosiness and feeling of mild euphoria that accompanies awaking after a solid, much-needed sleep. The thought of having to finish tidying up downstairs did not dismay her. She'd only need to fill the dishwasher, straighten chairs and cushions, and whizz around with the vacuum cleaner. It would occupy her for the remainder of the morning, before she went to her parents' for lunch. Agreeing to that had been the only way she could get rid of them last night.

That sounded uncharitable. She loved her parents dearly and all they'd wanted to do was help their younger daughter through a time of overwhelming grief.

Except, that wasn't quite true. Cath hadn't felt overwhelmed during the funeral or wake. She'd passed through the various stages of grief—the denial and anger and all the rest of it—and arrived at acceptance before Paul had gone. It had given her the strength and calmness to comfort him during his last hours without crumbling into a sobbing wreck. It enabled her to prop herself beside him in the hospice bed and whisper to him while he slipped quietly into a coma, and cradle his head while his breathing grew erratic and then featherlike, before stopping entirely.

After another ten minutes of luxuriating in the warm afterglow of revitalising slumber, Cath swung her legs out of bed. She took her time using the bathroom and dressing, before opening the curtains of her bedroom to let in the light of a fresh autumnal day.

Her bedroom was at the front of her house and the window

looked out onto the tiny front garden and beyond to the street. A man was striding past on the other side of the road, in jeans and hoodie, hands swinging by his sides, looking straight ahead. A man on a mission.

It was Griff. Not returning for his coat, apparently. He had already passed her house and was making his way along the street towards where Rhys lived.

Cath shrugged. No doubt he and Dai would be back to collect their coats sooner or later.

She turned away. The house wouldn't clean itself.

Eleven: Die, Pig Whore

There was no reply to his polite knocking, and Rhys wasn't answering his mobile, so Griff resorted to hammering on the door. When that didn't summon any signs of life from within, he crouched, raised the flap of the letterbox and hollered.

"Rhys! Open up. It's Griff." He turned his ear to the open flap and was rewarded by the sound of movement.

A grumbling voice called down the stairs, "Fucksake, hold your horses. I'm coming."

Griff grinned. By the time an approaching dark shape could be seen through the glass panel, his expression had turned sober.

Rhys opened the door, blinking, hair sticking out to the sides like the bristles of a cheap paintbrush. He wore a dressing gown, hastily thrown on judging by the lopsided way it hung on his slight frame.

He peered at Griff blearily. "Wassmarrer?"

"Wakey, wakey. I need to talk to you."

"Wasstime?"

"After ten." Griff recoiled from the waft of stale breath. "Bloody hell, you smell like a brewery. Let's get some coffee down you. I need you to be alert."

He pushed past Rhys and strode to the kitchen at the rear. A half-drunk bottle of something alcoholic stood on the work surface, next to three or four empty ones. An empty glass stood next to them, its rim smudged with pink lipstick.

Griff filled the kettle and switched it on. Rhys shuffled into the kitchen behind him, scratching his crotch.

"It's an unholy hour," he grumbled.

Griff indicated the bottles. "Decided to carry on partying after the *Poacher's?*"

Rhys shambled over to the work surface and picked up the bottle containing liquid. He sniffed at it uncertainly. Griff took it off him before he could raise it to his lips and emptied it into the sink. Rhys's puffy eyes widened as an internal penny seemed to drop. "Hey! Where did you and Dai get to yesterday? You missed a good night. Well, you know, for a wake."

"That's what I need to talk to you about. Go and fetch Sarah. She needs to hear this, too."

"How did…? Ah, never mind. The glass."

"I don't know why you two don't move in together. It would save a mortgage and a set of bills."

"Nah. She doesn't like me when I'm sober."

"She likes you most of the time, then." Griff flapped his hands at his friend. "Come on, shift your arse."

While Rhys shuffled away, muttering under his breath, Griff made three mugs of coffee. He carried them through to the living room at the front of the house and opened the curtains to banish the gloom, before taking one of the armchairs.

Rhys reappeared in a pair of threadbare jeans and an old, baggy sweater. Trailing behind him, yawning, came Sarah.

"Do I smell coffee?" she said. "Come to mamma." She sat on the sofa. Rhys slumped into the spare armchair.

Sarah also wore jeans and one of Rhys's sweatshirts. Her blonde hair had been pulled hurriedly back into something resembling a ponytail. Loose strands tumbled over her brow, above eyes bright and clear.

She sipped at the coffee. "That's good. So, Griff, what brings you here on…" She glanced out of the window. "On this fine Saturday morning?"

Griff hesitated. Now that it came down to it, he wasn't sure where to start.

"Yeah," said Rhys, "what gives?"

"Er, let's see. Okay. Rhys, what's your favourite song by The Cranberries?"

Rhys frowned. "Huh? You came knocking us up to ask a pop quiz?"

"Answer the question. What's your favourite Cranberries song?"

"I don't know. 'Linger', I suppose."

"No. Your other favourite."

"'Dreams'?"

"For fuck's sake. Your absolute favourite. The one you insist on singing badly when you've been at the red wine."

"Um, 'Zombie'?"

"Yes!" Griff sat back with a satisfied sigh.

Rhys and Sarah exchanged a glance.

"O–kay," said Sarah. "Now we've established Rhys's favourite Cranberries song, what has it to do with anything?"

"Ah," said Griff. He sat forward. "Well, it's like this…"

Reverend Hopkin unlocked the oak door and swung it open. Before he'd fully entered the church, he sensed something was wrong.

After closing the door, he walked to the end of the rear pew. To his left, the stone font lay on its side. Mercifully, the ancient stone appeared to be intact, though he doubted the tiles beneath where it had toppled would be whole. The font was heavy; he would need help to replace it in its upright position.

He turned into the aisle formed by the two rows of pews and began to make his way to the front of the church, to the apse, in front of which stood the altar.

On his way, he noted the hassocks upon which the faithful knelt for prayer had been flung about as though tossed by a violent storm; a few had split, their escaping stuffing resembling rusting wire wool. Pages had come loose from prayer books thrown about in the same storm.

The vicar passed the carved wooden pulpit and the choir stalls; behind the left-hand stalls stood the pipe organ. As far as he could tell, none had been disturbed.

His tread faltered when he approached the altar. If any part of him had been doubting his intuitive sense of approaching menace, the doubts were banished as his gaze took in the altar and apse.

A couple of steps led up to a shuttered brass rail which stretched across the entire width of the apse; members of the congregation knelt at the rail to take communion. The gate allowing access to the apse had been yanked off one hinge and hung drunkenly. The brass crucifix normally hanging on the wall at the head of the apse had been wrenched from its fixings. The half-life-sized plaster figure of Christ had been torn from the cross and bashed against the wall— powdery scuff marks showed pale against the stone. The figure lay to one side in a drift of pulverised plaster, its head and outstretched arms missing. The cross leaned against the wall, upside down.

Bottles of communion wine had been smashed on the floor of the apse. A tangy, fruity smell filled the air. The bottles were stored in the north transept where Reverend Hopkin's service raiments were kept. This was also where the choir kept their robes and there was a door leading outside, which seemed the most likely place the intruder had found a way in. It had been known for members of the choir to leave the door unlocked after practice, so it could be that the intruder hadn't even had to force entry.

Thankfully, none of the stained glass windows had been smashed, but the vicar only noted this absent-mindedly. His atten- tion was taken by the altar. Set back a few paces behind the brass rail, the altar was draped in a snow-white cloth inlaid with gold em- broidery. The cloth was still in place, though crumpled. The brass collection plates and candlesticks normally occupying the surface of the altar had been flung to one side. Broken glass littered the altar top and red wine stained the cloth. Wine had been used to create crude letters on the face of the cloth. It had dried the same dark shade as blood.

There were not many people living who could have translated the words the letters formed. Reverend Hopkin was one of them, but not because he was fluent in the ancient language represented by the letters. Rather, they formed words which had been replicated, alongside their approximate Welsh translation, in the fading manuscript sitting on his study desk in the vicarage; words which had been found inscribed into petrified wood carvings from the times of the druids; words which had first been uttered by something not of this world.

He mouthed them.

ADBALO RUXTO LUTTA

Aloud, he spoke their English translation.

"Die, pig whore."

There could no longer be any doubt: it had found a way to return.

Griff led them on a circuitous route to Dai's house, one that avoided passing Cath's. Despite initially being insistent upon their telling Cath about the apparent return of her late husband (he still couldn't bring himself to fully accept it was Paul lying on Dai's sofa), after witnessing his eyes glow yellow and his broken hands heal themselves, and after Dai pointing out what the news might do to Cath, he now accepted that telling her might not be the best thing for her. He still believed she, more than anyone, had the right to know, but he agreed with Dai that waiting until they knew more about what was going on made sense. So he led Rhys and Sarah away from Cath's house so Sarah wouldn't take it into her head to check Cath was all right.

They hadn't believed his tale and it had taken him twenty minutes to get them to agree to accompany him to Dai's house to see for themselves. They walked behind him; whenever he glanced back and shot them an encouraging smile, they regarded him with worried expressions.

It was after eleven when they turned into Dai's street. Local children were taking advantage of the dry weather to begin construction on the bonfire built each year on the common. The landowner and the Fire Service allowed the bonfire to be lit on November 5th provided it was under the close supervision of adults; the village Community Watch had formed a committee for the very purpose and Bonfire Night was allowed to go ahead with a proper bonfire, although children were not allowed to go near until it had been reduced to a pile of embers. Griff attended each year—the jacket potatoes cooked in foil amidst the bonfire's remains were the best he'd ever tasted.

He turned to address Rhys and Sarah. "Look at them. They spend so much time inside these days, it's bloody great to see the kids working together out of doors."

Rhys merely grunted.

"You're right, Griff," said Sarah, "but we don't really care about Guy Fawkes and all that shit just now."

Griff opened his mouth to say something, thought better of it and shut it again. He turned back to complete the remaining few yards to Dai's house. He knocked the front door and waited.

Rhys gulped in deep breaths as though trying not to hyperventilate. Sarah looked so pale, Griff was reminded of Paul's face when they'd found him sitting on the bench in the churchyard. He shot her what he hoped was a reassuring smile; she tried to return it, which was something, though it was a weak effort.

The door opened.

"Hi," said Dai. "I'm really glad to see you guys."

With a start, Griff noticed that his lower eyelids brimmed, ready to start spilling tears down his cheeks.

Rhys must have noticed, too, for he stepped forward and gripped Dai's forearm. Dai breathed out heavily and motioned Rhys inside. Sarah reached forward and gave him a hug. He looked grateful and embarrassed in equal measure. He waved her inside after Rhys as though no longer trusting himself to speak.

"You okay?" Griff enquired in a low voice.

Dai nodded and brushed away the moisture from his eyes. "Fine. It's just getting to me a little."

Griff stepped past him. Rhys and Sarah stood in the hallway, shooting nervous glances at the closed living room door.

Dai followed him in and closed the front door. He looked at Rhys and Sarah.

"Griff's filled you in?"

They nodded, wide-eyed.

"Are you ready?"

They glanced at each other, before nodding again. They had barely uttered a word since leaving Rhys's house.

Dai opened the living room door and went inside. Griff nodded to them and motioned after Dai. With a last nervous—no, terrified would be more accurate—glance at each other, they followed Dai into his living room. Griff stepped in behind them.

Rhys uttered a low moan. The noise Sarah made was higher, longer, more drawn out. A whimper.

The curtains remained closed, but all could see that Paul no longer lay huddled on the sofa. He was sitting up, bare feet on the floor, the duvet flung aside.

The yellow glow from his eyes spilled down his tee shirt, illuminating the faded skull beneath the faint, stylised words 'Black Sabbath'.

Twelve: Dead Man Talking

Sarah and Rhys clung to each other like two children lost in the forest, listening to the splintering noises of something big drawing near.

"It's okay," David said in what he hoped was a soothing tone. "The glow's fading." He nodded to Griff and mouthed *Open the curtains*.

The light coming from Paul's eyes dimmed. He became difficult to make out in the shadows.

David wrinkled his nose. The odour of spoiling meat was not overpowering, but remained noticeable. There was another smell, a new one, which he hadn't noticed earlier. Now he had fully entered the room, the other smell could be detected: sharp, fruity, not entirely unpleasant. More aroma than odour.

Griff drew back the curtains and daylight flooded the room, making them all blink.

Rhys and Sarah still resembled scared children, but both peered at Paul.

"Shit on a stick," muttered Rhys. "It *looks* like him."

Sarah nodded, but appeared incapable for the moment of speech.

"It's okay," David repeated. He stepped past them. "Come and talk to him. See if he recognises you."

They looked at each other with wide, frightened eyes. David beckoned gently to them.

"Come on. It'll be fine."

Without letting each other go, Rhys and Sarah shuffled forward. David moved aside to allow them to stand in front of Paul where he sat with head bowed towards his feet. David nodded at them encouragingly.

Rhys cleared his throat. "Er, Paul. Is that you, mate? Er, how are y—" He choked off the words. "This is frigging ridiculous. I'm standing in front of someone whose coffin I bore yesterday, asking him how's he's feeling…" His words tailed away as Paul slowly raised his head.

"Rhys," said Paul.

"Aw, *fuck*…"

"Hey, Paul," said Sarah. "It's wonderful to see you. I don't know if you remember me…"

The head turned towards her. "Sarah."

Her lips turned into a tight, forced smile. "It *is* you. Oh my God, this is so amazing." She let go of Rhys and took a pace forward, stooping to lean down and put an arm around Paul. Strands of loose blonde hair dangled in his face. He gave no reaction to the hair or the hug.

Sarah pulled away, her expression sober. "You're so cold." She glanced at David. "And there's a smell. A couple of smells, actually. One of them is wine."

David looked more closely at the seated figure. "Paul, your hands are stained. It looks like blackberry juice. Your feet… they're stained, too. And what's that? Mud? They look as if you've been running barefoot through a field. What's happened?" He recalled what he'd assumed to have been dreams, the sound of doors opening and closing. "Did you go out in the night?"

Paul shook his head. "My body but not me. It."

David felt a chill beginning to work its way up from the base of his spine.

"It? What do you mean?"

"It went out in the night. It's using me to get around. And now it's gone again. Without me." Paul's voice sounded like his old one, except it remained without inflection. It was like hearing a familiar song performed without feeling by an unfamiliar singer. "It can't do anything on its own except observe."

"What can't?" asked David. "What are you talking about?"

"I told you. It brought me back. It's gone, for now. But it will return. I can tell you now, but I'll have to be quick."

Paul spoke unhurriedly, his voice shorn of passion. Yet David could sense an urgency in the shape of his words, if not in their timbre. "What is *it*, Paul? What will be returning?"

A hush fell over the room. Griff came and stood next to Rhys. Four pairs of eyes gazed down at Paul. He gazed back impassively.

"Something ancient. Something evil."

The vicar stood back from the altar and surveyed his work. He had righted the cross and rehung it on the rear wall beneath the stained glass windows—it seemed incomplete without the plaster figure of Christ. The altar looked resplendent once more under a fresh white cloth complete with golden embroidery. One of the candlesticks leaned to one side and the collection dishes bore a couple of dents, but they remained functional. He had cleared away the broken glass and mutilated cast of Christ, and washed down the flagstone floor and wall to remove plaster marks and blood-like stains. The tang of communion wine had been replaced by the lemony scent of cleaning fluid.

He had also removed the crooked brass gate—they could manage without it until the hinge could be replaced. The gate served a ceremonial purpose; it wasn't as if it was necessary to keep back over-zealous worshippers.

Reverend Hopkin nodded, about-turned and walked down the aisle to the pews. He began to retrieve the flung-about hassocks and prayer books, and replace them in the box shelves in the back of the pews. Hassocks with protruding stuffing he placed to one side. He knew plenty of parishioners handy with a needle and thread who'd be glad to repair them. He'd have to make up a story about boisterous choir boys using them for an impromptu pillow fight, but thought he could wing it well enough. In a sense, he'd been winging it every Sunday for his entire career.

He reached under a pew to grab a stray hassock. As he straightened, the hairs on the back of his neck stood to attention and a sense of being watched swept through him. There was someone, or something, behind him. Clutching the hassock to his chest like a shield, he turned.

The church remained empty, yet every instinct told him he was no longer alone. Something unseen was observing him.

He stood unmoving. His breath grew shorter—more gasps than breaths. They plumed in air that had grown frigid, despite it being a reasonably warm autumn Saturday.

Whatever had entered the church—and he sensed it was a 'what', not a 'who'—was in front of him, in the space beyond the frontmost pew, before the pulpit.

Although he had dreaded this moment for most of his adult life, a calmness enveloped him. He had prepared for it, all the while hoping it would not be he, as the most recent bearer of the Burden, who would have to face what he suspected had come into his presence.

"You have found a way," said Reverend Hopkin. "You have come."

He stared at the empty space before the pulpit. Although there was nothing to see, nothing to hear, he knew it was the source of the cold, the source of evil regard, the source of the feeling of ancient malevolence.

He continued to stand still, staring at the space, clutching the hassock to his chest, though a cushion would do him no good in this confrontation. Yet, what sort of confrontation could there be with a being that was incorporeal…

"The way you have found is imperfect." He uttered the words while he worked it through in his mind. "You *have* found a way to take form, a way to influence physical matter—the damage you caused proves it—but it must only be temporary for otherwise you would not be here now like this. Inchoate."

The presence did not move, but continued to radiate rancour. So strong was the feeling of oppressive maleficence, so icy the coldness washing over Reverend Hopkin, he could sense the being as clearly as if it were a cloud of coloured gas suspended in the air before him.

"Impotent." He nodded slowly. "Yes. You can generate frigidity. You can emanate spite and hatred. But, when all is said and done, you have no power. Not here. Not now. You are quite, quite impotent."

It wasn't the vicar's intention to provoke the entity—he was merely thinking aloud—but he immediately sensed the change. Amidst the malevolence, a new emotion formed. If the entity had appeared in the form of a cloud, it would now be pulsating with rage.

"You don't like that, do you? Being described as impotent. Yet it's what you've been for more than two millennia. Since you were cast into chains by those who occupied this land before me. Know this: their knowledge has been passed down, generation to generation. Guardian to guardian. Knowledge of what you are and, should you ever reappear, how to send you back to the abyss from whence you came."

The sense of rage increased, became a seething core of resentment and fury.

Reverend Hopkin rocked back on his heels as the presence blasted past him, his grey hair lifting from his brow as though in a squall. He gasped at the iciness of the wind and gagged at its foulness.

The interior of the church grew calm. He was alone once more.

"I don't have long." Paul's demeanour remained unruffled, as though he was no longer capable of expressing emotion. "Let me speak without interruption."

David nodded and glanced at the others. Three more nods.

"Okay," he said. "Go for it."

Paul spoke quietly. Without inflection, without passion to provide emphasis and tone, David found he had to concentrate deeply to follow what he was saying.

"I died. It brought me back. The first thing I remember is coming to in the dark. I reached up and could feel wood above me. All around me. I knocked on the wood for no particular reason, except maybe to confirm it was wood. I wasn't knocking to be let out. I didn't want to be let out. But it sensed what I was doing and made me stop. It didn't want me to escape the coffin. Not then. It's weak, but it can take control of me."

"The yellow glowing eyes," murmured Griff. "That happens

when it's in charge."

David nodded and made a shushing motion to Griff.

"It makes me drink water to thin my blood," continued Paul. "It makes me eat to provide energy to make it stronger." He held up his hands. "These were ruined breaking out of the coffin. It used all its strength to make me do it. Then it had to make me eat to provide the energy to heal them. It needs them whole. It has use of them."

In the pause, Rhys spoke. "What does it want?"

David didn't shush him because he wanted to know, too.

"Although I can see its thoughts," Paul replied, "as it can see mine, it doesn't think in English or any language I recognise. But I sense its desires. They burn as bright as a star. And although nothing else about it is familiar, its desires are plain. Vengeance, power, domination."

He hesitated. "I don't understand the details, but I can see its needs as clearly as I can see your faces. It once—long, long ago—was free to roam the world. It was a time when the land was sparsely populated; the number of people here now bemuses it. And excites it. It was, and is, a doer of evil things for the thrill of being evil, not with any higher purpose in mind other than to hold dominion over all. Back then it took physical form, but its shape is unclear to me. All I can sense is solid muscle and great strength."

"Horns and cloven hooves?" asked Rhys.

"You'd think, but I cannot sense them." Paul looked down at his hands. "It now seeks to return to its physical form. To do that, it has to—through me—shake off its shackles. There's a priest… no, that's not quite the right word, but it's the same sort of idea. A priest will try to stop it."

"A priest?" said Griff. "Father Moran?"

Paul shook his head. "The church where I was buried. It's the priest there."

"Reverend Hopkin," said Sarah.

Paul looked up. "Is that his name? Well, the church acts like a prison. Not so much the building, but the ground upon which it stands. It's where it was originally banished. We're talking many centuries ago, before the Romans came to Britain. In the time of the Celts. It needs to destroy the church and defile the ground upon which it stands. Then it will be free. Then it can resume its physical form. Then it will seek to wreak havoc."

There was silence for a long moment. Sarah broke it, her voice quiet yet filled with something. Yearning?

"Where did you go? In the three days before it brought you back, where did you go?" She gazed at Paul with a strange intensity, as though anxious to hear his response yet, at the same time, dreading it.

He looked at her, his face and voice without expression. "Have you ever awoken from a dream? One you can't remember, only the way it made you feel. Deepest contentment, and happiness, delirious happiness. All you want is to be able to return to that dream, even if it means never waking up. Have you ever experienced such a dream?"

Sarah nodded, tears running down her cheeks. Rhys and Griff were nodding, too.

For the first time since he'd returned, Paul's face broke into something approaching a full expression. It was brief, gone almost as quickly as it had appeared, but David knew he didn't imagine it. For a moment, Paul looked wistful.

"All I want," he said, "is to return to that dream."

Sarah sobbed, but choked it back. Through her tears she spoke, her voice faltering as she tried to master her emotions. "What about Cath? She needs to know you've come back. She *has* to know."

Paul shrugged. "To what end? I know I love Cath, but I cannot feel it. I can feel nothing, except the certainty that I no longer belong here. I have nothing to offer her, except more heartbreak."

"How, mate?" asked Rhys. "How can you return to where you came from?"

"By not resisting it. Once it has used me to achieve its aims, it will have no further use for me and will discard me."

David gasped. Sarah and Griff stared down at Paul in wide-eyed horror.

Rhys said what David was thinking. "No, Paul. You can't just let it do what it wants."

Paul nodded. "I may be devoid of feeling, but I remember that I knew love and compassion. I cannot simply stand aside and allow it to destroy the world which contains my family and friends. Which contains Cath. But it is growing stronger. There may be little I can do to resist."

"There must be something you can do," said Rhys. "That *we* can do."

"Perhaps there is another way I can return to where I belong without it winning."

"Go on, Paul. We're listening."

"We can help the priest defeat it."

"How?"

"I don't know. We need to speak with this Reverend Hopkin. He may—" Paul's words cut off abruptly. His eyes glowed momentarily yellow before returning to normal.

"It has returned," he said. "And it's not in a good mood."

Part Three: Fire

Thirteen: Bugan

David let out a heavy sigh. "I need a fag."

He went into the kitchen, grabbed his packet of cigarettes and lighter from the worktop, and let himself out of the back door. Much of the rear garden was taken up by a garage, which let out onto the lane running behind the property. David had extended the garage to the side to create a workshop. An early 70s Norton Commando motorcycle stood inside, mainly in bits. When he'd finished restoring and rebuilding, he reckoned to make a cool four-figure profit at auction. David shot a rueful glance at the workshop. So much for his plan to spend the day refitting the exhaust.

He had barely taken a drag on his cigarette when Sarah joined him.

"Can I mooch one of those?" she asked.

"How long since you gave up?"

"Seven months." She shrugged. "It's a little early to hit the vodka so nicotine will have to do."

David handed her the packet and lighter. "What's he doing now?"

"Paul? Not a lot. Slumped back in the sofa, staring into space." She gave a short, humourless laugh. "Yesterday, we buried him. Today, we're discussing what he's doing now. This is beyond crazy."

Sarah lit a cigarette, took a deep drag and coughed. She took another drag and this time gave a sigh. "That hits the spot." She looked at David; held his gaze.

"What?"

"I know what Paul said about not telling Cath. I know your feelings on it—Griff explained. And yet…"

"You still think she ought to know."

Sarah nodded. "I understand all the reasons not to tell her. Truly I do. Seeing him now, like this, is going to cause her unimaginable anguish. And then she'll lose him again and have to start the grieving process all over again. I get it."

"But…?"

"But consider the alternative. If we don't tell her, but she finds out anyway. Later, after he's gone for good. Knowing that her husband came back from the grave, knowing we knew and didn't tell her, knowing she had a chance to see him again but it was kept from her. That will surely destroy her."

"So we make sure she never finds out."

"How? There are already four of us in the know. Four of us who are also friends with Cath. More are likely to find out before this is over. And it will get back to Cath. It may not happen soon; it may take a year or more. But someone will be careless, or unable to contain themselves any longer, or simply have too much to drink. Someone will let something slip. This is too mind-shattering for it not to happen. And Cath's not stupid; she'll notice. And she's a lot like Paul—very single-minded when she wants to be. She'll chase it down until she finds out the truth. When it's too late."

David took a long drag on his cigarette while he pondered Sarah's words. He let the smoke out along with a deep sigh. "I told Griff you're more sensible than Rhys."

Sarah grunted. "That's not difficult. So do you think I'm right? Do you think we have to tell Cath?"

David stared at her, his mind in turmoil. He opened his mouth to reply to her question, unsure what that reply would be, when the back door burst open.

"Come quickly," Rhys said. "It's Paul. He's run off."

While David swapped his moccasin slippers for a pair of trainers, Rhys filled them in.

"No warning. He suddenly leapt to his feet and ran out of the house. We both called after him, but he ignored us. And it happened too quickly for us to even think about trying to stop him."

"He's out in the streets? In broad daylight?" Sarah looked at David. "Still think we can keep this from her?"

David grimaced. "Were his eyes glowing yellow?"

"Glowing, yes," said Rhys. "Yellow, no. More orange, like flames.

Griff followed him, though Paul was moving a damn sight quicker than Griff can shift these days."

David stood. "Right, I'm ready. Let me grab my house keys. Did you see which way they went?"

Rhys nodded. "Left."

"In the direction of the church," said Sarah.

This time, David's grimace was deeper.

Reverend Hopkin checked the church once more. Apart from the toppled font, nothing remained out of place. In the morning, he would call Emlyn Rees, a hulking villager who'd be happy to pop along first thing and help him replace the font before worshippers began to arrive for the first service of the day. He would have called him straight away, except it was Saturday and Emlyn would be playing rugby for Taiwyn today. Will Hopkin had turned out a few times for the village himself in his younger, spryer days and kept himself abreast of the team's fixtures and results.

Today Taiwyn Rugby Club was playing away to a village in the Swansea valley, a journey of about thirty-five miles in a rickety old minibus. He didn't want to call Emlyn and risk him missing the bus or holding the team up. No, it could wait until the morning. And if the tiles beneath the font were damaged, well, he'd have some explaining to do anyway when members of the congregation noticed the missing figure of Christ and the brass gate. He'd probably open the service with mention of a spot of vandalism by some passing opportunist, though stress the petty nature of the damage and that it hadn't been serious enough to warrant involving the police. He'd say the intruder had entered through the unlocked transept door and it might prompt the choir to be more careful in future.

The north transept door *had* been unlocked, though Reverend Hopkin felt reasonably sure that even if it hadn't been, this intruder would have found another way in, probably with a lot more resulting damage.

He decided to leave by that same door and locked the main door from the inside. As he walked up the aisle towards the apse, he heard the door in the transept creak open. A moment later, it banged shut. He stopped in front of the choir stalls and waited.

A young man walked silently into the church, dressed in a faded dark tee shirt, hanging loosely from bony shoulders, and sweatpants which must have been tied tightly or they surely would fall down. He reached the aisle and turned towards Reverend Hopkin, coming to a halt within a few paces of him. His feet were bare.

The man gazed at the vicar with an expression of twisted contempt. His eyes resembled the amber of traffic lights, emitting an unearthly glow.

Reverend Hopkin swallowed. The calmness he had experienced earlier when faced with the incorporeal presence had gone. It was a different matter seeing the entity in the flesh, even if the flesh belonged to another.

"Bugan," said Reverend Hopkin, pronouncing it 'Bee-gun'. He forced his voice to remain steady, not to betray his fear. "So this is how you return. In the shell of some unfortunate."

He recognised the man whose body the entity occupied. Not a member of his flock, but a local, a villager, one whom the reverend had seen amongst the congregation at weddings and funerals. And, with a jolt, he realised the man had attended a funeral only yesterday—his own. Anger rose inside him like welling groundwater. He welcomed it; it displaced his fear.

"How despicable," he said, fury lending his voice strength. "How contemptible. To rip from its eternal rest a vessel for one of God's children and defile it with your foul being. God will surely not suffer your return. Begone, beast!"

A sly smile broke over the man's face and the eyes glowed brighter. A low, throaty chuckle sounded. "*Priest.*" The voice was gravelly, but otherwise the voice of a man, not of an otherworldly intruder. "Whore. Pig." The chuckle came again. "You think me impotent. I shall show you impotence when I feed off your liver."

"Oh, so you know English."

"Fucking priest. I have access to quite a vocabulary. And some colourful new words. *Cunt* of a priest."

From behind him, Reverend Hopkin heard the sound of someone trying to open the main door to the church, but his attention did not waver from the man. "Begone, fiend. There is nothing for you here. Even were you to regain your true form, you are bound and can never leave this place."

"Only while this temple stands. Only while the ground which it guards is hallowed. That shall not be so for much longer."

"You shall not prevail. I shall banish you once and for all."

"You shall die. It is what humans do. It is what this human did. It is not happy I have returned it to this plane."

"What… No. You have not disturbed that poor man's soul. Not even you would dare."

The eyes flashed red. "I dare! Oh, yes, I dare. It squirms and writhes while I delight in its anguish. Let me show you…"

The light in the eyes dimmed and was gone. The sly malevolence of the expression cleared, leaving a look of blankness in its place. Reverend Hopkin had been trying to think of the man's name. Now it came to him.

"Paul? Paul Duffy? Is that you?"

The man nodded. "It is watching, Reverend. You must be wary. It is gaining strength. It will come for you."

The eyes began to glow again, yellow this time, like the eyes of a sick seagull. "Enough. I did not come here to bandy words with you, priest. I came to end your miserable existence. Whether I have sufficient strength to best you while trapped in this clay cell… It shall entertain me greatly to find out."

The eyes flared orange once more and the man stepped forward. He moved much quicker than Reverend Hopkin anticipated. When the fist pistoned out, the vicar did not sway backwards fast enough to avoid it. With a thud like a mallet on steak, the bony knuckles connected with his cheek. Pain exploded in the side of his head and for a moment the world wavered.

The second blow caught him on the forehead as he lowered his head to try to clear it. He rocked back on his heels. A drunken step backwards saved a fall, but his assailant was coming again, arms swinging.

Reverend Hopkin managed to raise his arms and cover his head in some gesture of defence. Blows rained onto them and he staggered back, his forearms turning numb under the pummelling.

Uttering a roar of frustration, Will Hopkin ignored his instincts yelling at him to flee and moved, instead, forwards. He pushed his raised arms against the man's thin chest, forcing him to take a step back.

It provided a moment of respite, no more. Panting, his face and arms ablaze with pain as bright as toothache, Reverend Hopkin stared at Paul Duffy. It wasn't Paul Duffy who stared back, who turned Paul's mouth into a rictus of triumph, who growled from his throat, "This is too easy, priest. After all these long centuries the only sport I find is *you*. Now I think it will pleasure me to tear out your heart."

Reverend Hopkin raised his arms, although he had started to believe he was merely delaying the inevitable.

Ian Griffiths lumbered around the side of the church, breathing heavily. It had been a few years since a knee shattered in an accidental collision had forced him to retire from playing rugby. The knee had healed well after reconstructive surgery, but ached furiously after any attempt at prolonged exercise. As a consequence of lack of regular exercise and a fondness for calorific food, he had piled on the pounds.

A concrete path led from the locked main door along the side of the church and curved outwards around the rectangular protrusion which formed one arm of the cruciform shape of the building. A small door was set into the far side of the rectangle.

Griff skidded to a halt, panting with exertion. He grasped the worn brass handle tightly—his palms were slick with sweat—and turned. He swung the door open carefully, trying to dampen the noise of his laboured breathing.

He stepped inside, leaving the door wide open behind him, stopped and listened. He was in what seemed to amount to a large cloakroom. Dark robes and white cassocks hung on hooks along both walls. Another door, standing open, led into the church. Through the doorway came dull grunts and a rhythmic thudding, like that made by a boxer training on a punchbag.

Griff stepped through the doorway and lengthened his stride as the sounds grew louder and more frantic. He drew level with the altar and turned to face down the length of the church. About halfway down the aisle, Paul crouched in a curious half-standing, half-stooping pose, his back to Griff. His arms moved rhythmically, elbows drawing back and driving forward. Someone cowered on the floor in front of him, largely obscured from view by Paul's crouching figure.

"Paul!" Griff called and began down the aisle.

The crouched figure didn't pause; gave no indication it had heard.

"Paul, stop!"

Griff broke into a lumbering trot. He reached Paul and gasped when he saw more clearly what he was doing.

The church vicar lay on the floor before Paul, curled into the foetal position, arms clutched tightly around his head. Paul rained blows onto the vicar's arms, his thighs, his side. The vicar appeared to be conscious, still aware enough of what was happening to keep his head protected, but he would not be able to maintain it for much longer under such relentless, focused assault.

"For God's sake, Paul, stop! You're going to kill him."

Paul continued beating the curled figure of the churchman, but spoke in a matter-of-fact, hoarse tone which chilled Griff. "That's the general idea, you fucking halfwit."

"No! Enough!"

Griff grabbed Paul by the shoulders and yanked him backwards. His slight form stood no chance against Griff's bulk. Paul toppled to his back with a snarl of rage and immediately scrabbled onto his front to get back to his feet.

"Uh-huh," said Griff.

He poked out a foot and yanked away one of Paul's forearms

which he was utilising as support to lever himself upright. His shoulder thudded back to the tiled floor and he uttered a thin shriek of rage.

Griff hesitated for a moment, time enough for Paul to start levering himself upright again, before doing the only thing he could think of to subdue him.

Fourteen: It's Watching

They were approaching the church when David's mobile rang.

"Griff! Where are you? Did you find him?"

"Yes. I'm inside the church. You'll have to come around the back. I left the door open."

"Is Paul with you now?"

"Yes. I'm sitting on him."

"Sitting on him?"

Rhys and Sarah looked at David, eyebrows raised.

"You heard correctly," said Griff. "It was the best I could come up with at short notice." David heard him let out a long breath. "Trouble is, I'm no featherweight and I think I might have sat down too heavily. Heard a few of his ribs break."

"Why— Oh, never mind. We're coming into the grounds of the church now. Be with you in a few moments."

David disconnected the call and shot the others a worried glance.

"It doesn't sound good. He said we need to go around the back—"

"I know the door," said Sarah. "Follow me."

She led them to the back of the church and in through the open door. They passed what looked like a lot of choir outfits before entering the main building.

Griff was sitting low to the ground, facing them about halfway down the aisle. The still figure of Paul Duffy lay underneath him. Sitting at the end of a pew near them was a man who David vaguely recognised from the occasional wedding or carol concert he'd attended at the church.

Sarah, a regular churchgoer, bounded forward. "Reverend Hopkin? Are you all right?"

As they drew closer, David could see the vicar's face was red and puffy. One side was particularly bloated, the purple stains of the start of a spectacular bruise emphasising the swelling.

The vicar tried to offer Sarah a smile, but it turned into a grimace.

"I'm fine," he said. "A little battered and bruised, but it doesn't hurt too much. So long as I don't try to smile."

"Guys?" Griff was bending and twisting around to peer into Paul's face. "His eyes are back to normal. It should be safe to let him up now."

Reverend Hopkin began to nod but that, too, seemed to create more discomfort; he winced, stopped moving his head and spoke instead. "Yes. That's fine."

Griff eased onto his knees and rose with a grunt. He rubbed at his right knee. "That's going to give me gyp later."

David stepped forward and stopped by the prone figure. "Paul? Are you okay? Let me help you up."

He straddled Paul and lowered his hands beneath his armpits. The heat he would expect to find beneath someone's upper arms remained absent; the odour of rotting meat was stronger. It wasn't until he began to tug upwards beneath his shoulders that Paul began to move. David got him to his feet and walked him to a pew on the other side of the aisle from where the vicar sat. He sat him down and peered at him.

"Are you okay?"

Paul glanced up. His eyes had indeed returned to their normal pale green. He nodded.

Remembering what Griff had said about cracking some of Paul's ribs, David asked, "Does your chest hurt?"

Paul shook his head. "Nothing hurts. Not even these." He held up his hands. They weren't in as bad a condition as they had been when David had first seen Paul fresh out of the grave, but they were lumpen and deformed, the knuckles twisted and swollen. A little like the vicar's face.

"I guess now we have to call the police," said Griff.

Reverend Hopkin didn't hesitate. "No police. Paul is innocent of any wrongdoing. The one that is guilty is beyond the reach of the law. Human law, at any rate. God's law is another matter."

"What happened?" Rhys asked, looking at Griff.

David turned to listen. He was aware that Paul's head turned slightly as if he, too, was interested in the answer.

"When I got here, the vicar was lying on the floor with Paul bent over him, beating the shit out of him." Griff seemed to remember where he was and shot Reverend Hopkin an apologetic look. "Um, sorry."

The vicar waved away the apology. "If you hadn't arrived when you did, I fear he would have killed me."

Sarah gasped and her hand flew to her mouth. "No! Paul would never do something like that."

"Not Paul, no," said Rhys quietly.

"Your friend is quite right," Reverend Hopkin told Sarah. "That wasn't Paul who attacked me."

There was something about the vicar's manner. "You know what did, don't you?" said David.

Reverend Hopkin began to nod, but remembered himself before the motion caused him to wince. "Yes, I know what inhabits your friend."

David felt a tug at his shirt and glanced down. Paul mouthed at him, *It's watching.*

"Um," he said, "I think me and Griff ought to be getting Paul back to my house." He looked hard at Griff, willing him to agree.

Griff didn't look thrilled at the prospect of going anywhere with Paul, but nodded.

"Not yet," said Rhys. "We need to ask Reverend Hopkin…" He tailed away at David's frantic hand gestures.

"Why don't you and Sarah make sure Reverend Hopkin is all right?" David made a face he hoped Rhys would interpret in the right way.

"Um…"

Sarah came to his rescue. "Of course we will," she said brightly. "We'll make sure everything's secure here and see him back to the vicarage."

"Oh," said Reverend Hopkin. "There is one thing before you

go." He looked at Griff. "I hate to ask for another favour after what you've already done, but the font is rather heavy. I had intended to ask Emlyn to help me to lift it in the morning, but I'm afraid I'm no longer up to the task…"

Griff smiled. "Ah, heavy lifting I'm good at. Come on, Rhys, gissa hand."

They were both red in the face by the time they'd heaved the stone font upright. The tiles where it had fallen were cracked and sunken.

"Thank you, boys," said Reverend Hopkin. "The church is in as fine a condition as it can be for Sunday morning service. Which is probably the best that can be said for its vicar, too."

"Let's be on our way, then, Griff," said David. "Come on, Paul."

Paul stood and glanced at the vicar. His eyes flashed yellow. "I'll see you again, priest."

A chill ran up David's spine. The voice had sounded like Paul's, except for the gravelly quality. Yet the eyes had returned to green. Perhaps, after all its exertions, whatever inhabited Paul's body only retained sufficient strength for the occasional flash of yellow and snatch of hoarse discourse.

"Okay, then. Rhys, Sarah, see you back at mine. I hope you're not in too much pain, Reverend Hopkin."

The vicar gave a strained half-smile. "Oh, I've suffered worse on a rugby field. Although, that was quite some years ago." He looked at Griff. "Thank you, once again, young man."

Paul accompanied them willingly enough, unspeaking and head bowed, dragging his feet—his bare feet, David realised with a pang of anxiety. That prompted a thought.

"Griff." David had no idea if 'it' was continuing to watch them, and didn't know what the implications might be if it was—he felt he was stumbling about in the dark, blindfolded—but instinctively kept his voice low so that Paul would have to strain to hear his words. Not that Paul seemed to be paying him or Griff the slightest attention. "On the way to the church, when you followed him. Did anyone see Paul?"

Griff also seemed reluctant to speak at normal volume in front of Paul. "There were a couple of kids carting an old wardrobe to the common for the bonfire. If they knew Paul, they didn't act as if they recognised him. They just shouted something after him about his bare feet and laughed. He soon went out of my sight, but I didn't see another soul until I got inside the church, so hopefully he didn't encounter anyone, either."

David gave a sigh of relief. It seemed they'd been lucky.

"What are we going to do, mate?" Griff's expression was as grave as it had been while carrying Paul's coffin. "We can't have him running around assaulting vicars. And it appears we can't involve the police." He pursed his lips and blew out in exasperation.

"I don't know." David lowered his voice further. "Let's get him back inside as fast as we can, hopefully without anyone else seeing him. Then wait to see what Sarah and Rhys have to say. After that…" He matched Griff's sound of exasperation. "Fuck knows."

Cath Duffy drove through Taiwyn. Her parents lived on the edge of the closest town around two miles away through narrow lanes. She was running a little late—she'd taken her time cleaning the house and then enjoyed a long shower—but that was fine. Her mum would only be cooking a frozen pizza and would wait for Cath to arrive before popping it in the oven; the salad that was probably already sitting on plates might wilt a little, but… first-world problems.

This Saturday had turned out to be the sort of autumnal day Cath loved: fresh, dry and blowy, the sun appearing often from behind scudding, cotton-wool clouds. A marked contrast to the gloomy previous day and rain-soaked evening, although that had been the perfect weather for burying your husband.

Cath's face twisted into a sad smile and she turned on the car radio. An old Spice Girls hit was playing and she began to hum along, her expression growing less melancholy.

The village streets were almost deserted. She saw a few kids collecting for Bonfire Night—she'd given those who called to her house earlier some cardboard she'd saved for them—but otherwise the place was quiet. Usually the case when the village rugby team was playing away. As she turned down the road which would take her past the church and out of the village, she caught a glimpse of three men walking away from her, in the direction of the common.

One of them looked like David—he lived near the common—and she was certain another was Griff; she couldn't mistake his bulk and he was dressed as she had seen him earlier when he'd passed her house.

The third man looked familiar, but in a way she couldn't quite place and that, for some reason she couldn't fathom, caused her a deep pang of disquiet.

It had been no more than a glimpse—she had passed beyond sight a moment later—and the men had been distant with their backs to her, but there was something about the third man that reminded her of…

She shook her head. That was silly; probably an overwrought reaction to what she had been through the past few months. The man's head had been bowed slightly, as though watching where he was stepping, and there were lots of men whose hair was tawny.

The notion crossed her mind to turn around and drive past the men, pull over and say hello to Dai and Griff. Remind them to call round to collect their coats. It wouldn't be, she told herself, to find out what the third man looked like from the front; that would merely be a consequence of stopping to say hi to a couple of friends.

"Cut it out," she told herself out loud. "You've held it together so far, girl. Now's not the time to start losing it."

Besides, she was already late for her parents.

Cath turned the radio louder and drove on.

Fifteen: Myths and Legends

They turned into David's road without incident. Although they'd heard a couple of vehicles going by on adjoining roads, no cars had come directly past them. It was around lunchtime; many villagers would have driven to Swansea to watch Taiwyn play rugby. The club was tiny in comparison to the town and city clubs—it was a minor miracle it survived at all in this age of professionalism—but its support was large, loyal and vociferous. There would be more activity on the approaches to the pub and village shop, but they were streets away and Taiwyn was a sleepy village at the best of times. It's what made it an attractive place to live. There were plenty of livelier attractions for those who wanted them within easy reach in town. And the city of Cardiff, with its cultural and sporting attractions, its restaurants and nightlife, lay only twenty miles to the east.

David felt himself stiffen when he saw two youngsters walking along the pavement towards them. A boy and a girl, probably of junior school age. He tugged the sleeves of Griff and Paul to motion them onto the road in a break between parked cars. The children were both engrossed in their phones and walked past without a glance at the men. *Without even noticing they were there,* David thought as he relaxed.

They were almost there when they heard someone calling.

"Cooee. Hello there, boys. I hope Martin has recovered."

David glanced to his right and saw Mrs Jones standing on her doorstep. *Probably noticed us all going past earlier and has been stood there ever since, waiting for us to come back so she can find out what's going on.* David did not consider himself to be uncharitable, but couldn't help adding, *Bloody nosy cow.*

He whispered to Griff, "Deal with her. I'm taking Paul inside."

"Who the hell is Martin?" Griff whispered back.

David nodded at Paul. "You know. Martin. Paul's cousin."

"Oh, yeah," Griff muttered. "How could I forget?" He turned towards Mrs Jones.

Without breaking stride, David steered Paul along the pavement and into his garden. Before ushering Paul into the house, he risked a glance to where Griff was talking to his neighbour. Mrs Jones wasn't paying Griff any attention. She was staring at Paul, her mouth partly open. Even from a distance of the width of three houses, David could tell that her skin had grown pale with shock.

Paul made straight for the kitchen. David suspected his eyes were flashing yellow, but found he didn't have the inclination or energy to confirm his suspicion. He was suddenly bone-tired. He trailed in Paul's wake.

"I'm guessing you're hungry again," he said with a sigh.

Paul had opened the fridge and stood gazing into it.

"I doubt there's much left in there, but let me see what I can find. Go and sit down."

Paul shuffled aside and took a seat at the kitchen table.

David pulled out a half-eaten pack of bacon and unwrapped it. He sniffed at it uncertainly. "Not sure how long this has been open. Still, I don't suppose you're fussy."

He placed it on the edge of the table. "I'll grill that in a minute. Let's see what else is there."

When he turned back to the table clutching a chunk of cheddar, Paul was tucking into the bacon. Strips of raw meat dangled from his lips, reminding David of the chicken he'd stopped him from eating the night before.

He sighed again and removed the packaging from the cheese. He placed it on the table alongside the fast-disappearing bacon. Barely sparing it a glance, Paul picked up the cheese and began gnawing at it.

"That's it," David said. "Until I can get to the supermarket, there is no more food. We'll have to order in a takeaway later." His stomach rumbled. "Or perhaps sooner."

He filled a pint glass with water and left it on the table. Unwilling to watch his friend chewing raw meat and a slab of cheese, he wandered through to the living room. The smell of decay had gone;

it was in the kitchen now.

The front door opened and closed. Griff walked in, his expression sober.

"She's not buying it," he said, shaking his head. "I did all the remarkable family resemblance bit, gave her a long spiel about how Paul's mother and Martin's mother are identical twins and that's why he and Paul look so much alike. I was quite inventive, pretty persuasive, I thought, but I don't think she was even listening. She couldn't keep her eyes off Paul. When you took him inside, she just stood and stared towards your house. I was afraid she was having some sort of seizure. Eventually, she turned around, went inside and shut the door without even looking at me." He shrugged. "She knows. She might have trouble believing it, but she knows."

David grunted. "Let's hope Reverend Hopkin has a way to banish this thing from inside Paul. Whatever it is."

"And if we can do that? Perform some kind of exorcism? What then? Dai, you have to face it. The smell coming from him says it all. Paul's rotting away from the inside out. There's no medical help for that."

"Since when did you become a doctor?" David knew he was being unfair, but couldn't help himself.

Griff didn't seem to care. "Don't need to be a doctor to know that." He pulled a face. "The only doctor that can help him is a witch doctor."

Rhys and Sarah did not return for a couple of hours. David peeked into the kitchen about an hour before they arrived. Paul was slumped forward on the kitchen table, head on arms, fast asleep. Of the raw bacon and cheese, there was no sign apart from a few crumbled flakes of cheddar. The glass of water was empty. David wrinkled his nose at the smell. He opened the kitchen window wide and closed the door firmly behind him when he returned to the living room.

He and Griff sat with the television on showing snooker, the sound off. They spoke little while they waited.

Sarah and Rhys came bearing gifts. Sausage rolls, pasties, crisps and chocolate bars. Bottles of cola and lemonade.

"We took a detour to the shop," Sarah explained. "We guessed you'd be hungry. We brought some for Paul, too." She frowned. "Still find it hard to believe we're talking about Paul as if he's alive. Speaking of which…?"

"In the kitchen," said David. "Asleep." His stomach rumbled once more; it had been, off and on, for the past couple of hours. "Good job bringing food. He's scoffed what was left in my fridge."

He delayed asking the burning questions until they had started to eat. He began by enquiring after Reverend Hopkin.

"He'll live," said Sarah. "He'll be sore for the next few days, but I don't think there's anything broken. He won't look a pretty sight delivering tomorrow's services, but I've offered to pop around in the morning with my concealer and hide the bruising to his face." She winced. "Can't do much about the swelling, though."

"That vicar's a plucky guy," said Griff, spraying pastry crumbs.

"He's far more than that," said Rhys quietly. He glanced at Sarah, eyebrows raised. She nodded for him to go on. "At first, I didn't know whether to believe the strange tale he told us, but by the time we left, he'd convinced me."

"Me, too," said Sarah.

"That thing inside Paul," continued Rhys. "Reverend Hopkin gave it a name. Bugan." He grunted. "Sounds like a device for spraying insecticide. He said many ancient legends have been passed down over the millennia originating with this Bugan, and its name has become corrupted into other forms, but he was adamant it's the modern English translation of what inhabits our friend."

Griff pulled out his phone and tapped at it. "Buggane," he read from the screen. "B-u-g-g-a-n-e. A Celtic creature similar to an ogre that has a strong dislike for churches. Especially prevalent in the my-thology of the Isle of Man."

"Yeah," said Rhys, "I googled it, too. Reverend Hopkin said there are elements of truth in that and other monsters from ancient legend. Many of them originate with this Bugan. He said it's far, far older than the Celts."

"From when we all lived in the forest," murmured Sarah.

Rhys nodded. "That's what he said."

"Okay," said David. "So what is it? A demon?" He half-smiled at how ridiculous the question sounded, but then remembered the way Paul's hands had healed in front of their eyes and the smile faded.

"We asked the same question," Rhys said, looking at Sarah.

She nodded. "The reverend said it's not exactly a demon in the sense we think of them. Although he clearly found it difficult to explain precisely what it is, I got the sense it has many similarities to what we think of as Lucifer."

"Although," added Rhys, "he was at pains to point out it's not the traditional Devil, either, despite possessing many of the same characteristics."

"Huh," said Griff, his phone back in his pocket. "What, like evil?"

Sarah nodded. "He implied that the idea of the Devil and the traits we associate with it are at least partly based upon Bugan. A hatred of all the things we hold dear, like love and compassion and kindness. It comes from an ancient time when humans were few and unsophisticated. Their primary drivers were, basically, finding food and shelter."

"Survival at its most elemental," added Rhys. "Bugan roamed huge land masses largely free of humans. Those he encountered, he might kill for the sheer fun of it, or he might tolerate them. It was only as millennia passed, continents formed and humanity proliferated, grew more intelligent and sophisticated, that it developed a hatred of us."

Griff lowered the lemonade bottle from which he had been taking a long swig and uttered a loud belch. "Oops, pardon. I have a question. This vicar is, like, well, a vicar, right? A man of God. What's a man of God doing talking about ancient demons and suchlike? And how does he know all this shit?"

"Well," said Rhys, "this is the part I found most difficult to swallow. I mean, the stuff about a quasi-demon from ancient times I could believe in the sense it's based on tales people used to sit around the fire in their caves and tell each other in grunts and hoots. That's how most folklore has been passed down, becoming embellished during each telling." He shrugged. "A bear with eyes glinting by starlight could, millennia later, have morphed into a fire-breathing demon with glowing eyes."

"Hmm," said David. "No bear could have brought Paul back from the grave or made his torn hands whole again or make his eyes glow like they do."

"That's true," said Rhys. "Seeing is believing. But let me continue with what the good reverend told us. He reckons he's the latest in a long line of guardians which stretches back to the time of the Celts. It was the Celts who banished Bugan from Earth more than two millennia ago. They knew it was only banished, not destroyed, and so set a guardian to watch for its return. A circle of wood already occupied the site where the church now stands. It has been sacred ground for millennia. The Celts replaced the wood with a circle of stones. In time, that was replaced by the earliest Christian chapels. Eventually, the stone church that's there now was built on precisely the spot where Bugan was banished."

"Reverend Hopkin isn't really a man of God," said Sarah. "More a man of gods. He said it's his greatest secret, but one he now feels compelled to share with us since we have become caught up in Bugan's return. He showed us a faded manuscript written in old Welsh." She gave a short laugh. David fancied it contained an edge of hysteria. "It's basically a handbook. How to Slay Ancient Demons."

"Ah," said Griff. "At last we come to it."

David nodded slowly. "So how do we slay it?"

Sarah looked at Rhys.

"There's only way to destroy Bugan," he said. "Through purification. In other words, by fire."

A movement made David look up. Paul was standing in the living room doorway. Listening.

Sixteen: Consumer of Carrion

David grabbed a sausage roll and led Paul back to the kitchen. Griff followed them.

"How are your ribs, man?" he enquired, looking at Paul with concern. "I cracked a couple playing rugby when I was seventeen. Hurt like hell to even breathe for a week or two."

Paul gave a slight shrug. "Can't feel a thing." He regarded the cellophane-wrapped sausage roll in David's hand with a curious lack of expression.

"Okay, that's good," said Griff. "Look, I'm sorry for sitting on you so hard, but I didn't know how else to stop you getting back up. And you were laying into the vicar, though I guess it wasn't really you…"

Griff tailed off. Paul wasn't paying him the slightest attention. Then Paul's eyes flashed yellow and he grabbed at the sausage roll.

David didn't try to prevent him snatching the food from his hands. "Hey," he said, "chill, man."

Paul had already resumed his seat and was tearing at the cellophane. Tearing at it with fingers that were no longer swollen and misshapen from pounding away at the vicar. David glanced at Griff and motioned with his head towards Paul's hands. Griff looked and his eyes grew wide.

As soon as the pastry was free of wrapping, Paul began to cram it into his mouth and chew. He glanced at David and then towards the work surface. He repeated the motion and David followed his gaze—his green-eyed gaze, he was relieved to note.

A notebook and pen sat on the worktop beneath the phone attached to the wall. Though he rarely used the landline any more, David kept them near the phone for making notes of parts numbers when motorcycle dealers returned his enquiries.

David stepped to the worktop and picked up the pen and notepad. He raised his eyebrows at Paul, who gave an almost imperceptible nod. He had nearly finished the sausage roll.

"Griff, do us a favour, will you, and fill his glass with water?"

"Sure. What are you going to do with—" He broke off at David's curt shake of the head. He busied himself fetching water for Paul, while surreptitiously watching.

David opened the pad to a blank page and removed the top from the pen—it was a black marker, perfect for noting strings of numbers and letters in permanent legibility. He returned to the table and casually placed pad and pen on it within Paul's reach. Retreating to lean with his back against the worktop, he also watched, while trying not to make it obvious his attention was on Paul.

Without looking directly at the tabletop, Paul reached out and picked up the pen. Not once glancing at the pad, he wrote something on it in block capitals. Then he dropped the pen and picked up the glass of water Griff had placed close to hand. After tilting back his head and draining the glass, he slumped forward, head on hands, and went back to sleep.

David grabbed the pad, motioned to Griff and they both crept from the kitchen.

"What happened?" asked Rhys.

"He rammed down the sausage roll, drank a pint of water and promptly fell asleep," said Griff.

"His hands have healed again," said David. He held up the notepad. "Paul was trying to tell us something without Bugan knowing. He wrote something on this pad without looking at the page. Maybe Bugan can only see what he sees."

He turned the pad so everyone could see the page. On it was printed three words.

DONT FEED IT

David broke the silence with a grunt. "Well, there's not much chance of that, anyway. There's no food left in the house."

"Except for this pasty and bar of Snickers," said Griff.

"Eat them up, then," said Sarah.

Griff looked around. "Nobody else?" When he received three headshakes, he grinned. "Okay, then. Don't mind if I do." He grabbed the pasty and began to munch on it.

"You know," said Rhys, "I've been thinking. About how it's even possible for Paul to be walking around. And this apparent obsession with food. Yet he's not peed or pooped?"

David shook his head. "Not as far as I know."

They all looked at Rhys.

"I reckon," he said, "that Paul's digestive system isn't working. Not like ours do, so there's no waste removal. Perhaps there isn't even any waste to remove because Bugan completely consumes everything that passes Paul's lips. His nerves are dead, thus no sensation of pain. I'll bet his sexual function is non-existent. Probably his auto-immune system, too. When Bugan resurrected Paul, it was only interested in his motor functions, but needed his brain to be working to allow him to move around. So it got his lungs and heart working to provide oxygen for the brain; his eyes to see; his tongue and vocal cords to allow him to communicate. Everything else—Paul's liver, kidneys, intestines, whatever—are still dead."

Griff nodded enthusiastically. "It's what I was telling Dai."

"That would explain the stink coming off him," said David. "It's getting worse."

"Yep," agreed Rhys. "It can't keep Paul going for much longer, even with the limited functions he has. And now Paul wants us to stop feeding him, he's going to deteriorate even quicker. Bugan has obviously been utilising the food Paul's been eating to make it stronger. I suspect sleep also allows it to muster its reserves. But it depleted most of its resources in attacking Reverend Hopkin. And that sausage roll isn't going to help a great deal. If we don't give Paul more food, Bugan is going to struggle to replenish its strength."

"Maybe that's what Paul is trying to do," said Griff. "Starve it out."

"Perhaps," said Rhys, "but that won't kill it. Reverend Hopkin was clear on this: only fire can destroy it. No, I think Paul is trying to bring matters to a head. To force Bugan into acting quickly, while it still can." He glanced at Sarah and frowned. Tears ran freely down her cheeks. "Sar? What's wrong?"

"I'm thinking ahead," she said, her voice hitching with sobs. "It's something you all know, but are trying to avoid facing. It's the fucking twenty-foot elephant sitting on the coffee table."

Her sobs tailed away as she brought herself under control.

David looked from Rhys to Griff. They all knew to what Sarah alluded. It was Rhys who gave it voice.

"We're going to have to kill Paul. Burn him."

Since it had been such a fine autumn day, night seemed to take a little longer to fall. By six o'clock, it had grown completely dark. David sat at the kitchen table, his stomach making noises like distant thunder. The effects of the pasty and chocolate he'd eaten earlier had long worn off. Griff sat across from him, browsing the internet on his phone.

Sarah and Rhys had left around four. David had insisted they go and do whatever they needed to do on a Saturday; at the very least, to make sure they ate properly. Griff had been adamant in his refusal to leave him alone with Paul.

"I'll be okay." David tried to sound resolute. "I don't think Bugan is going to waste the last of its strength attacking me."

"I don't care." Griff folded his arms and stuck out his lower lip.

David had reluctantly given in, but continued to insist that Rhys and Sarah take time out. He'd had to almost push them out of the front door.

"Really, guys," he said. "Go and eat. Do your shopping. Watch TV. Whatever."

"I could do with a bloody stiff drink," said Rhys.

"Go have a drink, then. But keep your phones to hand. I'll call if there's any problem. It's not like you live far away. You can get back here within minutes."

"We'll come back by seven anyway," said Sarah. She held up a hand to stem his protests. "We'll sit with Paul while you two go to Rhys's and eat. I'll make you each up a plate of whatever we have.

Say yes, or we're not going anywhere."

David glanced at Griff, who was already nodding.

"Okay," he said with a smile. "Yes. And thank you."

A few minutes later, David received a text from Rhys: *Your nosy neighbour was in her window on the phone. The jungle drums are beating.*

After ensuring no snacks or fizzy drinks remained in the living room, David made up the makeshift bed on the sofa. In response to Griff's raised eyebrows, he replied, "I want to bring all this to a head, too. If that thing inside Paul gathers energy while Paul sleeps, let's make sure he sleeps well."

Griff considered for a moment. "I suppose. Whatever this is, I think it's going to end tonight."

"I think it must. If it doesn't, the fact of Paul's return will be blown wide open now that nosy parker down the street has cottoned on."

Griff shrugged. "At least it will no longer be our problem."

"That's true. But I don't think Taiwyn is ready for this, never mind the world. I doubt it ever will be." He patted down the duvet. "Right. Draw the curtains while I fetch him."

The stench in the kitchen, despite the open window, made David want to gag. He shook Paul by the shoulder.

Paul lifted his head and his eyes flashed yellow. "Food," he said in the gravelly tone.

"Later. Now, sleep." David beckoned for Paul to follow and began to walk away.

With a popping sound from his knees, Paul rose and followed.

He slumped onto the sofa without complaint, turned to his side and fell immediately back to sleep.

That had been almost two hours ago and they hadn't heard from him since.

Griff put his phone back in his pocket and sighed. "I'm ravenous. And I need a pee. I'll look in on Sleeping Beauty on my way back."

David listened to Griff clump upstairs. A few minutes later, he heard the flush, followed soon by the descending clumps. Light on his feet Griff wasn't.

The next sound he heard was a yell. "Dai! Come here! Quick!"

Paul was sitting up. Griff had switched on a lamp, bathing the room in muted light.

"What's wrong?" David looked closely at Paul, expecting his eyes to be aglow, but they were their normal colour.

"Take a deep breath," said Griff. "Through your nose."

David frowned, but closed his mouth and inhaled. His frown deepened. He took a few more paces into the living room, skirting the coffee table, until he stood next to Paul. He breathed in deeply again.

"The stink. It's there, but faint. Stale." He shook his head wonderingly. "Just about gone."

Griff nodded. "Yep. That's a residue you can still smell. Like yesterday's curry." He glanced at Paul. "He's stopped rotting."

Paul slowly raised his head and shook it.

"Not stopped rotting," he said.

"Huh?" said Griff.

"Not rotting. Consumed. In the extremity of its need, it has consumed the organs for which it had no use. It has feasted on carrion."

Griff swallowed. "I think I just lost my appetite."

Paul shrugged. "Taste is not one of the senses it has returned to me. Nor smell. I remember that smelling and eating good food was one of life's pleasures."

David peered more closely at Paul's face. There was no sign of yellow in the eyes. "Has it left you again?"

Paul nodded. "But I don't think it will go far. It's gone to hunt out something combustible. Like a canister of gas, or something."

"Shit," said David. "It won't have to look far. There's an almost-full can of petrol in my workshop. What does it want it for?"

"It intends to burn down the vicarage with Reverend Hopkin inside. Then it's going to destroy the church."

"How do you know?" asked Griff. "Can't it keep anything from you, like you did with the writing?"

"It grows desperate. It is not concerned with masking its thoughts from me and I have grown more adept at reading them. Nor is it concerned with examining mine. It considers me almost spent and no threat." Paul almost smiled, but he seemed to have lost the ability. "Therein lies its weakness. Will you help me finish this?"

David shot a glance at Griff. They both looked down at Paul and nodded.

"Thank you," he said. "I know you were both good friends to me, even though I can no longer feel what friendship means. Now listen. This is what you must do…"

Seventeen: A Plan in Action

David hurried to tie the laces on his trainers. He grabbed a hoodie from behind the kitchen door and shrugged it on; it might have been a mild day, but it was now November and the evenings were turning chilly.

Seeing his cigarettes and lighter on the work surface reminded him; he opened a cupboard and took out a box of matches. He pocketed his cigarettes and lighter, leaving the matches in their place. Next he grabbed his keys and rushed out of the kitchen door. There were no outside lights, but he didn't need any to find his way the short distance to the workshop door. He fumbled with the keys until he found the right one through touch. It slid in easily and he unlocked the door. He switched on the light and froze.

Every nerve-ending pinged an alarm; every hair on his arms and neck and legs tingled as they rose; a shiver began from the base of his spine and ran up to his head, making the hairs there want to stand on end, too. The evening *had* grown chilly, but not enough to frost his breath. Yet it plumed in front of his face like cigarette smoke.

He wasn't alone in the workshop, although he could see no one else. Not see, no, but all his other senses confirmed the presence of another. A sound at the furthest point of hearing, like a distant buzzing of angry flies; a smell, also so faint as to be almost imagined, of dusty mausoleums; a suggestion of a taste of something oily, something foul; and, the strongest of all, the touch of icy regard.

Above his fear, David felt something else; a rare emotion for a generally happy-go-lucky type of bloke. Anger, fuelled by a sense of indignant violation.

"I know what you are," he said in a level tone. "Now get the fuck out of my workshop."

The air moved. Pulsed, as though the invisible presence had drawn in a huge breath that sucked all the air from the space.

David gasped, his anger already dispersing, then flinched as frigid air flooded past him and blew into his face like a gust fresh from the Arctic.

He fumbled in his pocket for his phone, activated the screen and dialled Griff's number.

"Yeah?"

"It was here, in the workshop, but it's gone. I think it might have returned to Paul."

"Tell me about it. His fucking eyes are glowing orange."

"It will take a few minutes to fill the can. Can you try to hold him there?"

"I'll try. Hurry. Got to go—he's getting to his feet."

David disconnected and thrust the phone back into his pocket. He ran to the back of the workshop, skirting the bits and pieces of dismantled motorcycle. Three ten-litre plastic petrol containers stood against the wall. Only one contained anything: it was two-thirds full of petrol, ready to pour into the Norton's tank when he had finished restoring it. He grabbed one of the empty ones.

Leaving the workshop door open to allow light to spill into the garden, he ran to the rear wall of the house where a tap protruded. He screwed the top off the can, thrust the opening under the tap and twisted the tap on.

"Come on, come on," he muttered as the water sloshed into the container.

When he judged the container was around two-thirds full—he didn't want to overfill it and risk Paul being unable to lift it—he turned the tap off, replaced the lid on the container and lugged it back to the workshop. He left it next to the other empty container, hefted the one containing petrol and carried it to the side door that let into the garage. He closed the door behind him and edged around his car in the darkness until he reached the main garage door.

He had to put the petrol can down while he fumbled in the dark for the catch on the door that enabled it to be opened from the inside.

The door opened silently and he thanked his lucky stars he'd oiled it only a few weeks earlier. He hefted the sloshing container, stepped into the lane and closed the door behind him, being extra careful not to let it bang shut. Moving sluggishly due to the weight of the container, he turned and began to make his way along the lane.

Griff put his phone on the coffee table and stood. He moved to block Paul's path to the living room door.

The glowing orange eyes turned towards him. "Do not interfere." The voice was croaky.

Griff resisted the urge to take a step backwards. "Tell me where you're going." He already had a shrewd idea where it intended to go, but felt that stalling by talking to the creature seemed preferable to having to restrain it physically again. His knee still twinged and complained from the morning's encounter.

"It is no concern of yours," grated Bugan's voice. But it did not step forward, which Griff took as an encouraging sign. Perhaps it remembered how easily Griff had been able to subdue it earlier merely by sitting on it.

Griff shrugged, but stayed put.

"Step aside," said Bugan. Paul's hands bunched into fists and Griff tensed.

But Bugan hesitated.

"Step aside," it repeated, but the hands relaxed. It made Paul's eyes and head swivel, swinging his gaze around the living room.

"I'll move out of the way when you tell me where you're going."

Paul gazed into the corner of the room. At the old-fashioned standard lamp that stood there.

It had belonged to David's grandmother and he'd agreed to take it when she'd died as a memento, though he professed not to like it. Griff didn't blame him. It was an ugly thing, made of heavy, turned oak.

Paul walked over to it, squeezing between the edge of the sofa and an armchair to reach it. He yanked off the yellow shade, allowing it to fall to the floor, and gripped the shaft with both hands. He turned back towards Griff, holding the lamp like the shaft of a spear. The shadeless bulb seemed to stare at him like a lidless, alien eye. The heavy base appeared not to bother Bugan; evidently, the consumption of Paul's rotting internal organs had imbued it with a fresh dose of strength.

The lamp shaft was constructed of solid oak. The base, too. If it came at him swinging, Bugan could do Griff some serious damage. A broken ulna was likely to be the best he could expect; a fractured skull seemed more probable. Griff took a step back, then another, until his back was to the living room door.

The weight of the lamp and its uneven displacement made Paul's movements ponderous. Awkwardly, he manoeuvred himself between the sofa and chair and stood gazing at Griff with eyes which flared like living flames.

"Step aside."

Griff shook his head.

Bugan advanced.

Then stopped when the electrical lead pulled taut. Paul tugged at it, a puzzled frown on his brow. He looked down at the base of the lamp.

Griff took his chance. He darted forwards and grabbed his phone from the coffee table. Before Paul's head had swivelled fully in his direction, Griff had made it back to the door and was reaching behind for the door handle.

Paul swung the base of the lamp around in an arc. Its weight and momentum yanked the cable free; whether the plug had pulled free of the socket or the wires had torn away from the plug, Griff couldn't tell and didn't care. He was already backing out of the living room and pulling the door closed in front of him. The last glimpse he caught of Paul's face was of flashing red eyes.

Griff caught hold of the door handle and braced himself, leaning back in anticipation of the door being yanked from the other side. With his other hand, cursing under his breath when his thick fingers pressed the wrong part of the screen, he called David.

"Griff. You okay?"

"Yeah, but not sure how much longer I can hold—"

Crash! The door shuddered and a chunk of cheap veneer fell out at chest height. The dark base of the lamp protruded from the hole left behind.

"Shit!" exclaimed David down the phone. "What was that?"

"You really need to get better quality interior doors, Dai. Where are you?"

"I'm clear. Get out of his way."

"I'll be glad to."

Griff pressed down the door handle. The lamp base had disappeared, leaving a jagged hole through which Griff caught a glimpse of movement. Before Bugan could damage the door further, Griff gave it a shove and moved smartly to the stairs. He climbed halfway and paused, looking back down. If Bugan had a mind to come after him, Griff doubted the upstairs doors would present any more of a barrier, but he felt confident Bugan would show no further interest in him, provided Griff did not seek to obstruct it any further. At least, that was his hope.

Paul came into sight and Griff tensed in readiness to complete his dash up the stairs. But Paul continued past the foot of the staircase without sparing him a glance. He no longer carried the lamp.

"Dai?" Griff stage-whispered into the phone. "He's gone into the kitchen. Hold on…"

Griff crept down the stairs and peered into the kitchen. It was empty. He moved cautiously forward. The back door stood open. "He's out the back," Griff said into the phone.

"I left a box of matches on the work surface. Are they still there?"

"Nope."

"Good. It must have taken them."

"Wait. I can see Paul. He's coming out of the workshop. He's struggling to carry something… Yep, it's one of your petrol cans."

"That'll slow him down. Get yourself off to the vicarage."

"Shall I lock the back door to slow him down more?"

"No! God knows what it'll do to gain entry and I'd quite like a house to return to when all this is over."

"Okay. Shit, lugging that container isn't slowing him down as much as I'd like." Griff moved hurriedly away from the back door, out of the kitchen and to the front door. "He's coming back inside."

"Get going," said David. "You know what to do."

Griff opened the front door and was about to disconnect the call when a thought struck him. "What about Rhys and Sarah?"

"I'll call them. You just concentrate on getting to Reverend Hopkin before it does."

Rhys was in the kitchen replenishing their drinks when his mobile rang in the living room. Sarah answered it.

"Hi, David, it's Sarah."

"Is Rhys still— Never mind, this is his phone so of course he's still with you."

"Are you okay? You sound a little breathless."

"Yeah, I've been lugging something heavy... Look, it doesn't matter now. I'll explain when I see you. Can you both come?"

"Where are you? Doesn't sound as though you're inside."

"I'm at the end of my street, but Paul's just left my house and is heading towards the vicarage so I'm going to move across the road to the common. Meet me there?"

Rhys came back into the living room, carrying three glasses. "Um, he's left your house?" Sarah said into the phone. "Heading towards the vicarage?" Rhys's eyes widened. "What about Reverend Hopkin?"

"It's all in hand," said David. "Griff has gone to warn him."

"Warn him?"

"Yes." David was beginning to sound exasperated. "Look, it's all coming to a head. Just get here as fast as you can and I'll explain then. The common opposite my house, yeah?"

"Okay, but—"

"Oh, and if you've got a torch, bring it."

"Um, sure, but..." She was speaking to a dead line. Sarah looked at Rhys. "Do you have a torch?"

"Er, I think so, but why—"

Sarah silenced him with a curt shake of her head. She looked at their visitor. "I think you'd better come with us."

Cath Duffy bit her lower lip and nodded.

Eighteen: Water Doesn't Burn

Throughout the long afternoon of inactivity, Griff's knee had stiffened from where he had twisted it while halting the attack on the vicar. Fluid had started to accumulate around the joint, causing the skin to grow tight and giving him a pronounced limp. Still, he didn't have miles to hobble to reach the vicarage and, unencumbered with an almost-full, ten-litre container, he could still move faster than Paul. Nevertheless, Griff cast frequent glances over his shoulder. Apart from the first couple of peeks, when he was still in David's street and could see in the glow of the streetlights Paul Duffy making his ponderous way in his wake, Griff had seen no one.

The church loomed ahead, its grey clock tower lit faintly by floodlights dimmed with age and grime placed along the roof guttering. The vicarage was directly across the road, a light shining in an upstairs window.

Griff hobbled to the garden gate and swung it open. It gave a creak which he might have found satisfyingly spooky at any other time, but that now unnerved him. He glanced back the way he had come, but there was no sign of Paul.

Although still limping, the walk had done Griff good; the knee had loosened a little like a lubricated nut. He hurried along the path to the front door and hammered on it with his fist. Then he backed along the path, neck craned, until he could see the illuminated first-storey window and the light from it fell onto his face.

A shape of a man appeared in the window. Backlit, more a silhouette than a person, but Griff had lived in Taiwyn for most of his life and knew that Reverend Hopkin lived alone. He'd heard whispers of a wife and child, but if they had existed, it had been when Griff was too young to remember. He waved frantically at the silhouette and pointed at the front door. The figure disappeared.

Griff stepped back to the door, shooting anxious glances towards the road while he waited; it remained empty, for now.

The sound came of locks being undone and the door swung

inwards. Griff gasped. The swelling had begun to subside, but the bruising had developed, spreading across the flesh in a rainbow of colour. Reverend Hopkin's face resembled a basket of plums in varying stages of ripeness. But there was no time to ask after the man's comfort or exchange any other pleasantries.

"Reverend, you must come with me this minute."

The vicar's eyes narrowed a fraction. "What's happening?"

"It's Paul. No, it's Bugan. It's on its way here. It's coming for you."

The vicar nodded. "Let me put something on my feet and grab a coat. These old bones feel the evening chill…" He tailed away in face of Griff's impatient nods.

While Reverend Hopkin bustled about inside the hallway, Griff stared back at the road. A figure came into the wash of the furthest streetlight, leaning back to bear the weight of the plastic container it clutched, stiff-armed, before it.

Griff called through the gap in the door. "Reverend, we're out of time. You must come with me now."

The clergyman reappeared, boots on his feet, buttoning up an outdoor coat. He pulled the door closed behind him and turned a key in the deadlock. With the door shut, they were cast in darkness.

"Is there another way we can leave?" asked Griff in a hoarse whisper. He doubted Paul Duffy was close enough to hear him if he'd spoken in his normal voice, but didn't want to take any chances. "So we can avoid the road running past the church but can then circle around to it?"

Reverend Hopkin glanced at the road and his jaw tightened. "Is that a can of petrol it bears?"

"No, but it thinks it is. We've played a trick on it. When it finds out, it's going to get really pissed off. Paul's plan depends on it. You see, we need Bugan to come after us. Rather, to come after you."

The vicar blew out heavily. "Paul, you say? Okay. I have no idea how Paul has managed to formulate a plan, let alone communicate it to you without Bugan's knowledge. I have even less idea how I was going to beat Bugan on my own so I'm willing to go along with a plan that involves me as the bait. To a point, in any case. I would prefer to know more before committing fully—we're not playing games here, as I hope you boys appreciate."

"Oh, rest assured, we appreciate it," said Griff with feeling. "I can explain properly as we go. But we really, *really* need to move now."

Reverend Hopkin nodded. "Follow me."

David waited until he was certain Paul Duffy had disappeared from sight before emerging from the lane, struggling with his own heavy burden. He lugged the container of petrol across the road and onto the common. The ground was soft underfoot after all the rain that had fallen during October, but the top surface was dryer than it had been in weeks thanks to the sun and wind that had shone and blown for most of the day. The common here consisted of rough grasses and sedges, trampled and worn from dog walkers and, at this time of year, from the toing and froing of local children constructing their bonfire. That was situated around twenty yards in from the road, just before the grass gave way to gorse and ferns, to minimise the risk of strong winds blowing sparks onto the houses along David's street.

Although the streetlights did not penetrate that far into the common, David could make out the dark shape of the bonfire; he had deliberately stopped opposite it. It rose as tall as an upended car, a black void against the star-pricked canopy of night.

He shivered, although he was not cold.

Occasionally, he glanced at the houses. He couldn't see anybody watching him from a window—there wasn't even any sign of nosy Mrs Jones. The bonfire site was opposite the end of the terrace and so, thankfully, her house stood thirty yards or more away.

The next time he looked, a man was walking along the pavement towards him, his face pale in the streetlights. Rhys. A little way behind him came two women. David squinted to see them better and cursed silently. As soon as Rhys approached him, he grabbed him by the forearm.

"What the hell is Cath doing here?"

"She came to the house. Paul's mother rung her about some rumour she'd heard. Someone going around impersonating Paul. Our names were mentioned. Griff and Sarah, too."

"Ah, shit." David let go of his arm. "Well, you're going to have to get shot of her. If things go to plan, Paul should be here soon. And she won't want to see what he's going to do."

"Why? What's he going to do?"

David shook his head. The women had arrived. "Hello, Sarah. Cath."

"David," said Cath, "what's going on?" *David*. She only called him that when she was upset.

The small amount of light which reached this part of the common made Cath look insubstantial. Ghostly.

"Cath, you really shouldn't be here."

"Yes, she should," interjected Sarah. "If anybody should be here, it's her."

"Will someone please tell me what the fuck is going on?" Cath looked at David with an intensity he could not deny.

He sighed. "I don't know where to start." He looked in appeal at Sarah.

She shook her head. "Just say it, Dai."

He looked at Rhys, who shrugged. He looked at Cath, whose gaze seemed to pierce him like a laser.

"Oh, God. Okay. There's no easy way to say this—"

"So give me the difficult version." Cath's tone held no hint of mercy.

"Okay." He looked her in the eye. "I heard the sound of knocking during Paul's funeral. It was coming from the coffin. Griff and I went to investigate and found that Paul had broken out of his grave."

Cath's mouth opened wide in shock and her hand came up to cover it. Her eyes filled with disbelief, then tears of bewilderment. Sarah linked an arm through hers.

David blundered on. "Something brought him back against his

will. Some ancient being that lived in these parts thousands of years go… Shit! This sounds ridiculous, but it's true."

Cath's eyes opened wide in, what, horror? Yes, but something else, too: comprehension. Tears spilled freely from them. Her voice came in little more than a whisper. "I saw him. Today. With you and Griff."

David breathed out deeply. "It's Paul, yet it's not. He doesn't want to be here. And he intends returning to wherever he was dragged from as soon as he has destroyed the thing inside him. Otherwise, it will make him kill Reverend Hopkin and destroy the church and then it will be able to escape and take its own form and wander where it likes." David shook his head. "The more I say, the more ludicrous it sounds. And I really don't have time for this." He glanced at Rhys. "Did you bring a torch?"

Rhys nodded.

"Where is he?" Cath's voice had gained some strength; she really was a remarkable woman, David thought, not for the first time. "Where's Paul?"

"He'll be here. Soon."

Cath's glance darted to the petrol container at David's feet. She looked at him, her eyebrows raised.

David could no longer meet her gaze. He looked instead at Sarah. "I have things I must do. It's Paul's plan. He told us about it when Bugan left him again for a few minutes. You'll have to fill in Cath more."

He looked at Rhys and jerked his head for him to follow. Hefting the petrol container, he started towards the dark shape of the bonfire.

Reverend Hopkin led Griff around the side of the vicarage, through the back garden and into a lane via another gate. By following a muddy, shadowed footpath that ran off the lane, they regained the road near the church. They emerged onto it in time to see Paul Duffy lug the petrol can through the front garden gate of the vicarage.

Griff pointed up the hill to where the road bent around out of sight. "Reverend, please go and stand under that furthest streetlight so he'll be able to see you. I suppose I should say so *it* can see you. I'm going to make sure it doesn't set light to the vicarage. It's okay, there's no need to look so concerned. Water doesn't burn. When it realises it's lugged a can of water all the way here, it's going to get angry. I don't think it will be able to move quickly—Paul's joints are deteriorating—but I'd prefer it if you were by the bend. We have to make sure it comes after us so wait for me to join you."

The vicar nodded, his expression grim and resolute. "Be careful." He turned and began to walk up the road.

Griff made his way as quietly as possible to the vicarage and peered over the gate. It was too dark to make out much, but he thought he saw movement before the front door. Two sounds came: a grunt of exertion, followed by the glug-glug-glug of liquid being poured. He waited. The strike of a match sounded, accompanied by a flare of light which quickly died. Another striking match; another flare of light. In the afterimage, Griff saw Paul crouched in the vicarage porch, the petrol container by his side. Another match flared, guttered and went out.

The next sound made Griff's blood run cold. A thin wail that rose higher, higher, impossibly high until it seemed it must shatter the vicarage's windows. In the days that followed, Griff was to hear tales of infants throughout Taiwyn waking up inexplicably and crying uncontrollably to the consternation of their helpless parents.

The wailing dropped, turned into a guttural cry of pure rage. Two red, glowing embers appeared in the porch. Paul had turned to face him. *It* was looking at Griff.

"Oh, crap," Griff muttered.

He took off in a half-run towards where Reverend Hopkin waited for him beneath the streetlight. Griff's knee was still sore and swollen, but the exercise had loosened it and he managed to move, if not entirely freely, then without debilitating discomfort.

He didn't look back until he reached the vicar, and didn't need to then. The reverend was staring down the hill past him and his expression told him all he needed to know. Paul—Bugan—was following. As Griff had suspected, it did not move quickly. Although no longer encumbered by the container of water, Bugan was struggling to make Paul's body proceed at speed. It looked as though Paul's knees had seized, judging by the stiff-legged gait with which he ascended the hill. Nevertheless, he was moving quickly enough to reach them within a minute if they didn't get moving themselves.

"Come on," Griff told Reverend Hopkin.

They began to walk along the pavement. The bend soon hid Paul from their sight.

"Where are we going?"

"The common." Griff filled the reverend in as they walked. He kept glancing behind until Paul came into sight. By increasing their stride slightly, but not to an uncomfortable level for either of them, they were able to maintain a good hundred-yard distance between them and Paul.

The vicar, despite his beating that morning, was able to keep up the pace with only the occasional grimace to betray the odd twinge of discomfort the bruising to his legs and arms must have been causing.

Once he had heard Paul's plan, Reverend Hopkin nodded. "It might not work, but I suppose it's as good as any other plan we could come up with."

"Yep," said Griff. "It has its flaws, not least of which is its dependency on Paul being able to take control of his body against Bugan's will, if only briefly."

"Yes, that's the part which most concerns me."

"Me, too, Father. I mean, Reverend. Sorry."

Reverend Hopkin waved away his apology. "If we destroy Bugan this night and I'm still alive come the morning, I shall be a reverend no longer. I'll be plain old Will Hopkin. It's time Taiwyn's flock had a shepherd who believes in wolves but doesn't know for a fact they exist. Knowledge rather ruins the nature of faith."

"And what will plain old Will Hopkin do?"

"Oh, there's a woman out there a tad younger than yourself who has little or no memory of her father. He would very much like to find her." He gave a heavy sigh. "And if she wants nothing to do with him, at least he will be able to satisfy himself that she is healthy and happy."

"I wish him all the very best with his search. And I'm sure it will end happily for them both."

Reverend Hopkin smiled a sad sort of smile. "Let's hope you are right, young man."

Griff drew in a sharp breath. "Damn it. There's somebody coming."

A couple were walking towards them. Griff glanced back. Paul was still a hundred yards back, moving in that peculiar, yet determined, stiff-legged manner. He still wore the Black Sabbath tee shirt, baggy sweatpants and nothing on his feet. Griff shrugged to himself. There was nothing to be done about it now.

The couple drew closer. Griff recognised them—they lived near him the other side of the village. He nodded to them as they passed and they called, "Good evening," looking curiously at Reverend Hopkin, the bruises to his face apparent under the streetlights.

"Good evening," returned the vicar in a casual tone. Griff found himself feeling a grudging admiration for the man.

He looked back. Paul walked past the couple without sparing them a glance; they stopped, turned and stared after him, the woman's jaw agape, the man gazing down at Paul's bare feet.

"I think the woman recognised Paul," Griff muttered. "Oh, well. Can't be helped."

They turned into the street upon which David lived.

Nineteen: Flames

In the light of Rhys's torch, the bonfire looked quite impressive and there were still four days to go before Bonfire Night. Old planks and deadfall branches had been thrust into the ground to form a rough framework in the approximate shape of a tepee—a fat, broad-based tepee. Broken-up pieces of small furniture and odd bits of wood had been used to fill the space within, and strips of cardboard poked from the gaps. A battered wardrobe leaned drunkenly against the framework, its doors removed and leaning next to it, like wooden ramps. An old mattress, with protruding springs, had been balanced on top of the frame, supported by the top of the wardrobe.

At David's instruction, Rhys lifted one of the wardrobe doors and carried it to the opposite side of the bonfire, creating a second ramp on the other side. David walked around the structure, liberally splashing petrol at its base. As the container began to empty and grew lighter, he lifted it and splashed liquid over the wardrobe, the doors and the parts of the mattress within reach. He went around the bonfire once more, dampening the middle section until barely a litre remained in the container and it could be lifted by a child. He screwed the top back on and left the container next to the nearest wardrobe door.

"What now?" asked Rhys.

"Now we wait," said David. He glanced down the road. "Though we won't have to wait long. Here comes Griff with the vicar." He indicated the torch in Rhys's hand. "I'll need to borrow that, please."

They walked back to where Sarah stood hugging Cath. Judging by her glistening cheeks and swollen eyes, Cath had been sobbing, but she cried no longer. Her expression had become one of fearful anticipation.

She broke out of Sarah's embrace as they approached and looked at David.

"I'd never have forgiven you," she said. "If I'd found out that

Paul had come back and you'd kept if from me."

David dropped his gaze; he didn't know what to say.

"Why were you pouring petrol on the bonfire?" Cath asked. "November fifth is four nights away."

David forced himself to stop shifting from foot to foot like someone desperate for a pee. He had never felt so uncomfortable under another's scrutiny. Still, now that she was here…

He forced himself to look at Cath and held her eyes with his. "It's the only way to destroy the thing inside him. It's what Paul wants."

Cath's jaw set into a determined line David had seen before. She shook her head. "No, Dai. We have to stop him. Get him to the hospital." She drew in a deep, juddering breath that, despite her expression of grim resolve, told David she was barely keeping it together. "I'm going to ring for an ambulance." She drew her phone out of her jacket pocket.

David slowly reached out and placed his hand on hers. He pressed her hand gently but insistently back to the pocket, gazing intently at her the whole time. He paused and then drew her hand from her jacket. It came away from the pocket empty.

David looked to his right, down the street, then back to Cath.

"He's coming," he said.

As Griff and the vicar drew near, David beckoned them away from the others. Another figure had come into view farther back. A man, walking in a curiously upright posture as though too inflexible to bend at knee, elbow or spine.

David shot Griff a look of gratitude. "Okay?"

Griff nodded. "It's not happy about the water trick."

"Good."

Griff glanced in Cath's direction and raised his eyebrows.

David pulled a face and shrugged, before looking at Reverend Hopkin. "Griff's told you Paul's plan? Good," he repeated when he received an affirmative nod. "I'm coming with you."

"Me, too," said Griff.

David shook his head and lowered his voice. "I need you, Rhys and Sarah to keep Cath back." He grimaced. "This is going to be worse on her than on anyone so it might take three of you to restrain her."

"Oh, man…" murmured Griff, but he did not otherwise demur.

A cry echoed into the night. "Paul!" Cath had clearly set eyes upon her late husband.

David hissed at Griff, "Keep her back!"

Griff nodded unhappily and made his way to the others.

David motioned to the vicar. "Come on."

They walked across the common towards the bonfire, David lighting the way with Rhys's torch. The vicar's nostrils twitched when they approached the structure. "Petrol?"

"It should go up like, well, like a bonfire doused in petrol." David indicated the container. "There's enough left for Paul to finish it."

"If he can overcome the will of Bugan."

David nodded grimly. He shared the uncertainty he detected in the vicar's voice. "We'll soon find out. Here he comes. You ready? Stay at the bonfire's edge and keep moving out of Bugan's reach to give Paul chance to take control. I'll stay close to help you out if he manages to catch you."

Reverend Hopkin breathed out heavily and set his jaw into a determined line. "We come to the moment for which I, and countless others before me, was placed here in Taiwyn."

"Good luck."

David turned to face Paul. His approach could be seen by the double orange glow of his eyes. Cath called to him again as he walked within ten yards of her, but he didn't so much as slow his stiff stride. Griff and Rhys had hold of Cath's arms, gently restraining her, while Sarah stood behind her, arms around Cath's neck to offer what comfort she could.

The torchlight illuminated Reverend Hopkin when David turned back to him. He wanted to make sure Bugan did not lose sight of him, though he doubted he needed to worry—Paul's orange eyes were fixed upon the clergyman and nothing else.

As Paul drew within five yards, Reverend Hopkin began to edge around the perimeter of the bonfire. Paul followed him. Thus began one of the most sedate games of tag ever seen.

Though Paul's body was failing, Bugan kept it moving at a steady pace which meant the vicar had to keep moving to avoid being caught. Something about the relentless nature of Paul's stride told David the vicar would tire first.

Paul circled the bonfire, moving through petrol fumes, not seeming to be affected by them. The clergyman, by contrast, coughed once or twice and his eyes looked as though they had begun to smart and stream.

"A pyre," came Paul's gravelly voice, addressing Reverend Hopkin almost conversationally. "I can burn you as well here, priest."

Unease caused David's brow to crease into a frown. Paul had Bugan where he wanted it and yet there was no sign of him being able to take control. His eyes glowed a constant orange and his stiff-legged stride didn't falter as he pursued the vicar around the bonfire. Reverend Hopkin was beginning to noticeably struggle to maintain a safe distance.

"Bollocks," David muttered. Louder, he called, "Stay clear of him, Reverend. I'll be back in a minute." Without waiting for a response, he turned and hurried back to the others.

Griff watched the bobbing torchlight coming their way.

"Why's he coming back?"

"I don't know," replied Rhys, "but Paul's plan obviously isn't working."

Griff let go of Cath's arm. She had stopped struggling and stood with head bowed, sobbing uncontrollably. Rhys let go of her other arm and they both turned towards Dai. Sarah moved to Cath's side, her arm around Cath's shoulders. Sarah wore an expression of deep concern and she, too, watched Dai's approach.

"Bugan's too strong," said Dai without preamble. "And Reverend Hopkin is flagging. What the hell can we do?"

Sarah slipped her arm from around Cath and stepped past Dai, peering towards the bonfire. "We'll have to get Reverend Hopkin away from there," she said. "If that thing catches him…"

Griff shook his head. "Our only chance is to keep it by the bonfire. Otherwise…" He left the thought unspoken. They were all aware this might be their only chance to destroy whatever Bugan was.

"We have to set the bonfire alight," said Rhys. "I hope you have your lighter on you, Dai."

"No!" exclaimed Sarah. "The fumes from all that petrol will light up the whole thing instantly. Reverend Hopkin will be caught in it. And whichever of us ignites it."

"You're quite right," said Rhys. "But you were with me when the good reverend was telling us about his burden. You heard how passionate he is about keeping Bugan from returning to this plane of existence. He may be quite prepared to suffer some serious burns to achieve that aim. To die for his cause, even."

"If one of us sets light to that bonfire, he or she will be facing some serious jail time," said Dai. He nodded towards the houses.

Griff turned to look. The commotion on the common had been noticed. A number of upstairs lights had come on as residents went to their bedroom windows to see what was going on. A small crowd of people was beginning to gather at the common's edge. At least one person held up a phone, recording the event.

"I don't know," continued David, "if it's possible to be convicted of murdering someone who's already been certified as dead and been buried, but we'd at least be guilty of seriously injuring Reverend Hopkin."

They all looked at each other. Then Sarah frowned. "Where's Cath?"

David turned and flashed the torch towards the bonfire. Cath was running across the common. He set off after her, aware the other three were following.

Cath made a beeline for Paul, who looked to be gaining on Reverend Hopkin. The vicar was stumbling away from him, sweating profusely, the colours in his face lurid in the flash of the torchlight.

He was almost spent.

As the reverend came past the wardrobe for the umpteenth time, he glanced at David and gave a brief shake of his head. Sarah was right: they needed to get him away from there.

Paul stiff-trotted into the torchlight, eyes glinting red as he gained on his prey, at the same moment that Cath reached him. She flung her arms around his neck, forcing him to a halt.

"No!" David yelled and increased his pace. He would reach them within seconds, but that might be too late.

David's feet almost slipped from under him as he skidded to a stop. The torchlight bobbled before settling on the couple. Cath had pulled back from Paul so she could gaze into his eyes. With a start, David realised the eyes were no longer aglow.

"My love," Cath murmured. She leaned forward and placed a tender kiss on Paul's lips.

David felt he ought to move away, give them privacy, but he was afraid to in case the eyes began to glow again. He sensed Griff, Rhys and Sarah draw up alongside him. The vicar had noticed his pursuit had stopped. He wheeled away from the bonfire and came to stand, stooped and panting, next to David. They all watched breathlessly.

"It's you," Paul said to his wife. "It was too strong for me. I couldn't gain control. But you… You've ignited something inside me, deep inside where it cannot reach. Something more powerful than all the gods and demons combined. I have control. For now."

Cath moved her hands across Paul's cheeks as though trying to convince herself he was real. "Come away from here. Come home. With me."

Paul shook his head. "There is too little left of me to return home. Even now it feeds. It has started on my brain. Already my oldest memories have gone. Soon the memory of loving you will disappear. And that is the sweetest memory of them all. When all that remains is the ability to control motor function, it will begin on my blood. There is much energy in human blood, even the partly congealed stuff which runs through my veins. That will keep it going long enough to achieve its ends."

Paul glanced away from Cath, towards his friends. "Dai, it will not stop until the church lies in ruins. It will not stop until it has desecrated the hallowed ground. It will make me murder a child there, or something equally as vile. After that, there will be no stopping it."

David was aware of Reverend Hopkin nodding his head beside him.

Paul gazed back into the face of his wife. "Only I can destroy this abomination. And I must do it now while I still have the strength you have given me." For a split second, his eyes glowed yellow and David took half a pace forward. "Only now has it turned its attention to my thoughts. Only now has it realised I am yet capable of harming it. And it musters all its power to wrest back control. You must retreat beyond reach of the flames."

He began to gently push Cath away, but she clung to him, beginning to sob once more.

"We shall meet again in the most beautiful dream." He bent his head, causing a crackling sound from his neck, and kissed his wife.

She returned the kiss, then moved her lips to caress his cheeks when he turned his head to look at David.

"Take her," Paul said.

"Come on, guys," David muttered and stepped forward.

Griff and Rhys passed him, each taking hold of one of Cath's arms. She began to shriek, struggling against them. Acting as gently as possible, Sarah pried her hands from Paul.

The three of them began to pull the struggling woman back towards the road.

Reverend Hopkin drew alongside David. "Paul Duffy," he said, "among those who are aware of my true purpose, I shall ensure your name is known as the man who saved the world from a deadly darkness. The man who relieved me, and humanity, of the Burden. For this you have my eternal gratitude. And, though it does not know it, of the whole of humankind."

Paul's eyes flashed yellow. "Retreat, Reverend, for if it regains control, it will come for you. Pray to whatever higher power which exists that it does not."

Reverend Hopkin gave a small, stiff bow and began to back away from the bonfire.

"I must act quickly," said Paul to David. "I need one final act of assistance, my friend."

Paul stooped, making his spine crack like dry wood, and picked up the petrol container. He stepped towards the nearest wardrobe door, his movements jerky as though a conflict was raging inside. At the foot of the door, he looked at David.

David moved to his side and gripped his arm. "It was a great honour to have been your friend," he said, a hitch developing in his voice.

Paul's eyes flashed from yellow to orange, before settling on pale green. "You really bore my coffin to the sound of 'Tequila'?"

David nodded. He no longer trusted himself to speak.

Paul grunted. "Fucking ace." He looked up. "Now help me onto that mattress. These legs no longer have functioning knees."

David placed the torch on the grass and stepped onto the wardrobe door, yanking his friend's arm until Paul stood in front of him. Then he got his hands onto Paul's bony backside and boosted him. David's feet slipped backwards and he slid to the ground, but it didn't matter; Paul had grabbed hold of the mattress and swung the petrol container onto it. With both hands, he dragged himself after it and, to the accompaniment of the sound of snapping twigs, turned to face David, sitting on the edge of the mattress, his legs resting on the wardrobe door. David retrieved the torch and watched while Paul removed the cap from the container and upended it, emptying the contents over himself. From somewhere behind, David could hear Cath begin to scream.

"Hey, Dai," Paul said. Petrol made his face shine in the torchlight.

"Yes?"

"I can see your house from up here." Paul grunted. "Now get back with the others. There are people over there recording this shit with their phones. And the police are probably on their way. I don't want you anywhere near me when I go whoof."

"Goodbye, my friend," was all David could manage. He retreated, walking backwards towards the sound of Cath's hysterical sobbing.

Paul's eyes began to flash, skipping yellow and orange and going straight to red as bright as a traffic light at night. His hand kept moving towards the pocket of his sweatpants and yanking back again when Bugan temporarily regained control.

But as David drew level with the others where they struggled to restrain Cath, safely out of range of petrol fumes, Paul's hand came up holding the box of matches from David's kitchen.

Judging by the rate at which the eyes flashed—green to red, like a Christmas light display—and the hand struggled to open the box to withdraw a match, the internal conflict was gaining pace.

David held his breath, thinking he might have to dart forward with his lighter at the ready and damn the consequences, when the glow once more dimmed. Paul held up a match and drew it along the side of the box.

The night abruptly grew bright.

An unearthly screech rent the air. The same parents whose infants had mysteriously awoken an hour or so earlier and had taken until now to settle down, were later to report their offspring all awoke once more and this time there would be no settling them for the rest of the night. Dog and cat owners reported their pets leapt to their feet at the same time, fur bristling, throats grumbling like two-stroke engines, ears laid flat to skulls, and were out of sorts for the remainder of the evening.

The screech rose to a deafening crescendo and died as abruptly as if a switch had been thrown.

Amidst the flames atop the blazing mattress, Paul gazed at his wife. Before they blistered and popped, to run down blackening, splitting cheeks, his eyes appeared to her as emerald-green as they looked in their honeymoon photo in Corfu.

A deep sense of calm flowed from her husband and washed over her. Through her. She stopped struggling against her friends' well-intentioned clutches. In his gaze, Cath found peace.

Paul Duffy smiled.

About the Author

Sam Kates lives in South Wales, UK, with a computer, a family and *way* too many books. To connect on social media:

Website: samkates.co.uk
Facebook: www.facebook.com/writersamkates
Twitter: @_Sam_Kates_
E-mail: contact@samkates.co.uk

Note

Please consider leaving a review—reviews can be of immeasurable help to authors in gaining visibility and running promotions.

Thank you for purchasing and reading this book.

To sign up for news of releases and special offers, most of which are only available to subscribers (no spam, promise):

samkates.co.uk/stay-in-touch/

– Sam Kates
July 2019

www.ingramcontent.com/pod-product-compliance
Lightning Source LLC
Chambersburg PA
CBHW060948190726
48286CB00005B/1486